The Sand Fly

Oliver B. Williams

The Sand Fly

Oliver B. Williams

Copyright © 2010 by Oliver B. Williams, All
Rights Reserved.

First Edition 2010   First Printing 2010
Second Edition 2014
Third Edition 2019

Zeitgeist Publishers
Oxnard, CA
www.zeistgeistpublisher.com

Jacket Design by Oliver B. Williams

ISBN-13: 978-0-578-59064-6

Fiction

Published in the United States of America

10 9 8 7 6 5 4 3 2

ACKNOWLEDGEMENTS

Thanks to Dr. Gary Emery for reading as I completed every three or four chapters, and providing encouragement and feedback.

Thanks to Irmgard Williams for such meticulous and scrupulous copy editing. She trudged through the forest, checking each and every tree.

DEDICATION

To my wonderful children: Oliver, Christopher, Adrian, and Avery. I have to love every second of my life, because by any other path you would not have existed.

Chapter 1
The Panty Fiasco

The beast was upon him once more.

Marzee's armpits twitched; his heart pounded; his pulse surged. *Please, let me be. Just let me go home. Or go to the library to study. But don't do this again. I'll waste hours doing this. It's still light. I can't look through windows in the daylight. It's too risky. I'll be seen. But, it's a sunny day. Girls lying about, girls doing their laundry. I'll just look around the laundry room. Things will be there—personal objects. I can look around.*

He knew fighting the mounting temptation was useless. A demon possessed him; it had always won out, since his early teens, when he first delighted in peeping in the bedroom window of a neighbor girl, Cecilia Golden. The sunny, early Autumn day and warm air bred his infestation, spawning an uncontrollable urge. The apartment complexes across the street from the campus beckoned him.

All of the sudden, he panicked, realizing he was standing in the middle of the campus staff parking lot with no apparent purpose. He feared casual observers would perceive him as a nefarious, ethnic sort, casing cars to ransack or steal. He spun around, checking his surroundings, only to confirm his paranoia: two white students five cars away were just entering their car. Their unsmiling gaze lingered in his direction for an uneasy period of time.

Hoping to thwart their racist suspicions, he walked with a nonchalant determination toward his goal. They eyed him fleetingly as they drove by. Out of their eyeshot, he picked up his pace, bounding across the parking lot with resolve.

The mid-afternoon classes had adjourned, and students were abandoning the campus. Upon exiting the parking lot, he reached the street. The increasing boulevard traffic was a river, separating him from the object of his obsession.

He stood at the curb of the busy four-lane boulevard, anxiously awaiting a hole in the traffic. He had abandoned whatever resistance he had mustered; he forged forward with zombie-like tenacity. He had no intention of turning back.

The two-story apartment building complex sprawled for one block. Though serving primarily as student housing, many of the occupants were teachers, former students, or local eight-to-fivers. Marzee knew the layout very well, having been here many times before. A gated gap between two structures allowed clandestine access into the complex. The gate lock had been disabled in order to provide a short cut for tardy students and a quick route for people wishing to avoid the main entrance. The main entrance consisted of a public-accessible front lobby, beyond which was a locked set of double doors under the watchful scrutiny of a surveillance camera. He jogged to the vicinity of the gate, pausing on the sidewalk. He looked around, verifying no one was watching, then casually walked closer. He put his arm over the top to unlatch it, opened it, and slipped in. He carefully closed the gate behind him, not wanting to arouse suspicion from casual observers, or from the property manager who might be surveying the grounds.

He crept through the narrow path between the stucco walls, and paused behind a tree. To his left was a path leading to the main lobby; to his right was a narrow concrete path, meandering through rainforest landscaping into the main apartment complex. Ahead of him was one of two swimming pools, surrounded by more landscaping and a wrought iron fence.

With wolf-like intensity his eyes locked onto the pair of female legs supported on a chaise lounge. Part of a building blocked his view of her torso. He garnered all he needed to know in the partial view: she was white and attractive, as were so many of the female students living in this complex. His thirst soared; he had to soak her up, to fill up with her image.

Adaptation and blending in—he could act as if he belonged there, and was not a foreign body. The first rule of belonging: appear to know where you're going and maintain the flow and rhythm of a resident. In order to get near enough to the pool, or inside the fenced pool area, he had to be part of the scene. Half of the challenge had already been fulfilled: he was a student, he sported a backpack, he didn't look homeless or derelict. His skin color was light. To the casual white observer, he could be white, or Arabic, or from somewhere in Southern Europe. He had experienced only socially keen white people who suspected that he was mixed black and white, and not an exotic racial blend from another part of the world.

He slipped his keys from his pocket, and walked to the right pathway. After a few feet, the path split, the left one leading to the pool area. He rattled his key chain, examining it as if readying his apartment key—the casual observer would ignore him, accepting him as another tenant. The college-aged tenants were not threatened by the presence of strangers; only older, more conservative people are alarmed by the unfamiliar. His heart raced as he turned up the path toward the pool.

He approached the pool area entry cautiously, knowing his target was on the other side. He hoped her looks made it worth his effort. He peered over the gateway, gleeful at what he observed: a single, attractive, female occupant sunning on the pool deck.

Pausing at the gate, his throat became parched at the visage before him. She was an early-twenties brunette wearing a knit string bikini—not the Brazilian cut—rather the style of the Seventies and Eighties, using a strand of yarn to secure the bottom and the top. It was tiny. *Goddamn. Two Band-Aids and a cork*, he mused, smacking his lips.

She had positioned her top carelessly over herself so that a crescent of her left breast's areola peeked out. Her skin glistened from suntan lotion and sweat. *I hit the fuck'n jackpot.* She was asleep, and wore earphones from her iPod. She would not likely be aroused by his entry.

The pool gate was unlocked, secured only by a simple latch. He eased the latch free, opening the gate slowly, but not so slowly as to arouse suspicion from possible onlookers. Focused, but cautious nevertheless, he scanned around cursorily, reckoning the surrounding foliage hid him from outside view. He scanned upward toward two apartment windows on the second floor, worried that they were in line of sight. The curtains were drawn, easing his concern. He closed the gate behind him, carefully re-engaging the latch. His prey had not budged.

He positioned himself directly behind her; he didn't want her to open her eyes suddenly and catch sight of him. Thinking through each move, he was careful not to cast a shadow over her, causing her to cool and stir. He twirled around for another 360 degree surveillance—nobody.

Her body lay before him—her legs fully extended, concave abdomen, glimmering navel ring, hip bones protruding slightly over the tops of her bikini bottom string, and the crescent of areola still poking out. She had smooth, porcelain-white skin that resisted tanning.

His mouth was too dry to water. *She's probably trying to soak up the last summer's sun. Damn, I'm lucky.* He needed to hurry while still unfettered by passersby.

His penis was not erect, not even tumescent. His heart beat furiously—his breaths, short and shallow. He looked around again, unzipping his pants slowly through the turn. Extracting his flaccid penis, he massaged it with his fingertips, hoping to pump in some life. The female form sprawled before him seared an image into his brain. He milked his withered member gently, attempting to coax in some rigidity, but to no avail.

He focused, fixating on her skin, on her stomach, on the inside of her thighs, on her long lithe arms, on the crescent of areola teasing him. He was the conduit for a relentless flow of energy, a resonance between her passive form, and him silently and slowly masturbating behind her.

Suddenly, she raised a knee; she lifted her head. She had awakened untimely. He jolted around, and stuffed his penis into his pants, wincing as he snagged it on the opened zipper in his panicked haste. A soda vending machine stood against the wall of the pool veranda facing him. He stepped forward a few steps, knelt in front of the vending machine, and pretended to search the soda depository for an undelivered soda, feigning frustration. He twisted around, noticing she was seated and disoriented from her nap. He returned to the vending machine, ever the faker, digging around in the receptacle for the nonexistent soda can.

"Damn machine!" He stood up with a victim's resignation. He rattled the machine, and then banged on the return change button. He turned to face her, suspecting he had attracted her attention by now.

"Did it eat your dollar?" the girl asked, holding her hand like a visor.

"Yeah. Second time this month," Marzee responded.

"Tell the manager. She'll take your name, and get the money from the vending machine guy when he comes to refill it," the girl suggested.

Marzee's penis hurt, and he was self-conscious about blood on his crotch. More so, he was disappointed she was awake. "Sounds like it happened to you before," Marzee replied.

"Oh, yeah," she responded with confirmatory exasperation.

"Yeah, well, guess that's what I'll have to do. I just wanted a Pepsi before I went to class," he said, sighing.

Marzee eyed her as she sat sideways on the lounge chair. She turned back to filling her beach bag, which she had propped between her knees.

She didn't catch me. She has no idea. Oh! Those thighs. If only she had stayed down another five minutes.

"Well, thanks for the tip," Marzee commented as he headed toward the gate. "Hope you didn't get sunburned."

"Yeah, thanks," the girl replied laughing without looking up. "I do burn easily."

Tempted to stay and make conversation, he would have liked to know this girl. She seemed friendly enough, though he was careful not to misinterpret programmed chit-chat from an unfamiliar, young white woman as genuine interest in him. The gate rattled, closing behind him.

He was very familiar with these apartment complex grounds, already reaching a stride. Along the main walkway, a monotony of identical windows and doors filed past him. The rainforest-style landscaping in the center plaza filled the void between the pool area and another small structure he aimed for. The aroma of laundry detergent and fabric softener excited him. The sounds of buttons and zippers tumbling and echoing from inside clothes dryers refurbished the rush he had felt before his unscheduled exit from the pool. A side path led to the opened door of the apartment laundromat. He dropped his keys, stopped to retrieve them, and knelt in the direction of the opened door. The laundry room was empty. He collected his keys and returned them to his pocket. He assured himself nobody was headed in his direction as he ambled inside.

Only four washers and four dryers served the forty units in this section of the apartment complex. The washers faced the dryers across a narrow aisle. A thin, high table ran perpendicular to the aisle along the opposite wall. A bulletin board hung on the wall over the table. He trod unhurriedly into the laundry room, and stopped in front of an operating dryer. He opened the door; the dryer stopped, and the still wet clothes splat to the bottom of the rotating tub.

Rummaging through the clothes, he surmised the age and sex of the clothes' owner. He found men's jockey shorts, men's shirts, a pair of men's jeans, t-shirts, but no female garments. He side-stepped quickly to the door and looked both ways along the pathway—still nobody in sight.

A basket full of clothes sat atop the table, causing his heart to palpitate. He anxiously fingered the contents as if they were gold doubloons. They were dry, but not warm. He deduced they waited not for a free dryer, but for a free washer. *A basket of unwashed clothes! Another jackpot.* His head buzzed as he plucked a female tank top from the basket. Making a cursory check behind him, he commenced to ravage the basket—shorts, jeans, a bikini bottom, a skirt, a couple of tops, thong panties. His mouth went dry; he licked his lips; he looked around again.

He yanked the panties from the basket, turned them inside out, and exposed the crotch area with his fingers pressing from the other side. He meticulously situated the garment over his nose and mouth like a gas mask, and inhaled slowly. He closed his eyes, and moaned. He retracted the panties from his face, grasped the ass-crack string between his fingers, and while stretching the connecting fiber gently, held it to his nose, moving it back and forth, inhaling like a wine connoisseur. He closed his eyes dreamily.

Excited about his epic relic, he would not delay the gratification this rare find would bequeath him. He checked the door once again, still gripping his treasure. He remained close to the door with the intent to immediately detect potential intruders. He turned sideways to the door, attempting to obscure himself with the adjacent wall. He placed the undergarment over his head, covering his nose and mouth. He unlatched his belt, unfastened his pants, unzipped his zipper, and released his tattered penis. He was electrified, but not sexually aroused. He slowly and carefully manipulated his penis with his fingertips, hoping to draw some blood into his deflated member. He lapsed into fantasy.

Who wore these panties? Was she blonde? Brunette? Red head? Was that her by the pool? Yes! She dropped her laundry off here, then went to the pool, and fell asleep. I can smell her pussy. These panties were pressed against her pussy. Now these panties are pressed against my face. I could almost see her pussy by the pool—soft, tight, moist with sweat. Her soft pubic hair was bunched inside these panties; now it's on my face. Did she play with herself while she had them on? She did. She slipped her finger along her inner labia, and spread them

open like delicate flower petals. As she became
more lubricated, she wiggled her finger inside her
vagina. Her juices flowed, saturating these panties.
I can smell her; I can taste her; I can feel her on my
tongue. I want to drink her.

His barely tumescent penis oozed seminal fluid. He emitted a near audible moan, interrupted by a frumpy, mid-sixties woman approaching the door. He startled, snatching the under garment from his head. He stuffed his penis into his pants, and fastened the top latch of his pants without re-securing his belt. He compressed the panties in his hand, hoping to soak up the ejaculate. The woman confronted him at the door.

"What are you doing here?" she demanded.

"I...I...I'm checking to see if there's a free machine before I bring my laundry down. I need to wash my clothes," Marzee replied, stammering.

"You don't live here. You're the one slipping around here stealing laundry, and peeking in people's windows," the woman proclaimed with escalating emotion. "What's that in your hand? What are you doing?" She turned to face the door. "Help! Help!" she screamed, blocking the door.

"Please, ma'am, no. Don't yell. I'm not hurting anything," Marzee pleaded. He panicked, pushing by her, so she was knocked against the door frame. He ran out to the pathway, turning to retrace his exit. The woman's yells were shrill.

"Help! Help! Stop that man!" she shouted.

Marzee's pulse peaked; he felt trapped. If he could only make it to the street, and across campus, he would hop on his moped, and go home. He heard a male voice behind him.

"Hey, you. Stop! Hey! You fucking asshole. Stop!"

He ran by the pool area he had visited earlier, ages ago. He turned the path, and darted toward the secluded gate through which he had first gained entrance to the grounds. A police officer was inside the main entrance foyer, his back toward him. *Someone saw me and called the police!* He ducked between the walls leading to the outside gate to avoid being seen. The man who had yelled after him had not given chase.

Panting, Marzee paused to assess his position. *Don't fool yourself. Pigs are here. My ass is known around here. They've been looking for me. I've been bullshitting myself, thinking I've gone unnoticed.* He dashed to the gate leading to the freedom of the boulevard, and the campus beyond. Another police car had just pulled up, and parked directly across from the exit. He was trapped.

He turned back, but remained behind the building wall. The police officer in the lobby had still not gained entrance. He could hear voices from the direction of the pool and laundry room. His only chance was to retreat to the adjacent building. He had to retrace part of the path to the pool, and then cut through some doors leading to the parking lot between the main buildings. He peeked around the

16

corner, noticing that the police officer had been distracted from the door by his newly arrived cohorts. Taking the opportunity, he sprinted down the pathway. As he back-tracked to the next building, he caught sight of a small assemblage gathered close to the pool area.

"Is that him?" he overheard.

"Has to be. Look at him run," another said.

He burst through the door leading to the parking lot. He was in the shadow of a roofed car port along side of the building. Another car port structure extended between the two main buildings, bisecting the parking lot. He scanned the area, mapping a route of flight and deliberating tactics. If he ran toward the street, he would be in line of sight of the police, who probably had already fanned out to nab him. He was uncertain if he could trigger the motorized security gate to open, and it was too tall for him to jump or climb.

He zigzagged across the parking lot, using parked cars as cover, and took refuge in the second building. Guessing he had evaded his pursuers for the time being, he felt slightly relieved. They would certainly swarm to the second building soon enough, so he slowed down not to attract attention in these new environs. With alternating pace, he forged forward scouring the area for an exit route. Upon reaching the far side of Building Two, he emerged into another parking area bounded by a motorized gate sealing the driveway, and a high, brick wall running the lot length. Garbage dumpsters lined the wall.

He was no stranger to these property grounds—he had roamed its groomed pathways, explored the nooks and crannies, and noted the occupants' habits many times. The mid-nineties Mustang parked in the center of the carport was like a landmark. It lacked the scruffy look of abandonment, but no one seemed to drive it. Day or night, he had noticed it parked in the same place. Maybe the owner was out of town, or perhaps it was someone's backup vehicle. Curious, he had once tried its door, and it was unlocked.

Hunched like a soldier on a battlefield, he scurried to the lone car, relieved to find the passenger door still unlocked. He dropped the glove compartment, and pressed a yellow button inside. The trunk popped opened. He closed the glove compartment, slammed the passenger door shut, and slinked into the trunk. He closed the trunk door over himself very carefully, making certain the latch did not engage, locking him in.

Fortunately the trunk was empty, allowing him room to stretch, but he was aware that remaining folded inside here would be crippling. He was committed—he had to hide in the trunk for several hours until the heat was off—and now the heat was just starting.

He heard the jangle of the security gate opening. Marzee peeked through the narrow seam of the unlocked trunk door. A police car entered and parked close to where he was hiding. Two uniformed police officers greeted an older man, probably the manager.

"My wife caught him in the laundry room. A couple people saw him," the man told the officers. "He matches the description of a guy who's been creeping around the building day and night."

"And what's he do?" one police officer asked.

"At night he peeks in people's windows. He also goes in the laundry room, and steals women's underwear. If there's a woman lying around the pool area, he sneaks up behind her, and stares at her, and plays with himself," the man replied.

"When he plays with himself, what does he do? Does he ask her to look?" the other officer asked.

"Hmm. Nah..not really. I don't think she said he pulled it out. He tried to hide it when she noticed him," the manager explained.

"So he never showed his genitals to any of the tenets?" Officer One re-confirmed.

"No. The guy's a Peeping Tom, and a general, creepy pain in the ass," the man replied. "My wife said he looks like an Arab. He may be a terrorist."

Upon overhearing this diatribe, Marzee's pulse soared. He could feel his heart thumping at his insides, beating against his chest cavity. If they only knew he was just a few feet away, they would yank him out, cuff him, and beat him. About this occurrence he had no doubt.

He was so scared. His barely lit bungalow in the trunk of a 1997 Mustang would be his living quarters for the next few hours. He had resolved to remain still and quiet for as long as it took—until the frenzy to apprehend him had subsided. He contemplated slipping away under the cloak of darkness, scurrying across the campus, arriving at his Vespa, and going home.

The two officers and manager parted. Each officer went in different directions; opening garbage bins, looking under cars, and checking storage compartments in the parking stalls. He heard a helicopter overhead, surveying and circling the vicinity. Appalled that his behavior merited the presence of a police helicopter, he thought a murder would have warranted equal public scrutiny. He took solace knowing K-9 teams were not combing the area; they had probably considered it. They had no intention of letting him escape.

He wanted to cry. He wanted to snuggle with his mother while holding his teddy bear. He never hurt anybody; he didn't want anybody to hurt him. What was all the fuss about? Where'd all this energy come from? What did he do to instigate such a public outcry? Police search teams and aerial surveillance had been summoned to corral this public menace. He cowered, shivering and contorted in the trunk, occasionally braving a peek, ever so gently cracking open the trunk to glimpse at the ruckus he had caused.

Time passes—I hear them; they still search. I am fortunate. God looks out for me. I thought of hiding in that trash dumpster, but I saw a movie: the dude hid in a dumpster, and the cops found him. Where you gonna hide, motherfucker? In a big box where everyone can look? Of course not. You hide in something that appears closed, locked, and inaccessible. Then you peer out, and watch them look for you. How long will it take them? What did I do so wrong that they want me so bad? I didn't kill, rape, steal, rob, assault, molest a child, deal drugs, or embezzle money. I didn't cheat on my taxes. I'm honest, frugal, and forthright. These people hate me. This fiasco will probably be on the news, or in the paper.

Hours passed. He remained huddled in the car trunk. The commotion of the hunt waned, the helicopter whir disappeared, the police officers dispersed, and the tenant posse went back to their beer and television. The background noise reverted to returning commuters—their sole desire, a few hours of suspended animation, seated before a TV in their one bedroom apartments, then sleep it off until tomorrow morning, when they must repeat the cycle for fifteen dollars per hour.

He had persevered for hours, huddled in a car trunk. He had evaded a search, including several police officers, an overhead helicopter, and a few zealous tenants. Wisdom, luck, and providence had

21

delivered him from handcuffs, a booking station, a line up, humiliation, and incarceration. He was numb from trauma. The consequences of his behavior—as mundane and innocent as he believed it was—were eroding his well-being. These last four hours had changed him.

He yearned to leave. The drone of parking cars had diminished as day turned to night. Besides, he rationalized, those just returning would not recognize him as the one being sought. He doubted a sentry had been posted to maintain a lookout. He eased the car truck opened an inch, perusing the area through the slit. All appeared clear. He opened the lid a foot, and stuck his head through, twisting his neck to view the second floor windows in the building facing him. He pushed the trunk fully opened, and attempted to support himself on his knees.

His limbs were numb, reminding him of the times when he had become engrossed, reading, while sitting on the toilet. He'd lose track of time, eventually realizing that his feet and legs were lifeless, later to agonize in the tingly, prickly sensation of his limbs reawakening. Emerging from this trunk surpassed those extended, lavatory reading lapses. His over-riding concern superseded the pain: regaining alacrity and stealth. He could not afford to dally about the area.

He hoisted one leg out of the trunk, lifting it with his arms. He assisted the other leg so that both drooped over the bumper. He maintained constant vigilance. Being sighted now would put him at a worst disadvantage—he couldn't move. He stood, stretching both legs. He jumped up and down, squatted and twisted. The pain of reactivated circulation was excruciating.

With cat-like stealth, he avoided the floodlight-lit areas, staying in shadow and hugging the walls until he was close to the security gate. A hose stretched across the asphalt a few feet away from the gate. He jumped on it, activating the gate; it cranked open. As the gate parted, he squeezed through. He scanned up and down the street, scrutinizing the parked cars on the block—no police cars, no sentries. He darted between two parked cars closest to him, and ducked down. He waited for traffic to clear, and then sprinted across the street. Once on campus, he bounded through the parking lot, behind a fake Lipchitz statue, over to a covey of park benches, through a classroom building, across campus, passed the student union and cafeteria, passed the building where his psychology class would be, and finally to the east parking lot where his moped awaited him. He would go home at last.

Chapter 2
Home

Dazed from being hunted like an escaped convict, and hiding in the truck of a car for hours, he was numb to the rapidly cooled night air. After a half hour ride in a t-shirt, he arrived at his house. His moped puttered to a stop as he bounced up the driveway, and coasted into the backyard. With one fiasco behind him, he still had to persevere: dealing with his parents, his neighbors, his neighborhood, and the tactics of coming home.

He wanted to avoid a commotion putting his moped away, but the garage door was closed, and made an awful racket if opened. Mopeds were foreign, even alien, in his neighborhood. The likelihood of it getting stolen was low, but the likelihood of vandalism was high: the unknown and unapproved were prime targets. He parked it in the shadows behind some lilac bushes for camouflage. He had to awaken early to return to school anyway, so his vehicle's security was sound for now.

After locking the wheel chain, he stood for a moment and breathed a deep sigh of relief. He had escaped to the shadowed seclusion of his backyard, to the freedom of his amber-lit street, and soon to the uninspired probing of his parents. He soaked up the darkness. The lightless sky gave thanks to the new moon, clouds moved in to block the stars, and his wearisome day, though still disturbing, segued to unimposing memory. He stood in silence, attempting to collect his nerves and demeanor. His parents must not sense his lingering inner turmoil.

He pondered the difference between the environs from which he had just escaped, and his own neighborhood. His predominantly African-American community had not received the renovations bestowed upon other areas of equal socio-economic status. On some streets the pavement was so worn and unkempt, you could see the bricks from the original century-old street. The power lines hung low from wooden poles, and electricity outages were common occurrences. Incandescent bulbs still burned in the streetlamps, casting a yellow hue over a squalor and formless backdrop of tree-camouflaged, wood- frame dwellings. The neighborhood ambiance was particularly conducive to Halloween, especially if the wind were harsh and cold. Barren branches shook and rattled in shadows cast by the unnatural yellow light, and an occasional power failure rendered everything pitch black.

His mind drifted as he recalled one Halloween evening of his boyhood traveling to a white neighborhood. His disguise was Al Jolson— black face, top hat, and cane. The residents thought he was white kid in a clever, ingenious costume, and they doled out extra candy for his entertaining shuffle-and-dance presentation. For punctuation, he ended his performance with a "yeow-sah," met with pats on the back and confirming, silent applause. The spurious memory flushed out a grin.

25

He wished he could go straight to his room without interacting with his parents, but they hung like vultures inside, waiting to pick information out of him. Having to conceal the truth from them increased his unrest. He loved them, but he did not like interacting with them. Remaining outside for the time being offered a moratorium between what he had done, and what he had to do.

His eyes scanned the darkness in a familiar direction. The light shone from Cecelia Golden's bedroom a few houses away. For ten years he had been drawn to her window with moth-like attraction. Like the lure of the apartments across from campus, his pulse raced, and he immediately abandoned having to go inside, talk with his parents, or tackle his studies. Her window was an old friend, offering a fortuitous respite.

I am not a robot, a machine. I am not an animal, driven by thoughtless instinct and uncontrolled behavior. I do not have to act on these thoughts. I will go inside, greet my mother and father with respect, share a few social niceties, retire to my room, and commence my schoolwork.

He abandoned his inner objections. He checked the windows at the back of his house. No one had noticed him arrive. He dropped his book bag next to his moped, ran across the yard, jumped the back fence to the alley, and then snaked along the paths and short cuts between houses to Cecelia's window.

Marzee had known Cecilia most of his life. They had attended the same grade school, junior high, and high school. When they were twelve, he convinced her to remove her shirt and training bra, so he could examine her with the medical kit he had received for Christmas. He told her the only way to really hear her heart, especially if her heart had problems, was to position the cup of the stethoscope directly over one nipple, while holding the other nipple in his hand in order to keep it steady and reduce noise. After the procedure, he informed her it was time to examine all the parts in her underwear, so she had to remove her panties as well. She declined, unconvinced, and revealed Marzee's maneuverings to her mother. The respective parents decided that Marzee and Cecilia should desist in un-chaperoned playtime.

He reached the shadow alongside Cecilia's house, and crouched below the rectangular light beam radiating from her window, positioning himself to pop up for a quick peek. If the light were on, she was usually present, sporting various states of undress. He raised his eyes to the bottom of the window, as he had repeated this routine so many other times. Her bathroom door was closed. He put his ear to the window—she was taking a shower.

He had witnessed Cecilia naked through her bedroom window so many times, he had an indelible movie of her in his brain. Each time his pulse raced; each time he pondered the logistics. How long would she take to come out? Would she dry herself in the bathroom, and emerge in a robe? Would she remove the robe in the bedroom, and then dress herself? Or would she dress at all— sometimes she slept naked. All questions bore this identical scenario, whose plot and climax had been repeatedly rehearsed. Perhaps the plot had a twist: she had known of his presence outside her window these many years, and did not feel threatened, violated, or disturbed. Perhaps she was not the victim after all; perhaps he was.

Cecilia emerged from the bathroom, showered. He weathered an initial jolt of disappointment—she wore her bathrobe. She had bundled her hair in a towel. She closed and locked the bedroom door. She disappeared into her bathroom for a minute, and then re-emerged without the bathrobe. Naked, she stood in front of her dresser mirror with her hands on her hips. She winced, expressing slight displeasure. She raised her arms, clasping her hands together, and rested them on her head. She twisted slightly to the left; paused; then to right, with her feet planted firmly on the floor. She turned around facing away from the mirror, and twisted far enough around, contorting her neck so that she could view the reflection of her elongated, hour-glass, brown-skinned figure. She faced the mirror again. Her left hand edged toward her right breast, and her center fingers slowly rotated around the perimeter of her bulging nipple. Her right hand slid toward her protruding mound of pubic hair. Her eyes rolled back as she cocked her head sideways and parted her lips. She maintained this stance a few moments, and then she walked over to her bed. She lay down so her head was on the pillow, and placed her feet astride each opposite corner of the mattress. The obstruction-free foot of the bed faced Marzee. She arched her back, raised her hips, and her middle finger disappeared within a bollix of hair, flesh, and mucus.

Marzee's excitement dissipated rapidly. Watching her naked thrilled him; watching her have sex with herself—a new development—disappointed him. He retreated from her window, creeping along the edge of the house to a point where was out of eyesight.

After retracing his path, he jumped his backyard fence and verified his parents were not in their bedroom where they could catch sight of him. He scurried along the side of the house to the steps leading to the porch and his front door. "I was at the library studying," he whispered to himself. Trying to maintain the emotional balance they expected—in light of the tumultuous circumstances of his day—edged him toward his most dreaded precipice: losing control. He fumbled with his key, turned the lock, and gingerly coaxed the door opened with his foot.

Musty, grease-laden air assaulted him. His mother sat in her usual easy chair, feet propped up on the Ottoman, wearing her dingy, white, ankle-high socks, reading the newspaper while she watched television. She was probably doing the crossword puzzle, he thought. She stopped, lowered the paper, and glanced at him over her glasses.

"How come you're home so late? I was starting to worry about you," she said sternly, but without anger.

Cool, calm, collected. "I had to go to the library to study," Marzee replied, noticing the tension remaining in his voice.

"Library? This late? Can't you just check out the books you need, and read them at home?" his mother challenged.

Guilt overwhelmed frustration. Her questions reminded him of what he had really been doing. "Well, Mama, it's not like that. I didn't need books. I needed to use the library database," Marzee explained with hesitation.

"Database?" she queried skeptically.

Fuck. I can't do this. Another explanation of the twenty-first century is out of the question. "Yes, Mama, the library research database. You can only access—get to it—using the computers in the library. Books weren't involved; it was all computer stuff," Marzee replied.

Ione Banks shook her head slowly in disbelief. "I remember the Dewey cards. Seems like they were easier. Anyway, dinner didn't stay warm for you. You'll have to heat it up yourself. And I already cleaned up the kitchen once. I don't mean to clean it twice today," she admonished.

Barely maintaining a steady stance, he felt faint. He was desperate to get to his room. "I'm not

30

that hungry, Mama," Marzee responded. "I've got a lot of school work to do, anyway.

"You better eat something. You're too skinny as it is. No girl's gonna want a skinny, little man like you," she chortled. "I fixed fried chicken, some boiled potatoes, and some green beans. Go heat some up. Daddy's in the kitchen," she said as a benevolent command.

Marzee felt vulnerable, guilty, and under intolerable pressure as he stood before his mother. He yearned for disengagement and privacy. "Thanks, Mama. I'll heat up some chicken," he replied, hoping to bypass actually doing it.

Mrs. Banks put down her paper, raised her eyebrows, and opened her mouth to issue another directive. Something stopped her, abruptly resuming the state in which Marzee found her when he had walked into the room.

He sauntered into the kitchen, his book bag still in hand. He greeted his father, who predictably sat at the kitchen table working a scrambled word puzzle from the newspaper. He probably wanted to isolate himself from his wife, who enjoyed working crossword puzzles with the TV blasting. Mr. Banks was nearly comatose in concentration when Marzee entered the room.

Tempted to simply say hello, and go upstairs to his room, he feared such asocial tactics would lead to unwanted curiosity about his temperament. "Another puzzle, Daddy?" Marzee asked.

His father grinned—a grin that meant he had given up, and wanted his son to solve it for him. Morgan Banks didn't want to know the answer—not immediately—he simply wanted to know Marzee knew the answer. He was fascinated and proud that his son could solve a puzzle in one minute, a puzzle that took him an entire evening of futility, re-juxtaposing letters. To Marzee, it was a matter of looking at the puzzle with a fresh perspective. He had no vested interest in solving it. Challenged with puzzles, he dispatched them quickly, not aware of the effect his facility had on others.

"I've been working on this one for about two hours now. I haven't given up yet," his father replied almost monotonically, still concentrating.

"Ok. Hope I don't bother you. I'm going to heat up some chicken," Marzee said.

"You have some potatoes and beans, too!" his mother yelled from the other room.

Marzee winced at his mother's intrusion. His stomach twisted from distress, he was far from hungry. "Guess I'm heating up some potatoes and beans, too," Marzee remarked, sighing.

The trauma of the day had more of an impact than he was aware. He could hardly concentrate. Robotically, he extracted three Tupperware containers from the refrigerator, and collected a clean dish from the cupboard. He stood behind his father, aiming to minimize the interference. His single selection of fried chicken was the portion with the least amount of coagulated

32

grease. He added a small spoonful of green beans and boiled potatoes. His mother annoyingly spread butter on the potatoes, and then sprinkled parsley flakes on them. He did not like boiled potatoes; he cared less for mushy, over-cooked green beans; and the parsley flakes punctuated his disdain. He ripped off a length of cellophane wrap, covered the dish, poked several holes into the film, put the plate in the microwave oven, and set the timer.

Barely able to stand upright, he supported himself with his elbows on the kitchen counter. If he could manage to heat the food and eat quickly, he could lessen his torment, and escape to his room. If he lingered, his father would initiate some inane conversation, or ask him a question about something he had explained a dozen times.

The Banks family kitchen was drearily cramped and miserly lighted. Any edge of the kitchen table was less than three feet from a counter, sink, cupboard, or stove. A tiny alcove housed the refrigerator. Marzee compressed himself between the stove and the table. His father sat as referee; his mother served remotely as coach.

Reflecting briefly that he could be in jail this very instant—this dinner table repartee not taking place—he shivered in partial gratitude. He had to pull himself together, else they would suspect something was wrong. He decided to consume his meal—as wretched as he believed his family's culinary habits were. He would converse a bit more with his father, and he would retire to his room upstairs where he would contemplate the day's happenings.

Deciding to process his misery in large gulps, the large potatoes hindered his expedition, and he was forced to cut each in half. He ate the chicken rapidly, but he despised the tell-tale glossy wreath of grease encircling his mouth. He would have wiped his mouth more frequently, but his father did not want him to waste napkins. Still, he was able to devour his supper within three minutes, remaining mindful not to give the impression of eating so fast he wanted to leave their company.

"You shouldn't eat so fast," his father admonished.

"He finished eating already?" his mother chimed in from the other room.

Marzee loved his parents, but he detested their interference and micro-management in details of mundane behavior. As the years passed, he had become increasingly impatient with them, maintaining a silent and unexpressed anger. "I have work to do. I need to get upstairs, and get started," Marzee replied loudly enough so both could hear.

"What do you have to study?" Mr. Banks asked, unaffected by Marzee's announcement.

Swallowing his frustration, he squelched an outburst of anger. "Psychology and philosophy," Marzee responded in a low voice, suppressing the terseness.

"Those the two classes you had today?" his father asked.

"Tomorrow. I bought the books today. I just wanted to get a jump start. I've been looking forward to both subjects."

He was torn between the urgency to escape, and impressing them with his class schedule he had picked up today. His parents were intelligent, but uneducated. Psychology and philosophy were words with little meaning to them: psychology meant "nuts" and philosophy meant "full of shit".

"What's psychology like?" his father inquired. "What sort of things do you learn in that class?"

"Well, I'm not sure yet. The class is tomorrow," Marzee responded impatiently. But from what I understand, the subject is the function of the mind."

"How's somebody going to study the mind? You mean, the brain?" Mr. Banks asked.

As he scrutinized his father, he felt disconnected from his surroundings. Even his father's words sounded distorted. Though compelled to disengage and retire to his room, he was obliged to persevere this unique sensation, if simply for the experience. "Daddy, I really have to study and shower," he told his father politely. "Studying the brain would be neurophysiology. I think we'll study how we sense things, how we learn things, why everyone is different. You know, different personalities, intelligence, stuff like that. Maybe something about mental illnesses."

Mr. Banks chuckled slyly, ignoring his son's protestation. "So, you're telling me, when you're finished taking this class, you'll be able to explain why your friend Freddie is nuts?"

"It's just an introduction course, Daddy. People get doctoral degrees to treat people," Marzee replied, chuckling similarly. "Anyway, I don't think two doctorate degrees in psychology could tell Freddie why he's so nuts," Marzee retorted, noticing his dad nodded with agreement at his come-back.

"How about that retarded child down the block? I know he's working with some psychologist. Ain't done noth'n for him," Mrs. Banks inserted from the other room.

"And how about Boo Jack Pickens?" Mr. Banks said with animation. "They found him sitting in his car with his brains blown out. Now that's crazy, blowing your own brains out. What's psychology going to do for him?"

To avoid rage Marzee had lapsed into a stupor—a harbor of safe refuge. He had described his coursework, and they challenged the veracity of the subject matter. They knew nothing about it, but they had an opinion. Neither of his parents had ever taken the subject, but they were qualified to provide examples of its failure. If he left now, they'd be hurt and angry. His best defense was an offense. "Well, medicine doesn't always work, either," he offered as a response.

36

"There's a pill, or a shot, or some cream, or a cast, or an x-ray, or something. What's psychology going to do—talk your ass into not being so crazy?" Mr. Banks blurted. A loud guffaw erupted from the other room.

"Actually, there're pills for psychological disorders," Marzee calmly retorted. "I know there're pills for depression, anxiety, even schizophrenia."

"So, you're telling me you're taking a course in why crazy people are nutty. Problem is: they stay crazy. Never, in my entire life, have I have seen someone I knew was crazy get un-crazy. They stayed crazy 'til they died," Mr. Banks pronounced.

His father's recital represented an attitude, an ignorance, that repulsed Marzee, but he could not voice it; he could not display it. He had to get out. "Yes, I suppose you're right," Marzee replied softly, taking a step toward the door leading to his bedroom.

When he was not stressed or recoiling from near incarceration, he was more adept at handling his parents. Still, he knew what to say to win them over. They sanctified the pinnacle of black, middle-class professions: being a doctor. "Courses like psychology and philosophy are necessary to transfer to the university. Maybe I'll study law or medicine. You have to study psychology and philosophy to study medicine," Marzee replied pensively, waiting for his father's reaction.

"Medicine? You mean, be a doctor?" Marzee's father asked incredulously.

The prospect of her son being a medical doctor prodded Mrs. Banks out of her easy chair. She appeared in the door well. "I always thought you were a smart enough boy to become a doctor. You make me very happy you're thinking about it." She hesitated with a stern, but proud expression, looking downcast and a bit forlorn. "But it's very expensive."

I've got 'em. He gloated inwardly. "They have scholarships for promising African-American students. But you have to study hard, and get good grades," Marzee paused, turning to his father, "Even in courses like psychology and philosophy." Mr. Banks looked away at Mrs. Banks. Both bore expressions of people who had just won a large sum of money.

"But speaking of good grades, I'd better head off to my room. I need to get some studying done," Marzee interjected with perfect timing.

"Before you go, take a look at this for me." Mr. Banks opened his paper to the page with the Jumble puzzle. "Don't tell me the answer."

Marzee complied affably, taking the paper from his father. He studied it for a few minutes. Mr. Banks had unscrambled all the words, but he had not solved the puzzle, even with the clue provided.

"Ok. Got it." Marzee said, shoving the paper across the table.

"You got it? You solved it that fast?" his father exclaimed, astonished.

The staircase door leading to Marzee's attic bedroom was adjacent to the kitchen. He grabbed his book bag, which he had dropped next to his chair on the kitchen floor, and climbed the creaky, wooden stairs, closing the door softly behind him.

Once upstairs, he threw his book bag on the floor beside his desk, turned on his computer, and flopped on his bed. He contemplated what was more stressful: tolerating his parents' uninformed beliefs or being chased by the police. Both tested his emotional stamina. Having had lifelong exposure to his parents might explain his ability to survive being chased, he mused. His arms over his head, he whiffed his armpits. "Jesus, I need a shower," he muttered.

Curious about the commotion he had caused, he sprang from his bed to look online. Perhaps his escapades had made the news wires. His heart raced as the anticipation grew—reading about an unknown suspect being chased through the apartment complex across from Cal State Long Beach. *Oh shit! What if someone identified me? What if someone recognized me?*

Using Google's search engine, he typed various terms, attempting to bring up any news regarding his escapades earlier today. Unsuccessful, he logged into Long Beach State's website, sniffing for hints of his activities there, but he found nothing. The notion that someone in that apartment building knew him seemed far-fetched. Nevertheless, he decided to curtail future forays in the locality of the college, given that he was a student there. Whom he does not know today, may be a classmate tomorrow. Someone could still recognize him on campus tomorrow. Or what if the Long Beach police persuaded the campus newspaper to publish a description? Or what if the campus police go from class to class, looking for suspects?

The wooden stairs outside his room creaked. His father had given up. Mr. Banks solved the word puzzle only two or three days out of the week without his son's assistance. Marzee never gloated, nor did he ever infer any superiority to his father. But this evening, the stresses of the day had taken their toll. He was tired and upset, and wanted to be left alone. A humble and nonintrusive knock sounded at the door.

"Come in, Daddy," Marzee said.

Mr. Banks sported his usual sheepish, obsequious grin whenever he sought the solution to his evening's toil. Marzee knew his father came to him hat-in-hand. He was a proud man, so for him to repeatedly request the aid of his son was an accomplishment of character to which Marzee conceded.

"Do you want a clue, or the answer?" Marzee asked, anticipating the reason for his father's visit.

"A clue," his father answered, sounding determined to conquer the task.

"Ok. Let's see. There's a clue that might be too obvious. Here—what does the earth do around the sun, year after year?"

Marzee's father thought. "Orbit. Revolve Rotate. Circle. I don't know," he responded.

"You're so close. The answer to the puzzle is *recycle*," Marzee told him.

Mr. Banks shook his head, as the answer was now clear. He turned, exited Marzee's room, and closed the door. The look on his father's face told him that his father loved and appreciated him in his own way. He felt a pang of guilt for the negative thoughts he had ruminated downstairs moments ago.

His psyche had calmed from when he first came home, though he was mildly concerned about someone from the apartment building seeing him on campus. He opened his book bag, and extracted the syllabi he had collected. An obstruction blocked his concentration: the body of the girl lying by the pool; the aroma of the panties on his face. He stood up, undressed for bed, and lapsed into masturbatory fantasy.

I am the sand fly. I spy her from my hiding place among the dried kelp. One knee extends toward the blue sky; her other leg is outstretched. I take flight, hovering over her. Fine hair lays flat in the clear oil film enveloping her upper thigh. The wind has calmed, steadying my flight. I take care,

*moving along her leg, landing in a tuft of hair
pointing to her upper torso. I edge my way down
ever so gently, and settle on a curved crevice. I look
down, noticing delicate protrusions. They make
their way above the surface of the finely curved lip
up upon which I rest. I want to see inside; I want to
immerse myself in the nectar brimming beneath.
The gentle, irregular undulations beckon me
onward.*

His ejaculation was powerful. He muffled
his moan, but he wanted to cry out, exalting an
undefined demarcation between pleasure and pain.
He wanted it again, but the hour was late. He wiped
himself with some tissues, and soaked up the spots
on the carpet with the same. He turned out the
lights, going to bed without showering. Exhausted,
he dozed off, thinking of his friend's mother's
gumbo he would have for lunch tomorrow.

Chapter 3
The Mind's Eye

What is it about these bitches?

She squatted on the floor, her back against the wall. The blue jeans melted into the stretched curve of her upper thigh. Her calves bulged upward, kissing the longer curvature of her hamstrings. Her knee formed a squared curve unlike any knee he had ever seen. Her bare ankles, framed by the orange Levi's stitching and her scuffed pumps, lured him—from the drone of the Psychology 101 lecture in a cramped classroom to a few square inches of exposed flesh.

The voice of the lecturer faded in the background as his eyes strained, searching for the subtle, ubiquitous ridge that would run like a fault line around her upper hip. Tight jeans could not compress the tell-tale landscape revealing the geology milli-inches below the surface. His stare pierced every weave, searching like an orbiting spy satellite, penetrating thick cloud cover with radar, scooping up concealed secrets. Heart pumping faster, the object he sought was not discernible; it was invisible; the tell-tale bulge was not there. She was not wearing panties.

Reality intruded as background crept to foreground—*psychology quiz*. Holding his pen motionless in a tight grip, Marzee's hand slipped down the barrel, his sweaty hand sliding to the paper. His eyes darted from the unknown female classmate to his notepad.

"We will have our first quiz on chapters one and two next week. You are responsible for the material I discussed in class, and the material in the book," the professor repeated.

"Shit. Quiz already! The semester just started," Marzee muttered to himself, having not fully focused on his class. The student next to him laughed under his breath. Marzee looked around sheepishly, realizing he had spoken aloud. The squatting girl smiled at him as well; he quickly averted his eyes.

The first class of the semester adjourned, and he had barely written a page of notes. Fifty minutes had elapsed in a trance. Desks scraping the floor, conversations, cell phones being reactivated, ruffled papers, and noises from the adjoining hallway encroached on Marzee's senses.

"Excuse me," the student next to him said. Two students needed to get by. His trance had obscured his full-sized erection until now. His quandary was apparent: he did not have enough room to push back; he could not draw in his legs far enough to let them by. He had to stand to let them pass.

Marzee acknowledged the request, motioned that he was packing his notes, placed his jacket over his lap, and furtively stuffed his penis along his leg in a pressure fit against his inner thigh. He stood up with his right leg slightly tilted forward in order to insure that the precarious lock remained secure.

"Sorry. Take it easy," he commented to the passersby.

"Yeah, easy bro," the two students responded in kind.

What is it about white boys saying bro? They say bro; they wear baseball caps backwards. They're damn fools. Are they trying to imitate black people? I wonder if they're even aware that bro comes from brother, and the use of brother came from the Nation of Islam, and from the Black Power movement of the Sixties. White boys need to stick with dude. Maybe if they knew bro aligned them with black Muslins, they'd stop saying it.

He twisted around to check who else was in his vicinity, and was glad to see he was alone. He sat down, concealing his socially sensitive protrusion. Students continued filing out of the lecture hall. A few lingered in their seats. Three students had darted toward the front to converse with the instructor. A girl wearing tight, thigh-length, workout pants and a halter top had zeroed in first. Marzee recognized her type: serious, studious demeanor—a fake—her underlying intent was to make herself known to the instructor. Two male students formed a loose perimeter, waiting for workout girl to finish her spiel. Marzee did not approve of her; she was bouncy and animated. Her body reminded him of the girl around the pool. He winced with restraint, forced to behold her narrow waist and chiseled muscular shoulders. *Animation equals issues,* he thought.

I should have a chat with the professor. Everyone likes his ass kissed. I'm sure this dude is no exception. Show some personal interest; tell him I liked the organization of the material; tell him I've been waiting to take psychology since I was in high school, but they didn't offer any psychology courses. No psychology and no philosophy in high school. What's with that? Too much bullshit for gullible youth?

He pulled out the syllabus. Though he had perused it last night, the instructor's name had not registered. He continued amusing himself with his ruminations.

Larry Butler, M.S. What! No PhD!? Shit, I'm being gypped. That's what I get for going to a jive state college. Poor ass parents, and no athletic ability. What's a nigga to do? They should at least have some special scholarship for being high yellow! He chuckled, unaware of the effect his own inner-ruminations had on him. A friendly voice percolated into his consciousness.

"You waiting to talk to me?" his instructor asked.

Startled, his trance was broken. "Huh? Oh, yeah." "How'd you know? I was just going to wait it out for the others to finish," Marzee replied.

"Sixth sense, I guess," Butler answered, smiling. "Actually, there's no such thing as a sixth sense. Your body language told me—your posture and expression. Most importantly, you didn't leave when the hot girl left, so I figured you were sticking around to talk to me."

Embarrassed about daydreaming, he reassured himself his psychology instructor could not read his mind. "Sharp of you. That what you learn when you get to be a doctor of psychology?" Marzee asked, hoping to elicit an explanation for why the guy didn't have a doctorate.

"Me, doctor? No. I'm working on it. Whatever natural sensitivity about human behavior I might possess now, will probably get trained out of me," Butler remarked sarcastically.

Marzee had only perused the syllabus since his real intent was to schmooze. Not wanting to be perceived as a sham, he scrambled to pose an authentic question. "Yeah, I was wondering. Will we spend much time learning about drugs and drug abuse?" he blurted.

"Yes. On the syllabus—I believe in week ten we discuss addictions and addictive behavior." Butler paused and smiled, taking a moment to assess Marzee a little closer. "You know the most heinous drug of all?" Butler asked.

"Heinous?" Marzee asked curiously.

"Heinous—yes! Dangerous. Evil—if a drug can be called evil," Butler responded.

He knew what heinous meant, and it bothered him Butler assumed he didn't. "I don't know. I guess heroin," he responded.

"It may come as a surprise to you, but it's alcohol," Butler replied, grinning with calm resolve, as if he had expected Marzee to respond in kind.

Discomfited, Marzee needed to compensate for his apparent ignorance of heinous and alcohol. Appearing to the white professor as if he were the uninformed African-American kid trying to get an education because someone told him to do it was unacceptable. "Damn! And I was going to ask the local wino outside the neighborhood Seven-Eleven to go in and buy me a bottle of Thunderbird. You just ruined my evening!" Marzee retorted. He watched Butler loosen up, reacting to his comeback.

"What's your name?" Mr. Butler asked.

"Marzee. Marzee Banks," Marzee replied.

"Marzee. Interesting name. How's that spelled?" Butler asked.

Marzee's gay alert was orange, going to red. He preferred Butler as a disinterested white professor. "M-A-R-Z-E-E," he spelled it out.

"You're part black, aren't you?" Butler asked unabashed.

Butler's inquiry caught him off guard. White people had asked him that question many times, but never so brash, usually preferring the more circuitous, euphemistic approach: "What nationality are you?" To which he'd answer, "American."

I like fucking with white people when they're trying to gloss over their inherent racism. This guy puts it right out there.

48

"Yes, I am," Marzee replied momentarily.

"Sorry. I hope I didn't offend you for being so forward. My doctoral research is cultural identity, and how skin color and self-esteem are connected." Butler hesitated, assessing Marzee's reaction to his candor. "The research involves collecting data, people answering questionnaires, and doing interviews. I'd like to interview you sometime."

Butler rattled Marzee. Never had a teacher been so forward with him; never had a teacher express interest in what it was like being black, let alone being light-skinned black. "Interview me? What do you mean?" Marzee asked skeptically.

"For my research. Ask you some questions. Maybe video tape it, if that would be OK with you?" Butler replied. "I'd be willing to pay you. I have a budget for research participants."

This shit sounds gay to me. I just wanted to kiss the teacher's ass; I didn't want a fucking date. "How much?" Marzee asked with reserved interest.

"Hmmm. I don't know. Twenty dollars?" Butler responded.

"Twenty bucks?!" Marzee chuckled defensively. He had no idea one could be paid to participate in psychological research. He figured the experience was payment enough. "How long will it take?"

"No longer than an hour," Butler answered.

Marzee had made up his mind before he came to college to keep an open mind, deciding not

49

everything that seems strange is gay. "I'll do it for free. No one ever interviewed me before," Marzee responded with resolve.

"That's great!" Butler squealed, pleased with Marzee's response. "I'm a part-timer here, but they gave me a temporary office I can use. What's your schedule look like next week, when you can spare an hour?"

Marzee did not trust why a white professor would take an interest in him. Still, he subdued his skepticism, thinking maybe Butler did see genuine value in him as a student, or maybe he was just telling the truth. "I think any day next week after class is OK," Marzee replied.

"By the way, I meant to mention in class that if you haven't already bought your textbook, I'd suggest you buy it online. It would save you lots of money. Have you used Amazon.com before?" Butler inquired.

"Yeah, but only to buy some new gloves. You know, to protect my hands while I'm pick'n cotton," Marzee replied with a mischievous smirk.

"Well, lots of white kids don't know how to use Amazon.com," Butler replied defensively. "Many don't even have computers—or email accounts."

All white folks don't think all blacks are dumb. I've got to drop this ghetto shit. He embarrassed himself once more, this time for white stereotyping. "Sorry. You're off the hook. I better get going. I need to hook up with a couple of *mah*

50

homies at the cafeteria," Marzee said, sarcastically emphasizing homies.

With his backpack over his shoulder, he turned and headed through the door, raising his free hand in a half-hearted wave as he strolled into the hallway. He felt uneasy about Butler's genuineness. The first day of class, and his instructor seemed to take a personal interest in him. *Is he gay, or what? He wants to interview me about being high yellow? Or does he want me to freak out on camera: jack off; rub my balls; shit like that. Research, my ass. He needs original jack off material. Damn. He could put the shit on the Internet. I can see it now. Richard, Freddie, everyone cracking up looking at me being a freak on YouTube. What was I thinking?*

He strode the short distance down the now not-so-crowded hallway to some sliding glass doors. He loved the authority he commanded when automatic doors sliced opened for his passage, conjuring images of Captain Kirk on the Enterprise. The tepid air of the Southern California autumn grazed his face. The sunlight crackled through the patchy sky. Hunger pangs assaulted him. The walk to the cafeteria would take less than five minutes, but the fear of someone recognizing him from yesterday concerned him. The route did not provide enough concealment. Outside, he felt exposed and vulnerable. He bowed his head, and hastened his gait.

The student center building loomed ahead, forcing him to unfurl his head to navigate through denser student traffic. He entered the building to meet his two childhood friends, Richard Ball and Freddie McCain. His mouth watered, anticipating Freddie's mother's shrimp gumbo, which they had agreed to share. Meeting his friends socially had less appeal—he anticipated another round of *the dozens*, a "ghetto-ish" practice which he felt he had outgrown. He sighted them seated at a corner cafeteria table.

"We ate yours already. Don't even stop!" Freddie commented seamlessly as they observed Marzee's approach, both cackling feverishly.

"That's right!" Richard confirmed, grinning. "I was too hungry to wait for your skinny, narrow little ass. I had mine, then kicked this nigga's ass over yours, too!" Marzee noticed three white students at an adjacent table, smiling nervously and continuing their subdued chatter.

Whenever black folks are loud, white folks get jittery. It should be the other way around. When white folks got loud, niggas got hanged. What upset these chucks and annes anyway? I'll bet they leave within two minutes. They're stupid. They don't know what I am. Probably think I'm another white boy or Arab or Italian, or some shit like that.

Marzee remained expressionless, totally ignoring his friend's comment. He sat directly across from Richard, positioning his face one foot from Richard, and stared directly at him.

"Get out mah face, fool!" Richard demanded.

"True, I am late." Marzee said unflinchingly with a tempered voice. "But I'm late for a good reason. Yo mama, Betty, told me high yella dick was hard to come by, so she made me fuck her extra long today. She told me she wished I had been available twenty years ago when she had to fuck yo daddy. Then at least today, you wouldn't be so black and ugly—and at least you'd know who your daddy was—me."

Freddie rolled out of his chair, doubled on the floor laughing. Richard absorbed the insult, grinning stoically.

"The problem with having you as a daddy would be the piss-colored tint. Nah! I'd rather stick to what I got," Richard replied.

Marzee had backed off from Richard only slightly, still maintaining an expressionless glare. "Yo mama likes the nickname I gave her. I call her Five-B: big, black, burly Betty Ball," Marzee retorted smoothly. He sat back in the cafeteria chair, crossed his legs, and folded his arms. "She even shouts it out when I'm fuck'n her doggy-style. The flabs of fat rolling off her big, fat, black ass, they slosh around, slapping me in the stomach! Bitch is loud, too. 'Yeah, baby! Call me Five-B again! Yeah, baby!'" He paused to assess Richard's demeanor. His goal was to eventually say something to tip his friend's emotions, and make him lose his cool. "And how'd that pussy get so cavernous? You ain't so big, nigga, so it didn't happen when she popped you out. Shit. The last dude who fucked her was still in there, lost. He was yell'n to me to help him out! Problem was, he couldn't find his car keys."

Freddie picked himself up off the floor. He was still hunched over in spasms of laughter as he precariously reseated himself. Richard grinned sheepishly, exuding an air of resilience: whatever Marzee said would not make him flinch. Nonetheless, his eyes glassed over.

"Say what you want," Richard responded resolutely. "Being piss-colored, and going home to a piss-colored mother and father is like living, breathing, and drinking piss all day and all night. Look at you! Your hair is piss; your skin is piss. It's even leaking into the whites of your eyes. Your teeth don't turn yellow—they turn piss. And nigga, your hair! It ain't nappy; it ain't straight. What do you call that shit, anyway? Shit looks like piss-colored poodle hair."

"Piss-colored poodle hair!?" Freddie yelped maniacally, contorting over the dining table, banging his fists and drooling.

Marzee and Richard discontinued their diatribe and turned in cadence. Both stared at Freddie.

"Nigga, I don't know what you're laughing at," Richard warned. "You're next."

Marzee glanced at the white students at the next table. He, Richard, and Freddie played the dozens through entire lunch periods in high school with lots of white students around, and he never gave it a second thought. Here he felt uneasy. "You know, I could sit here wasting time with you niggas all day, but I have another class soon, so I have to eat something," Marzee remarked.

"Eat, then!" Freddie replied, extracting himself from the table.

"Gimme that five dollars you owe me!" Marzee ordered.

Freddie reluctantly dug around in his pockets and pulled out two dollars and some change.

"That's all I got," Freddie exclaimed, displaying the pathetically crumbled bills in his palm.

"You better have Claretta work that old, tired, skinny ass of hers harder then," Marzee retorted, referring to Freddie's mother as he held out his hand. "Give me the two."

Freddie tossed the two dollars on the table, deliberately by-passing Marzee's hand. Marzee snatched the bills, stood up, and marched to the cafeteria line. He returned after a few minutes with a bowl of chili, a Pepsi, a bag of potato chips, and a Baby Ruth.

"You niggas were wrong for not saving me any gumbo," Marzee complained as he returned to his seat. "I was looking forward to that, too. I got delayed after psychology class. Teacher wanted to talk to me."

"Talk to you about what?" Richard queried skeptically. "'Bout be'n yella?"

"No," Freddie interrupted. "About how his sweet, tender, young ass could be used if he wants to get an A!"

"Well, actually, yes. That's exactly what he wanted to discuss," Marzee answered matter-of-factly, fidgeting with the cellophane-wrapped saltines.

"What?!" Freddie and Richard looked dumbfounded. "He wants to freak out with you?"

A sense of pressure—of flight—lingered in the background. He wanted to get up and leave. The satisfaction, the rush, he used to receive from his daily mutual-parent-bashing repartee with his friends eluded him. "No, fool!" Marzee snapped back. "He wants to know what it's like being light skinned, and having to survive in a world full of orangutans like you." Marzee paused to observe the effect of his insult. "No, really. The man said he's doing research on variations of skin color among African-Americans. He's particularly interested in what it's like being—light," Marzee added. He withheld a cringe as he saw Richard sneer.

"He can watch me kick'n yo ass. Then he'd know what it's like being you!" Richard remarked.

Marzee smirked. Other than taking a few sips from his Pepsi can, he had not eaten a bite. He opened the saltine cellophane, and dumped the crumbs over the chili. With obvious intent, Freddie attempted to manipulate a spoon in a trajectory toward Marzee's chili bowl. Marzee slapped his hand away like a pesky fly.

"Nigger!" Marzee snapped.

Freddie's hand and spoon made a hasty retreat, slumping back to an empty bowl of gumbo. Meanwhile, Richard's attention was directed elsewhere.

"Man, that sista is fine." Richard smacked his lips as he commented on an attractive African-American female student walking outside, passing the large pane window of the cafeteria. Both Freddie and Marzee twisted, looking in the direction of Richard's gaze.

"She's too light for you," Marzee said factually as he resumed slurping his chili.

"Too light for me?!" Richard rebuked piously. "You've never seen a sista as light as her with a nigga as light, or lighter, than her. If the nigga ain't black and ashy, he don't get the pussy. That means you—" Richard pointed tauntingly at Marzee with his finger in his face. "—pussy!"

"Then why go light at all?" Marzee offered philosophically. "Why not get the real deal? Why not go white?"

"White? You mean fuck white girls?" Freddie hissed incredulously.

Marzee's impatience momentarily waxed to rage. *What is this anger? I can't tolerate these fools any longer.* "Yes, that's what I mean. If you want light, why not just go to the logical extreme?" Marzee replied.

"Now the nigga's going all intellectual on us. Listen to him—logical extreme! When was the last time you even had any pussy?" Richard demanded, folding his arms mockingly. "I'll tell you. Never. That's because no sista would ever fuck you, unless you count that fat ass Cheryl Biggs back in the tenth grade. So now, since you can't get no black pussy anyway, what are you saying? White girls will fuck you?"

Suppressing the urge to simply get up and leave, he feared saying something he'd regret later. "I'm not saying anything. I merely posed a question. If you like light-skinned women so much, why not take it all the way?" Marzee replied with forced monotone.

"All the way?! Then by what you are saying, I should fuck an albino," Richard retorted with courtroom lucidity.

Freddie doubled up, and fell on the floor again with clown-like antics. The white group at the adjacent table had gotten their fill. They cut a silent and subtle retreat, attempting to feign an air of urgency about getting to class so as to not offend their black neighbors.

"It's a good retort, but my argument is linear. Yours is not. An albino is unnatural. They lack melanin, the protein responsible for skin coloration. Please keep the argument reserved to the pool of women without genetic defects." Marzee dropped his spoon in his now empty bowl, and commenced to peel open his candy bar. "Damn! This is a Baby Ruth. I meant to get a Butterfinger."

"Ok, let me ask your yellow, melanin-coated ass a question then. What would Mr. and Mrs. Banks say if you strutted through the front door with a white girl on your arm? You gonna say, 'Oh. I looked around at all the possibilities, and I figured, you two, as yellow as you are, are still too black for me, so I figured I'd just go to the logical extreme.'"

Marzee sat stoically with his arms folded across from Richard. He barely concealed a grin at the scenario Richard had presented. He had imagined the very same situation, dozens of times, as he explored the curves, skin, torsos, and hair of nameless white girls while he sat in class, or as he perused the surroundings while sauntering across campus, or while peeking through windows. Richard bore the torch of the rules, and Marzee resented his friend's self-assigned role as cultural overseer. He foresaw Richard's reaction as soon as he made mere mention of a hypothetical transgression across sexual-racial lines.

Marzee leaned over the table, confronting Richard, placing his nose five inches from his friend's. "You know, I think the darker a nigger is, the more entrenched he is in his color rules. He's less likely to explore options that are readily available to him. Listen up. There's no lynch gangs here. This is the twenty-first century. You're still thinking and talking that old, old, old nigger shit. That bullshit comes from your mama. She keeps your daddy's dick in an old pickle jar upstairs in the attic, far away from those dreaded white women," Marzee retorted.

Marzee did not throw a cream pie—he threw a dagger. The intent of the remark was not the usual fun and buffoonery of the dozens. Marzee had crossed the line, manipulating their standard joust as a means to lash out at Richard's beliefs—beliefs which Marzee thought were defended with religious ferocity. Marzee's query triggered a disproportionate amount of resistance. The question pricked the veneer of an emotional reservoir, burgeoning toward overflow.

"Leave my mama and daddy out of this. This discussion is just between you and me," Richard demanded with atypical sensitivity.

Marzee smelled blood, and he liked it. He smashed through the unsatisfying facade of the dozens, exposing the underlying animosity. "There is no discussion. I'm finished," Marzee replied, hesitating momentarily. "What's wrong? You afraid of white people? Damn, nigga. You act like you live in the South in the Thirties, or some shit like that. Really. Where'd you get that old-ass nigger shit? You can gawk, peer, eyeball, and drool at any bitch you want. It's legal. You ain't gonna get lynched. You see any hooded white men in here? Your mama has you on a very short leash. That woman is looking over your shoulder right now. I can hear her; so can you: 'Boy! You better leave those white girls alone!' Let me tell you something: If you learned your lessons in school as well as you learned yo mama's lame ass lessons—shit—you'd be an honor student!"

"I won't tell you again. Leave my mama out of this!" Richard warned menacingly.

"Civil rights didn't come this far so you can remain a slave to black-perpetuated bigotry meant to keep black men hooked to black women. You're a free man. Look at who you want; fuck who you want. In your case, you might have more luck with white girls. At least they may view you as a novelty, or as a tragedy, and give you some mercy pussy. Nigga, let me tell—" Marzee continued relentlessly.

Without warning, Richard tossed the remaining ice in his soft drink cup in Marzee's face. Marzee stopped and silently assessed the damage. He took a napkin from his tray, wiped his face, and brushed the few ice cubes from his lap. Freddie ceased his side antics, and awaited the outcome. Having acted impulsively, Richard froze in shock at what he had just done.

Marzee was relieved. He felt vindicated; his message was acknowledged. "You know I'm right. You just can't take the truth," Marzee stated apathetically. "You're pathetic." He slid his chair back, brushing off any additional debris, stood up, collected his backpack, and strutted away.

He burst through the automatic sliding doors into the courtyard commons, and hit a stride. The confrontation had exhilarated him. His friends had belittled and ridiculed him for furtive glances, peeks, and stolen glimpses. Now his secret passion

61

for white girls was out in the open. He was free; Freddie and Richard were not. They were bound by mores whose source permeated through Jim Crow and straightened hair. It propagated a social class defined by plastic-covered carpets, lamp shades, and sofa cushions.

His emotions triggered unintentional associations. The source, he did not know. He could not be aroused without consequences. An unwanted salve oozed in, intent upon distracting him from pain and pleasure. Subverting a renewed flare-up of voyeuristic obsession, he pushed toward his early afternoon class with forcefulness.

Disappointed that the door did not swing open before him, and not accommodated by other students transiting through, he repositioned his books and backpack, and opened the heavy wooden door. The brick building was a classic academic structure, older and majestic, fitting for a philosophy class. Physical, biological, and information sciences were housed in buildings whose architecture made a statement about the contained subject-matter—evolved, cutting-edge, twenty-first century. Nevertheless, those subjects' essential foundations originated generations ago in the venerability symbolized by this brick and ivy-laden earthquake trap.

The hall floor was wood, composed of long, warped, polished slats of interlaced cedar. The smell and color variation was unsurpassed by the contrived, repetitive geometric patterns of commercial vinyl floors. The wood gave and creaked under his footsteps. Wooden lockers, though no longer used, still lined the walls, the consistency interrupted by classroom doors.

He located his classroom, Room 121, halfway down the hall. The door was already opened. The classroom had desks—not the auditorium-style chairs with retractable writing surfaces. He had difficulty taking notes with tucked-in elbows. He sighed in disdain; wondering what is was about him, always attracting the more portly female students to sit next to him. His meager frame seemed to invite flesh overlap. He had adapted to taking notes with his elbow welded to his ribcage. He selected an aisle desk half-way from the front, guaranteeing left arm freedom.

With a few minutes remaining before class began, he decided to re-read the course description from the student catalog. He had waited years to take philosophy. Starting as a sophomore in high school, he had self-schooled himself in Spinoza, Kant, Hume, Marx, Nietzsche, Descartes, and Voltaire. He lusted for answers to the classically mundane timeless questions: What determines good and evil? Right and wrong? Grotesque and beautiful? Reality and fantasy? Science and religion?

Five minutes before class, and he was the first one there. He hoped the class would not be very full, but enough students had registered to assure the class would not be cancelled. The instructor had not arrived, though other students were finally meandering in. A fat girl squeezed by Marzee, and sat next to him.

A blond, lithe woman in her late thirties breezed by Marzee's side to occupy the front of the classroom. She owned the classroom. She dropped her shoulder bag on a long table, unzipped it, and extracted a manila folder, a textbook, and some other loose papers clipped together. She placed the manila folder and papers on the podium, shuffled through them, and then briefly scanned the class.

Marzee's jaw plunged. Such a woman cannot exist. Her tied dark-blonde hair hung long and thick to the small of her back. She appeared German or Nordic, but her skin was not the pale, pasty complexion he associated with Teutonic types. Her skin was naturally tanned and sensuous. Her full and spacious lips, not round and pucker-shaped, scorned lipstick. Her eyebrows, unplucked and unblemished, framed her crescent, blue-green eyes with perfect arches. Their definition highlighted her distinct nose. The cheekbones rose as monuments to her facial landscape, but not so high as to wave an Aryan flag. Her forehead typified a well-proportioned pallet, setting off her unbanged hairline from her not-too-round, not-too-square face.

His goddess' hemline rested about an inch above her bare knees. Her sculptured legs were greater than the sum of the parts: calves contoured and developed, knees symmetric and flush, ankles highlighted by smooth transition from her calves, and absolutely no hair stubble. Marzee thought she had to be an athlete—maybe a runner, or some other track and field event—not swimming or bicycling.

Her hourglass figure was not reminiscent of the Fifties Marilyn Monroe form, defined by full breasts, robust waistline, and wider hips. Rather, she was solid and hard with a soft coating. Her broad back and chest, and her full breasts, contributed to her upper body dimension, accentuated by narrower, though substantial, hips. She defined the antithesis of pear-shaped.

The drool on Marzee's chin cooled. He unconsciously wiped it off with his sleeve. He felt physically and emotionally aroused—not sexually aroused—but rather a tingling sensation, no erection. His body presented a novelty to which he had no reference. He was afraid to look at her. He opened his spiral notebook, and prepared to write.

Chapter 4
Utte Thorndike

Introductory Philosophy; Instructor: Utte Thorndike, PhD. Each syllable she spoke lingered in his ears. Her voice was melodic and crisp, highlighted with a mild German accent. The rhythm and cadence of the German language enraptured Marzee. The rapture was not a melodic quality, like Spanish, but rather, it had a beat, a rhythm, a code, a complex machination; not of tom-tom drums, congas, hollow sticks banged together, or tambourines—no one jumping, hooting, hollering, and yelling. His senses welled: he heard the chimes of human evolution. His mind's eye peered back at his life and circumstance: the accented voice induced loathing for his brethren's guttural utterances, and self-loathing from which he shrank away.

Utte had lectured for five minutes, her essence freezing him in the moment. She advanced from the recluse of her lectern to face the class unblocked and unhindered. Her movement and sheer sex appeal aroused Marzee, breaking his trance. Her skirt was tight around a narrow waist, tastefully gripping her hips, the hem creating a halo around her golden legs. Her sleeveless blouse exposed sleek, tan, muscularly toned arms and well-defined shoulders. Her hair was waist length, draping in a loose pony tail just grazing the small of her back.

*How old is she? She doesn't seem young;
she doesn't look old. She might be in her late
twenties. But her face—her face looks wise and
intelligent. Some pain, maybe, but not the lines of a
woman in her forties. Women I know in their forties
are out of shape, fat, burned-out, angry, and tired.
Freddie's mother, Richard's mother, most of my
friends' mothers are in their late forties. They are
fucked up, and fucked over. Life has taken its toll.
This woman does not have the lines of age and
frustration, the lines of collected disappointments
and lies. Maybe she's from a rich family. Is she
married? Ahh, the ring on her finger says yes! Only
a rich man could have such a woman. A bounty of
beauty not yet depleted by the ravages of time and
the onslaughts of bullshit. I'd say she's thirty-five.
Look at those legs. Look at that ass. My god, those
tits. Her chest size is at least forty.*

    *Married? Yes. Not just the ring, her name.
Thorndike is not German. She's married to some
white asshole. Certainly not married to a bro. She
should be, though. Only black dick could satisfy and
maintain a woman like this. I never met anyone with
that name before. It's British. I'm sure some
plantation owner had the name, Thorndike.*

    *The other female instructors here must hate
her. I noticed them; most are fat, ugly, pale, and
proletarian-looking. They look as if they had just
crawled out of their cracker-box production houses,
condominiums, or trailer-park tin cans, and*

waddled into work, dragging their book bags on wheels behind them.

"…this course requires student discussion of various philosophies. Throughout the semester you will be assigned weekly reading worksheets. These worksheets will prepare you to think critically about philosophical essays. The reading and discussion we do will culminate in three argument papers. This class will give you an opportunity to ponder and question ideas you've probably grown up to believe are true. Philosophers often challenge the beliefs we otherwise hold sacred," Utte announced, holding her audience steadfast.

Utte paused, surveying the class. She dragged a stool from the side of the lectern, centering it in front of the class. She hoisted herself on the stool, instilling an apparent aloof casualness.

He sensed Utte was dissatisfied; she wanted to say something, but could not strike the correct tone for her listeners. She needed to communicate a concern other than course guidelines.

"You can read the course outline in the syllabus. You can all read. No need to repeat it. But I need to emphasize something else—" Utte hesitated, looking for words to express herself, seeming uncertain where to begin. "The goals of this class are aimed toward engendering philosophy only—your ability to think critically and honestly about philosophical ideas. Writing is a critical part of your ability to express how you think. I cannot teach you how to write. This is not a writing class.

On the other hand, if I cannot understand what you are attempting to convey, if you do not express yourself in a clear and cogent manner, your point will be lost, as well as your grade. If you do not feel it is within your current capacity to write expository, I strongly suggest you take a writing class before you take this course," Utte announced with stoic clarity.

His gut churned as forlorn eroded his mood. He would die unfulfilled, as he could never have her—never, in his entire life. He was out-classed, out ranked, out-raced, and spent before ever applying. Like a starving beggar groveling outside an upscale restaurant—happy diners enjoying meals and warm social intercourse inside, unaware of his destitute despair—he was barred from entry. *Never, ever, ever would it happen. Never. Not in an alternate universe. Not in this life. Not in the next. I can have her only in my dreams, my fantasies. I can look at her when she is unaware.*

"All right, let's begin. On this first day of class, I'm going to propose a question for you to consider. I want you all to write several paragraphs in response to the issue I'll write the question on the board. You'll have one half hour to compose your thoughts and write. I'm not looking for a book chapter, just a few paragraphs. Is everyone prepared to write?"

Shuffling and grumbling commenced as students dug around in backpacks and purses. He was disappointed he had not sat in the first row so

Utte would be impressed with his preparedness. The fat girl next to him elbowed his arm.

The power and command of her words—the sumptuousness of her calves, legs, and ankles, framed by the wooden stool—created an ambivalence. The contrast seared itself into Marzee's mind. The sensory ensemble overwhelmed him; he found himself longing for more. He knew at a level out of his immediate awareness that all his senses—more than eyes and ears—had to consume this woman.

Utte extended her legs to slide off the stool. Her feminine quadriceps formed a conch-like tube, culminating at her knees. She dropped to the floor, went to the whiteboard, searched for a marker, and began to write.

She has to know what she does to people. She probably even turns on some of these girls— these lipstick lesbians. Marzee cut a side glance at the fat girl next to him. *She's not turned on—she's turned off. She's disgusted. She didn't take this class to have her self-esteem challenged. Problem is, she gets her self-esteem challenged wherever she goes. A young, fat-ass girl can't go anywhere without asking herself: what the fuck is going on with me? How come I'm such a fucking loser? The fat bitch looks sick, and it ain't 'cause of this little in-class assignment. She's sick from seeing this beautiful woman—a professor—and the experience is an affront to her very being. I've noticed how fat women react to good-looking women they see in public. The fat bitches become momentarily ill. And if the fatty's with a man, he better not look. To be a man stuck with a fat-ass bitch has to be the worst punishment of all. Like, what the fuck did I do to deserve this? A motherfucker must ask himself: How can karma be real, 'cause I didn't do enough evil in my life to merit this much punishment?*

What is terrorism? Utte wrote on the board. She spun around to assess the class. "Questions?"

A hand flew up in the back. An animated Latin male student in his mid-twenties proceeded before he was actually acknowledged.

"Yeah. Like, what do you mean, 'what is terrorism.' Like, you mean, blowing up sh…I mean…stuff?"

"If you believe terrorism means 'blowing up stuff,' then write about it, but give it some thought. You raised your hand one second after I wrote the question on the board," Utte responded with a smirk. "There is no right or wrong answer."

Marzee felt pressure to perform. He realized the ethical and political implications to the question. He was not prepared to compose such a treatise, but he wanted to impress. *In a half hour, what can I write? What's the best way to discuss terrorism? I remember from somewhere—maybe it was a movie—someone said, 'one man's terrorist is another man's freedom fighter.' The course catalog said this course would discuss ethics, good and evil, so then terrorism becomes an ethical issue: is it good or bad, right or wrong? Shit, I'd like to raise*

71

my hand, say something, but I might seem like a
fool, so I better be cool.

"Any other questions?" Utte inquired.
"Then, if there are no more questions, everyone is ready. Start writing. When you are finished, please put your paper up here in a pile. And remember, put your name on the paper," Utte instructed, reflecting some exasperation.

His head was his enemy, not allowing him to focus; causing him flights of fantasy, pondering her. *She's like sweet and sour. What's the word for that? I don't know. Synergistic? Two opposites going together to create a different thing. Yin-Yang? Damn. I wonder what she looks like naked? I must see her naked. I better concentrate on this writing assignment.*

He stared at his opened spiral notebook, griping his pen over the page, forcing his thoughts to the lined surface. The theme of his essay struck him after several moments. He would discuss terrorism from a utilitarian viewpoint, as a means toward social and political cleansing. Realizing few, if any, of his classmates would justify terrorism, he relished getting her attention. He fretted how to express his theme succinctly. His aim was to impress without appearing provincial, contrived, or pedantic.

Once he began, he tapped into a rhythm, a source of energy, a channel through which his intellectual creativity streamed without his thinking and involvement. His writing hit a stride, scrawling five pages in fifteen minutes. The sooner he could finish, the sooner he could think about her, unrestrained.

His frantic writing had worked up a sweat. The moisture on his forehead became increasingly uncomfortable in the un-air-conditioned classroom. The day was the gift of a Southern California autumn: a warm, Indian summer afternoon. As girls shed their outer garments, Marzee's thoughts drifted to the beach. Such a sunny day would generate a wealth of beach enthusiasts, wanting to take advantage of one of the last beach days before the rainy season begins.

Finished with his essay, he rested his head in his hands and found an inconspicuous angle from which to stare at Utte while she was preoccupied. His thoughts drifted. *Her accent—it sounds German. She's from Europe. They have topless and nude beaches in Europe. They aren't so uptight about titties there as they are here. With a body like hers, she must lie out nude on the beach. Then again, since they are not so uptight about bodies, that means little old grannies and grandpas with tits and ball sacks dragging in the sand probably run around naked. I need to go to Europe; I want to go to Europe; I deserve to go to Europe. I gotta escape these monkeys. They badger and plague me constantly. Fending them off drains me. They create noise in my psyche, drowning out the pleasantries of the world.*

Fuck these black motherfuckers! I'll think about her, lying on the beach.

I am the sand fly. I flitter along the footprints and ripples in the sand. Ahead of me a bronze, shiny mound protrudes over the rest of the grainy landscape. I zigzag my way to the glossy oasis to study the wondrous dunes before me. I light on a crop of dried kelp washed up from this morning's high tide. Other brethren buzz and dart around, unaware of the aesthetic wonder inches away, legs fully stretched, arms extended above her head. She glistens with oil and beads of sweat. Her skin is blemishless, smooth, clear. If I light, I will become entangled in the film of oil bound to her skin.

A bead of sweat accelerates from the peak of a deeply tanned brown nipple, and hesitates down the slalom of her naturally round breast, curling around the transition to her ribcage. Her succulent nipples culminate her breasts' summits, elongated by her up-stretched arms. Her nipple is more than a mere topical confluence, more than a landmark noted and passed too hastily. I must hold myself steady in the sea breeze. As he sat in a daze, daydreaming, impervious to the sights and sounds around him, he was unaware of Utte's approach from the aisle.

"Sir," she said, attempting to stir Marzee. "Sir!" she whispered loudly, nudging his shoulder.

Startled and embarrassed, he gathered his papers nervously, looking around as if he had lost something. He noticed his full erection, and closed his thighs around it. *Fuck! Busted*, he screamed at himself silently.

"Daydreaming?" she posed cryptically. "Or just dreaming?"

His erection evaporated quickly to the shame of being caught. He overcame the guilt and came to his senses, realizing she cannot read his mind. His self-consciousness followed the erection to oblivion. "I finished," he responded defensively. "I'm just resting."

"I'll take it now. Save you a trip to the front," she said, holding out her hand to receive his intellectual toil.

He was caught between flattered and disconcerted, wondering why she had singled him out for special attention. *Maybe she thought I was sleeping? Or maybe she knew I was thinking about her.* "Certainly," he responded with restrained composure, gathering and collating the notebook sheets. "Here you are, a gift for you," he added coyly, placing the papers in her grip.

"I noticed you wrote feverishly for fifteen minutes. Then you stared in space for another fifteen. I figured you were either finished or needed medical attention," Utte responded, answering Marzee's puzzled expression.

Students in their immediate vicinity became fidgety at their discourse. Some scribbled with fever pitch, while others were engaged in silent composition. Suddenly aware of disturbing the students writing, she took Marzee's papers, and returned to sit at the front of the class behind the table.

"You still have ten minutes to work," she announced. "If you are finished, please bring your work up here, and put it in a pile. Again, don't forget to put your name on the paper."

Trapped between paranoia and glee, his misgivings nullified the incident. *Why me?* he pondered. *What the fuck did I do to get her attention?* She had not approached other students. He was not seated front and center, demanding classroom limelight; nor was he the most attractive, nor ugliest, nor oddest, nor pierced, nor tattooed, nor most flagrant accoutrement-wearing person in the room. But the situation had created an opportunity to approach her after class.

Three-fourths of the class deposited their strained productions in front of Utte after another two minutes. With finalized resolve, they probably faced the culminating realization that profound thoughts would not ensue; that one was uninspired, and should accept an awakened tribute to self-actualized mediocrity. The few who remained caricaturized students frozen over unknown test items, praying, pondering, searching, probing their souls for answers to questions for which they drew a blank. An operationalization of terrorism eludes many. Others have intercepted the term over barking heads spewing Britney Spears and McDonalds. Given the benefit of the doubt, perhaps performance anxiety hinders undiscovered artful prose and truly erudite ethical insight.

Pragmatically, they simply do not possess the cognitive wherewithal to produce lucid expository.

Remaining conspicuously behind, Marzee felt like the fart in the elevator. Pressure mounted to offer a gesture explaining his dilatory departure. He offered a midrange whisper, not necessarily to avoid disrupting his cohorts, but rather to signify to his teacher that he was, indeed, mindful of others. "I'd like to discuss something with you after class, if you have time?" he asked obsequiously.

"Sure," Utte replied friendly, but a bit curt.

One by one the lingering students floated to the front, each laying his essay on the pile. Utte sat, perusing selected works as they departed. She looked up as each one passed, smiled briefly, and bid each student a civil farewell. Finally, the last student, an obese girl, waddled out, dragging her feet. Utte frowned as the girl departed.

Tense—almost panicky—he repeated to himself he had nothing to be nervous about. Rejection was not a potential outcome of this interaction. He wasn't going to ask her for her phone number; he would not be laughed at, or referred to as puny; he would not be disparagingly compared to a neighborhood peer who could run faster, shoot more hoops, or tackle, block, and catch passes with lackadaisical grace. Pejorative commentary would not be on the agenda. Her comments would be commensurate with her role.

She did not know him, and even if she became acquainted with him as a student, she would not judge his walk, talk, shoes, hair, eyes, skin color, or any of a plethora of personal characteristics which had fallen under critical review in his past. He decided he should be at ease, but his body would not comply with his mind's advice.

"I'm sorry. I hope I'm not delaying you," he said sheepishly as he gathered his book bag.

"No problem at all. It's my job. Usually there's a lot more students waiting to talk to me on the first day of class. I think the pre-test scared them away," she replied, smirking, as if that were her intent.

"I was just wondering. Did I do something wrong?" Marzee asked.

"Wrong?" Utte asked contemplatively. "Oh. You're wondering why I approached you during class. I'm sorry if I embarrassed you. No, nothing wrong. In fact, you may have done something right," she replied looking up, delivering a consoling smile.

Traumatized by his social awkwardness, the conversation seemed surreal, leaving him feeling dissociated and without frame of reference. "Something right? That'll be different," he replied with dejection.

"What's the matter? Not used to things being right?" She raised an eyebrow, and grinned a mischievous grin. Marzee stood directly in front of her, self-conscious about an impending erection.

With his self-esteem plummeting to new lows, he wished he could launch into jocular monologue, impressing this woman, convincing her that he was a man of the world, one worthy of her respect and body. "No, I just didn't know if...what...I should do when I was finished writing," he explained, faltering.

"Sorry. I didn't explain what to do when students were finished. You appeared to have completed your essay. I wanted to get a class sample...not that you're representative of the class, mind you." Utte replied, winking. "Have you ever taken a philosophy course? Perhaps this class will be too basic." She looked back and forth between him and his essay.

He surged inside, stirring with colliding emotions. He had never spoken with such a woman. *Please, don't say something fucked up,* he chided himself. Marzee's heart raced. His opportunity to impress was now, but anything he might venture could be a mistake. "I've never taken a formal course before, but I've read a lot. I have a keen interest in the European existential thinkers— especially Hesse, Mann, and Kafka."

"German writers?" Utte asked startled.

He felt exuberant, like he hit the right nerve. "Yes. Like, I've read Hesse's *Siddhartha and Steppenwolf,* Mann's *Death in Venice*, and a bunch of Kafka's short stories," he relayed with enthusiasm, then hesitating. "Aren't you German?"

79

Marzee noticed Utte looking askance. His momentum turned to sludge. Had his question disturbed her?

"Yes, I'm originally from Germany," she answered stoically, pausing. "Before your state elected its current illustrious Austrian governor, I noticed when Americans encountered a German accent—and 'I'll be back' really isn't exemplary, anyway—the speaker was a sadistic Nazi interrogator, a rocket scientist, or a bearded psychoanalyst," she commented, studying Marzee to see if he comprehended her insight.

While they conversed, his eyes darted in furtive scans, trying to detect details of her body— more skin, curves he hadn't noticed during class, signs of undergarments. He stopped suddenly when she looked at him directly. "Yeah, I noticed the same thing. Like in James Bond movies, the bad guy always has a German accent. You know, like 'T minus sixty seconds, and counting,'" Marzee pronounced with superb German-accent elocution.

Utte erupted in laughter. She laughed so hard, she snorted. "My husband and I were just discussing the very same thing the other night. He mentioned what you just said—a character in Bond movies always announces the time to the big explosion, and the accent is always German. He even imitated the accent," she described, animated.

His earlier sense of dissociation had dissipated. She had turned so that her bare leg was in eye-shot. He strained not to look. *Is she doing that on purpose?* he thought, toiling to not stare. "How long have you been here? In America, I mean," he inquired half-heartedly.

"Four years," Utte replied, returning to her terse demeanor.

Fighting an impending erection, he longed to see her naked. When he looked at her, her clothes melted off. He had to see her naked, but how? *Does she know what I'm thinking, that my dick is going to burst out of my pants?* "That's something I've dreamed about doing—going to another country, like Germany, or France, and going to school there. Immigrating to another country—I wish I could do that," Marzee said dreamily.

"Why don't you?" Utte asked with matter-of-fact directness.

Restraining his pent up emotions, he had to concoct a rational response. He sported a pensive expression after mulling over what she had proposed. "Money, I guess. And I really don't know where to go, or how to do it." He paused, boiling inside from his first eye-to-eye look at her. "But those are excuses, aren't they? That from which I escape, pulls me back, telling me I can't leave," Marzee responded, aware he had just divulged a personal flaw. A shadow fell across his face. "I just had a disagreeable discussion with my friends about the beliefs they cling to. That would explain their reluctance—and I suppose, mine—to change or leave," he added.

81

"You have to take action. You could plan a trip to Europe with your friends. Make it a group trip," Utte suggested enthusiastically.

Sensing her desire to disengage, he needed to entice her to remain longer, maybe with some personal color. "My friends won't go downtown to see a play. Matter of fact, they specifically told me they would not go to Europe: 'not to see a bunch of old buildings, museums, pictures of dead white folks, and hear some language they don't speak' were their exact words," Marzee recited with down-trodden expression.

"And what did you tell them?" Utte asked, reflecting the effect Marzee had sought.

"I told them they don't speak English themselves, anyway, so what difference would it make?" he answered.

"That's interesting," Utte replied introspectively, looking troubled. "One of the reasons I left my country was because of the same narrow-minded thinking. I found Americans to be much more open-minded."

Utte's comment caused him to bristle. Black history and his personal experiences had yielded a paucity of open-minded Americans. "You found white, educated, middle-class Americans to be much more open-minded," Marzee corrected abruptly.

"I suppose you're right. Most of my contacts were with Caucasians in university settings," Utte replied, glancing at the wall clock. "I better get going. I'll be late for my client." Utte gathered her papers, loading them in her leather carrying bag.

Uncertain whether she recognized he was black, he hoped his criticism had not disturbed her. "Client? You're a tutor?" Marzee asked.

"Tutor? No, nothing to do with school. I'm a personal fitness trainer," she said, distracted by her preparations to leave. Marzee looked puzzled. "You know—in a gym. Weight training. Body building," she explained, busy with her bag.

His mood tumbled. Embarrassed and mortified, he had hoped his enlightened discourse— his rap—would beget more face time. "Oh," Marzee mumbled. "Well, thanks for taking time to talk with me. See you next week," he said, already backing out to leave.

"Sure. Have a good week," Utte responded, displaying a perfunctory smile.

His friends' deriding badgering buzzed in his head. Perhaps they were right—he was inept. If he could only depart without tripping on his shoe laces, he'd be happy. "Bye," he said nervously, exiting with the stride of someone having completed a heavy leg workout. His fast pulse and churning stomach: the demon took control.

The empty hallway beckoned him. His body reacted ahead of his blind-sighted awareness. He took a sharp right turn, hastening his pace. The intense focus blurred his vision. The hall became a dim tunnel, the sunlight shining through the door at the far end. Classroom doors were recessed into the

83

wall, creating a series of cubbies along the hallway. Passing the adjacent classroom, he saw a class in session, so he ducked into the next available doorway. He poked his head out, checking both directions. *I must maintain stealth; not attract suspicion.* He had waited for her to emerge, but sitting cross-legged and alone in front of the door would look too peculiar. He withdrew into the empty classroom, and crouched below the door window, holding it slightly ajar, so he could hear footsteps. He had heard her footsteps in class only briefly, but he could recognize them over roaring falls. He would shadow her once she passed his position. If she went the other direction, he could still follow.

He remained squatting behind the door, heart pounding—breathing short, fast, shallow breaths—nervous sweat in his armpits. The sound of floppies became louder, then receded in the other direction. The potential intruder vanished.

He heard his beloved's cadence, coming in his direction. Her rapid gait was distinctive as she breezed by his position. He jumped up and scrambled through the door. Staying low to the floor, he cautiously poked his head out, checking in both directions for observers. As she approached the exit door, the bright sunlight created a stark cameo, irradiating her form. He came from hiding, running down the hall after her so as to not lose track.

Pedestrian traffic on campus was light, not offering Marzee much cover. He glimpsed Utte cutting across a grass-groomed plaza. *She must be headed for the staff parking lot.* He chased after her, utilizing available cover to obscure his pursuit—trees, a statue, a group of benches. Cars in the parking lot would provide camouflage thereafter.

He scurried in a power walk toward some benches, and then sat quickly with his side toward Utte's direction. He feigned rummaging around in his backpack, appearing busy with mundane activity. Looking toward her as she reached the parking lot, he was intent on not losing sight. His blood surged as he anticipated his next move. He darted toward a statue on the edge of the plaza bordering the parking lot. He admired the statue's artistic splendor with one eye, and the splendor of his prey with his other.

After taking refuge behind the statue, he attempted to appear inconspicuous. She had halted abruptly to search for her keys. If she turned back, catching him behind this Lipchitz knockoff would not be good. He could hear his valves opening and closing in his ears. His tongue stuck to the roof of his mouth. He had to get closer.

He ran toward the parking lot, scurrying between several parked cars, and dove to take cover. He was within fifty feet of her position. He planted his belly against the pavement, taking aim under the cars. Her perfect ankles and calves made easy targets from his vantage point. A cursory scan assured no one was around. If someone spotted him, they would be certain he was a thief.

Peeking over the trunk of a parked car, he raised himself for a better look, like a gopher from a hole. She opened the trunk and tossed in her leather tote bag. The parking lot exit was in his direction. He decided to remain crouched between two parked cars, allowing him to observe her undetected as she drove by. Timing was critical: he had to come out of hiding long enough to view her car, and hopefully, memorize her license plate number.

Utte started her engine. The whir of her convertible top going down excited him. He peeked around the rear bumper of the car hiding him, relieved that his assumption was correct: she drove in his direction. He raised his torso high enough to observe the late model white convertible BMW. The sun's reflection from her side view mirror blinded his view of the license plate number, glimpsing only a small bumper sticker with a "D". She rounded the corner, and disappeared.

Utte. Utte. Utte. Her name consumed his thoughts. Desperate for more, he had to discover where she lived—the only way he could watch her, unfettered.

I'll find her on the Internet! He turned tail and jogged toward the library building. Looming in the distance, he couldn't get there fast enough. Such a majestic structure— wide marble stairs and pillars—it reminded him of Rome or Greece. Still strapped with a phone line connection at home for Internet access, he often used the library computers instead. After checking his wallet for his pass card with his student ID, he scurried toward his favorite workstation. He dropped his book bag next to the desk, and sat down like a piano maestro preparing to play a sonata.

Utte. Where is she? What is she? She is German; she teaches philosophy at a state college; she is a fitness trainer; she drives a convertible, white BMW; she is married, and her last name is Thorndike. After switching on the monitor, he entered his student ID and pass code at the prompts, and began.

He stared at the icons on the screen. "Where do I start?" he muttered. He tried generic telephone number lookups first, but that search was unfruitful. Next he pulled up Google, but all combinations of her name and locations yielded nothing.

"What!" he hissed, at the empty hit list. Perhaps Internet traces of her would be more likely on a German search engine. He changed the Google URL to 'http://www.google.de,' submitting her name to the German Google search engine.

"Not one single return!" he gasped in disbelief. "It's almost as if she didn't exist. Just being a teacher at Long Beach State should have produced something."

He logged into the Long Beach State web site, and scanned the 'Course Schedule' listings until he found her philosophy class—'TBA' was listed under 'Instructor.' "Well, that's not her name either," he mused silently frustrated.

The Internet channeled the world's knowledge to your fingertips—he relished that fact. If the information was not readily available through publically accessible databases—free ones—one could pay a search service to find what you're looking for. His investigative resourcefulness was put to the test several months ago when some new neighbors moved on his block. They were elusive, avoiding questions regarding where they had lived, what the husband did for a living, how many kids they had, and other personal queries normally posed to those seeking neighborhood rite of passage. Marzee's mother fretted, ranting about this unacceptable lack of candor. No one in the neighborhood knew anything about them. Mr. Banks had exhausted his pool of informants. Naturally, in the absence of clear evidence and hard facts, rumors and speculation flourished. Marzee had taken it upon himself, quietly and covertly, to discover the true nature of the mysterious new neighbors.

He pried the new neighbor's name and previous address from the postman, who liked Marzee. He had read about a security Internet service, performing detailed background checks for a price. The hype lured him to the search agency's website, where he registered, obtained a user name and password, provided his PayPal account information, and entered the information his postal-worker friend had provided him. For $29.95 the company promised former addresses, bankruptcies, credit reports, aliases, criminal records, and any sex offender registration. Within twenty-four hours the company delivered as promised. They emailed a document listing his neighbors' residences for ten years, and the bonus addendum: the man had been registered as a sex offender in Maryland eight years ago. Armed with this additional information, he narrowed his search within relevant news archives. He discovered the neighbor had been involved in a Catholic seminary scandal. Several of the seminarians had lured boys into their dormitory rooms to pose for nude photographs. He decided to keep this finding to himself, never disclosing it to anyone.

Acquiring Utte Thorndike's history presented a similar challenge. He logged onto the search company's website, entering his user name and password. *She has to live near school. How long? No longer than a year. How old is she? Mid to late thirties. I don't care about this other bullshit. I just want to know where she lives.* He entered her name, the state, estimated her age to be thirty-six, and agreed to the $29.95 fee. A message stated his order had been processed, and an email confirmation would be sent to him along with the order number. Now he had to wait. He went home, dreading the familial routine awaiting him.

Upon waking the next morning, he immediately turned on his computer, and impatiently waited for it to boot up. He logged into his email service, anticipating the answer to his query from the day before. He found one unread message in his mailbox with the subject line: Utte Thorndike.

"The following is a history of reported addresses for Utte Thorndike. In most cases the current address is the first reported address; however, it occasionally it appears elsewhere in the list."

1. 148 Conch Way Seal Beach CA
2. An unknown address in Washington, DC
3. An unknown address in Virginia
No other addresses were listed.

Chapter 5
Munich

"Zwanzig zerquetschte Zwetschgen und zwanzig zerquetschte Zwetschgen machen vierzig zerquetschte Zwetschgen," Utte shouted over the beer hall noise while she laughed encouragingly at John Thorndike. "A German tongue-twister many Germans have problems with. If you can repeat it aloud—no mistakes, no hesitations, fluently, own it—then you will have mastered the language. Forget reading Schiller and Goethe."

John took another swig of beer, and leaned across the table closer to Utte. "It's too noisy in here to talk—too public to fuck. I don't understand this place," he hollered two inches from her ear, straining for her to hear him.

Bringing John to Munich's Löwenbräu was a field trip, not a date. She had hoped this American would evince more cultural empathy. "You don't understand it because you don't understand the German psyche," Utte responded. "We don't need to hear every word; we do not need constant discourse to be entertained. It's the camaraderie, the reverie. The commotion is the reason to be here."

"It doesn't make a difference. I'm here with you. That's all that counts," John replied, leaning even further over the table, so he could kiss her ear when he talked. The four boisterous college-aged boys sitting next to them at the stretched indoor picnic table departed, cheerily patting and slapping

91

John and Utte on the back as if they were all returning to the same dormitory.

"You see?" Utte proclaimed, referring to the departing boys, then acknowledging John's peck of affection. "This place is not about drinking beer. This hall engenders a mood, a feeling, an ambiance. We call it *Stimmung*. This place is not about closing deals, it's about being German."

"I don't want to close a deal—I want to open one. Let's go back to my place," John yelled as he swilled down what was left in his stein.

Utte smirked, realizing no lessons were to be taught, no cultural insights conveyed. She playfully spidered her hand across the table, then captured his hand. She caressed it, and then hoisted it to her face, sucking each of his fingers individually, sensually. She leaned over the table, placing her mouth over his ear. "You just want to go home and fuck, don't you?"

John's eyes shone agreement. "That's what I love about you. You can read my mind, even in all this noise."

"Your mind? No. I could tell by your fingers. Your fingers have an erection. Didn't you know fingers give the same tell-tale sign as a lump in a man's pants?"

"You're sooo full of shit," John remarked, tugging her chin and withdrawing his hand.

Utte plunged her hand under the table, thrusting it along his thigh to his crotch. "You see!" she exclaimed haughtily, "I'm right."

"Bullshit. You were sucking on my fingers and gave me a hard-on."

She wondered why his brilliance had not generalized to other areas beyond particle physics. Afsane was right again. "Let's just go to your place," she responded assertively.

Utte and John side-winded, contorted, and finagled themselves through the standing-room crowd to the outdoor lobby where the autumn coolness had beset the Bavarian evening. John buttoned his coat, and pulled up his collar, attempting to transition from the body-heated warmth and congeniality within the Biergarten. As inconspicuous as he tried to be, Utte noticed him admiring her form. He admired her constantly: eating breakfast, taking a shower, getting dressed, walking—from front or rear, short skirt, slacks, naked, or underwear. He insisted upon turning on all the bedroom lights when they had sex, and he chose positions giving him optimal vantage points. Utte's firm body under her shear blouse and slacks stiffened against the cool air.

The couple walked quietly along Frauenhoferstrasse, and headed toward the U-Bahn station. The wind whipped up from the Isar, causing Utte's hair to electrically swirl above her head. When she was a girl in Simbach, the Inn breeze had the same effect. The sting of the wind stimulated a flashback: The image of her father beating her sister with his belt caused her to cringe.

"Cold?" John asked, using the occasion to put his arm around her.

She did not want the physical closeness, especially while walking. It caused a contrived bond, imposed by the presumption of the presence of masculine protection. It was a role-lie; it did not exist. She nestled closer to him. He had to believe she was genuine.

"Maybe, a little," she answered. If he were truly perceptive, he could have detected the difference between a shiver and a cringe. She put her arm around his waist. She was grateful John did not stink from the arm pit like so many other men. The recalled sensation remained with her. *Why did he beat her? She was stronger than me. I was weak and helpless. I was blond; she was dark. I was frail; she was robust. I hate him. I hate his memory. I'm glad he's dead. I hope my sister went to urinate on his grave, as she had promised him she would do.* Her memories only reconfirmed her conviction to her cause. *Someone must uphold the banner of the weak and oppressed. Who can form armies and buy weapons? Nations with weapons are occupied oppressing their own people. And people oppress themselves by their own proletarian hedonism. Their so-called freedom is their slavery; their trite ideas of righteousness are their blinders. John is perfect for our cause: smart enough to hear; not aware enough to see. I sought him, found him, and lured him. Now I must convince him.* Forlorn flashed through her, as if she had committed the worst sin. *I must eventually kill him.*

They rode the U-Bahn to Universität, intertwined emotionally during the entire ten minute ride. Even the drunk who got on the train at Marienplatz, and sat across from them, did not disrupt the couple's trance. They emerged from the U-Bahn station, and walked the two hundred meters to John's apartment, adjacent to the University of Munich. His third floor flat was the largest unit in the five story building.

"Like the new picture?" John asked after opening the door, gesturing to a striking black-and-white nude female photo sprawled across three meters of an otherwise bare living room wall.

Utte gasped noticeably, not at the subject matter, but at the exquisiteness of the rendering. She was aware her body was beautiful, but John Thorndike portrayed it as a monument to artistic expression. He was an accomplished amateur photographer, and this piece belonged in a museum.

"I was a photographer in search of a model. Not only did I find my soul mate, I found the point of focus for my artistic expression," he remarked, throwing his coat on the sofa, and embracing her from the rear.

He's truly enamored with me, but will he help me kill millions? Philosophically unsettled— socially resentful. "I'm impressed. It's a magnificent work. Have you masturbated to it yet?" Utte asked drolly, reaching around to unzip his pants.

She screwed herself about-face within his grasp, burrowing her face into his neck—breathing, kissing, sucking, licking, biting—unleashing the sublime power of her oral attributes. He bared his neck to the vampiress, closing his eyes and readying himself for the sensual onslaught. After a few moments, her skin beckoned. He peeled her blouse over her head, inverting it as it bared her upper torso. He kneeled before her, praying, worshiping, making tribulation to his false, but beautiful, god. Her slacks melted off, like hot wax, and she lifted each foot, shaking it to rid herself the encumbrance. He inhaled her soft, compact, well-groomed plot of pubic hair, using his nose to embellish the part.

Utte possessed effortless control. She evinced intense sexual passion while manipulating each apparent reflex action—instantly deliberating meanings and contingencies for every expression, blurring spontaneity and premeditation. Teaching philosophy, writing about Schopenhauer, discussing Nietzsche, or negotiating a play of sex and passion—she was the model of fluent, flawless self-management.

John inched Utte toward a sofa from the top of which he yanked a silk sheet. He effortlessly manipulated the silk, spreading it loosely over the rug, while holding Utte with his head over her abdomen.

"No more rug burns," he commented while slipping out of his clothes.

From a kneeling position, he hoisted her left leg jack-knife fashion, and rested it on his shoulder. He kissed and nibbled the inside of her leg from her ankle, up and down, taking a different track each time until he had circumscribed her entire leg. He repeated the same motion for the other leg. He made similar strokes along her torso, back and forth, up and down. Then her arms. Not a square millimeter of her body was unadorned by his lips and tongue. The process took an hour.

Men adored Utte, but John was the first to put the adoration to skillful practice, expressing the passion with clear and deliberate style. She was not an object for ejaculatory release. His adoration resulted in a transfer of pleasure—a sophisticated, yet unrestrained, banquet of tactile delight.

Utte lapsed into sexual abandon. She jerked herself back to awareness, feeling careless that she had allowed herself to drift away. She excluded herself from a moment she would have enjoyed. She had tempered her orchestrated outsides to not match her regimented insides. Concerned about her careless lapse, she checked to see if John had noticed the sudden disruption in her flow. "You're not going to cum?" she asked.

"No. I'll save it until later—maybe in the shower. Coming is such a crude finale to such an exquisite experience." He paused thoughtfully. "German captures it perfectly: *speisen und fressen,* culinary, artful dining versus animal-like engorgement."

Utte found it difficult not being impressed with John's level of self-control. He defined hedonism. She did not want to trust him, but she had to. "You've elevated having sex to a new level. I'm not just telling you this to flatter you: I've never come so hard, so many times, with anyone else," she announced.

John Thorndike was average height, lithe, with long, well-defined muscles under pale, clear skin. He stood, his still erect penis protruding obtusely to his flat stomach from Utte's floor perspective.

"Put it back inside me and cum," Utte whined uncharacteristically, as if trying to convince a sick man to remain bed-ridden and still.

"I want to show you a sketch—something I'm designing. It's an invention," John chanted, ignoring her request. He disappeared into a back room, and returned shortly with several pieces of paper. "You ever see Woody Allen's movie, *Sleeper*?" he asked.

John's persistent erection, and his apparent indifference, distracted Utte, and excited her. The incongruence titillated her. "You're designing a real orgasmatron?" she exclaimed, not at all serious.

He looked at her puzzled, disappointed. "Well, yes," he replied. His penis drooped languidly.

She lost sight of her purpose. A childish effervescence overcame her. "Let me see those papers," she demanded, giddily extending her arm straight up from the floor. "You really didn't design a device that controls sexual brain function," Utte exclaimed, flipping over, supporting herself with her elbows to peruse John's schematics.

"You didn't let me finish. It's not an orgasmatron—not like in the movie. It senses what your body is doing—your autonomic nervous system, and to a degree, your brain waves—and it moves you accordingly. It facilitates the process; it amplifies it, makes it resonate."

If I were to have a child, I would have it with this man. What a waste. "These look like pulleys," she replied, pointing to the drawing. "And this, a harness?"

"Right. The woman—in this case, you—sits here. The man—" He postured modestly, gesturing to himself. "—lies face up, below the harness. The woman's vagina is exposed through here." He pointed. "These pulleys and harnesses are unique, a blend of bungees, pulleys, cords, and servos. I'm looking into patenting them. They simulate smooth muscle coordination—true muscle fiber simulation. The harness senses blood pressure, electrodermal conductivity, pulse, muscular tension. But here's the key: the infrared laser in this ceiling mounted control box follows the woman's scalp. It picks up very low amplitude voltage signals— electroencephalographic waves, brain waves. The autonomic and EEG information feeds back into the processor which controls the motors and servos which control the harness suspension. It moves her in perfect rhythm, resonating with her body's orgasmic crescendo. It should produce the most powerful orgasm ever. I'd like for you to be the first to try it."

Utte strained her neck, staring up at John. She realized women were John's weakness. And in that category, the field was narrowed to her. The time was ripe to present her pitch. She feared Afsane's brutal henchman, Mansour, would kill him within a few days if he did not accept; much later if he did. She stuffed her ambivalence, knowing the cause prevailed.

"Your mind could be put to a higher purpose other than helping women have orgasms," she remarked as she did a push-up off the floor.

"I know. The defense department wants to hire me to do all kinds of helpful things," he replied with a cryptic snort.

"Come take a shower with me," Utte commanded, grabbing his penis and pulling him along toward the bathroom door.

"How can I resist?" John replied, reluctantly dropping his design papers on the floor.

They had showered together frequently, so the process was a choreographed dance. Utte scrubbed his back gently with a loofah while he arched forward, hands pressed against the tile wall. She was uneasy. A negative response would be unacceptable; indifference would render similar results. Rejection had consequences, and the outcome was not in her immediate control. "I've always told you the truth. You know I'm allied with a freedom fighting organization here in Munich," she stated matter-of-factly.

"I know you've got terrorist inclinations," John replied as he turned to face her.

"I like you very much, John. But there's a reason we're together."

"I know," he responded, clearing his throat nervously. "I took a big chance being with you. I couldn't help myself."

The gloom disturbed her. She repressed her conscience—early-instilled social curricula programming proliferated by a flawed system. "Initially, we wanted to test our cover. We knew your security agencies would check out anybody you fraternized with, and especially anybody with whom you were intimate. If they checked me out, and didn't find anything, then our cover was sound. They never approached you about me?"

"They asked me how much I knew about you—whether you talked about your politics. I told them to mind their own fucking business. I'm a private citizen, and I'll fuck whomever I please."

Utte winced. It was to John's disadvantage—and theirs—to react so. "I'm sure they did not take that comment lightly. Did they threaten you with reprisal?"

"They told me unscrupulous types, such as yourself—" He put his arms around her waist, squeezing each butt check firmly, "—would attempt to win my trust. That I should be ever vigilant about

101

potential infiltrators attempting to coerce me to procure nuclear materials. It's a moot point. They restrict my access to nuclear materials, even in the low quantities I use them. But about you? After I made that 'go fuck yourself' remark, they never came back to warn me. That was about four months ago. "

Utte braced herself, fearing the worst. "We want. No, I want you to join our cause. If not to join, to earnestly help us in our mission," she announced unabashedly.

"I figured we'd have this conversation eventually. You know I'm not interested in killing anyone, innocent or otherwise. And I'm not really political."

Standing naked and wet in the shower, she had to present an articulate and convincing argument. With disdain, she launched into her soliloquy. She turned to face him, placing her palm against his chest, and nudged him back gently against the wall out of the shower spray. She remained in the stream, the water splashing against her belly. "Our mission is to create a situation requiring the underlying forces of world government—not simply the US State Department or the United Nations or China or the European Union, but the prime mover of world economy— require the global cultures to alter the direction of economies over the next century."

"You would have to wield a very large stick—the largest stick ever—to accomplish that goal. What you propose is pure idealism—fantasy. It's trite rhetoric, at best," John retorted calmly and without cynicism.

Her affect became even more serious and staunch. She had to convince him. "The people responsible for the shape of global economies are very real, with names and families. They want you to believe their existence is paranoid folly, long-winded conspiracy theory without any credibility. The explosion of communications media, the Internet, and statistical profiling in the past forty years has given them immense power: the power to make you believe, without wielding a single weapon. We know who these people are. We can turn the tide. Our mission is humanitarian, utilitarian, in every sense of the word. At the risk of sounding grandiose, our goal is the most noble in all of history."

She noticed her naked speech had excited him. John turned off the water and stepped out of the peculiarly large shower stall for a European bathroom. He handed Utte a towel, remaining silent while drying himself. Her heart fluttered. She wanted him to believe in her, to take her seriously. She knew he was intelligent beyond the capacity to understand what she had explained. But intelligence and early-seeded beliefs were often diametrically opposed: the devout Islamic astrophysicist; the faithful Catholic evolutionary biologist; the fundamental Christian tectonic plate geologist.

"I'd like to meet your family," John remarked, breaking a five-minute silence.

Surprised by John's request, he had expected a comment in-line with their discussion. "I told you about my family. My father is dead. I haven't spoken to my mother in over ten years. My sister, even longer."

"You have no other siblings, relatives, early childhood friends? How about your hometown? The grade school you attended—I'd like for us to visit it."

Flustered, she had not prepared a contingency. She was at a loss for words. "You don't know what you're asking. I haven't been there in years. It's gone. The ties are severed."

"You're asking me to sever entrenched beliefs; join you in a cause that could very well end my life, and you deny me access to your past?" he implored.

John had pin-pointed her flaw. Her current agenda was only possible because of familial attrition. Absence did not mean resolution. Her past was a landfill, and seeping gas from the rot underground would eventually lead to devastation.

"You ask me to convert. All religions claim the higher moral ground; all expound the greatest good. That is what you just said: 'the most noble goal in all of history.' He nudged her shoulders for her to rotate, so he could dry her back. "I would not be the first to convert to the religion of a loved one. But I feel the love is imbalanced. If I were to ask you to convert to my religion, whatever that might be, you'd walk out the door."

She choked down her defensiveness, hoping John had not detected it. "You have no religion," she retorted calmly.

"Yes, I do. It's rationalism. And you've replaced whatever misery you've abandoned in your past with this fanaticism you claim holds the highest moral value. Your cause is not absolute—you've merely distracted yourself. Its truth is powered by your need to survive."

She had underestimated John. He knew her better than she had figured; perhaps better than she knew herself. Her resolution was a façade, a house of cards. Its foundation was an optical illusion, real until challenged with empiricism. She had to tidy her past, tie off the loose ends. *What would Afsane say?* "I agree; you're right. We'll go back to my hometown. I'll show you my school, the house I grew up in, we'll even look up childhood friends. Simbach is not too far away, about two hours from Munich, on the Inn River."

John dropped his towel across the tub and pulled Utte close. "I've looked for you all my life. Perhaps we can live through this."

She kissed him deeply, secretly pining for the normal life from which she was deprived. Afsane's voice intervened, warning her of the *wicked, soothing voice of her culture.* Social norms had corroded her. She needed further work, scraping out the remains of what others would deem true humanity: love, caring, feeling for others—delusions to keep the middle class in place; proletarian ideals duping many to abide the few.

"Isn't Braunau am Inn across the river from Simbach?" John asked after disengaging from the kiss. "I've always meant to visit that town. You grew up across the river from where Adolf Hitler was born."

For someone as passionate as John, he could change emotional gears quickly. Utte's momentum was less agile, and she faltered to get back on track. "Not many Americans know that little fact. It's funny—they all visit Salzburg, Mozart's birthplace. But Hitler, probably the most notorious, nefarious character in history, his birthplace goes unnoticed. Yes, we should visit. There's just a granite plaque outside the house, warning against fascism. I had a childhood friend, Eva. She lived around the corner from there. I wonder if she's still there."

"I'll wrap things up here in Munich in about two months," John responded as if a successful business negotiation had been concluded. "My research should be complete here, at least for awhile. I'll continue in Los Angeles—a research grant at UCLA—next fall. Maybe we can hang out here until your dissertation is complete. I'm pretty sure you can get a teaching job at one of the universities around Los Angeles."

Utte toweled herself. She blow dried her hair lightly, and finished dressing, delaying commenting on John's suggestion. John distracted her; Afsane's rhetoric and vision of the future kept her out of her past. She lapsed into memories.

As I cross the bridge to Braunau, the phallic church steeple's reflection in the water prompts me to a jog. Eva awaits me. Her mother is warm; her father friendly. They smile when I arrive, greeting me as a family member. At home I'm not allowed to drink Almdudler—and nothing cold. Eva's mother hands me a cold bottle. Eva hugs me, and shows me the new Men at Work record album she purchased. I cannot buy record albums; I cannot listen to popular music; I cannot view television programs imported from America. My father beat my sister with his belt until she bled because she watched a National Geographic feature on natives of Madagascar. He yelled, cursing as he struck each blow. She screamed in terror. My mother would not stop him. I cannot bear it.

She was beyond tears. Like the battle-fatigued soldier, traumatized by his buddy's viscera splattered about, the memories compiled an armor of numbness over the years. She could think and speak of atrocities as if she were giving someone directions to an address. She felt her lover's grip on her shoulder.

"You didn't answer me. Any comment about Los Angeles?" John stated.

His voice spoke to her from the distance, drawing her back to his bathroom. "I'm sorry. You caught me in a daze. I'm going over what we were talking about earlier. I'm still in Simbach—and

Braunau. Yes, I would like to go to Los Angeles with you. I mean that sincerely." She walked into the living room to collect her clothes. John was glued to her words and her form. "But Simbach is much further away for me than LA," she commented as she got dressed.

John leaned naked with his back against the hall wall, his arms folded, and doted on her words and her image. "You've got that committee meeting in the morning. You need your rest. Want me to call you a cab?"

Utte struggled to conciliate an intermingled sense of accomplishment and loss. Without discussing the specifics with him, she knew he would follow her anywhere. The visit to her hometown was a painful necessity—a show of genuineness. "No, thanks. The U-Bahn's still running. It's only twenty minutes." She swooped up her shoes while walking toward him. She propped herself against him to put on her shoes. "We'll visit Simbach. I just have to sort things out. We'll work out a schedule later this week." She put her arms around him and caressed his shoulders and back. "It will all work out," she added, kissing him briefly, and turning for the door. Grasping the door knob, she looked back, smiled coyly, and departed.

She broke into a fast stride as she hit the sidewalk. The damp evening air and Isar mist blurred the tear. She still had thirty minutes before meeting Afsane at Munich Hauptbahnhof, the main train station. Control through fear—whether couched in comforting benevolence or violent reprisal—achieved the same ends. Perhaps Afsane was that Janus. Utte loved her anyway.

Subways fascinated her. As a girl she had traveled alone to Vienna and Munich, spending hours going from station to station within the city, neighborhood to neighborhood, stopping only for coffee and something to eat. She'd catch the last night train back home. Her father trusted her more than her sister. Her day sojourns prompted curious, but oddly pointed and specific queries from her attorney father: "Can you make unlimited transfers with a day pass?" "Did you see any gypsies on the train?" "Was anyone caught for *Schwartzfahren*?" She had surmised the term *Schwartzfahren* had racist overtones—a peculiar word for passage without buying a ticket—since the literal translation was "black riding," and her father was a racist.

Emerging from the subway car at Munich main train station exhilarated her. The doors slid open to a collision of sights, sounds, and smells. The energy was a spirit, enveloping her, wrapping its ethereal tentacles around her, coaxing her from the subway car. She had traversed the multiple levels of this complex train station all of her life, so finding her bearing was automatic. She would meet Afsane on the *Fernzug* level, at a bar in a secluded alcove of the crowded station, served by her favorite bartender, a friendly Asian man.

Utte had arrived ten minutes early, as she always preferred early over late. Afsane was always punctual. The Asian bartender greeted her as an old friend, though neither knew one another's name. He knew her life history, and that she was a doctoral candidate in philosophy at the University of Munich. She knew he had immigrated to Munich from Hong Kong with his family when he was four years old, he was married with two small children, and he and his wife had almost saved enough money to buy a small condo on the Munich outskirts near Markt Schwaben.

They were talking about housing prices when Afsane put her hand on Utte's shoulder, greeting her in English. Utte sensed Afsane's presence before she had touched her, and she turned her head, smiling to acknowledge her friend's arrival. Afsane ordered an espresso and Utte a bottle of sparkling water. They turned to one another, looking intently, not breaking eye contact for fifteen seconds.

"You've been crying," Afsane commented, finally interrupting the silence while gently stroking Utte's cheek with the back of her middle finger.

Utte usually prepared herself emotionally for Afsane, but this evening she had been remiss. "One tear, thirty minutes ago," Utte replied defensively.

"Why only one tear? You deny yourself. Self-control is not the answer. You either are, or you are not," Afsane said as she moved a few strands of hair from Utte's face, and then caressed her ear with her thumb. "But I think I know the difference between one tear and a sob."

Making decisions about her own destiny was simple; making decisions about another's disquieted her. "He's in love with me. He's disillusioned with life, career, country. He's willing to help us." Utte stopped, studying Afsane's reaction. "We did not discuss the details, the expectations. He's absolutely against killing anyone, as you predicted. I told him there would be no murder—our intent is to scare and threaten."

"If you were not in love, you could have sold him murder as well," Afsane replied, inferring a deeper insight into Utte's emotional status.

Utte's love for Afsane and her love for John were different—opposed—and the conflict frustrated her. Her clarity of mind had been shattered. Afsane's comment was uncharacteristic. It sounded like jealously. "My goal was pragmatism, not submission. He wants me to move back to Los Angeles with him. I hadn't expected moving to the States, let alone moving to LA."

Afsane's expression lit with unpredicted satisfaction. "I do not take these little favors of the universe for granted. It's as if he had been secretly briefed on our project, and he wanted to surprise you," Afsane remarked, the corners of her mouth turned up in a Cheshire cat smile. "You have done very well. We have the operation in place and ready to execute in four years, given your betrothed delivers," Afsane replied, squeezing Utte's shoulder.

"Please don't think my confidence in you has diminished by asking: Are you up to the task?"

Utte flinched inwardly, recognizing a pulse of panic. Afsane had never questioned her capability before. "He loves me; he loves my body; he loves sex. He's a hedonist. Keeping him focused will not be difficult," Utte replied, turning back to Afsane after gesturing to the Asian bartender that they would like to pay.

"Do not underestimate him, my love. He loves more than your body and sex," Afsane advised, touching Utte's hand. "He loves you: the way you think, the way you talk. It's more than physical. That you do not see his love is disturbing. Or is it, you do see it, but you deny it for my benefit?"

Utte resented her own transparency, yet resentment toward Afsane was untenable. How was she to resolve this inner conflict? Stuffing it guaranteed future rage. Re-examining her relationship with Afsane was not an option. Honesty was the remaining choice. "You're right. He loves me; I love him. Call it what you may, he's the first man for whom I've felt more than sexual craving. I say this not as an excuse, but my relationship with him does not diminish my love for you, or my devotion to our goals."

"I'm getting tired. I've had a trying day. Could we go to your apartment? Holding you during the night would be very restful," Afsane

112

responded, signaling satisfaction with Utte's explanation.

The two women left the seclusion of the bar, and merged with the still bustling late evening travel mire. Afsane clutched Utte's arm, and put her head on her shoulder. "We have had him under tight surveillance for three months. We trust you. I trust you implicitly. We had installed several listening devices in his house. He's discussed you with friends and family. We knew of his plans to ask you to return with him before he told you. Our cover in the United States has been prepared. We are ready when you are."

Chapter 6
The Spy

Marzee was frantic. He had to see Utte. He checked the class schedules, discovering she taught two classes today. He yearned to hear her voice, to feel her majestic presence. The husband hounded him as well. *Was he German? Maybe he was an American, and she just married him for green card.*

Since he possessed her home number, he ached to use it. Since his parents' number was not blocked, he could not call from his home phone. He'd call from a public phone, preferably from Utte's neighborhood.

He opened the Venetian blind covering the single window in his tiny bedroom to be greeted by another sunny, off-season day, a Friday. He relished and abhorred days like today: the warm, sunny weather induced the demon. Girls would skip class to catch the last natural rays of summer sun. He had one class, a help section for calculus. He'd skip it, rationalizing he had already worked out the last problem set, and he wasn't impressed with the TA.

He turned on his computer, waited for it to boot, and pulled up MapQuest. He keyed in her address. The demon spoke to him—his breathing hastened. Finally the results unfolded onto his screen. More excited than a child on Christmas morning, he desperately awaited the detail.

Just a half block from the beach, he thought. He magnified his screen, first studying the directions to her house, then switched to satellite view. With a clear perspective, her house looked as if it was about seven houses west of Beach Street. A series of parallel alley-like streets connected the main boulevard to the beach frontage road. Walkways separated the backyards of the houses of each street from the backyards of the houses on the next street.

In Google Maps typed in her address: 148 Conch Way, Seal Beach. As the image assembled laboriously on his slow computer, he imagined seeing her naked, lying privately on her roof sundeck, unaware of his stratospheric perspective. He zoomed to a full screen image of her block, with her house in the center. Conch Way looked more like an alley than a street. The Google satellite view confirmed a sidewalk directly behind her house. His heart pumped furiously. He had to see it for himself. He had to go there. He craved experiencing her neighborhood—be close to where she lived.

He switched to the Long Beach State website, went to faculty search, and typed her name in the search window. "Thorndike, U." appeared, followed by a list of classes. She taught one course today from noon until 2:00 PM. Assuming it took her a half hour to get to work, and another half hour to get home, he had three hours of free sailing from 11:30 AM to 2:30 PM The clock on his computer read 10:15 AM. He had just enough time.

Marzee undressed, and hastily slipped into his bathrobe and floppy slippers. He dashed down the stairs, feigning even more urgency than necessary in order to keep the conversation with his mother brief. Relieved his father was at work, he would be obliged to create a convincing tale explaining his demonstrated exigency. He showered more quickly than usual, skipping masturbating, thus shortening his showering routine.

Back in his room, he planned his logistics. *Remember the six P's,* he recalled, grinning. *Proper planning prevents piss poor performance.* After printing the black and white map image on his antiquated laser printer, he studied it for accuracy.

"Oh, shit! I almost forgot to write down her phone number," he scolded himself. He scribbled the phone number on the map, folded it neatly in quarters, and slid it in his left rear pocket. He looked around the room, making certain he had everything he needed for his quest.

In order to appear convincing, he needed to take his book bag. He removed the class-related contents, filled it with nonessentials, and then slammed his door, leaping three-steps-at-a-time down the stairs.

"Mama. Sorry. Gotta go now! There's a study group at school waiting for me. If I don't leave now, I'll be late."

"No breakfast?!" his mother responded, agitated.

"I'll get something to eat later. Maybe at the school cafeteria."

"You're too skinny already. With all this rushing around you do, and no eating. Humph. Boy, you gonna disappear!" Mrs. Banks reprimanded.

He felt guilty, lying to her, but his mission supplanted any remorse. He kissed her on the cheek, and grabbed his helmet. "Thanks, Mama. I'd love to spend some time. Sorry, I gotta go." He ran down the back staircase.

Concerned about his Vespa's security, he was relieved his moped had not been tampered with by neighborhood vandals. Since he was the only local moped driver, he was the target of verbal abuse and opportune vandalism. Locals jeered him, challenging him to go get a real motorcycle, or go back to his tricycle.

His route of travel required street navigation, and he had only cursorily planned his course. He pulled the carefully folded map from his rear pocket. Sensing his mother observing him from the window, he didn't want to appear that he was doing something out of the ordinary, or contrary to what he had told her. After all, what planning is required to go to school? His heart throbbed, and thoughts of being around where Utte lived were unyielding. He refolded the map, carefully returned it to his rear pocket, started the engine, and drove slowly down the driveway.

The Santa Ana condition, with its steady breeze and stark sunlight, created an unusually warm mid-morning. He stopped at the corner light and gazed briefly down the street toward where his friend, Frank Sanders, lived. A fleeting voice encouraged him to visit Sanders instead of Utte. Already sweating from the heat, he unzipped his jacket. The light changed, and he raced across toward his destination, disregarding the voice.

After dealing with some avenue traffic jams, and detours through side streets, he reached Pier Street, the major thoroughfare running north-south through the beach district. He still had two miles to go before he got to Utte's street. Flustered, he looked at his watch—11:45 AM, placing him well within the window of opportunity he had planned. He still had to make sure she was not unexpectedly at home. He spotted a phone booth on the next corner, and parked by the curb.

Scrupulously, he had packed coins for the public phone. His heart raced as he dialed her number. *What if she answers? What if her husband answers? Simple. I'll hang up quickly. Or should I say, "Sorry, wrong number?"*

The signal rang—once, twice, three times, then a man's voice: an answering machine. "Hello. This is the Thorndike residence. Please leave your message and number at the sound of the tone. Thank you." The voice didn't have a German accent. In fact, he sounded very much American. Marzee replaced the receiver.

After returning to his moped, he cruised past each block, counting down how many more blocks to Utte's street. When he reached Conch Way, he pulled very close to the curb to carefully assess the best parking place. The walkway he had viewed on the Google satellite view was exactly as depicted. The parking signs gave him free reign: unrestricted parking today.

After parking, he paused a moment to inhale his state of panic and exhilaration. Two giggling girls in bikinis, balancing towels and Boogie boards, had just emerged from the corner house. As they walked toward the beach, he felt dejected, knowing he was invisible to them. One of them was brazen enough to wear a Brazilian cut. His temples pulsed as he absorbed her fully exposed, swaying butt cheeks.

He walked at a subdued pace for fear of catching up with the girls, who kept pausing, giggling, and reorganizing all their paraphernalia slipping from their grasp. Finally, they were far enough away that he could pick up his speed.

The gates facing the walkway appeared to be rear entrances, and not front gates. Some had addresses, some did not. A wall or fence secluded each property. Concrete, brick, and wood provided variation. A few were slats of wood with separations so wide he could see inside the backyards as he walked along. He slowed his pace to get glimpses through the fences as he passed them. Sun patios, Jacuzzis, hot tubs, and children's swings personalized these alien backyards. The houses were not addressed on his side. He would have to venture around the front to verify her residence, and then match her house from the rear.

I'm scared shitless. What am I doing,
pimping down my philosophy instructor's street?
I'm exhilarated, challenged, frightened. Where are
all the people? For this fine, Indian summer day,
where is everybody? People who live at the beach
are used to the beach. If it weren't for us ghetto
motherfuckers, Mexicans, and white trash, these
people would be alone and happy.

The sound of a car behind him, or the appearance of an approaching car, wracked his nerves. Being identified with the sinister-looking silhouette on the "Crime Watch" sign at each street corner would interrupt his adventure swiftly. He suspected that on the other side of each beach house window, white eyes peered at him, and the head behind those eyes asked, "I haven't seen that weird-looking nigger around here before. What's he doing here?"

Remaining steadfast in his quest, his spell of paranoia would not deter him. Here, he was unable to concoct an innocuous cover, like in the apartment complex across from campus. In this neighborhood, the most believable cover for him would be Jehovah Witness, but he lacked the literature. He scrutinized each address. Fancy addresses pissed him off, but the house with the most basic numbers was Utte's.

Discerning what Utte's house looked like from the front was important, so he could identify it from the rear. How mortified he would be if she saw him from her window. Her two-story house was blue-gray with white trim, and a ceramic tile

120

roof. The house just to the east had brick trim, and a shake roof. The house to the west was also two-story, but light blue stucco.

The day turned warmer than he had expected. Uncomfortable lugging his backpack, he returned it to his parked moped. He idiosyncratically checked his pockets. *I should only carry my ignition key—quick getaway.* He knelt to retie his sneaker laces, then checked his watch— 12:35 PM.

The giggling, bikini clad girls were long gone, though he figured he might search for them later on the beach if nothing turned up at Utte's house. Many buildings along the beach were constructed on pilings, so adequate cover for peeking should not be a problem.

Once more on the sidewalk behind Utte's house, he tuned his peripheral vision to peering eyes and suspicious gestures. Recognizing her house from the rear, he stopped. A six-foot wood slat fence with interspersed knotholes barricaded him from her backyard, and tall hedges jutted over the top of the fence. Large, bushy plants protruded from opposite corners of the fence, offering him more cover. He rotated mechanically in the center of the sidewalk, turning and stopping like a clock gear. He had to account for every possible angle that might compromise his position. He scrutinized all windows—curtained, stained, shuttered, and opened. Any neighboring gate could unexpectedly fling open, presenting skeptical and inquisitive intruders, or busy neighbors out and about, tending to their yards and gardens. No one was watching him.

One of the fence knotholes was about a foot from the ground. He knelt down, peeked through with his right eye, and gasped. The bottom of a female foot confronted him. He drew back shocked, not registering to whom the foot was attached. He went back for a second look, pushing his eyeball as far as it could protrude without detaching itself. A sunbather adorned a bright orange towel atop a close-cropped mowed lawn. He had called earlier, but no one answered. Maybe she was asleep, or just didn't feel like answering.

He returned for a third view, studying all within range—foot, toes, toe ring, ankle, calf. He had memorized Utte's legs, and this leg was not Utte's. The shapely appendage behind the peephole lacked the muscle tone, tan, and sheer dynamics of Utte's form. And this leg had freckles. The sunbathing woman repositioned herself, giving Marzee a better perspective.

He crept back on his belly, trench-soldier style, and double checked each direction of the walkway. He stood up, searching for a better vantage point. He spotted another knothole higher and closer to the center.

Peering through this new peep hole, Marzee observed a thin, shapely, redheaded woman in her late twenties. Freckles covered her white, smooth body. She had just applied suntan lotion, and she squirmed around on her towel to get comfortable. She wore an unremarkable bluish colored bikini— sort of Brazilian cut, sort of string.

Ever watchful about being detected, he suddenly fretted about losing track of what was around him. He stepped back from his observation post, and re-examined the fence. Since it was constructed of two layers of wood, the layers interlaced, assuring Marzee more obscuration, but more difficulty seeing through. She would have to suspect a spy; she would have to eyeball the fence. Vigilant, he remained ever so quiet.

He returned to his knothole. Suddenly, a bare-foot man in shorts and an unbuttoned Hawaiian shirt appeared from the side of the house. He seemed quite animated, waving around a bottle of suntan lotion.

"That stuff you covered yourself in was just number eight," the man exclaimed. "Here's some number 30." He approached the supine woman, and knelt beside her. "You'll turn beet red in no time just using number eight." He bent over, kissing her briefly on her tummy.

"Ohhh," she replied, sighing. "I wish you'd found that sooner. I just finished coating myself. That was a lot of work!"

The man settled next to her. "Tell you what," he said. "Let me do the work for you. Take that goddamn swimsuit off. I'll rub this oil all over your body. You won't burn anywhere. I guarantee it," he said with a reassuring demeanor.

"You mean you want me to get naked? Now? Here? What if your wife comes home?" the redhead asked, giggling.

"Just a sec. I'll call her." He pulled a cell phone from his pants pocket, punched in a number, and held the phone to his ear. "Utte! Whew. Good. I'm glad I didn't get the voice mail. You still at that school, hun?"

Time paused as Marzee tunneled his attention to the unfolding scene in the backyard. A wave of panic struck him, causing him to jolt backward. He hurriedly checked around him, verifying all was clear.

"You're going to be stuck in a meeting on campus 'til 6 PM? What about Krispin and Renee? Weren't they supposed to come over tonight for dinner at about 6:30? Think you can skip out a little earlier?"

"Ok. I'll just entertain them until you get here," he said cheerily. "No worries. See you later. I love you." He snapped his phone shut and looked toward the redheaded woman on the towel. "She won't be home until at least 5:30. Like I said—get out of that swimsuit," he commanded.

Marzee looked at his watch. It was 2:15. He scanned up and down the sidewalk again. No one was in sight. He had been careful to not lose his balance or rattle the fence for fear of letting his presence be known.

The redheaded woman giggled, sat up on the beach towel, reached behind her back, and untied the bikini string. She pulled the top over her head nonchalantly, and dropped it at the edge of the towel. Then she rolled back on her back, and pulled her bottoms over her knees and ankles, and added them to her discarded top.

"Let's defy convention, and do the front first!" he said.

She giggled. "Ok." She lay back, naked on the towel. Fascinated by her body, Marzee had only seen freckles and red pubic hair on the Internet.

Utte's husband poured the oily lotion into his cupped left palm, placed the bottle on the grass, and slapped his hands together dramatically. He started massaging her face, very slowly, very gently, in circular motions with the expertise and style of a trained masseur. In tiny precise circles, it took him five minutes to complete her face, including her forehead, closed eyelids, cheeks, chin, nose, ears, and neck.

After obtaining more lotion, he moved to her shoulders and arms, using both circular and elongated strokes over the entire length of each arm. With jeweler's precision, he completed each of her hands, caressing oil into each finger so that not one pore was uncoated. Marzee heard her moan softly.

Utte's amorous husband repositioned himself behind her, centering his companion's head between his legs. In longer strokes he applied lotion across her clavicles. His hands moved under her arms, then around the sides of her breasts simultaneously. The fingertips of each hand, held firmly together, gently orbited each breast, at first carefully avoiding her nipples and areola, but then gradually spiraling inward. Each index finger dwelled over her nipples, making micro-circles clockwise, then counter-clockwise, orbiting her areola in the glistening, frictionless oil.

Marzee had been glued to the spectacle through the peephole. Suddenly, he caught movement from the corner of his eye. He stepped back stealthily, and took aim toward the distraction. Someone had appeared on the far west end, and was walking in his direction.

He cursed silently, not wanting to leave his spot. Now he had to feign some unsuspicious activity for the intruder to observe as he passed by. He would have to greet the person as well. *I belong here. I have to act that way. I have to say something neighborly. I better move down a couple houses.* The pedestrian, a man walking a small dog on a leach, approached. Marzee, blessed with a seasoned sense of survival, reached in his pocket, found the few coins he had used at the public phone, and dropped them on the ground. He stooped down in a Mr. McGoo-like posture, deliberately and slowly retrieving each coin. The dog walker passed him, making some comment about "how every penny counts these days." Marzee smiled and affably agreed, hoping he would not have to deal with a return trip.

As soon the intruder had distanced himself, Marzee hastily perused the perimeter, then returned to his peep hole. During the time he had missed, the redhead's upper body was covered in oil. Her masseur had repositioned himself, now kneeling between her legs. One of her legs was outstretched on the towel to his side; the other was extended upward, resting on his left shoulder. He watched as Utte's husband's hands encircled her oiled thigh, churning it, creating a ring of pressure slowly sliding from her knee to her hips. As he continued this motion up and down, the oil squeegeed between his fingers and her skin, causing him to pause at the bottom of a stroke to redistribute an accumulation of oil from her outer labia. She cooed.

"You didn't mention your hubby," Utte's husband whispered, maintaining the thigh massage's rhythm. "When do you expect him home? I thought he was the family-man sort."

"Business trip," she said, barely audible.

Marzee noticed the man had removed his shorts, probably during the time he had detached himself from the peephole. He stopped the massage to shed his Hawaiian shirt. Still kneeling, he placed the woman's other leg on his right shoulder. The sex play mesmerized Marzee, and he watched them have sex in this position for several minutes. He witnessed the red-haired woman writhe, experiencing multiple orgasms from multiple positions. Marzee positioned his hand over his zipper, and eased it down. His erect penis had demanded release, and it unfurled defiantly from his pants.

The woman had moved to the top, rocking back and forth. Her motion accelerated into another orgasm. She rolled off Utte's husband, and convulsed in a fetal position. Marzee's ejaculation was powerful. Several waves of seminal fluid battered the fence. He choked down his moans. The yard performers were too preoccupied with their activity to notice the muffled noises from the other side, anyway.

The late afternoon beach coolness crept eastwardly. Marzee's ejaculatory frenzy cooled him further, causing him to shiver. Utte's husband and his companion had both fallen to the orange towel. He kissed and caressed her nipples, as she continued to convulse in smaller orgasmic waves.

The three members of the sexual event— Utte's husband, the neighbor, and Marzee—had spent their energy. Marzee backed from the fence, ready to find his Vespa, and meander toward home. Watching these spectacular gymnastics primed him for more. His moped transported him home, the return trip lacking the adrenaline-charged anticipation. He opened his door, greeted his mother and father, went to his room, did some reading and homework, rethought his day, and went to bed.

He had substituted tofu for filet mignon. He was still hungry. He craved Utte. In the dark, stretched under the covers, he massaged his penis into a maximum erection, fantasizing the red head had been Utte. He ran the mental video as he preferred it, with Utte writhing in orgasmic bliss.

He could never take Utte's husband's place. He ejaculated, rolled over, and slept.

Chapter 7
The Good Student

Marzee's morning hard-on, usually welcomed, awoke him, interrupting the extra time he could have slept. The etched images from the day before had created an overlay of indelible visions, allowing him to think of nothing else. They were powerful, potent images, not to be avoided or evaded. The craving enveloped him.

He had to go to class; he wanted to go to class, but Utte's backyard beckoned him. Psychology class was today, and he was keen about the subject. Other factors mitigated his yearnings: the air was cooler, and more clouds dotted the sky; yesterday's performance was once in a lifetime—no chance of him seeing an encore so soon. He could look into another five hundred fence knotholes, and never see what he saw yesterday. He threw the blanket off, and sat up in bed. The erection had to subside before he could put on his bathrobe, head downstairs, and take a shower. His mother would definitely be in the kitchen waiting for him, making sure that he did not leave home without first having a "good breakfast."

He scoffed inwardly at a "good breakfast," consisting mostly of animal fat, salt, and starch. Being home-cooked and prepared with motherly love and provisions of previous generations made it good. Were he to simply eat a protein bar, the goodness would be omitted. The ingredients, and inability to pronounce many of the them, detracted from the goodness as well. Bacon, eggs, sausage, and grits were easy to pronounce, easier to remember, and taste better anyway.

Utte's husband was a conundrum. *Why would he jeopardize his relationship by fucking another woman?* he pondered. His wife was exceptional, the most beautiful woman Marzee had ever seen. Her body was far superior to the redhead's, even though memories of the redhead aroused him instantly. Jacking off in the shower would help.

He sprang from bed, put on his bathrobe, and ran downstairs, again feigning desperation as he jogged through the kitchen. Predictably, his mother was sitting by the window reading the newspaper— probably looking for a crossword puzzle she had not done.

"You're not getting out of here without eating breakfast," his mother said steadfastly. "I already scrambled the eggs."

"I know, mama. I'll eat breakfast this morning. I have some time. I just need to be at class by one. And I need to go to the bookstore first," Marzee responded with a reconciliatory tone. "Let me take a shower and get dressed first, though."

His showers took too long for his parents' taste. Saving hot water ranked up there with eating a good breakfast in the things-to-be-concerned-about hierarchy. This morning he jerked off, soaped off, rinsed off, dried off, and completed his usual hygienic routine in record time. He returned to his bathrobe, and scurried through the kitchen to the door to his upstairs bedroom.

"I'll be back in ten minutes. Wait for me?" he asked teasing.

"Go on and get dressed. You want sausage or bacon?" his mother retorted.

His craving to re-enact yesterday had eliminated his hunger. His vigilance to conceal his ruminations had become more pressing. "Bacon," Marzee replied. "But I'm pretty hungry this morning. How about both? Some grits, too, if you're up to it."

He jolted upstairs, and quickly dressed himself. A myriad of images continued to assail him. He wondered about Utte's marriage. He disliked her husband, being a philanderer, liar, and cheater. He was appalled at her husband's gall, that he could talk on the phone with Utte guiltlessly, with the redhead three feet away, waiting primed to have sex with him. Utte deserved better. He didn't have her class today, but he hoped he might run into her somewhere on campus. Her extra job as a fitness trainer pricked his curiosity. He had fantasized about having a female professor who moonlighted as a stripper or prostitute; fitness trainer would have to do for now. He lamented—he could never reveal his feelings. He descended the stairs to consume his good breakfast.

After chatting up his mother and piling on compliments, he wiped his mouth, patted his belly, got up, gave his mother a hug and kiss, and bounded up the stairs two steps at a time. He needed to prepare for his day: books for today's courses, notes in order, homework or material due today, money for incidentals and lunch.

A kaleidoscope of lust-filled memories interfered with his concentration. He was dressed and ready to go, with just enough time to get to school, find a parking space, and head over to the bookstore. Perhaps he could park in the lot where Utte parks, though the limited student parking in the western lot was usually taken by early arrivals.

He arrived on campus to have his suspicions fulfilled: the western lot was full. He spotted Utte's car, pausing as he cruised toward it. The glimpse he got a few days ago made an indelible impression— the car was splendid, enticing him to move closer. He dropped the kickstand of his Vespa, and sauntered closer. Except for the European styling, the car dashboard was unexceptional, presenting a blatant paucity of accoutrement, not even an audio system. Ever aware of being watched, he figured he spent enough time nosing around a parked car. He returned to his moped, and crossed the campus to the eastern lot where his usual parking spot awaited him.

Memories of yesterday's backyard sex display had over-shadowed events occurring just two days ago, when he had spent several hours in a car trunk, evading angry apartment tenants and the police. The girl at the swimming pool was a poor second compared to what he had spied through the fence knothole. Nevertheless, as he parked he recalled his trauma just two days ago, shuttering at almost being apprehended. His friends, his parents, his teachers, maybe even Utte, would have found out. He would be removed from normal society, and placed in a jail, or worse yet, a state mental hospital prison for the sexually deranged.

"Marzee!" a friendly voice called behind him as soon as he removed his helmet.

The moped engine had barely stopped puttering. He looked around to see Larry Butler just emerging from his car. He approached Marzee with a briefcase in one hand, and an unknown apparatus in the other.

Marzee raised his hand, acknowledging he had heard Butler. He lowered his bike's kickstand, chained the wheels, and stood quickly to greet his psychology instructor. He thought it odd that Butler parked in a student parking lot. He carried a brief case and a device that looked like a Geiger counter.

Apprehensive about Butler's research questions the day before, his curiosity was tweaked nonetheless. "How you doin?" Marzee asked in a friendly, if not obsequious tone. "Haven't seen you for awhile!" He laughed nervously. Butler seemed nervous as well.

"You have a class now—something pressing to do?" Butler asked with guarded assertion. "I wanted to speak with you about that research I mentioned," he hesitated, "and something else."

Butler's request was like a cold shower, and the water sizzled off him. Disappointed he had run into him at this inopportune moment, he had to balance the onslaught of intrusive thoughts about Utte with not letting down his psychology professor. "Well, yeah, I guess so. Where do we go?" Marzee asked awkwardly.

"I share an office over in Bronze Hall, the psych building, with a couple other part-timers. We could walk over there. I also want to give you a little questionnaire to fill out, and also sign an Informed Consent form—for the research. What do you say?"

Fuck, I'm caught. No way to get out of this. I could lie, but he'd know I really don't have a class immediately. "OK, sure." Marzee responded cautiously.

Marzee and Larry Butler walked ten minutes to a five-story, rust-colored building named, though not officially, Bronze Hall. Nervous during the trek across campus, he was apprehensive about what to expect from his somewhat eccentric and assertive psychology instructor. As he strolled across campus, he feared being recognized as the one they were chasing a couple days ago around the apartment building across the street. Foremost, his friends' caveats of buggery and freakiness were still looming uncomfortably in his memory, although he had dismissed most of what they said as buffoonery and envy.

Butler's office was on the fourth floor of a building exemplifying contemporary campus architecture of the mid to late 1960's. Its creativity existed in the ease and quality by which the architect created geometrical designs with his mechanical pencil on a drafting table. They breezed from the elevator amidst other students and faculty, and briskly walked left to the end of the hall. Larry Butler stopped in front of the office adorned with the most taped-on, pasted-on, and tacked-on cartoons, headlines, and bumper stickers. He studied the various cartoons, laughing aloud while Butler unlocked the door. One comic grabbing his attention depicted a stereotypic image of a psychotherapist sitting behind a patient lying on a couch. Though the cartoon amused him, the underlying message depicting a troubled and angry patient as an "asshole" created a disturbing incongruence between a helping profession and a morally judgmental helper.

Butler finally found his office door key and they went in. Except for the window, bookcases obscured the walls. Books, papers, magazines, and pamphlets were strewn on filing cabinets, boxes, and desks. Doubtful Butler owned all these books, he concluded that the library was probably the office mates' combined collections. He scanned the subjects: abnormal psychology, addiction, relapse prevention, theories of therapy and counseling, assessment of children, assessment of adult personality, life-span development, death and dying, love and anger, family therapy, cognition, depression, anxiety, obsessive-compulsive disorders, and sexual deviations. He stopped here.

"May I?" Marzee asked, pointing to the books inquisitively. Butler looked around.

"Of course," Butler confirmed, as he intently searched for a file in his computer.

Marzee extracted a book entitled *Sexual Deviance*. He perused the table of contents: Bestiality, Necrophilia, Exhibitionism, Voyeurism, Pedophilia, Frotteurism, Sexual Sadism, Transvestic Fetishism. He was drawn back to the subject of voyeurism. He flipped to the first page of the Voyeurism Chapter, and read: "As defined in DSM-V the essential feature of this disorder is recurrent, intense, sexual urges and sexually arousing fantasies, of at least six months' duration, involving the act of observing unsuspecting people, usually strangers, who are either naked, in the process of disrobing, or engaging in sexual activity." His pulse hastened. His demon had a name.

Fearful of exposing his secret life, he was hesitant asking about what he had just read. "What is DSM-IV?" Marzee asked with a tremulous voice.

Butler disengaged his head from his monitor. Whatever he sought on his computer had unintentionally lured him away from Marzee. "It's the Diagnostic and Statistical Manual of Mental Disorders. It's a book that defines all the mental disorders. It's like the bible of psychology when it comes to diagnosis. Why do you ask?" Butler replied.

Needing to create subterfuge, Marzee did not want to be obvious about his interest in this subject matter. He felt self-conscious even having read what he had just read. "This book here references it," Marzee replied, obscuring the title.

"There's a DSM-IV right there," Butler responded, pointing nonchalantly to a book on a shelf to his left.

Marzee stretched to pull the book off the shelf. In the table of contents he found DSM-IV classifications of mental disorders. He zoomed in on the heading: Sexual Disorders. Voyeurism was prominent among the list. He turned to the page indicated, and read the description of voyeurism as quickly as he could. Reading this was like running over hot coals: one does not dare to light until the course is complete. He had always considered the powerful urges overcoming him as some sort of possession of mind, though he really did not believe in demon possession. The cravings seemed more like flights of fantasy, the sand fly coaxing and guiding his sight over the bodies of young women in various states of undress. The passages he had just absorbed indicated more than flights of fantasy—he was truly mentally disturbed—and he bristled at this notion.

"There! I found what I was looking for! I thought I had lost it." Butler rejoiced. "I'm sorry for leaving you alone for so long. Rude of me, since I invited you here," Butler stated apologetically.

Marzee placed the two books on the desk adjacent to Butler's so that the book, *Sexual Deviance* was on the bottom, and the binding title faced away from Butler's view. "Not a problem," Marzee replied sincerely. "I'm curious about something you said, anyway. I've thought about this a lot in my personal life. You questioned the other day: 'Does an African-American's skin color affect his or her personality? But before you answer that question, don't you have to answer another first? From where does the referred African-American come?' If he's socialized as black, no matter how light he may be, you're only gonna get 'blackness' out of him. You know what I mean?"

Marzee detected a sick, almost pallid, heaviness befall Butler momentarily, and then the aura disappeared before he was sure. "I know what you mean. That's the main reason I approached you in class—I believe you would provide empathetic insight. One obvious subject to be addressed in the research is what is 'blackness' anyway?"

Marzee's attention shifted away from his self-consumed interest in voyeurism, facilitated by his even more self-consumed interest in race and skin color. "Why does it interest you to begin with?" Marzee asked bluntly.

"'Cause I'm black myself. I know it's hard to see, but I'm about 20% black, and I was raised in a black neighborhood. Compton, in fact." He paused apologetically. "A lot of research in psychology is really aimed at self-discovery," Butler added, not deviating from Marzee's eyes as he answered his question.

Marzee remained expressionless, not reacting to Butler's disclosure, but he was in fact shocked—even awestruck. Butler looked white as white can be. But then again, on closer examination, his skin color was creamier and tanner than most white people's. And his hair was not straight and formless, but rather wavy and wiry. It still boasted a "good hair" look.

"What do you do with your hair?" Marzee responded, not flinching.

"I blow-dry it," Butler responded.

"I know many a nigga who would blow-dry his ass off if he could have hair as good as yours," Marzee commented, remaining straight-faced.

Butler casually flipped up the books Marzee had earlier studied so intently. He replaced them with equal casualness. His temperament turned somber.

"Race aside, I want you to be able to trust me, because I have something serious to talk to you about," Butler announced.

Butler's sudden change in mood alarmed Marzee, reminding him of times he had gotten into trouble as a boy, his mother sitting him down to scold him. He did not trust sudden changes in emotion, and he had just started to feel comfortable with Butler. *Here it comes— the freak out. Richard and Freddie were right.*

Butler himself seemed agitated, nervous about what he was preparing to say. He toiled over adjusting his seat, facing Marzee, clearing his throat, uncrossing his legs, licking his lips, folding his hands together on his lap. These were the gymnastics of one readying himself to ask for a date or a loan, and Marzee was assured he wouldn't ask for a loan. Finally, Butler gathered his composure, and spoke.

"I live across the street, in the apartment complex across from Campus Avenue. I saw you from my window there the other day, when you were running away. Later I saw police swarming the grounds. I saw the bulletin they displayed for the trespasser and peeping tom who has been—and these are their words—'harassing the women who live in the building.' Obviously I didn't report you to the police."

Awash with outrage and mortification, Butler's disclosure paralyzed him between these two extremes. He had been set up. Butler had prepared unloading this revelation on him—even since the first day of class. He was mortified that he had been exposed. He cringed, having absolutely no place to hide, especially at school, a place Marzee sanctified and revered. His world, his reality, shrank to the small space he occupied, to the few seconds surrounding Butler's words. "Are you sure you saw

141

me?" he replied with a broken voice, hoping to refute the person Butler saw was him.

"How old are you, Marzee?" Butler asked, ignoring Marzee's question.

"Twenty," Marzee replied.

"Have you ever been arrested?" Butler continued.

Marzee lost touch with reality whenever he went on his voyeuristic forays. He knew his behavior was illegal, but he partitioned it, deluding himself to believe repercussions were not forthcoming; that he was immune to consequences. Indeed, that his behavior did not merit consequences. "No!" Marzee answered with indignation.

"Marzee. Let's cut the bullshit! I know I saw you. And I know people have complained of a peeping tom running around the apartment grounds for several months. The person they describe fits your description. It's you, and I saw you," Butler responded sternly.

He had never been confronted with his secret behavior. It was his secret life, his private world. He never, NEVER, let anyone inside. Yet this stranger, this white man sitting across from him, had full knowledge of his world, full access to his core. Marzee crumbled. Torrents of tears gushed from his eyes. His body quivered; he cowered, throwing his face into his hands. He could hardly speak as he combusted into an amalgam of emotion and memories.

Vehement sobs stifled his speech, as he released years of restraint and denial. "I don't know what to do. I don't know what to do. This—this—thing—is a demon. It gets me, and won't let go. I have to do it. But it's not me. I don't want it!"

Butler remained sympathetic, but calm. "How many years have you been doing this? How long has this problem bothered you?" Butler asked in a soft voice.

"Prob'ly since I was eleven or twelve. Almost for as long as I can remember. But it started with looking in my neighbor's window at night," Marzee's answered between gushes of tears.

"You've been looking in her window? What are you looking for her to do?" Butler asked.

For the despair his exposed secret provoked, he felt oddly relieved. "Get undressed. Get dressed. I just liked watching her naked. I liked looking at her bare body. I don't know. Sometimes I think she knew that I was there, watching her, but she never said anything about it."

"Did you masturbate while you watched her?" Butler pressed.

His admissions offered more than relief—sparks of exhilaration lifted him. "Yes. I jacked off while watching. Sometimes she just looked at herself in the mirror. I jerk off," Marzee admitted.

"So this behavior—this peeping—has moved to others? Other houses? Other neighborhoods?" Butler asked, seeming to probe for specific information.

"As soon as I got my first bicycle, I would cruise different neighborhoods at night, or real early in the morning before the sun came up. I'd look in people's windows when they got up in the morning," Marzee replied, continuing to weep sporadically.

"No one ever saw you? No one ever chased you?" Butler questioned with concerned intensity.

Talking openly was novel, breaching his inner sanctuary. He could rejoice or cringe. His emotions were in stasis, as both extremes tugged on him. "Well, yes, they saw me, but nobody ever came after me. Couple times people would shout, 'Hey. Quit peep'n in my window!' But nobody actually came running after me. No, that never happened until a couple days ago." He paused, and the sobbing intensified. "But I don't like it. It like...it controls me. I get the idea in my head, and I can't shake it. I have to do it. I have to find somewhere, someone. Then I found those apartment buildings across from campus. And those fine white girls tanning around the pools."

"So you masturbate while you watch the girls sun around the pool?" Butler asked monotonically, displaying no outward judgment to the account unfolding.

He averted an immediate response, sensing danger. To answer such a question was to acknowledge the reality; to acknowledge the reality was to admit his role; to admit his role was to accept accountability. "Yes—but also I found the

144

laundry rooms in the apartment buildings. Then I started to—" Marzee stopped, paralyzed by the onslaught of candor. His body shook, heaved, and quivered. He could not stop crying. His thoughts, his feelings, the things he did—all exposed. *Keep Utte a secret.* He collapsed into deeper weeping.

"I have a friend, a counselor, a psychotherapist. He works at the student counseling center part time. I believe he could help you. I know he's worked with clients with problems like yours before," Butler said, trying to edge his words in between Marzee's sobs. "Would you be willing to speak with him, Marzee?"

"Counselor? A psychologist?" Marzee asked with a broken response.

"Yes. He's a psychologist. He's worked with this sort of problem before. He's a good guy. You'd like him. I'd like to set up an appointment for you later? Say, sometime after class today?" Butler replied with an encouraging tone.

Marzee mulled over Butler's request. He had never thought he would have to see a shrink. But he understood he was at Butler's whim—he was busted. "Yes. Yes, I'll see him. I guess this thing of mine could not stay my secret forever," Marzee whispered, shivering.

"We're only as sick as our secrets," Butler replied.

Between the torrent of shame and embarrassment, misgivings about Butler percolated in and out of his awareness. Butler had manipulated him into his current circumstance, staging the events leading to this confrontation. He resented being obliged to trust Butler. But he was busted, giving him no other choice. And though Butler made no mention of the consequences of noncompliance, turning him in was the unstated outcome. "What's the plan? You're going to call him after class, or the appointment will be after class?" Marzee asked.

Butler squared himself with Marzee, remaining silent while he strategized his response. "After I saw you running from the police in the apartment complex the other day, I realized who the peeping tom was. I didn't want to turn you in. I thought you needed help, not punishment. So I took the liberty of calling my friend. We discussed you at some length yesterday. I told him I would talk with you about the situation. He said, based upon your agreeability, he had an hour available today from three to four. So, to answer your question, your appointment is already set up for after class—at 3 PM. But I still need to call him to confirm it, and let him know that you and I have talked. Is that OK with you?"

Marzee looked up, peering at Butler. He wanted to ask, "What happens if I say no, it's not OK," but he refrained. "Why are you being so nice to me, anyway?"

"Nice? No. I'm being what I consider professional and moral. I see a distressed, intelligent young man who needs psychological help. If law enforcement gets their hands on you, you might have to register as a sex offender. It would ruin your life. So I'm not being nice—I'm being the citizen of the world I want myself to be," Butler responded.

"OK, so, the counselor I'm supposed to see. You're going to set that up?" Marzee asked.

"Yes, it's basically already set up. I'll call him as soon as you leave and let him know you'll be there this afternoon," Butler replied. "He'll be expecting you at the Student Counseling Center. His name is Lorn Dance. Dr. Lorn Dance."

"OK, then. I'll see you in class. And—" Marzee said, stammering. "—thanks for not turning me in, and for talking to your friend."

Butler returned a modest nod and smile, reflecting an uncertainty that unnerved Marzee. Butler rose from his chair, squeezed Marzee on the shoulder, and opened the door for him.

Chapter 8
Where's the Couch?

Embarrassment dominated Marzee as he sat through Larry Butler's psychology class. He had avoided looking at Butler directly, preferring to avert his eyes toward his notes. Notwithstanding, Butler had glanced toward him during a comment about human behavior, a salient remark that stuck with Marzee. He pondered over the remark's simplicity—so simple it was complex: "all human activity is really an interaction of three factors: affect, cognition, and behavior. We feel; we think; we act. When they become out of balance, mental disorder arises."

Facilitated by a desire to escape, he drifted into rumination. *I wonder if these states happen so fast in sequence, that they only appear to occur at the same time. Maybe we really don't multitask after all. It's just that thought occurs so rapidly. Maybe our ability to be aware is slower than thought itself. Maybe the so-called unconscious mind is really just a time gap between thought and awareness.*

With class dismissed, he roamed across the campus, mulling over his thoughts about his psychology class and Butler. He garnered peace from the serenity of daydreaming about the past; he shuttered at the uncertainty of the future. He dreaded this upcoming counseling session—he had divulged his lifetime's secret involuntarily because he had been caught. Now he had to do it again. With a cooler perspective, he was in route to tell all once more. He speculated candor was the expectation of therapy. *How could I be helped if they don't know where it hurts? I need to keep an open mind. Don't bullshit yourself. Haven't you been waiting for this? Isn't that why you're all over psychology? Is relieving me of my distress the goal of the man with whom I will spend the an hour talking? Is his goal to yank me from my misery? That's more the goal of a preacher. Maybe there's a pill he could prescribe. Maybe there's a chemical imbalance; my brain's just fucking with me.*

As he neared the student counseling center, his stomach became queasier. He was being asked to say goodbye to an old friend. He had yet come to terms with himself, what he did, what he was, and more importantly, what he would do. He was not finished with peeping.

Psychotherapy was an enigma. He objected to submitting to a practice with unclear methods and tools. What was the active ingredient of the process? If it's pharmaceutical, then write him a prescription, and he'll be on his way. His sand fly beckoned.

I am the sand fly. I hover over this rotted, washed up kelp, and wait, flitting and fluttering in the beach sun. I see your cure. Lying on the beach, she is tan and round and all alone.

He stopped, pausing in front of the student counseling center. *I'm reporting for a prison sentence.* He stood, reflecting, muttering to himself: "What is it I fear? I'm gonna tell another white dude I like peeping in people's windows while they get naked. It's a bad habit I can't break. But what is it really?"

A wave of loneliness washed over him. When he was scared, when he was lonely, when he was bored—to whom did he turn?

I fear losing the sand fly.

The loss of his mother, his father, close friends—were circumstances too catastrophic to consider seriously. Losing the sand fly carried identical grave import. He shuddered at a sadness so deep; he dared not exhume it.

He had conveniently dismissed the existence of a student counseling center, conveniently disavowing that he belonged there. The center was on the first floor of the Humanities building. On a placard over a large glass double door, the words were inscribed: "The first steps toward change are recognition and acceptance." *Noble words,* he thought. *I wonder if it's bullshit or true.*

With ten minutes remaining before his appointment time, he leaned against some bike racks adjacent to the entrance; he did not want to sit in a waiting room. *What about the people who come and go? They'll wonder what my weird-looking ass is doing there. And the other patients? They must sit around wondering the same thing about each other. Maybe they want to compare craziness. They can't help from hiding behind magazines, peeking around for a glimpse, wondering what form of fucked-up dementia brings you here today.*

He realized—he recognized—he had a problem; he accepted that it was a problem, but the recognition was not the issue. He did not evade the issue: he simply did not want to get caught. His deepest desire: to continue as he had for eight years, remaining undetected. He had agreed to counseling under coercion, so the inscription over the entrance made no sense. Acceptance and recognition changes nothing, as far as he was concerned. The only factor changing things is change itself—and *change* is doing or refraining from something you otherwise don't do or do. *So how is counseling going to help? It's bullshit.*

Eager to get this over with, he looked at his watch—five minutes to go. He went inside, to be greeted by a smiling, friendly, horse-faced, buck-toothed, blond woman in her late twenties wearing glasses with Jacuzzi-sized lenses, making her pale blue eyes half the size of her head. She stood behind a semi-circular reception desk gabbing with two attractive women. As soon as she saw Marzee, she pushed some papers across the counter as if she recognized him.

He was uneasy that she seemed to know him. *We haven't been introduced.* She commenced to produce a stack of paperwork. *How does she know who I am? I thought this shit was supposed to be anonymous and confidential. Was I on the cover of the shrink newsletter this morning?* "You must be

151

Marzee. We're expecting a new client, and you seemed lost and befuddled," she chirped, apologizing for the inconvenience while she separated the forms into two piles. "I'm Joanna, by the way."

He scowled at the forms, instantly resenting having to do any paperwork. "No one said anything about filling out forms and questionnaires," he commented after clearing his throat.

She squeezed his arm sympathetically. "Don't worry. You can take this big stack home with you. No hurry," she added, maintaining her broad smile. "But these here you do have to read and sign before you receive services," she recited, patting the shallower stack with the palm of her hand.

Worried—almost repugnant about counseling now—he was at the brink of walking out. "I'm not very good at reading and filling out forms. I'll tell you that right now," he replied, with an irritated, forced smile.

"I'll explain each one, but you should still read before you sign." She paused, appraising him with a cocked head. "Didn't you learn that in Kindergarten?" she asked, joking and squeezing his arm again.

She's a touchy-feely bitch.

Feeling self-conscious, he wished they were in a private office or some confined space rather than standing in the open at a counter. And he despised filling out forms. "Please, explain them. I promise, I'll read them," he said.

She started her explanation as if she were a DMV agent divvying out application documents. "This form deals with payment for services rendered. Two pages. You can handle it," she said giggling, once again touching his forearm.

Jesus, she touches too much. She don't get no dick—that I'm sure of. "Hang on. Payment? I thought it was student counseling. Isn't it free?"

"It's close to free if your parents aren't wealthy," she replied, still too bubbly for Marzee's taste. "It's called a sliding scale. Basically, you pay what you can afford."

He perused the form, hastily filling in the blanks for parents' income, then scanned to the bottom, and signed. "Looks like I'll owe ten bucks a session," he said.

The receptionist looked the form over for missing information, relinquishing her otherwise permanent smile for ten seconds. "Yup, you're right. Soooo, your dad isn't Bill Gates?" she asked, resuming the levity with which tried to characterize herself.

"Nope. I wasn't at the adaption center the day he came by," Marzee retorted with a cynical hiss.

"I'll explain this second form, but your therapist will discuss it with you as well." She paused, again becoming serious. "This form explains where the confidentiality with your therapist might be compromised. It says that the therapist is required to report a patient to law enforcement if the therapist suspects the patient of sexually or physically abusing a child, or if a child's safety is threatened."

He felt threatened, being asked to sign such a form, as if they suspected him of such behavior. "So, if my problem is kiddy diddling, he'd report me. Is that it?" Marzee asked, hoping to shock some of that smile off of her.

"Yep, that's it," she responded unfazed.

He recalled spotting voyeurism listed with pedophilia among the list of DSM sexual disorders he had browsed in Butler's office. Anguished that his problem would be even remotely related to child molestation, he feared indecision about signing such the form would cast aspersion. He scribbled his signature just as Joanna was starting a comment.

"OK. We're almost done. This is a consent form. It states that you consent to the session with your counselor being videotaped," she explained dryly. "The tape is strictly confidential, if you're worried we'll post it on the Internet." She guffawed at the implication. Marzee remained silent, taking the implication seriously. "Don't worry. These tapes are just used for training. You know, by therapists in training. The students study and analyze them under supervision. We erase them after a year."

No wonder the prices are so low. This place is a fuck'n barber school, training psychotherapists. That means my ass will be scrutinized and analyzed.

A classroom listening to every fucked up thing I tell this dude. It's like some dude agrees his ass surgery can be taped for a reduced price. So his ass is in the middle of a surgical room, a bunch of doctors and nurses sitting around watching the ass operation, taking notes for when they have to perform the same ass procedure.

Toiling over whether or not to sign, he finally relented. "I feel a little nervous about people viewing my private session. It's sort of like someone reading your diary," he remarked, shoving the form toward her across the counter.

"We really ought to change the form so it's clearer for people to understand. Some people simply don't want to be recorded." She paused and leaned furtively across the counter to Marzee. "And I'd be one of them," she whispered.

Goddamn! How could anyone so ugly be so friendly and happy? "So, you would decline?" he asked hastily, pulling the form back. "You just convinced me." He crossed out his signature on the consent line, and signed on the decline line.

She snatched up the three forms, readied an unlabelled hanging folder, and while depositing Marzee's paperwork, checked the wall clock. "Oh. It's already five after three. Lorn is late. He's usually right on time," she commented, half talking to herself. "By the way, you've got the only non-student therapist here. Dr. Dance is a consulting psychologist, and he teaches forensic psychology—criminal psychology." She looked around at the

155

three clients already sitting in the waiting room, reading magazines, still, quiet, absorbed, straining to eavesdrop on Marzee's conversation with the receptionist. He scanned the room, noticing for the first time that others were behind him. One of the waiting clients, a woman wearing extraordinarily large sunglasses, her hair bundled in a knit cap on not such a cold day, got up and walked around the corner. Joanna looked at her curiously without comment.

"Don't forget your packet," Joanna reminded him as he left the counter. "You're not through filling out forms yet! Depending on how late he's running, maybe you could start one of them while you're waiting. They're each stapled together, and labeled at the top."

Blandly turning about face, he took the packet from Joanna's hand. He resigned himself to her request, rationalizing that filling out forms gave him as much cover as leafing through a *People* magazine. He rifled through the forms, alternating between scribbling and furtive glances around the waiting room.

At 3:15 a frail-looking man in his mid-fifties with brown hair—frantic and frustrated—burst through the double doors. He walked briskly toward Joanna who was already poised to reprimand him for his tardiness.

"You wouldn't believe what just happened to me!" he exclaimed wide-eyed. "I was at my West LA office. I went down to the parking lot to find I had—not one flat tire, but two!" Noticing that Joanna was going to interrupt, he added quickly, "So, naturally, I was going to call you to let you know I'd be running late. Then, my cell phone was dead. I couldn't even call the Auto Club. Luckily, a colleague in the office was leaving at the same time, so she gave me a lift here. I was going to call you using her cell—and guess what—she didn't have it with her!" He paused with an exhausted exhale. "I made it, though. I'll take care of the flat tires later."

Joanna's jaw dropped, accentuating her already elongated face. "You could have gone inside and cancelled your appointments from your office phone," she said. "I think all your clients would have understood," she commented, glancing toward Marzee.

"Nah. Besides—" Dance looked around, zeroing in on Marzee. "You Marzee?"

Dance's attention, and sudden shift in his direction, unsettled Marzee. He shuddered, wondering what Butler had said about him to bequeath Dance's instant recognition. "Yes, I am," he answered nervously.

"Then let's get started. You already heard all my excuses. Usually I'm the one listening to excuses," Dance commented as he approached Marzee and extended his hand. "I'm Lorn Dance." Marzee stood and reciprocated the hand shake without comment. "Joanna, what room do we have?" Dance asked.

"Room four," Joanna sang.

"Please." Dance motioned for Marzee to follow him. "I see the dreaded packet is still in your hand, so you probably didn't have time to complete any of the assessments in there," Dance remarked inquiringly.

Joanna's sing-songy mannerism grated on Marzee, delaying his response. *Does she take drugs, or a fucking happy pill? Maybe she's one of those religious nuts, always happy because Jesus is between her legs.* "No. But I was going to try to fill out one or two while I was waiting," he replied.

"I like to have them before I start with someone new. Saves time. I don't have to ask you stuff about your relationship with your parents, or how many siblings you have, or how many years of school you have, or what kind of drugs you take, or whether you've ever been treated psychiatrically. That sort of thing." Dance explained with a sincere smile. "Then there are some other psychological tests in there. They'll give me a snapshot of whether you're happy, sad, nervous, guilty—things like that. But then again, I can also gather those bits of information by just talking to you—right?"

Since this was his first therapy session—and under less than voluntary conditions—he figured *agreeable* was the best attitude. Yet he remained guarded. "I guess," he replied, smiling meekly and shrugging his shoulders.

Dance closed the door behind them. The situation did not meet Marzee's expectation of stereotypic psychotherapy, consisting of him lying on a couch while Dance sat behind him. They sat four feet across from one another in ordinary, cushioned chairs with arm rests. "OK, first off, Marzee. You are sort of a unique case. I say unique because my friend, and your teacher, Larry Butler, already called me, and told me a bit about your problem. But you should understand, Butler and I are not discussing you behind your back. Your comments to me are strictly between you and me. What you say here, stays here. Maybe, knowing that will instill a bit of trust in me. I know we just met one another, so it takes some time for any kind of trust to develop," Dance explained in a rote manner, as if he had rehearsed the speech.

The apprehension Marzee had experienced in the waiting room had changed—before he was at the edge of the cliff, looking down. Now, he had jumped, and the ground was getting closer. "Ok," Marzee said nervously. "I understand. That helps, what you just said. And you knowing why I'm here to begin with."

"I'd rather hear it from you, but I'll tell you what I know so everything's on the table. Butler told me the details concerning why he recommended you to me, and that you appear to have a problem with voyeurism. When he called me, he was very concerned. He believed you needed to get help before you run into law enforcement problems, and asked me to work with you," Dance recited.

Marzee's stomach churned the same as when he had to speak in front of an audience. "I assumed he told you the details. He said he talked to a friend of his who 'dealt with problems like mine.'" What you said just about sums it up." Marzee responded, shuttering and bowing his head. "And this is my first time ever talking about it. Talking openly about this is very difficult for me."

"Give me an example of what's hard about it," Dance asked, leaning forward in his chair, maintaining eye contact with Marzee.

Marzee choked back sobbing, determined to go through with this. "It's always been my biggest secret. It's something I'm ashamed of. I get these thoughts. No. Actually, they're more like images, pictures. Then my heart starts to pound. My mouth gets dry. I lose my appetite." He paused, seeking his next words. Then feeling uncomfortable with the silence, continued. "I feel like I'm possessed. Like a demon controls me. It's not me; it's something else. Then I plan my whole day around how I can make the image real. The desire. Whatever you want to call it."

"How horny do you feel when you have these thoughts and images?" Dance asked, now leaning back into his chair.

"Horny? Hmmm. More like desirous, nervous, scared," Marzee responded pensively. "It's hard to say. I never really thought about how I feel. I just do it. Sometimes, I don't want to, but I do it anyway."

"Good list. You said desirous. Would I be correct saying that you experience an overwhelming desire to make the image real?" Dance inquired.

Dance's description was succinct and accurate, helping to reduce his resistance. The apprehension he had harbored all day had evolved into tepid engagement. "Yes. That's true. I want the image. But it's not like I really want to be part of it. Like, I don't really want the woman, or the couple, or whatever. It's like I want to be part of it without really being part of it. I don't know. That doesn't really make much sense, does it? It's like I want something, but I don't really want it," he explained, his voice rising an octave as he talked.

"How do you feel sexually when this urge strikes? Do you get an erection?" Dance asked, opening his posture, still leaning back.

Direct discourse about sex flustered Marzee, especially when presented in such a clinical manner, though talking about sex with his friends stimulated him. He believed, with limited experience, that white people discuss sex differently than black people—but then again, they engage in it differently as well. *Here it comes—questions about my dick. I knew I would have to talk about my dick.* "No. Not at all. Just the opposite. My penis shrivels up," he answered, forcing himself to look at Dance in the eye. "Later, maybe, if I'm looking at something, and it's really nice, I might get a hard on. But I have to focus, to concentrate."

161

"How about masturbation? Do you masturbate later, after you've done the peeping, or there at the scene?" Dance asked, again leaning forward, maintaining eye contact.

His penis shriveling up when he was on the prowl had always confounded him. His actions, his thoughts, his feelings—all a secret. He could never ask or confide. He felt relieved and conflicted, being able to talk about it. "Both. Sometimes both. When I'm at home, alone, and I concentrate on what I saw, then I get a hard on—like in the shower later. But usually not when I am at the scene. Except—" Marzee said, hesitating.

"Except?" Dance said.

"Except a couple days ago. I don't know. Maybe later I can talk about it. It's heavy." Marzee responded. He noticed Dance's expression turned stern.

"I won't bullshit you, Marzee. You've been very lucky so far. What you do is not accepted well by the general public, and it's illegal. It's considered a sexual perversion. That's the way it is, right or wrong, fair or unfair. You're here with me, safe, talking about this overwhelming desire—this demon, as you described it—that possesses you, makes you do things that you don't really want to do. But if you get caught, you'll be in a lot of trouble. And the police, and the courts, they don't really care about why you do what you do. They simply see a pervert, a public nuisance. And that's how the courts consider a peeping tom—a nuisance.

Because you're not really dangerous, they may let you slide on the first offense with a charge of trespassing or disturbing the peace. But sliding sends a message to you: 'Hey, I can keep doing this, and that's the worst that will happen.' To make it stop, you have to stop. You have to want it. It just won't happen by talking with me a few times. So, my question to you is, do you want to stop? Or do you simply not want to get caught? Because if your answer is—and really, really think about this. If your answer is, 'I just don't want to get caught.' Well, you will get caught. The odds are against you because of frequency. You'll do it over and over again. The odds are against you. You will get caught. You were almost caught the other day. You've probably had other near misses. You'll get arrested. Your family will know. You'll be ashamed. But time will pass, and the fear and shock of dealing with the legal system will diminish. And people forget. And the demon will return. And the cycle will resume."

The direct and unwavering quality of Dance's decree disturbed Marzee. He felt indicted already, and he was frightened by the imminent nature of his proclamation. "You sound like you've seen this before," Marzee replied.

"Many, many times. I used to work at Atascadero State Hospital. Ever hear of that place?" Dance responded assuredly.

"No, sir. No, I haven't," Marzee answered.

"It's a prison hospital for the sexually criminally insane," Dance answered. "Most inmates are rapists and pedophiles—child molesters. Notice I didn't call them patients—although they're in a hospital, they're prisoners. But we had our share of peeping Toms. Usually for a voyeur to end up in Atascadero, he'd been arrested and convicted many times. The charges range from trespassing to prowling, breaking and entering, malicious mischief, petty theft, and whatever else the DA could throw in. But the main crime is prowling." Dance paused, scooted forward slightly, and assessed Marzee's wide-eyed angst. "And Marzee, make no mistake about it. Once you're in there, they throw you in with the rest of the pot. All the rapists, child molesters, and incest-doers. When you get out, you have to register as a sex offender, wherever you go, wherever you move. And that will follow you around for the rest of your life. Listen, I'm not trying to 'scare you straight.' It's just the way it is."

Ambivalent about Dance, he could cure him or imprison him. Either would stop him, though he preferred the curative route. He had known this man for less than an hour, yet Dance knew him as if he had watched him, concealed, since he was thirteen. His sand fly beckoned him, offering to transpose his fear. "I was hoping maybe some sort of medication , you know, might make it easier to control," Marzee asked, crossing his legs sheepishly. Dance's mood turned from somber to pensive.

164

"Possibly. Perhaps in your case, maybe meds can help. But we have more talking to do before we pursue medication. If you have all those questionnaires filled out by the time we see one another again, that will speed things up." Dance answered.

"So, you're saying there may be some medication that relieves this peeping urge?" Marzee asked, intensely interested in a pill to fix his ills.

"Let me ask you, Marzee. Once you go out and fulfill the image you get in your head, how do you feel?" Dance probed.

As he had hoped for a prescription today, he was disappointed. He didn't believe talking alone would help. "Hmm. If someone I know found out what I do, I'd feel ashamed. But how do I feel when I'm done? I feel—relieved. Sort of relaxed, or maybe just tired." Marzee answered.

"It sounds like you said as long as people you know don't find out about your secret life, you're OK with that. And after a round of peeping, you feel better? Not guilty or ashamed. Just relaxed or relieved?" Dance replied, summarizing Marzee's comment.

A subtle edginess slinked in—restlessness with which Marzee was all too familiar. He was ready to part company, but he dare not act impatiently. The sand fly flittered in his chest. "Yes. That sounds about right," Marzee confirmed.

"Here's a question: What do you think you'd do if you had strong urges—very strong

165

images and desire—but something prevented you from acting on them?" Dance asked.

Dance's description of the prison hospital for sex perverts had alarmed him. *Would he turn me in? Is that what that form I signed meant?* "Prevented? Like, being locked up?" Marzee asked cautiously.

"No. Not locked up, or bound. Well, maybe socially bound. Say you had commitments, like a job. Or some other obligation, limiting your ability to pursue your obsession. What would happen?" Dance responded.

"Hmmm. Well, I don't know. I don't think I'd explode, if that's what you're getting at," Marzee replied, causing Dance to chuckle.

"That's a good start. I'll make a note: worst case—exploding—not happening. So then what would you do?" Dance inquired.

Torn between telling Dance what he really believed he'd do, or giving him the right answer, he choose the later. "Well, nothing, I guess. I suppose I'd just have to cope with the discomfort since I couldn't get away," Marzee responded—the answer he believed Dance wanted. Marzee knew otherwise: He'd get away, whatever it took.

"So, you're saying, nothing would happen. You'd feel discomfort for a while?" Dance continued. "And how about the next day? Say, you had the same, or different, obligations the next day? You couldn't get away. What would happen after two days?"

166

Heed the man; he has a message. He's saying if I don't follow you, I won't die. If I don't do your bidding, nothing will happen. Your power over me will cease, and I can live without you. "Well, still no explosion!" Marzee exclaimed. "I think I know what you are getting at. Like the werewolf when he's a man, asking a friend to chain him during a full moon."

"What happens when you try to hold back? What happens when you don't do what your thoughts are telling you to do?" Dance retorted.

The urge pounded him now, and he forced himself to ignore it. He had to behave as if it were not pushing from inside. "I usually convince myself to go do it anyway," Marzee answered with earnestness. "It's like, the thoughts are really forces, and the forces are hard to resist. These thoughts, these images, they seem to have strength, a pull. Yeah, I know they're only thoughts, but they almost seem to come from somewhere else. Almost like demon possession. I don't know if that makes sense or not. I feel like I get struck. Bang! From out of nowhere. Then I'm hooked."

"So, you're bound and obligated to act out these thoughts, urges, images. You lose control. Would that be an accurate statement?" Dance pressed, like a courtroom lawyer converging on a confession.

"Yes, that right. It's like my whole body wants to do it. And my heart beats faster. And my armpits sweat a little bit more. Once I was riding my moped, minding my own business, enjoying a warm, Spring day, when all of the sudden—bang—the urge hit me. And I yelled, 'Leave me alone!' at the top of my lungs," Marzee recounted. "But I went ahead and did it anyway."

"Usually voyeurs don't want to be seen, so they look into windows at night, or early in the morning before the sunrise. You mentioned a Spring day. And you were chased the other day, not at night. So how do you peep during the day?" Dance inquired.

Discussing tactics incubated the demon egg. The tell-tale signs warned him of an impending storm. "Girls in bikinis lying around pools. Or at the beach. They don't have to be naked. And you'd be surprised at the number of girls who lie around topless at the beach," Marzee responded, trying to subdue his heavier breathing. He felt Dance draw closer.

"It sounds like you're saying nudity or near nudity attracts you. Then you conceal yourself to watch," Dance remarked.

Time seemed to drag. He was antsy, becoming more agitated with the subject matter. "I hide, even if I'm out in the open, even if I'm not peeping," Marzee explained guardedly. He noticed Dance glance at the wall clock.

"Marzee, our time is about up. I'd like to see you again in two or three days if that's possible. You can set up another appointment with Joanna. Another thing—please complete the forms and questionnaires in that packet you've got," Dance added, pointing at the manila envelope Marzee had placed on the floor. "It shouldn't take you more than an hour, given your intelligence."

Hearing Dance refer to him as intelligent, he self-consciously blushed. "In two or three days? I thought therapy was, like, once a week. I must really be crazy," Marzee exclaimed. Dance resumed his stern demeanor.

"Not crazy, but you're in danger. More danger than you care to realize. If you and I put our heads together, maybe we can keep you out of some serious trouble," Dance responded.

Marzee agreed to make the appointment and complete the paperwork. After they had exchanged a firm handshake, he was relieved he had cleared this hurdle. The session was over. Finishing was like completing a long anticipated examination.

Dance preceded Marzee, and approached Joanna at the counter. Marzee turned to study the empty room, glancing toward the wall-mounted cameras. He dismissed the tiny red pilot light dimming after the two had vacated the therapy room.

Chapter 9
The Sex Machine

Damn! He must think I'm seriously nuts, wanting to see me so soon. Once a week—that's a shrink's schedule!. But twice a week? Am I really that crazy? I need to be cool and go along with the program. Don't forget squeezed into that dark, cramped trunk for four hours. Damn! I didn't kill anybody. I didn't rob anybody. Nobody saw me with a gun. Why were they so determined to catch me? I heard the helicopter overhead from inside the trunk. Damn! I remember seeing some crazy nigger directing traffic in an intersection, naked. No one got out of his car, and chased his naked ass up and down the street. But I had armed police, and a tenant posse, searching for me. I owe Mr. Butler. He didn't turn me in. He could have easily. But damn! Twice a week! Maybe that's for starters, so he can know me faster, talk to me more at first. Later he'll ease off. What's going to happen from talk? The sand fly stays. The sand fly ain't goin' nowhere.

Marzee looked up, dazed from his impromptu reality retreat. Suddenly confronted with Joanna's smiling face, he jolted. *Goddamn! I hope whoever fucks her has lots of paper bags handy.* Speechless, he eked out a smile. She remained as bubbly and cheery as when he had first arrived.

Self-conscious about looking her in the eye—having thought what he had thought—he felt

170

a pang of sympathy for her. *I admire people having particularly challenging handicaps who maintain good dispositions—especially visually challenging handicaps*, he mused, mindful she might be able to read his thoughts.

"So, while you were in session with Dr. Dance, Marzee, we figured out your sliding scale," she whispered. She leaned over the counter toward Marzee, talking under her breath. Her contrived, secretive tone made it appear like he's getting such a deal, and the other clients in earshot should not hear lest they riot the waiting room. "You came in at the bottom end of the scale, so your sessions will be fifteen dollars each."

Marzee cracked a mischievous grin, wanting to impress her with his wit and rap. "Fifteen dollars!" he exclaimed. "That's pretty good. I thought it would be higher than that." He reached for his wallet. "I thought you guys might charge by craziness level—then I really couldn't afford to pay!"

"I never thought of it like that before. I guess some clients would be more work for the therapist than others, and therefore should have to pay more," she replied, cocking her head sideways, pondering the comment as if it were meant to provoke serious consideration.

She's not only ugly, she's stupid. Disappointed that she didn't get his dead-pan witticism, his grin ebbed to a smirk. "I was just joking." He counted fifteen dollars from his wallet.

"Also, Dr. Dance wanted me to reschedule with him for pretty soon, like in two or three days. Is that possible? It would have to be around this time again."

"It could only be around this time. He's only here in the late afternoons and evenings." Joanna replied, checking the schedule on her computer monitor. "How about Friday at 6 PM?"

Looking forward to his Friday evenings to unwind and socialize, her proposal soured him. *Friday at six! He must not have much of a social life.* "That's a little late, especially for a Friday. Anything else?" he questioned.

"Well, he's got another on Thursday at four. Would that work?" she asked.

"That's perfect. Put me down for that one, please," Marzee requested, politely smiling, still appalled at her exasperatingly upbeat disposition. "And I'll have all these forms filled out by then as well," he added apologetically as he held up the packet and eased away from the counter. He grinned obsequiously as he attempted a subtle escape, not wanting to hear another word from her.

"Great! Oh. Want your receipt?" Joanna called after him.

After depressing the door handle, Marzee had already picked up speed. He cringed at the sound of her voice. "No. That's OK. Maybe I can get a total when all this is over," he yelled back, determined to get away. The door closed behind him as he uttered his last syllable.

172

As he walked into the cool dusk air, thoughts of Utte smittened him. Primed by describing his escapades to Dance, he should have seen it coming. He had to see her. *Does she teach tonight? If so, where? If not, where is she?* Frustrated as he rifled though his backpack, he could not find a schedule of classes. *The stack of schedules near the library entrance—I need one.* He rose quickly, and jogged toward the campus library.

Resolute, single minded in his goal, he yearned to go back to her neighborhood. *The street. The sidewalk. The fence. The knothole.* The image—the ambiance—flooded his mind. He hoped she did not teach a late-night class. He wanted the subterfuge of darkness, without the suspicion creeping around too late could elicit. With racing heart, he longed to see her in her habitat. He longed to see Utte the same way he had savored Cecilia through her bedroom window. He craved his sight gliding over Utte's bare skin, smooth, glistening, unprotected from his eye.

A faint voice barely in the recesses of his awareness called to him. It exerted an opposing tug: *turn around, go back into the counseling center— Help me, please!* He dismissed it, overwhelmed by a vision of nude Utte.

With sure-footed steps, he hoped he did not encounter someone he knew, especially not Freddie or Richard. As the ambient light dimmed, the campus lights flickered on. The round, shining globes lining the edges of the sidewalk lighted his path to the library.

The broad stairs leading up to the library entrance doors gave the structure a majestic, classical appearance. Bounding up the stairs, he punched the "handicapped" handle, causing the door to swing open. He entered, only to execute an about-face after he had grabbed a schedule from the near-by stack. Leafing alphabetically to the Philosophy section, he found Tuesday night. *There! 5 PM to 6:50 PM. She teaches Existential Philosophy tonight. I have to wait it out for her to head home. Fine. I'm already in the library. I'll find a cubical; bide my time; study.*

Study cubicles lined the outer walls of the upper floors of the library. They formed a perimeter around book shelves, desks of administrative workers, computer services, and catalog stacks. When he had first used the library study facilities, he noted female students became careless while seated in these semi-private study desks. A side and front partition separated each study cubicle, imparting a feeling of privacy and blocking out distractions. The underside of the desk was unobstructed.

Marzee trolled the third and fourth floors, finally spotting his objective: a girl, writing feverishly, inattentive to her seated posture, her short summer dress clinging marginally to her mid-thigh. He discreetly occupied the cubicle in front of her, quietly opened his book bag, and extricated his study materials. He was meticulous, organizing his textbook and notepad on the desk. He propped open his book, then with James Bond stealth, stuck his head out of the cubicle to scan the area. *No one around. No one watching.* Retracting his head, he slowly, silently pushed the chair away from the desk, giving himself space to contort and bend downward. If the circumstance arose—another student appearing in his vicinity—he'd have to make a rapid retreat from under the desk to appear to be studying.

Scrupulously poised, he dropped his pen. He could still hear her pen scratching behind him. He reached down to retrieve his pen. He propped his hand on the floor over the pen, and peered through the open space behind him, straight up her dress.

Damn! She's wearing panties. But her legs are nice. They're opened, not crossed. Soft. Juicy. No tan. A little pale. But, mmmm. so juicy. Damn! She spread her legs a little more. She's not wearing thong panties. Pretty small, though. Brazilian cut. I can almost see where her ass crack starts.

Fearing he had lost track of time while staring between the girl's legs, he picked up his pen and sat up. Writing and the shuffling of paper continued behind him. The apprehension of being caught sharpened him, kept him preoccupied, kept him on edge. He didn't have an erection—he was scared. His heart was beating—not like when he was hiding in the trunk of the car; not like when he was peeping through the knothole of the fence outside Utte's backyard; not like the hundred times he stood in the dark outside Cecilia's bedroom window, gazing, waiting to see her—but the feeling was similar.

Impatient, he wanted to get on with his quest. *Only 6:15. At least another hour to go. Utte has to complete her class, pick up her stuff, go to her car, and drive home. Hopefully, she goes straight home. I could get some studying done here, but damn, those thighs behind me.* He dropped the pen again and kneeled down.

Afraid his heavy breathing would attract attention, he recovered the pen once more. He felt guilty, but not about looking up the girl's dress behind him: he wasn't doing his work; he wasn't tending to the business of his life. He pondered his pending math, psychology, and English assignments. A sudden commotion startled him. The girl behind him was leaving, none the wiser of his intimate knowledge of her tanless inner-thighs and panty design. Her departure relieved him: he could work now without the distraction of her thighs. After a couple seconds, he poked his head out to watch her depart.

Not so hot when they stand up. She's a bit chunky, needs some muscle tone.

He shuttered, reflecting on the risk he had taken. Her unexceptional appearance hardly substantiated the jeopardy he had assumed. *Why risk the embarrassment being caught might cause?*

176

Even if she were so, so fine, so what? At what cost is stopping?

He grew restless. The anticipation of spying on Utte naked had diminished his appetite. Normally with growling stomach by this time of evening, he'd steer toward the student center cafeteria, a vending machine, or home. He decided to check for Utte's car in the parking lot. If there, he'd double back, grab a Baby Ruth and bag of chips, go to his moped, and meander toward her neighborhood. If she had already left, then no food, and he'd speed to his destination.

As he packed his book bag, he stood up—pangs of guilt battering him momentarily—his vivid fantasy seeing Utte naked unceremoniously discharged his self-reproach. He strode through the double doors into the cool evening air. Hastening his pace toward the western parking lot, he remained vigilant of her presence. Were he to accidentally encounter her, amidst his plan to peep through her bedroom window, his plans would be shattered. *Passing by her classroom? Would that be too bold? I could just stay outside.*

Bushes and a few small trees divided the campus walkway from Utte's existentialism class on the first floor of Baker Hall. From his vantage point behind a tree, he watched as she articulated with her hands, her face, her body. Her energy and animation apparent, strutting and gesturing in front of her class, he ascertained the subject matter excited her. She turned and wrote "Hesse-Sidhartha-

177

pp.1-100" in red letters on the whiteboard. If he remained in the shadows, somebody noticing him was unlikely.

Gripping the rim of the desk behind her, she hoisted herself to sit on its edge. Her mini-skirted bare legs, contrasted from the fluorescent lights inside the classroom and his shadowed perspective outside, underscored the reason he had tarried on campus this evening.

They're leaving, she's still talking. She must have dismissed class. Lucky dude sitting in front of her. He can't take his eyes off her either.

He assumed Utte would go home directly from school. As he recalled her husband at work in her backyard, he hoped Utte did not have any similar external dalliances as well, which would impede her hasty return home. He intended being outside her window, ready to see it all.

Departing his observation post behind the tree, he darted toward the eastern parking lot. The rush of the pending spectacle consumed him. Logistics: her timing; his timing; time to here; time to there—he scoured each tactical interval. He wanted the spectacle, from beginning to end. He had to see; he had to see everything. Hastening his pace, he pictured her bare body and the details of her skin. His walk progressed faster, evolving into a jog, becoming a run. He sprinted toward the parking lot.

Winded, he reached his moped, having run the entire distance across campus. Heaving, trying to catch his breath, he detached his helmet from the rack, plopped it on his head, and started the motor. Carelessly, he pushed back from his parking place and sped to the exit driveway. As he merged with the flow of the heavy early evening traffic, a motorist flashed his high beams, and he switched on his headlamp.

Donned with a thin cotton jacket and t-shirt, he was impervious to the chilled evening air, as the forty mile-per-hour wind pelted him. He ran stop signs where he could, made split second left turns in front of on-coming traffic—inciting several horns and finger gestures—and darted down side streets and alleys, avoiding stop signs, signals, and pedestrians. Fifteen minutes later, he was incinerating in the ten-degree-cooler air in Utte's beach neighborhood. The anticipation—fulfilling the fantasy of finally seeing her naked—absorbed him, mind and body. The exhilaration glowed with a white-hot burn.

He parked his moped at exactly the same spot he had parked a few days ago. Retracing his steps to her backyard, he felt a nostalgic reunion—a familiarity, as if he were at home away from home. He recognized which fence to pick from the rear sidewalk. Because it was dark, he was free of scrutiny by prying eyes from adjacent houses.

Unknown territory awaited him, as Utte's backyard was his next aim. Getting over the fence presented a challenge. He was not yet certain about the house's rear windows through which he had assumed he would peek. He had a sixth sense—a mental image of where she would get naked, shower, dry herself. He pictured the layout: her bedroom window had to be at the rear of the house. He had dismissed logistics complications: the bedroom is elsewhere, window blinds closed, a dog in the yard, security sensors. Above all, he had faith in his intuition.

Bringing his problem-solving skills to bear, he considered the course before him: penetrate an unknown perimeter, the fence and yard; get close to the back wall of the house without being detected. The fence had a gate, but he was not sure how to unlatch it, or whether it was locked. Since he doubted it was locked, he figured it was a matter of unlatching a gate—a six foot gate—and the latch might be located well below his arm's reach from the top.

I might have to scale the fence, and jump from the top. What if I break my leg when I jump? No, better not do that. Then I'd be all fucked up in their backyard. I didn't notice any dogs last time I was here, unless it's in the house, and I doubt that. She doesn't strike me as a dog person. No dogs next door. I don't hear any barking.

He paused at the gate, stood in place, and rotated around slowly, checking every house and window in his view as he turned. Utte's gate was unlit, as was the backyard. The sidewalk lights were dim, allowing him to be concealed by night's cover.

Combing the surface of the fence, he found a familiar knothole, and peered through it to the rear of the house. The room was dimly lit through narrow, partially extended Venetian blinds. With no one apparently home, he dashed over to the other knothole for an alternate perspective, having to crouch even lower. Suddenly activity erupted from the front of the house—a car engine, tires on the road, the sound of a garage door opening. With a cat's reflexes, he stood at attention, his gray-green eyes piercing the darkness. The glow of headlamps—someone had just arrived.

After performing a military perusal of the vicinity, all seemed clear. He took aim through the fence hole providing the most straight-on view of the two rear windows. Then he heard the sound of the garage door closing. He repressed his impulse to bound over the fence, and rush up to the windows. *What if she goes into the backyard when she arrives home—to water some plants or take a walk or smoke a joint?* He lingered, hunched, until he detected activity in the bedroom.

Lights! And voices! Her voice, and a male voice. Damn. Hubby's home. They're *in there, moving around. She's not going to eat? Or watch TV?*

Desperate, yet controlled, he decided to make his move by first poking around for hinges and a gap in the fence. Finding no handle or outside latch, he assumed the latch must be on the yard side, opposite the gate hinges. He stood on his tip toes, reaching his arm over the gate, and extended his arm as far as possible, stretching it to its limit. His fingertips touched a metal protrusion. He jumped on the gate in order to hang from under his shoulders. After much finger wiggling and jiggling, the metal protrusion he had grasped, twisted, opening the gate with him dangling from it.

He eased himself the few inches to the ground, careful to obstruct the gate from closing. He lodged a landscaping rock in the gap to assure that the gate did not close behind him. The glow from the windows radiated. He hyperventilated.

In ninja-fashion, he approached the left window of the two rear windows. He embarked sure-footedly across the same lawn where, just a few days ago, he relished the sexual gyrations between Utte's husband and their female neighbor. Cursing under his breath, he caught his balance after tripping over more landscaping brickwork bordering the back wall of the house. From the indelibly implanted memory, he recalled seeing the small bushes and flowers planted along the wall. He didn't like moving through vegetation, especially in the dark. *Spiders. Spider webs. Bugs. Crawling things. All kinds of bullshit I can't see.* He crept along the wall, approaching the window from the side. Crouching to make eye-level with the two-inch gap between the blind and the window sill, he slowly panned sideways so that his right eye was first over the opening.

Overwhelmed, the brightness from the room obscured the detail. He moved over further to utilize both his eyes. As his vision acclimated to the light, the slowly focusing view astounded him.

Three studio lamps mounted on professional-looking tripods, spaced equally, were aimed at a larger than king-size, low profile bed in the center of the room. The square bed was the biggest he had ever seen—not even in any store or ad had he seen such a gigantic, trampoline-sized bed. Adorned with shiny red sheets, it reflected the bright light, creating a crimson aura.

Engaged by the inside decor, he felt more secure in his position outside. The bright light from within was likely to obscure his presence, and he did not sense that anyone would venture outside. Feeling more courageous, he edged to the center of the window. A large archway leading to what looked like an adjoining bathroom caught his attention. As his eyes adjusted to the light, he detected moving shadows and activity in a covey beyond the archway.

That's the shower! She's already in there. Damn. I didn't see her undress.

As more detail in the room became apparent, other furnishings attracted him. At the foot of the bed a tripod-mounted camera took aim at the bed's center. Squatting to change his angle, he was aghast, noticing one of the largest mirrors he had seen—mounted on the ceiling.

He squinted his eyes and twisted his head, trying to discern an object obscuring the center of the bed. Neither its reflection from the ceiling mirror nor a straight-on view helped to identify it. It was a device, seemingly hovering over the bed. To him, it looked like a black folding chair—the kind movie directors use—only it did not have legs. As he contorted, peering into the two-inch window slit, he recognized tube-looking cables attached to the each corner of the chair-thing and extending to the ceiling, attaching at the mirror's perimeter. A gray box about the size of a small television was mounted at one of the mirror's corners. Since it had little lights and switches on it, he thought it was either part of the camera equipment, or a security device.

Straining to improve his view, he inched backward to the lawn, then side-stepped six feet to the east window. He was pleased to find the gap between the drawn blinds and the window sill about the same. As he stepped over the landscaping bricks, and into a sparsely populated flower bed, he cringed as his feet sunk slightly into the soft dirt. Certain of his concealment, he propped himself against the window. It was opened slightly, allowing him to hear inside better. The sounds of running water were definite; someone was taking a shower.

His new perspective offered him greater resolution. The mysterious object was not hanging directly from the supports—a ring or disk mechanism supported the chair, and the tube-like struts supported the ring from the ceiling. To his amazement, he recognized photographs and posters of Utte plastering the walls—dozens of likenesses juxtaposed from floor to ceiling. *Ah! Makes sense. Dude's a photographer. All this stuff—lights, camera, tripods. Even that thing over the bed. She's a model, with her body, her face. Wonder why she wastes her time at school.*

Many photos were full length nudes mingled with close-ups of her face. One section of a wall was dedicated to black-and-white artistic renditions of singular body parts—knees, buttocks, breasts, a nipple, the curve from her ear lobe to her clavicle, an extreme close-up of her clitoris, her back, her toes, a shoulder, her abdomen, even her anus. *No part goes to waste*, he mused, grinning.

Suddenly activity filled the room, catching Marzee off guard. A sopping wet and naked Utte stood by the edge of the bed in his full view. She searched the area impatiently, focusing on the device hanging over the bed.

"Where's the remote?!" she yelled.

"Probably under the sheets," a male voice answered from the ante room.

She patted around on the sheets, bending, twisting, contorting—to Marzee's delight—as she looked for the elusive remote. She was more perfect than he had imagined—more beautiful naked than clothed. Feeling compelled to masturbate immediately, he knew if he did, it would drain him of the energy that brought him there, and he would want to leave. Within seconds she found what looked like a TV remote.

"John, are you coming soon?" she shouted, her German accent more pronounced than in class.

"Hopefully, for your sake, not too soon," he replied with a sly air, entering the room as naked as well. "I wanted to dry myself first, hun."

Marzee lacked experience guessing white people's attributes, but he figured Utte's husband was in his mid-forties, maybe five to ten years her senior. Though Marzee felt self-conscious about admiring a man's physique, he was in awe of her husband's superlative condition: no pot belly or gut, a chest almost requiring a bra, little body hair—not a carpet, but not an infant, ass cheeks that could hold on to a lottery ticket, bulbous, well-defined shoulders, legs not too thick and not too skinny, and a rock-hard, solid penis at least seven inches long.

So this is what a dude has to look like in order to have a woman like her, he lamented, feeling discouraged.

Utte pushed one of the buttons on the remote, and the overhanging contraption began to descend. Stopping it three feet above the surface of the bed, she handed the remote to her husband. With the grace and expertise of a trapeze artist, she hoisted herself on the chair part of the device, and secured a belt around her waist. Playfully, she stretched her body, hanging backward from the chair, until her long blond hair grazed the bed. Her

186

body formed a perfect arch: toes straight, quadriceps bulging, abdomen stretched and concave, her hip bones protruding, and her breasts forming natural ovals. Marzee unfastened his belt, unzipped his pants, and removed his penis, stroking it gently.

John stroked Utte's body, caressing and handling her as one might play a divine instrument—a quintessential harp, requiring alternating pressures, varying numbers of fingers, combinations of areas touched in unison or separately, and the occasional application of mouth and tongue. She arched, her husband played, and the melody: writhing, moaning, contorting. Eventually, the smooth arc of her body transformed into a vice of passion.

Reluctantly disengaging his head from between her thighs, Utte's husband took the remote-device from the bed and gave it to Utte. He laid facing up on the bed, his erect penis pointing almost vertically. He grasped its hilt with his thumb and forefinger, as if taking aim.

"I'm ready if you are," he said, muffling his lust to eke out the words.

Without responding, she wrapped the Velcro-fastening support straps around her thighs, which caused them to spread partially apart and up. She pressed a button on the remote. An invisible crane lowered her, his penis disappearing inside of her. The decent stopped automatically without her intervention, the device somehow sensing how far to traverse. Slowly the mount supporting her began to rotate—initially, a turn every thirty seconds. Marzee recoiled slightly as she looked in his direction when she turned toward his window. Drawing back, panicked, he regained his composure quickly, and re-approached the window. *There's no way she can see me. If she noticed me, she'd have reacted.*

"A little faster," her husband said.

Utte touched the remote briefly, which initiated a faster rotation. Her supported legs, travelling in a circle every ten seconds, were almost parallel to the floor. Marzee gazed in awe. He marveled at the unseen engineering design facilitating this wondrous spectacle. Her eyes were closed as she rotated toward Marzee again; her head hung backward. The sexual pirouette continued for several revolutions, at least five minutes.

"Now," her husband moaned.

Utte nonchalantly touched the remote. The harness supporting her slowly undulated up and down as it continued to turn, like a wooden horse on a carousel. Marzee could see her husband's penis appear and disappear inside of her. He contorted his neck for a better view, his angle blocked by a leg of one of the studio light tripods. As he edged more to his right, a gardening tool stuck into the ground hampered his path. He pulled it from the dirt, and gently replaced it further to the right.

The disconnected three-some achieved a crescendo of sexual harmony: Utte, her husband,

and Marzee. Utte and her husband approached simultaneous orgasm; Marzee masturbated furiously. Utte spun even faster. The vertical churning varied in stroke distance and intensity, as if the device could sense the couple's orgasmic waves. All three orgasmed simultaneously in a final burst of release.

Marzee's confidence, his sense of abandon, reversed instantly. Panicked, he felt ensnared and cornered, though his situation had not changed from fifteen minutes ago. The couple inside remained impervious to his presence. He was overcome with a desire to escape. He stuffed his penis inside his underwear, zipped his pants, and buckled his belt loosely. Maintaining caution while backing away carefully, he turned around and walked quickly toward the gate he had left ajar. He threw the rock aside he had used to prop open the gate. It made a thud impacting the ground. Then he closed the gate behind him, making sure the latch engaged. He ran toward his curbside moped, and rode home.

Chapter 10
The Rapist

A carnival of visions possessed him, as two image-filled days had passed since his evening outside Utte's window. Sitting in the waiting room of the student counseling center—his second visit with his psychotherapist, Dr. Dance—Marzee contemplated his lush memories, fresh and powerful, seething in his fantasies. Encroaching upon every thought and feeling, he mused that perhaps the heat of hell would give him more peace of mind. But then again, even the heat would remind him of Utte.

Pre-occupied with his thoughts, he panicked, remembering he had promised Joanna, the counseling center's receptionist, that he would complete all the forms by the time he had returned for his next appointment. He feared her reprisal should he arrive empty-handed. Dashing through ten questionnaires of varying lengths—questions about family history, whether or not he felt like crying more frequently recently, how nervous he became whenever he travelled away from home, were there any events in his past that caused him to have recurrent dreams—to these inquiries he pondered only briefly. The question: "Sometimes I get a thought in my head over which I have no control"—he answered "false." It was truly the only relevant question to his inner workings, and he felt of tinge of guilt responding falsely.

He glared at the *People* magazine on the table; he despised *People*. Filled with pictures and articles of people not like him, it aimed at entertaining people not like him as well. He pondered resentfully, *What kind of fucking life does a person have, finding any entertainment or amusement from reading about some fucking soccer mom's trials and tribulations with her retarded twins?* Although viewing it with disdain, he browsed the pages, occasionally garnering some guilty delight whenever he read about some celebrity committing suicide, or entering a drug rehab program, or being arrested, especially for a sex offense. *Most of these assholes are white, stupid, uneducated, trailer park trash, and somehow they picked up a big social lottery ticket*, he reflected, shaking his head. *It's not who you know, it's who you blow. For that kind of fame and fortune, there's too many people willing to blow anybody for anything.*

He hated the notion of luck or fortune or karma—especially karma. Feeling particularly angry about having to sit in a waiting room for therapy, he glowered about his own fortune. *How in the fuck am I responsible for the actions of someone one thousand years ago, having to pay for his bullshit by sharing his soul? It smacks free will in the face. Whatever I do in this life has no bearing on somebody's soul one thousand years from now. It's all bullshit. It's just another philosophy so people in power can fuck you over. Whether it's*

Pearly Gates, sixty-seven virgins, or karma, you're going to get fucked. He propped his hand on his raised, crossed knee, fully extended the magazine, and hid behind it.

After ten minutes Dr. Dance emerged from one of the therapy rooms with a frail, elderly, light-skinned black woman in her mid-seventies. He clasped her comfortingly around her shoulders as she departed, crying. Although weeping, she seemed happy—relieved.

"Shit. Happy…and crying," Marzee muttered, offering a cryptic head shake.

The woman seated at the opposite end of the row overheard his remark, and smirked. He recognized her from the last time he was in the counseling center. Eccentrically dressed, her trench coat did not match the wide hijab-style scarf concealing her lower face and the Elton John sunglasses covering the remainder. *Truly a nut-case*, he thought.

As Dr. Dance accompanied the weeping woman to the door, Joanna was quick with a box of facial tissues. "First line of psychotherapeutic aid," she commented, winking as she passed. Doting over her at the door, they both hugged her before she shuffled away. Joanna returned to her clerical duties behind the counter, maintaining what Marzee discerned as a smile of enlightenment, as if some kernel of great truth had been gleaned from the encounter with the old lady. Dance seemed less impressed, nonchalantly motioning to Marzee that he should follow him.

Marzee followed him into the therapy room, impressed Dance had so seamlessly detected his presence. "I didn't think you noticed me when you came out with the old lady. So I just figured you'd probably go up to the counter, and ask if I was there yet or not," Marzee commented.

"Your power of obscuration is not as effective as you think," Dance replied, grinning broadly to counter-balance any offense Marzee might infer. "I saw you when I first emerged from the door. What was it about your withdrawn posture and your head behind a magazine leading you to believe you were invisible?"

Returning a blank gaze, he had never thought about how he appeared to others. Whenever he skulked around the campus, he had sometimes fantasized that he was a camouflaged sniper, or a one-way mirror, or simply invisible. He assimilated the information around him via his peripheral vision—a skill about which he was very proud. "I don't know. We didn't make eye contact, I guess, so I figured you didn't see me," Marzee responded sheepishly.

Dance levied a refrained smile, as if concealing thoughts he seemed unwilling to share. "How have you been doing?" Dance asked.

The question irritated Marzee, as it circumvented his reason for being there. *What the fuck does "how have you been doing mean?"* It means *"have I been doing any peeping."* It doesn't mean, *do I have a cold, or have I been diagnosed with brain cancer since here last.* "Been doing OK," Marzee answered, fidgeting and crossing his legs. Consternation segued Dance's previously beguiled expression.

"Done any peeping since we last talked?" Dance inquired more sternly.

The unexpected candor jolted him to defensiveness. "You get right down to the point, don't you?" Marzee snapped. "You a therapist, or a probation officer?" Unperturbed by Marzee's comment, Dance's face relaxed as he grinned knowingly.

"I don't know if your comment was insight, perception, or just an accident. I used to be a probation officer many moons ago. Maybe that accounts for my abrupt style. You aren't the first to complain. I worked with people on alcohol and drug offense convictions. Sometimes I'd get a peeper or a flasher." Moving up in his chair, peering at Marzee, he continued. "But please don't think that I'm treating you like a criminal, or that you are coming in to see me just to stay out of jail. I hope that's not the reason you think you're here. I made that point clear the last time we met. What you say here, stays here. You understand that, don't you, Marzee?"

The words peeper and flasher flustered him. He disliked being labeled. And he certainly did not want to be distinguished as a pervert. "If you say

194

so," Marzee replied skeptically. "I've never been in therapy," making quotation marks in the air when he said therapy. "Being in therapy means that I'm crazy. Maybe I do some crazy things, but what is crazy? You can't control yourself? Your thoughts? Your feelings? What you do? I guess that's me."

"Sounds like you've given yourself some thought. Let's talk more about 'can't control oneself,'" Dance responded, readjusting his position. "When you say, 'can't control yourself,' give me a recent example."

Suddenly, the urge to tell Dance all overwhelmed him unexpectedly, resolved by a gush of conviction toward self-improvement through truthfulness. "OK. You remember I told you, when I peep, I don't get a hard-on. At least, not at first, when the urge hits me. Just the opposite happens. It shrivels up. But what happened the other night?" He paused, taking aim at the memories still cascading through his libido. "I looked through someone's window. What I saw, it made me so hard, no questions asked!" he exclaimed as if in a state of disbelief.

"What was different about what you saw the other night?" Dance asked matter-of-factly.

"This is sort of hard to explain," he responded, laughing nervously. "The whole thing is just too weird, but here goes." He paused, looking down at his shoes, rotating his feet. "OK. I was looking through the window of my philosophy instructor's window the other night. It's like, since

195

the first time I laid eyes on her, I couldn't stop thinking about her. She's on my mind day and night. Everything about her is pure sex. Her hair, her face, her eyes, her body, the way she moves and talks. Everything. I had to see her naked. And there was only one way I was going to see her naked, and that was to find out where she lived, and then go there, and look at her through her window. So, that's what I did."

"That must have taken a lot of planning and preparation," Dance remarked, edging further forward in his chair. He looked at Marzee with a broad and inquisitive face.

Delighted in Dance's recognition of his achievement, he took glee in expressing his accomplishment. "Fuck'n A, it took a lot of planning!" Marzee pronounced exuberantly. "But that wasn't the first time I was there," he added sheepishly, now aiming to release his Utte floodgate. "Last week I went there for the first time, the day it was so warm."

Anxious to recount his laborious quest, he was delighted that someone was there to listen to the details. "I found out where she lived though an Internet search. I used one of those search websites to find out where Utte lives," Marzee proclaimed with excited self-satisfaction.

Dance displayed muffled surprise. "Utte? Sounds German," he responded.

"Yeah, she is German," Marzee answered with enthusiasm. "And she's married so some chuck—he's American." He noticed an inquisitive—almost befuddled— expression overcoming Dance. "Chuck—means a white guy. It's a name me and my buds made up to exemplify the stereotypic white male," he explained nervously, realizing Dance was, more or less, a stereotypic white male.

"OK. Let's get back to Utte. You found her address through an Internet search. Please, continue," Dance urged.

Marzee rejoiced in recounting his adventure, like talking to an old friend, and forgetting he was in therapy. "I got the results by email the next day. I couldn't wait to find out where she lived. To go there—to look at her house," he said gleefully.

"What conversations had you had with her, other than in the classroom?" Dance asked.

Fantasizing about Utte vitalized him. The reality of talking with her in person made him uneasy. "I only really talked to her one time, after class, and she was in a hurry. She was friendly, but like, German. She's direct, says what's on her mind, doesn't hold any punches. She told me she's a fitness instructor at some gym. From the way she looks, I believe it." Dance seemed almost impatient for him to continue.

"After you got her address, you went to her residence twice, but on different days?" Dance inquired.

"Right. The first time was that hot day last week. I had to go there. It was all I could think

197

about. I spent most of the day planning how I was going to get there, mapping out the route. I used Google Earth. Got right down to ground level. Looked around the front of her house without even going there. I knew what everything looked like before I set foot in the neighborhood."

He paused, looking for a stopping point. He waited for Dance to comment, but his expression conveyed 'proceed.' From nowhere, a mental block hindered him from continuing, a resistance tugging at him. The friendly aura of the psychotherapy session switched to a legal deposition. "What I saw that day! Goddamn!" Marzee blurted.

Aware of an overwhelming self-consciousness—even paranoia—he had allowed himself to fall prey to a whirlwind of candor. A percolating dread pervaded his awareness. Did he feed Dance's voyeuristic curiosity? For Richard and Freddie, fabricating yarns satisfied them, and they provided him an audience. The template meshed well. But Dance was not an audience, and in this role, Marzee was not an entertainer. What he was telling Dance was neither fantasy nor fabrication. These tales were real. His life's lure since puberty came to focus. "I'm not here to entertain you," Marzee snapped. "I'm not a pervert, but that's what they'll call me. I'll get thrown into jail, some cell block with other perverts." Noticing Dance's eyes widen uncharacteristically, he realized he must have struck a nerve.

"You know that, and I know that. I won't bullshit you, Marzee. If you keep doing what you're doing, you're going to jail, guaranteed. You will eventually get caught, tried, convicted, incarcerated. Your friends, your family, everyone you know will know. But you don't want to stop. And you're not going to stop. If you wanted to stop, you'd stop. You're proud you were able to find your instructor's address and phone number. As long as you're proud of your actions, as long as you think you're special, and above it all, you'll never stop. So air it out. Tell me what you do. Let someone else know what Marzee thinks and feels on the inside— on the side that no one else sees—on the secret side," Dance proclaimed, reacting to Marzee's confrontation. "Hearing yourself describe what you do will turn the fantasy into reality."

Marzee gazed at Dance, and then looked away. He felt caught and embarrassed. *You can't out-bullshit the bullshitter,* an adage he had known since childhood. "You're right. I won't bullshit you. I planned everything, like I said. I could hardly wait. My heart, it was beating so fast. I felt like a burglar, executing a long-planned heist. I took two maps—street and satellite. I knew exactly where I was going," he explained. And although he had made the decision to open up, he felt the interplay between him and Dance was a game, a dance of give and take. He just gave. Now he watched Dance receive, process, and give back.

"So you executed getting to Utte's neighborhood. Then what?" Dance asked.

Opening up was exhilarating; a rush of elation tingled him. "Utte lives in a beach neighborhood. I knew I didn't belong there. All the planning helped. I was careful, cautious, and surveyed everything around me as I walked. I scanned for probing eyes and heads popping out windows. I tried to not attract suspicion. I tread a fine line between caution and relaxation. I was aware of attracting attention just by being too cautious. I moved in closer and closer until I got to her backyard fence. Then I looked through the knotholes of the fence, one by one." Marzee paused, taking a dramatic deep breath. "You asked me about whether or not I got erections when I did this stuff—peep. I got one this time, fast. The first time ever." He turned inwardly, his gaze directed into space, seeking a comparison, a similar experience, a description for what had happened. Turning to Dance with a look of cathartic discovery, he continued. "Watching niggas fuck donyas just always seemed nasty." He caught himself unintentionally saying 'nigger,' and he refocused to observe Dance's reaction. There was none. "They hoop, holler, yell. It turned me off. But the shit I saw through that fence that day! That was ecstasy."

"Donyas?" Dance asked, raising an eyebrow.

Marzee's foray into candor had facilitated his native slang and dialect, a characteristic he

200

normally controlled when talking with white people. "Ahh, sorry. Same thing I told you about chuck, only a term we coined for black females. Sort of an archetype of the black woman," Marzee replied. Dance seemed to grin in a millisecond, then went back to detached interest.

"Marzee, your racial taxonomy fascinates me. I'd like to hear more about it, but it would lead us astray," Dance remarked. "So, please proceed, you saw something through the fence that sexually excited you. And you had never been sexually aroused watching your African-American neighbors having sex?" Dance asked, attempting to summarize Marzee's remarks.

"Paraphrased nicely," Marzee responded with a cryptic smirk, maintaining flawless, white dialect. "That's correct. The famous apartment buildings across the street—the reason I'm here— were really my first experience watching annes. Excuse me—white girls—in various states of undress. When I first saw how they just lie around the pool in those little bikinis, I don't know. Before that, I just fantasized. Black women don't do that. Folks in my neighborhood don't even have pools. Shit, most of 'em can't swim." He saw in Dance an inquisitive stance that approached fascination.

"I don't quite understand—fantasized? About what specifically did you fantasize? About seeing nude white women? Or women in general? People having sex? What specifically is the fantasy?" Dance asked.

201

The risk of losing something precious to him caused him to falter. *Will I lose you if I tell him?* "I'm on a beach. It's a hot, sunny, sky-blue day, with just a little wind. But I'm not me. Well, I'm me, but I'm a sand fly. I have reign over the entire beach, and I can see far distances. I spot women lying on the beach. Sometimes it's a little windy, but I still manage to get close to a nude sunbather who's stretched out on the beach. She's covered in suntan oil from head to toe, making her skin glisten in the bright sunlight. If I light on her skin, and get stuck in the sticky suntan oil, she'll swat me. I find some dried kelp, or some driftwood close by for cover. Then I just concentrate, focusing on different parts of her skin, different parts of her body. She has some muscle tone, a build, not just some skinny bitch. She's sweaty from soaking up the hot sunlight. She lies on her towel with her eyes closed. As I'm flitting around—remember, I'm a tiny sand fly—her body takes on the features of a landscape: mountains and curves and contours and textures. It's like being in a trance. Then, like I said, I just focus on things: a bead of sweat rolling down her breast, a grain of sand in her pubic hair. I watch how the grain of sand moves back and forth with the breeze. If it's not too windy, I'll hover over her for a different perspective. In my mind's eye, I've gotten close enough to study her skin pores. I get into the contour of a flat abdomen, with the hip bones protruding to the side. I studied how the peach fuzz hair connects to the pores, around the navel, and down toward the pubic bone, or how the hair may be smeared by the suntan oil. But I never light. I might get stuck, swatted." As he studied Dance's expression, he sensed Dance struggling, resisting the captivation of the fantasy himself. Or perhaps that's what he wanted to see in Dance. Or perhaps that's what Dance wanted him to think. Whether it was coming from him or Dance, Dance seemed drawn in, and was making a fleeting attempt to retreat.

"When you were looking through Utte's fence, were you the sand fly?" Dance inquired with subdued voice.

Marzee squirmed in his chair at the pronounced erection he had evolved during his description of the sand fly fantasy. He crossed his legs to conceal the protrusion. "Interesting question. I don't think so. It was too real, but I did see a red-haired woman lying on a towel in the backyard. It wasn't Utte. Then a man joined her. I assumed the man was Utte's husband. Later he called Utte from the backyard. His conversation, and what he told the redhead cinched it. Then he told her, the redhead, to get out of her bikini, which she did, fast. He applied suntan oil to every inch of her body for about ten minutes. Then they fucked. I jerked off while I watched them. After I shot my load all over the fence, a strange thing happened. The energy, the motivation to stay there, vanished. Poof. It was gone. I switched back to being Marzee. The demon left me standing there. It deserted me." Marzee explained, recounting each detail as if living it again. As he glanced up at Dance, he saw him settle back into his chair, possibly recovered from the sand fly fantasy.

"And your second time there, two nights ago?" Dance asked. "You went there in the dark, so you took more risk, getting closer to the house, looking through the window?"

An image of a harnessed Utte, hanging—arched and stimulated—over a huge, caricatured penis materialized in his mind's eye. A bust of energy swept through his libido, priming him. "Two nights ago. What I saw was, like, I can't really describe. Pure sex. It was the weirdest thing I ever saw." Marzee answered enthusiastically. "I returned at night, hoping to see Utte getting undressed, maybe, for a shower? While I was on campus, I checked her class schedule, then I went over there, thinking that she'd head straight for home once she was finished teaching. And I was right. Close to the end of her class time, I raced there on my moped." he declared, chuckling. Dance laughed with him, but prompted him to proceed.

"Anyway, I got there just a few minutes before she got home. I figured out how to open their backyard gate. Damn, I was scared. I thought there might be a dog, or a nosy neighbor, or worse, she or her husband might come into the backyard. But none of it happened. Their whole bedroom was a stage for fucking," he commented, pausing, a sly grin forming. "It was a fucking set up! Their bed, their pictures, a mirror over the bed, and they've got naked photos of her everywhere. I guess he's a photographer. But, Dr. Dance!" He hesitated, incredulously shaking his head. "I saw this thing, a machine. It's a contraption mounted over their bed. It's more like a futuristic folding chair suspended from the ceiling, connected through tubes. A box on the ceiling seemed to control what the thing did by remote control. They were in their bathroom, showering. When they came out, naked, she got into this chair thing. The dude lay down on the bed, face up, with a very hard dick, and she sat above him, hanging above his dick, in this chair thing. Her legs were held up with some straps and harnesses. Then she touched some buttons on a remote control, and it lowered her onto him, like a crane. So then the chair started to rotate slowly, as if she was a ballerina." He stopped and laughed nervously as his fingers unconsciously edged toward his crotch, then pulled away. "Then she pressed another button, and the chair started going up and down, like a wooden horse on a carousel. But it seemed to *know* not to go too high or too low. They didn't have to stop for re-adjustments, if you know what I mean." Marzee paused and stared, thinking Dance had a question or comment. Dance returned the stare with expecting anticipation.

"My first three-way. Damn! Me, jerking off furiously outside, and them, inside. We all came at once." Seeming bewildered, he wavered. "But then the same empty feeling came over me, like the demon left me, and I was there all alone, scared. 'What the fuck am I doing here,' I asked myself. 'I should be at home studying, or helping my father with his Jumble puzzle, or anything but this shit.' I got the hell out of there as quickly as possible."

Dance's expression turned taciturn. "Since you departed in a hurry, did you leave any indication of your presence? Did you ever get the feeling they were aware you were there? Anyone chase you, or call after you?" Dance asked.

As he recounted Utte's bedroom window, the desire heated him. He wanted to return, but he dare not make his lust apparent to Dance. *The therapy makes me want to do the shit I'm here to get rid of. How's that work—like a vaccine? A flu shot makes you feel like you've got the flu.* "Funny you should ask. She was sitting in that sex machine, and while she was pivoting on his dick, when she turned in my direction, I sort of got the feeling she knew I was there. I panicked, but then said 'bullshit, no way she can see me.' So I regrouped and kept my cool." Dance turned aloof, his posture stiffened.

"We're approaching the end of our time together. But I wanted to summarize some of my thoughts with you," Dance said. "I'm not a big fan of diagnosis, giving what's troubling you a name, so to speak. You, Marzee, present an interesting mix of problems, some contradicting conventional wisdom," Dance replied, leaning forward as he spoke.

"So I'm really messed up? It that what you're saying?" Marzee remarked with a smirk. Dance's expression was a bulwark.

"We've got a couple things going here. On one hand, you display all the symptoms of voyeurism, which is under the classification of paraphilia in DSM-IV. It's the bible of psychological diagnostic classification. Paraphilias include voyeurism, fetishism, exhibitionism, sadism, pedophilia."

His heart jumped and his mouth went dry. He had never touched a child, and had absolutely no interest, real or fantasy. "Pedophilia!? Is that like a child molester?!" Marzee exclaimed.

"THAT's probably the most severe of the category, but hear me out," Dance replied, slightly impatient. "You also present with classic symptoms of obsessive compulsive disorder. Your behavior appears sexual in nature, BUT it occurred, at least until recently, without a sexual arousal component. You had recurrent, intrusive thoughts, fantasies, ideas. You tried to refrain from these impulses with other thoughts. You experienced symptoms of anxiety with the images: nervous stomach, palpitating heart, sweaty armpits—pure physiological anxiety, not sexual arousal. Your behaviors were repetitive, planned, organized, and aimed at relieving or eliminating the underlying images and fantasies," Dance recited, catching his breath. "What do you think of that summary?"

As he reflected on Dance's comment, he didn't hear anything he had not already researched. Whether to be a neurotic or a pervert was still undecided, but being both was unacceptable. "Seems about right. Keep in mind, the girls— women—I looked at in my neighborhood, I'd seen so many times, they just didn't arouse me. I WAS anxious. Damn right. I was scared of being caught. Boners and ass-kickings are on opposite ends of the sexual spectrum. But looking at annes, white girls. Wow, that's something entirely different. Maybe the change of scenery made things worse, huh, doc?" As he checked Dance for a change of temperament, he sensed a steadfastness instead.

"Fear," Dance pronounced with emphasis, "is what gives you a rush. It reinforces itself. It's as if you were a drug addict, and your drug of choice was adrenaline. Here's a proposal, and I'd like you to think about it: if you control the thoughts leading to the anxiety, then you control the behavior that results from the anxiety."

The concept of addiction appealed to him. He had never thought of himself as addicted to what he did. Addiction excused him. "So, you're saying I'm addicted to the possibility of getting caught— getting an ass-whip'n, being arrested, or worse, getting killed?" Marzee asked with reserved astonishment.

"Well, that's message number one," Dance replied as if preparing Marzee for more. Here's part two, equally important. If I recall correctly, you said you'd be 'minding your own business' when these urges, these impulses, would come out of nowhere, 'like a demon took control of you.'" Dance paused, squaring his posture directly across from Marzee. "Have you ever had a problem, one you spent hours trying to solve, but never could come up with a solution?" he inquired, not wanting a reply. "So you leave it alone. Forget about it. Then one day, bang! There's the solution. Where'd it come from? You weren't thinking about the problem when the solution popped into your head. So what part of your mind was thinking about it? Most of what the brain processes gets filtered out, else our thoughts and feelings would be one chaotic morass. It's the very top layer to which your consciousness is currently privy. The rest of your brain is busy doing other things. But the part of your mind out of your awareness continues to process memories, sensory input, problems. And it generates thoughts that percolate up to your awareness. THAT's the source of your urges. They come from YOU, not from some demon. What we have to figure out is, what thoughts are going on out of your awareness when these voyeuristic obsessions seize you."

Marzee was spellbound by Dance's animated elucidation. What Dance had described made perfect sense to him. Dance had delineated the concept in such an alluring and convincing manner—one matching his own sense of logic—he believed Dance was absolutely correct. He himself did not believe in demons, spirits, soul, the intangible nature of being, or God, for that matter. "If what you say is true, and frankly, I believe you hit the nail on the head, then how will I know what I'm thinking since those specific thoughts are out of my awareness?" Marzee inquired. Dance remained stoic at Marzee's insightful question.

"Briefly, we get there by taking careful inventory of what we are aware of at that instant. Then we slowly dig down further as more is revealed," Dance replied. "But, unfortunately, our time is up for now." His eyes gestured to the clock on the wall behind Marzee. Marzee turned around, confirming they had gone five minutes over their usual session time of fifty minutes.

At the reception counter Marzee scheduled his next appointment with Joanna. He left through the double doors. Uplifted, he was relieved that the problem vexing him for so many years may be solvable, finally freeing him of a bondage to which he had almost become numb. He sauntered to an adjoining grassy area, and sat on a bench under a shade tree. A young woman with tanned, bare, shapely legs, wearing a short skirt and a tank top passed him, smiling.

The sand fly lives. The sand fly is here to stay. The sand fly lives with you. The sand fly is you. You are the sand fly.

Chapter 11
W.M.D.

"Say, you! Yeah, you, you little chickenshit! You said those pills would make my dick hard. They didn't do shit. It's still limp as hell. I want my mothafuck'n money back, rat now," Jeffery, a local wino screamed at Marzee, who was walking from the neighborhood grocery store where he had shopped for his mother.

Aware Jeffery despised being called Jeff, Marzee's response was swift. "Fuck you, Jeff," he yelled back, though not with Jeffery's force. "They would've made your dick hard if you didn't drink so much Thunderbird. Motherfucker! I told you that. What'chu want? A fuck'n signed contract? Besides, why the fuck do you need a hard dick? Who's gonna fuck your drunk, wino ass anyway?"

"Yo' mama, that's who!" Jeffery retorted with a grunt. Kneeling, his back propped against an alley brick wall, he stood up, hobbling toward Marzee who had stopped for the verbal exchange. "I'm gonna kick your fuck'n yella ass if you don't gimme my money back!"

Two weeks prior, Marzee had sold five of his prescription pills—recommended by Dr. Dance and prescribed by Dance's psychiatrist colleague—to Jeffery for two dollars each, with the promise that each pill was good for a five-hour hard-on. He sold twenty to Freddie and Richard as well—who

211

enthusiastically split the purchase between themselves—guaranteeing each improved memory: they'd do better on exams, read faster, and retain more. Since the filled prescription bottle had contained thirty pills from the pharmacy close to campus, only five remained. He had stuffed the bottle with cotton to keep the pills from rattling around and crumbling. The cotton also served to subdue the clattering sound as he walked, attracting the attention of his parents who were unaware of the medicine bottle and its contents. He brought them with him, expecting a Jeffery encounter along the route.

"Say, man, you don't want to kick my ass. 'Specially since I know Miss Good Skull's outta jail. I heard she was look'n for ya. She's short on cash. She wants to suck your dick. You need your dick hard for her, don't ya? She don't want no wormy noodle dick. I know where she's at."

"I ran outta pills, motherfucker. All they did was put me to sleep!" Jeffery complained.

Marzee disliked Thunderbird wine. He considered it a crass beverage, even for a wino. He had urged Jeffery to change brands on numerous occasions. "I told ya! That's 'cause you can't drink Thunderbird. It has some anti-dick-hard shit in it. You gotta switch wine—MD20/20! Try that, then take the pills. Do that. You're good to go," Marzee said, reassuring Jeffery.

"I told you, I took'em all. You got more?" Jeffery inquired with an edge of desperation.

Selling drugs to winos was not his forte, but he had decided not to take them himself; he needed the extra cash, and he hated to see them go to waste. When the bottle was empty, he would fill it with aspirin—to a wino, pills dispensed from any prescription bottle were legitimate. *Expectation is ninety percent of the cure.* "Goddamn. I wish you'd caught me sooner. I got five right here," Marzee replied, patting his side pocket. "But Sidney, yo homie, down the block, I promised them to him."

"Fuck that wino muthafucka!" Jeffery cried, spitting and jumping. "I'll pay twice what he's paying!"

"Twice? He's paying more than you paid last time 'cause I cut you a deal. He's paying three dollars a pill. You telling me you're gonna pay six dollars a pill?" Marzee asked skeptically.

"Got the money right here," Jeffery answered, gloating and digging in his pocket. "Some bitch lost her purse. Cards, driver's license, money. Bitch even had condoms in her fuck'n purse."

No wonder Sanders does so well. He told me I'm wasting my time in college. He never understood—it's not for the money "Six dollars a pill. Five pills. That's thirty dollars. Nigger, you ain't got no thirty dollars. Let's see it," Marzee challenged, unconvinced of Jeffery's windfall.

Jeffery produced a musty handful of wadded bills of sundry denominations—ones, fives, tens, and twenties. "I hit a horse at Sanders' too," he exclaimed proudly. "All this didn't come from that bitch's purse! I earned some of it!" He tried to count out thirty dollars, repeatedly confusing the numbers on the bills.

Goddamn drunk-ass ignorant fool. I have things to do. "Here, let me help," Marzee remarked impatiently, reaching for Jeffery's wad.

"Get the fuck back!" Jeffery rebuked. "I'll count out my own goddamn money. What the fuck. You think I can't count? Shit, I was run'n numbers and mak'n odds on horses before you were born." After five minutes and much grumbling, he pressed two tens and two fives into Marzee's hand. He emptied the contents of the bottle in Jeffery's hand.

"I'll have some more pills next week. Better ones. They're white," Marzee yelled back at Jeffery as he separated himself hurriedly, aware his mother was awaiting her bag of sugar.

After fending off his mother's accusations of tarrying along the way, he went to his room to prepare himself for his English class. Though a core requirement, the course did not present a challenge to him. The instructor, recognizing Marzee's advanced aptitude and misplacement in a general English skills curriculum, had suggested Marzee need not attend class—just turn in the assignments. He lingered in his room, deliberating whether or not to go.

His obsession had already been primed. Like Dance said, the primal urge emanated from within. Its momentum percolated to the surface, its tentacles consuming his thought, emotions, behavior. Soon he would know its face. He contemplated it, like trying to recall a barely reachable memory. It spoke to him. *Seeing her alone, maybe undressing for a shower after she comes home. Not from here, but from her fitness job, all sweaty. Ohhh, if I could smell her essence then, plant my nose deep into her crotch, take a deep, long whiff. It's not going to happen. But, her panties, maybe.*

This singular fantasy etched itself into his imagery, carving a deeper presence as he sat. Utte's sweat-laden panties over his head— the site where her precious pubes had adorned, pressed over his mouth and nose—this notion now consumed him, a malignancy of instant proportions. The objective was clear—to enter her house and make the fantasy real.

Consumed by this new goal, his armpits were sticky, his heart raced, his stomach growled, and his appetite disappeared. Over-heated, heart at a gallop, he mulled over being alone inside her house. Considering all contingencies, he recognized planning, observation, timing, and patience were key to this undertaking. He fell into a trance, reflecting every detail, every consideration, before embarking on this latest quest.

Her prolonged absence from home was crucial to his objective. He didn't know, and he sighed in exasperation. Not wanting go back into campus for a schedule, he checked the campus

215

website. Disappointed—panicked—she did not have a scheduled class until tonight. He ran two blocks away, passed Jeffery who ineptly spat at him, and used the corner phone booth to call her house. He got the answering machine once more.

If she's not at home, and she's not at school, she may be at her second job as a trainer, he thought. He had to discover her whereabouts now, and hopefully confirm his hypothesis. He charged back to his bedroom.

Since he knew the name of the fitness club at which she moonlighted, he found the telephone number from an Internet phone book. He dialed it ravenously, his heart skipping as if he were calling a secret, unspoken crush for a first date.

"Good afternoon. Supreme Fitness and Workout. This is Susie. We're offering one month free trials and an extra two months with a one-year sign up this week only. Can I help you?" a nasal female voice answered, reciting the greeting.

Jesus. What the fuck happened to hello? "Uh, hi, my name is, uh, Chaz Smith. I'm, uh, I'm a student at Long Beach State, and I heard about a really good trainer there. She's German, and—"

"Oh, you must be talking about Utte," the cheery voice interrupted, rising two octaves.

"Yeah. That's it! A friend told me about her. Said she's really good. You know, friendly, easy going, but gets results," Marzee stammered, unprepared for his contrived story.

"Utte's here now, but she's working with a client. Hang on a sec," she announced abruptly, distracted by something in her background, and dropped the phone with a bang. He declared her a 'silly, no-social-skilled cunt' under his breath, and sighed in impatient exasperation. The woman returned to the phone. "Yes, like I said, Utte's here now, but I've only seen her with one client, a woman. Maybe you could talk with her about working with you. Are you a member? What was your name again?"

He hesitated, struggling to recall the name he used. "Chaz. Chaz Smith. Really, I just wanted to work with Utte. Like I said, she came highly recommended. She's there, right now? You see her now?"

"Yup. I didn't get your number, Chaz."

He hung up. Heart pattering, armpits sticky, stomach growling, he was suddenly besieged by a painful onset of diarrhea. He bounded down the stairs, where he once more dodged his mother's ambush of questions and concerns.

Given his class schedule—English class in an hour—his reason for leaving the house was established. He'd take his book bag for appearance's sake. Outside, he donned his helmet, started his moped, and paused, pondering in the backyard. He thought about Dance, the conversations with him—the pain they had discussed. The pain emerged now, but it was not imminent. *If I was taking the meds like I was supposed to, maybe the drive to make this journey would not be so strong. But it is, and I have to do it. I can't wait to get there.* He felt as if he were on a trajectory, fired from a cannon—his path determined by the laws of physics. Jolted by the familiar bump to the street, he exited the driveway from his parents' house.

He parked his moped, motor running, by the Ocean Avenue phone booth and made another cautionary phone call to Utte's house. After four rings, the answering machine picked up. *I've never called when someone answered the phone, so this proves nothing. He ain't home. No way she's home. She couldn've made it back so fast. She's still at the gym. Damn, I'd like to find a way to peek into THAT locker room. Then again, maybe not so pleasant. Bunch of fat chicks trying to slim down.*

Now on his third visit, he had systematized his approach to the house. The cool air and overcast reduced the local pedestrian density, lowering his vigilance. Nevertheless, he repeated his usual look-around precautions. Then he jumped up, straddled the fence gate to gain access to the latch, and stood inside the backyard, and listened for sounds from within. All was still.

The beat of his heart resonated in his chest. The potential of an unoccupied house assailed him, bringing his fantasy more to life, more to reality. *They can't suspect anybody was in their house. My entrance has to be undetectable and untraceable. No footprints. Don't drop anything. I have to go slow. Make sure I go out the same way I came in. If someone arrives unexpectedly, I have to make a dash for it. I have to hear them before it gets to that. I can tread upon that hallowed ground: where she showers, where she gets undressed, that bed, where they fuck, that sex machine, smell her.*

As he had expected, an unlocked patio sliding glass door awaited him. Taking stock of the patio, he marveled at the Jacuzzi on one side and a BBQ grill and counter on the other side. The drone of an overhead airplane irritated him, as it interfered with his vigilance for signs of life within the house. *Maybe the dude's inside, asleep, or maybe he decided to fuck the redhead indoors for a change.* He chuckled silently. *Give the skank a promotion,* he mused. He tip-toed to the door, and peeked inside, placing his face to the glass. He was prepared to bolt if he heard or saw anybody.

The fantasy was stronger than any rumination about his inner-shame, and he shrugged off whatever veil of misgiving haunting him. The stillness prompted him to continue. With two fingers he applied an uncommitted shove to the door handle. The disengaged latch gave way; the air from within caressed his face. The house beckoned him inside.

He pressed his elbow against the sliding door's edge, and slid opened a three-foot gap. Like an Apollo 11 astronaut, he placed one foot inside, then the other. His vigil intensified, though the stillness disarmed his tension. The sound of a car passing in front of the house momentarily alarmed him, but it continued along the street, and out of his concern. The uncertainty between his intense anxiety and the house's solitude disquieted him. Fantasy visions he had conjured while daydreaming percolated to the forefront, helping to clear his mind of recalcitrance from his target. Utte's essence awaited him.

Though he had never hunted, he had assumed a seasoned hunter's stance. Moving further from the door, he side-stepped toward the opposite wall. He continued along the wall until he reached an opening with an adjoining wall. Recalling suspense movies in which the character evaded gunfire from another room, he pressed his back to the wall likewise, and slowly poked his head around the corner. An uncanny silence pervaded his space, and only his beating heart set the rhythm to his stealthy procession.

Still hunched, ready for flight, he had gained enough conviction in the house's emptiness to straighten his stance. He rounded the corner of the wall, and stared down a short hallway into the bedroom he recognized from this opposite perspective. The window blinds remained in the same position as when he had hovered in stealth outside at night, and only a few planes of light sliced through the otherwise unlit room. Almost there, his fantasy was materializing.

Not side-stepping or crouching anymore, he crept cautiously forward, continuing to favor proximity to the wall rather than centering himself in the hallway. He noticed his shoulders were still slightly hunched. The carpet beneath his shoes was thick and soft, and the floor did not creak. This tactile sensation, a dichotomy of solid softness, elicited another reminder of Utte, and a fantasy of what it might feel like to touch her body.

He had trespassed upon the threshold of the kingdom through which he had gazed through a magic keyhole, a slit accidently left opened by the purveyors of the vision. The picture remained intact, just as he had witnessed it from the other side of the window—the round bed, the mirrors, the photos of Utte covering the walls, the studio lamps on tripods, the alien-looking instrument—box, tubes, and harness attached to the ceiling. It hovered over the bed, still, quiet, awaiting its virtuoso diva to return and play its sexual rhapsody.

He was on the inside, a tacit member, a part of the family. No longer excluded from the hearth; not forced outside into the cool night air, compelled to assume a clandestine presence, separated by a membrane of glass. He was free to explore, feel, and experience implicitly what he had craved and endured when he had crouched below the window nights ago. Now he could touch her. He could smell her most intimate parts, caress where they had been, and embrace intimate accoutrements. He spotted the dresser drawer in an opposite corner. It had been hidden from his view during his night visit.

He floated, as he was so possessed, he could not feel pressure on his soles. He glided toward the center of the room, and approached the edge of the bed. He spun in place slowly, around and around, taking in the pictures of Utte on the walls. The montage of images pelted his senses—hundreds, some framed, some poster-style, color, and black and white, mounted from floor to ceiling. Thin lines of exposed underlying white wall created a surrealistic checkered pattern. These photos didn't vie for positions in art galleries or museum displays, nor were they family remembrances, neatly measured, positioned and hung at eye-level— characteristic household adornments of the enduring black middle class homes to which he was familiar. These images defined the room's ambiance—her face, her body, the topology of her curves, the photographer's perspectives—angles, colors, shadow, highlight, composition—the pictures reminded him of large picture books he had browsed in the photography section of bookstores. Nudes, as he had never experienced them, a manifestation of a female form as both artistic and erotic surrounded him. *And her husband did it without portraying one gaping snatch or inserted dick*, he marveled.

The chest of drawers in the corner, his prize, diverted his attention. He skirted the bed, approaching the piece of furniture like Barnacle Bill the Pirate skulking toward a long-sought treasure chest filled with gold doubloons. There were no

222

locks to pick, no secret code to decipher, no
combination of numbers to dial. He faced a single
column of five drawers which, to his certainty,
contained a treasure more precious and esoteric than
Bill's most fervent, rum-filled adventure could
conjure.

His heart hammered at his ribcage.
Reverent, yet impatient, he opened the top drawer—
belts, small purses, some jewelry carelessly strewn
about. Tempted to examine the contents of the
purses, he deemed it a distraction, and closed the
drawer. He deployed the second drawer: scarves,
handkerchiefs, fine, silky things. He closed it
hastily. Upon examining the third drawer, a pang
bolted through this stomach; his underarms tingled;
his mouth turned to sand. A jumbled assortment of
female undergarments dazzled him.

He pressed his palms against the mass of
fabric, as if magically absorbing a power through
the contact. He wiggled his fingers—hands
stretched and extended—using slight pressure in
slow circular fashion, so that the garments slid in
unison under the pressure. Excited by the rubbing
sound on the bottom of the wooden drawer, he
weaved and snaked his fingers into the pile, as a
soufflé chef might fold stiffly beaten egg whites.
With two fingers, he randomly extracted a pair of g-
string panties.

What is it about these particular panties?
They stuck to my fingers. He extracted them
tweezer-style, grasping them between his index and

middle fingers—plain, white—with candy-cane striped border and band—Victoria Secret-style, g-string panties. A small, pink, embroidered symbol of a terrier dog adorned the front upper right side.

Transferring the garment gingerly in both hands, he rubbed and caressed the fabric between his fingers and thumbs. Examining the panties closer, he scoured the material for every microscopic detail. He followed the line of the fabric from front to back, finally settling on the rear tag. *Small, 92% cotton, 8% Spandex. Not one blemish, not one stain.* His body quivered.

Impervious to his surroundings and situation, his focus was the miniature garment in his hands. *This string adorned her anus.* He rubbed the panty string under his nose, oscillating it gently back and forth—inhaling—as having just uncorked a fine bottle of wine. He shivered.

He spread the panties carefully on top of the chest of drawers. Then he disrobed ritualistically—shoes, socks, shirt, pants, underpants—he stacked his clothes beside him. Naked, he returned to the chest of drawers, facing it as if it were an altar. He turned the garment inside out, and placed it meticulously over his head, spreading the front side over his nose and mouth like a surgical mask. Taking deep breaths through his nose, he sounded asthmatic. He slid into ecstasy—closed eyes and tilted head—he slowed his breathing, and with his right hand he manipulated his flaccid penis into an erection. With his right hand he massaged and stimulated his nipples and abdomen. In less than a minute, ejaculate spattered the chest of drawers and dripped on the carpet.

Dumbfounded, he lingered. The demon had not abandoned him. Rather than fleeing the scene, he wanted more. Though vitalized by this novel reservoir of energy, the fleeting reality nudged him—he had crossed the line.

He freed his face of Utte's panties. Then inspecting his penis, he carefully cleaned off the remaining drops of semen using the savored garment. He dressed quickly and stuffed his contraband into his rear pants pocket. He rushed into the adjacent bathroom, pulled some toilet paper, wet it, and wiped dripping semen from the furniture. He folded over the wad of toilet paper, and dabbed at the semen drops on the floor, making sure no residue remained. He dashed back to the bathroom, flushed the toilet paper, returned the toilet seat as he had found it, and returned to the bedroom, scanned area for items dropped or misplaced, and closed the drawer.

He retrieved his precious souvenir from his pocket, chiding himself for not tending to it more meticulously. He thrust it to his face once more. *I smell Tide. I want the real deal. That would only be in a laundry basket with unwashed clothes. I've got to find the laundry room.*

***

Lead by intuition, he sensed the laundry room was at the other end of the hallway. He panicked for not being panicked, and he heightened his awareness for noises and sounds during his return foray down the hall. Too focused upon his entry journey, he had not noticed the hall wall adornments. Clusters of three to four small, framed, nude photographs, drawings, and paintings of Utte decorated the passage. Other than the photos, the nude figure drawings were renditions of her body as well. *Is he an artist? A photographer? Maybe both?* He squinted, looking closely at the signature in the corner of one of the drawings: Thorndike.

He shook his head vigorously as if trying to stay awake while driving. The hall wall exhibition distracted him. Carefully skulking sideways along the hall wall, he skirted along the half-opened vertical blinds hanging over the patio door. They clicked and rattled, startling him momentarily.

At the end of the hall, the marble-tiled front lobby was on his right, the double-door front entrance clearly visible. A single closed door faced him, and another to his left. The quiet of the house and neighborhood was underscored by the sound of his thumping heart. An urgency impinged upon him, as if he were running out of time. Frozen in panic, he stood in place.

"Reality check," he whispered, the sound of his voice helping him cope. He glanced at his watch. "I called the fitness club about an hour ago. It's at least twenty minutes away from here. The girl said Utte was there, busy with her client. Even if she left shortly after I called, I should have another fifteen minutes, if not more. The husband, I don't know where he is. I guess he's at work. It's almost three o'clock, so assuming he works until five, he won't be coming home soon. I still have time to look around." He took a deep breath, then stretched his torso, twisting left and right. "Relax, Marzee," he whispered with a sigh. Continuing to inhale and exhale deeply, he practiced the relaxation technique Dance had taught him in a previous therapy session—to practice it whenever he felt the urge to peek in someone's window. Though not achieving its desired effect of expelling him from his present course, the procedure did aid him to continue.

The door facing me must go to the garage. Some people have their washing machines and laundry stuff in the garage. He paused with a suspicion: *Maybe this house has a security system. As soon as I open the door, an alarm will trigger, and pigs will surround the house within two minutes.* He disposed of his fear, rationalizing he had just entered the house by opening a door, and nothing had happened—no alarms, no police, no helicopters overhead, no megaphones demanding that he exit the house with his hands up. Gripping the doorknob courageously and fool-heartedly, he opened the door.

He stood in the doorway of an empty single car garage—hardly enough room for laundry paraphernalia. His recollection of the front of the house clashed with his current view. When he had cruised the street, he remembered a much wider

227

front with a three car garage. An unfinished plasterboard wall divided the garage to his left. A narrow door with a bright, round, gold-colored doorknob invited him.

The treasure must be behind Door Number One, he mused.

Immediately concerned the garage door could open at any second, him standing with a deer-in-headlights expression in the center, he scurried to the side door and twisted an unyielding knob. He turned and jiggled, but the knob held steadfast. He noticed light dispersed from the space under the door. Frustrated, he shoved, and the latch gave way.

Mouth agape, he stood in the threshold, awed by his discovery. Instead of finding more garage space, a tool shed, a ping pong table, or his much-sought laundry room, he beheld a scene reminiscent of science fiction movies. A briar patch of stands, mirrors, lenses, tubes, pipes, and wires woven through a labyrinth of benches and tables confronted him—all compacted within the space of an extended two-car garage.

"I thought the dude was a photographer, but damn!" he muttered aloud.

Edging inside the barely-standing-room area, he had to side-step between the multi-leveled counter tops. Odd objects and jerry-rigged components filled corners and hung from the metal-tiled ceiling. He felt as if he had been miniaturized, and now roamed amongst the components inside a television. *I recognize some of this shit from AP*

Physics, from optics lab. These stands are for mirrors. Maybe he's a photographer after all, just doing some way-out shit. He wandered about the room, spellbound, inching meticulously through the maze of equipment. At the end of the central counter, a cable as thick as his arm entered a large microwave-oven-sized box. Multi-colored wires of varying thicknesses, supported from the ceiling, dispersed throughout the room. All appeared connected to a gray, metal, refrigerator-sized cabinet covered with dials, knobs, gauges, and switches in the corner opposite his entry door.

Five bundles of cables entered the corner cabinet from the bottom. The cables' origins emanated from an area bounded by a framed chicken wire fence, protruding four feet from the wall, and extending the wall's length from the big corner cabinet. Hundreds of silver canisters—each about eight inches long and two inches in diameter—were precisely stacked in columns and rows from floor to ceiling behind the wire fence. Creeping around the work benches to get a closer look, he noted each silver can had two end terminals, each interconnected by smaller wires to the others.

He stood amidst this quagmire of technology, pondering its purpose. *This is too much shit for a photographer. Some shit's goin on here. What the fuck are these things? Batteries? And that big ass cabinet? Looks like it handles high voltage from the size of the wires and switches. These crazy white folks must be making Frankenstein*, he mused. *Sparks and shit rising through the ceiling. Where's Igor?* He chuckled.

From the myriad of apparatus on the work benches, he discerned round, larger-than-eyeglass lenses mounted inside elongated vacuum-sealed boxes with glass see-through tops. A fluorescent-light-bulb-looking tube—ten feet long, wrapped with a spiraled smaller glass tube—dominated a single center countertop. Multiple stands and brackets holding mirrors and lenses of varying thicknesses and sizes appeared ultimately related to the central tube, though the convoluted configuration created a circular maze that spiraled around the room on multiple levels. Other flexible tubes and wires crisscrossed one another, creating a network of indistinguishable components.

A dozen pressurized gas cylinders, each six feet high, lined the wall opposite the stacked silver cans. He recalled his friend, George Douglas, whose father owned an auto body shop; the acetylene gas cylinders they used for welding were identical—they looked like scuba tanks, but four times longer. A regulator meter and valve controlled each tank on the wall; hoses extended from each to a different direction, each losing itself in the tangle of tubes, wires, and cables. Three dark-colored, welding-type goggles hung close by.

Captivated, his gaze bobbed from side to side. Panning up, he noticed optical stands and similar equipment on counters and racks, supported at varying levels cascading above him. Long, rectangular copper tubes extended back and forth below the ceiling. Like solving his father's Jumble Puzzles, he gleaned order from what he had observed. From the apparent chaos, a cyclical pattern emerged. All converged on a desk-sized, glass-domed container in an unexplored corner. He inched toward the apparatus for a closer look.

He concluded it definitely was not cutting-edge cookware or a casserole dish. It appeared to have been designed with sealed brackets, tubes, and electrodes—all penetrating evenly around its perimeter. A singular glass tube emerged at forty-five degrees through the dome. The tube connected with one of the optical stands supported above the tables. The dome itself rested on the surface of a small, sturdy metal frame, also supporting a Collie-sized electric pump. Stacks of smooth, quarter-sized, dull, metallic discs were piled on a counter dedicated to the dome device. A thick lead box with its cover askew held a few of the disks as well.

Utte's husband—an enigma to Marzee— appeared to be a scientist. *This dude's a physicist, or something. This sure ain't no darkroom. Maybe his hobby lab, but what kind of hobby uses shit like this? Sure as hell ain't electric trains. What the fuck?!*

At that instant his fear converged to a single noise—the garage door opened in the room he had abandoned moments ago. Panic-stricken, he froze in place. Fearing the slightest unplanned movement or jerk could hit something, making a racket, he stood immobilized looking for a place to hide. The space under the tables was jammed—every inch of space was occupied with apparatus and gear. He had to hide immediately, and he whipped his head around wildly, seeking any concealment. Suddenly, he spotted a door which had been obscured by the pump and novelty. He could see a door knob, suggesting the door was not completely obstructed. He would have to climb over the pump. This door offered his only escape route. If he could not go through it, he would lie flat on the floor and hope they did not come through.

While shuffling to the pump-obstructed door, he heard the garage door motor stop and a car rolling into the garage. Though his destination was merely yards away, the span seemed enormous. He reached the corner, and he turned the doorknob. A gust of air refreshed him when the door opened. In a purposeful wide arch to avoid hitting any apparatus, he carefully lifted one leg over the pump and into the door opening—then the other. He clutched both sides of the door frame, and hoisted himself through. Quickly and silently he closed the door behind him, hearing the latch click unobtrusively.

He found himself in the laundry room. Small, shallow cabinets lined the facing wall. Opening one, he squeezed himself in with a vacuum cleaner and broom. Crunched and fetal, he pulled the cabinet door shut with his fingertips, and sat compressed in the darkness. His deeply pumping heart broke the silence.

His thoughts whirled into an abyss of anguish and self-recrimination. *What the fuck am I doing? Why didn't I take the meds? I could be at home, studying; I could be at school, attending my English class. My mother, my father. I owe them more. I owe myself more. I want to be a scientist, a politician, a writer, somebody contributing to the world. What am I doing. Oh, God, what am I doing?*

The rumbling from the garage door closing muffled the sound of two car doors opening and closing in rapid succession. He could hear a woman's voice—she sounded like Utte. *No signs of my presence. Car doors closed. Fuck, I hope she doesn't decide to vacuum the house.* He strained to listen to the voices.

"We believed this neighborhood provided the perfect cover, and John wanted to live close to the beach. Buying this house was a necessity. We couldn't take the chance of renting. Renting leaves you open to a nosy landlord snooping around," Utte said.

"Mansour and I—in fact, the rest of the organization—thought the four hundred thousand was excessive for living quarters, but it seems to have worked out well. You see, we do trust your judgment explicitly," another accented female voice replied. Marzee noted the accent was not like Utte's.

"John and I bought it as a married couple, legitimately with a mortgage, living the American dream." He detected the same cynicism in her tone as when she lectures in class. "The value of the property has appreciated; we've doubled the down payment in the time we've owned the house. We couldn't have planned it better—living quarters, laboratory space, seclusion, and the project expenses are offset by property appreciation," Utte replied.

"What about the neighbors?" the other voice asked in her unidentifiable accent.

"John and I are civil. We say 'good morning,' 'how are you,' 'have a nice day'—that sort of gibberish. But we don't really stop to engage them in chit-chat. I think we make it clear we want to stay to ourselves. The neighbors are reasonable and intelligent, most college educated, some professionals, so they don't push getting into our lives. They've got lives of their own. That was another deciding factor about this neighborhood that made it a good choice. Too much seclusion, like in the middle of the woods, and you invite suspicion. Americans want to know what you've got to hide. Choosing a proletarian or blue-collar demographic would elicit uninvited curiosity as well. Here we have people who respect our privacy, mostly, with the exception of a fellow at the end of the block. He's assumed the role of neighborhood watchdog. I believe he Google'd John, based on a comment he made to me several months ago. Something about 'what's it like living with a big brain?'" Utte explained.

"What!" the other voice exclaimed. "We don't want that kind of curiosity." She sounded deeply distressed. The accent was soft, but still more guttural than Utte's German accent. He couldn't place it.

"Let him search; he discovered the truth. John is a respectable particle physics researcher at UCLA," Utte responded, sounding defensive. "I think this neighbor wants more interaction. He's lonely. He's an older man. I haven't seen a woman about, so maybe he's a widower. Always a big wave and smile whenever I drive by. I nod politely, nothing more. He may be a retiree looking for entertainment, maybe ex-military. He's the only one on the block who doesn't get the hint that we want to be left alone."

"Point his house out to me when we leave. What's his name?"

"Chuck something. I really don't know," Utte answered. "But, please, don't get Mansour involved. That's all we need, a gruesome murder on our block. Then the police WOULD knock on the door, asking questions."

"You've been very patient, waiting for me to arrive." Abruptly, the two women stopped talking. *What are they doing? The bitches kissing? Shit! I wish I could see what the fuck's going on.* After two minutes, the conversation resumed. "Driving here, my dear Utte, I was thinking about Mexico. Being that it was the only way for me to enter this country; we should look to moving more of our operation there since many of our comrades have the same problems with American security."

"It's not a bad idea, but don't be misled by the apparent lackadaisical lapse of vigilance. They make up for it in corruption, meaning everything is harder to come by, and what you get, you pay for. And you can't pay enough for silence," Utte replied with soft assertiveness. "Afsane. You've come so far. Don't you want to see what we've done?"

"With great enthusiasm. I've been eagerly waiting to see what you've done," the other female voice said. "It's unfortunate the others couldn't join us on this occasion."

"Through this door," Utte said. "I couldn't risk emailing encrypted pictures, but we've made such progress. We're essentially finished. We converted the garage into the particle accelerator, as you'll shortly see."

Accelerator? I thought it looked familiar. Sort of cyclical. They're doing some sort of homemade particle physics project in there. That big fuck'n tube. I'll bet it's a laser.

"Seems unsecured," the other voice said.

"Secure from what? There's nothing to guard against," Utte replied.

"Aren't people suspicious that you don't use this part of your garage?"

"Most of the houses on this block—in this neighborhood—use part of the garage as a work room. These men, they spend their weekends and free time dabbling in mediocre woodworking and shop projects they learned in secondary school. Instead of bettering themselves, or merely being with their wives and families, they occupy themselves with this nonsense. This American way!" Utte paused, her temperament reminiscent of her classroom style—caustic and direct. "Never mind. I don't want to get started. I'll be happy to complete our project and leave this country. What they will get, they deserve!"

"What they get, we deserve!" the other female voice countered.

The interchange seemed to have facilitated another silent reverie between the two women. Marzee heard nothing briefly until the sound of footsteps and the door to the lab opening signaled they had gone into the lab.

"The quarters are cramped, but it works, Afsane," Utte said. "Results are the best markers for success."

"Please, show me," Afsane replied.

"John's set up a very efficient particle beam accelerator using CO_2 lasers to induce inverse Compton scattering. He can achieve very precise, high-energy beam focus, the kind only X-ray lasers were able to accomplish, and still not with the efficiency he's developed," Utte said boastfully. "In this lab we do what medieval alchemists dreamed of doing: we turn lead into gold, of sorts. We do it in a garage, in the middle of middle-class America."

Both women laughed as he heard shuffling footsteps.

"It's the type of gold I would not want to wear as jewelry!" Afsane exclaimed in a muffled laughter.

"Yes, exactly!" Utte joined in with the ecstasy. "Our gold is more precious than gold. Transforming lead into a radioactive isotope simulating uranium is much more valuable than gold. The governments of the world are busy watching uranium. But who watches the movement of lead, a common metal whose atomic number is only ten less than the heaviest natural metal, uranium?"

"Though you've raised an interesting question, my dear. Who watches the movement of lead?" Afsane asked in a serious voice.

"Maybe the plumber's union," Utte replied in jest.

"So, you're able to create the proper lead isotope already?" Afsane asked, unfettered by the levity and still serious.

"John completed the last bombardment a few days ago. He took some of the disks to UCLA to test them with their mass spectrometer."

"What? He took them?" Afsane said alarmed. "What if he is questioned?"

"He is a principal researcher there. He is trusted. It's not even a question. You are too paranoid," Utte replied. "Testing is as important as the production. Using the university spectrometer is ideal for our goal. We could neither afford the price of one, nor the curiosity it would bring."

"One cannot be too careful," Afsane responded didactically. "What are those silver-looking cans, stacked over there against that wall?"

"Ah, those," Utte acknowledged with a flair of pride. "Those are power supply filters, from discarded television sets. Electrolytic capacitors from hundreds of junked televisions. We used them, as they offered the most untraceable method to develop the capacitance required for the CO_2 laser. We connected hundreds of them in series and parallel. Together they create one large capacitor bank. John and I spent many hours soldering and dressing wires. The power supply controller is that gray cabinet in the corner. The transformers are under the tables."

"John transporting the radioactive lead still concerns me. How does he carry it?" Afsane asked.

"In his briefcase, in a small, thick lead box," Utte answered apathetically. "He's testing the last batch of the series from last week's bombardment. After this series we can complete the bomb. We've procured an excellent assembly site as well, a factory warehouse at San Pedro Harbor. I'll take you there next. This building could not be more ideal for the assembly of a radioactive device," Utte said with added zeal. "And we've already procured most of the raw materials for the chemical explosive detonation. We've been extraordinarily resourceful in this area. Our inside contact has helped us in this department as well."

Marzee strained to hear sounds whenever a pause ensued between the two women. He imagined them simply running out of restraint—not able to withstand the attraction to one other—grabbing, kissing, feeling, licking, sucking, diddling, or whatever two women do to each other's body. The fantasy and the reality split him. *What the fuck are they talking about? Radioactive? Bomb? Explosives?*

"Then the next logistics concern will be the transportation of the pellets to your facility in San Pedro," Afsane asked, hesitating, as if out of breath. "I'm intrigued. You mentioned it with such enthusiasm. Won't you tell me about it beforehand?"

"It would spoil the surprise. Here's a hint: think about your early years as an electronics engineer," Utte replied.

"How do you protect against the radiation once the pellets are en masse? Do you have suits, badges, Geiger counters, lead shielding adequate for the radiation emitted by three hundred pellets? And how about your final assembly crew? You'll have to use robot arms unless your assembly crew is expendable," Afsane commented, laughing as if not serious.

"They are expendable," Utte responded abruptly. "We'll use migrant workers. We can pick up hordes of them at certain hangouts where they wait for work. Their task is very simple, so they won't require technical skills. We have designed the final bomb so that it can be assembled with basic manual labor."

"They'll die of radiation poisoning! Don't you think that will attract attention?!" Afsane exclaimed with exasperation.

"Tens of thousands will die of radiation poisoning once the bomb is detonated, soon after assembly is complete. The workers' symptoms will not appear before bomb detonation, anyway," Utte responded.

Their discourse flabbergasted him, distracting him from his self-reproach and contortionist's discomfort. He entertained alternate explanations for what he had heard. *Maybe they're rehearsing lines for a play, or some shit like that. What they're saying, it can't be real. Ain't this a bitch? I come here to find some dirty drawers, and these bitches are talking end-of-the-fucking-world bullshit. These white women really can't be terrorists. I've seen pictures of terrorists on the Internet—dudes wearing towels on their head, sheets blowing in the wind, knife held to some shitting-in-his-pants chuck's neck. I can't believe I just overheard a terrorist plot to detonate a radioactive bomb in Los Angeles. What do I do? I could jump out, bust through the door, saying, "Ok bitches! I caught you!" Then what? They might have guns. I don't know what that other bitch looks like, or what she can do. Besides, Utte could prob'ly*

kick my ass, anyway. And who's this Munster
motherfucker? I need to stay cool. Call the proper
authorities once they're gone, once I'm out of here.
Out of here? I'm not supposed to be here in the first
place. How do I explain what I was doing here?
How about an anonymous tip to the FBI, or
Homeland Security, or whatever? Damn. They'll
ask too many questions, and they have ways of
tracing numbers, and finding out who called. Then
they'll be chasing my ass instead of the terrorists.

He contemplated his position while sitting in
his dark, contorted quandary—confused, befuddled,
numb. The words through the wall dizzied him; the
situation seemed nonsensical. He pulled his ear
away, and rested his forehead on his knees. His
arms ached. He strained, pulling his ankles toward
his body, remaining compressed in the tiny laundry
room closet. A tear rolled down his cheek.

The drone of the voices had stopped. He put
his ear back to the wall. The lab door closed; car
doors opened and shut; the auto started; the garage
door opened, then closed. He was alone. He waited
in the closet another five minutes, and then he
leaned against the door of the closet, allowing the
light to beam in. Releasing his balance, the closet
doors gave, and he toppled to the floor. He
remained in a fetal position, unable to move his
feet, legs, and arms. Numb, he stretched them
slowly. He compared the excruciating tingling in his
limbs to when he sat on the toilet too long, reading,
then stood up. He laid on the floor, outstretched,

dazed. Glancing up from the floor, he saw the laundry basket resting atop the washer and dryer in front of him.

Two voices screamed within him, both fighting for dominance. He had heard what sounded like the end of life as he knew it, and he alone had been privy to this discussion. Fate had handed him a toxic gift. He could save millions. Yet a miniscule shred of soiled fabric beckoned him with equal, if not stronger, attraction. *Madness. I'm crazy. I can't resist her dirty drawers, and I heard her talking about exploding a nuclear bomb in LA. I'm fucking nuts. I can't. Maybe, this time. The last time.*

He scrambled up, ignoring pain once incapacitating. He looked inside the basket filled with her clothing. He counted half a dozen panties. He selected the most dainty, turned it inside out, and pressed it over his mouth and nose.

The sand fly engaged him immediately.

He lifted the basket to the floor. Placing the panties meticulously over his head, he masturbated into the basket, delivering his ejaculate with ten strokes. He wiped the residual semen from his penis with the panties from his head, then stuffed the panties into his pocket. Eager to take his leave, he replaced the basket to its original position on the washing machine and left the house the same way he had entered, making his way back to his moped, and home.

243

Chapter 12
Reckoning

Tormented by dreams, Marzee opened his eyes. He was not dreaming; yesterday had really happened. Sunshine, sand dunes, and the sand fly skittered on the perimeter of his thoughts; escape eluded him.

Yearning for relief, instead he found isolation and loneliness. His mother and father were out of bounds; telling Freddie or Richard was not an option. He had already realized the person with whom he must confide: Dance. As he anticipated confessing to Dance the circumstances surrounding what he had heard, a cold wind of shame blew through him.

He avoided eye contact with his mother and father that morning. Having so little to say, his mother believed he was "coming down with something." Added to his mother's insistence that he eat "a good breakfast," and maintaining patience to avoid the certain drama that would unfold, tried his emotional resilience. If all else failed, his home life must remain intact. He could always return home, his sanctuary for sanity and stability.

Dazed and unaware, he barely remembered how he got to school. He paused in the parking lot, sitting on his moped for several minutes while the engine ran. Cars, students, ambient noise and traffic—distant rushes in his head. The urgency to call Dance isolated his focus, averting distractions.

He needed consoling, to be told everything was going to be OK. His shame overpowered him. He had lied in his therapy sessions, completely abandoning the cornerstone of the process—honesty. He shivered from the guilt of deception, and now he had to fess up to Dance pending a horrific terrorist attack. He had stalked his philosophy instructor—peeping through her bedroom window at night, breaking into her house during the day. These words, these memories, these behaviors tumultuously resonated through his psyche: stalking, peeping, breaking in, being a criminal, being a pervert. They struck him down; they lifted him up. His conflict was unbearable; it removed him from his pain. He hated it; he relished it. It tore him asunder.

Information anointed his torment. Whenever he searched for information, he felt closer to a divinity—a purpose that would protect him from lies and ignorance. He prized spending hours in front of a computer screen. The infinity of data at his disposal absorbed him. Sorting through novel facts and figures drew him into a vortex, away from the malaise of his life. Stealthily researching Utte on the Internet, he had sifted through public databases and search utilities. He could recall nothing corroborating the nightmare he had overheard yesterday.

Jolted by yesterday's vivid memory, he cringed: contorted into tiny broom closet, hiding like a roach, eavesdropping on a conversation inside a stranger's home into which he had invaded, into which he had criminally encroached—he grimaced, recoiling from the vision of the person he did not want to be. He had been told he was bright, resourceful, and tenacious; people had accredited him with the combination of traits leading to a successful career in almost any subject or business. Now his future eluded him: a family of his own, a wife, some children, a dog, a house in the suburbs—no more ghetto, no more Freddie and Richard, no more coveting what his white, middle-class cohorts took for granted—the path to his dreams crumbling before he had taken a step.

   The library computers offered sanctuary. His incursion into Utte's broom closet had revealed yet-to-be utilized Internet search terms, and offered justification to procrastinate. He would put off calling Dance's office pending new discoveries, then call him on the public phones in the library foyer. *Why didn't I ever look up John Thorndike? Was it, like, I was trying evade the fact that she was married? Hell, I watched the dude fuck their neighbor in his backyard, then I didn't even Google him. He's a scientist at UCLA, so I should be able to come up with something. And that bitch she was talking to yesterday. Af—whatever the fuck her name was. Maybe it's all bullshit. For all I know, they could've been rehearsing for a play. Maybe I don't have to tell Dance a goddamn thing. Then again, maybe I should anyway, just to keep the therapy on the up-and-up.*

Finding a secluded spot in the research section should be easy since it's a quiet Friday morning, he thought. *No distractions, no bullshit, and for damned sure, no Freddie and Richard.* Grumbling under his breath, he resented the unabated openness of the pool of research computers on the first floor. *Fucking Big Brother! Watching. Watching. Watching. Goddamn surveillance cameras everywhere. Fucking George Orwell. How'd he know? And who's on the other side? I should know WHO is watching ME. And if they're recording, who's going to see it later? Freedom, my ass. Most of these people don't know they're being watched. I guess it makes sense though. All this expensive equipment has to be protected. But who the fuck is going to walk out the door with a computer under his arm? It's more than theft and vandalism. They watch for other reasons. I don't want some dickhead observing me. Suppose he's gay? Jacking off with me on his screen, squirting jizz all over his monitor.* With that thought, he cracked his first smile for the day. *Especially knowing what I heard yesterday, I don't want to be watched.* He chose a workstation facing away from the domed ceiling cameras.

"Where to start?" Marzee muttered to himself. He laid his rucksack at his feet, and typed in his user name and password. Starting with Google, he entered "John Thorndike," and "UCLA." Listing too many hits, he added "particle physics" to the list of search terms. Fifty-seven hits

247

appeared relevant—the first linked to an Acrobat file, a paper entitled "Nonlinear Inverse Compton Scattering as an Inexpensive Polarized Positron Source," on which John Thorndike was listed as the second author. After perusing the other links, he surmised a common theme: John Thorndike *at UCLA* was associated with particle physics research and what was termed "break-throughs in inexpensive and efficient generation of particle beams using CO_2 lasers." Another article summarized Thorndike's career. *Six years ago he was at the University of Munich. Bingo! That's where they met! That's the connection!*

A picture might be useful, he thought. He clicked Images icon from the Google menu bar, and photos of John Thorndike cascaded across the screen. He printed the highest resolution image, jogged to the printer at the end of his row to pick it up, and returned to his workstation, hastily stuffing the printout in his pocket.

He deleted his search history, he typed "Afsany" into the box. Several hits sprawled down the page, but the list was preceded by "Did you mean 'Afsane?'" Clicking on "Afsane," hundreds of links resulted. *Fucking A! The common denominator: Iranian. That's why I didn't recognize that weird accent. She's from Iran. Afsane.*

Squinting his eyes, furrowing his brow, he tried to remember the other name. *Monster? Nah, sounded like Munster, like Herman Munster. With a name like that, I'll bet he had his share of ass-*

kickings in school. He typed "Munster," getting exactly what he had expected: links to the classic TV comedy, as well as "Munster, Germany."

OK, not Munster. How about Munser? No. I'll try Munser and Afsane together. Maybe the names will converge. The search result heading urged him to try "Mansour." Complying, the search engine spewed hundreds of results. *Iranians.*

The government is scared of Iran. Got their asses in too deep in Iraq, talk'n about weapons of mass destruction and terrorists. Didn't find a goddamn thing. Now they're worried about Iran. I didn't understand why they just didn't go after Iran to begin with. It wasn't nigger-give-an-opinion day, so they didn't ask me, and I kept my mouth shut. He bowed his head, eking out the day's second smile.

He had not considered terrorism a real threat. It was a remote concept, too far away. Richard and Freddie, peers in his neighborhood, those who menaced him all his life—they were more terrifying than remote antagonists produced by media and the US government. He had learned of the terrorism inflicted on black people by white people in Los Angeles and the US. He was familiar with images of lynching, the history of slavery, the legacy of Jim Crow, pictures of the race riots in Los Angeles, Detroit, and other cities in the Sixties, and videos of Rodney King being beaten by white cops. The terrorism was here, at home. *Why worry about foreign people from a small country thousands of miles away bringing terrorism here? What's the*

249

reason to import terror? The history of the United States, the history of racism, the history of the exploitation of non-white people in this land, exemplified terrorism. For non-whites, terror has been abundant.

Perhaps karma exists. Perhaps Carl Jung was right, he deduced, having recently read about the collective unconscious. *The concept seems like pure bullshit, but maybe it rings some truth. Maybe it's time for chucks and annes to pick up the tab for all they've ransacked, stolen, and consumed, as a race, and now they're scared as shit! Perhaps it's time to bring the terrorism to them for a change.* Averting from this reflection, he did not want to become awash in a tidal wave of karma against the white-ruled United States; he did not want to be a victim from guilt-by-association. His mother's and father's childhood admonishments retold themselves in his mind's ear: "Whenever you see trouble, don't stay there—go the other way. Get as far away as you can. Run!"

I've got to tell this shit to someone, someone who can do something, do something other than tell me I'm full of shit. Dance. I've got to call Dance. What about mama and daddy? I've got to get momma and daddy out of town before those crazy motherfuckers set off a nuclear bomb in LA. Crazy motherfuckers! I can't leave mama and daddy behind. How can I tell them, so they'll believe me? Do I fess up and tell them the truth? Tell them all the shit I've done in order to save their lives?

Engulfed by cold sweat, he shuddered. *They won't believe me anyway. They already think I'm full of shit. Maybe I can get Dance to back up my story. I haven't told him yet. Fuck! I hope he believes me. I know he knows I'm not telling him everything. It's a bullshit game. I gotta tell him about the panties. I gotta tell him about what I heard. A fuck'n particle accelerator in a garage? A meth lab, yes. But a particle accelerator?*

The cool demeanor and Teflon-coated style he had developed to fend off the emotional onslaughts of Freddie, Richard, and other ilk—those who had insulted and humiliated him all his life—did not apply. His world had changed, the situation was different. He had not learned maneuvering in this new world. Uncharted and unknown, his circumstances had altered abruptly. He wanted to cry; he wanted to scream; he wanted to be nurtured by his mother.

He gripped his book bag by the top hook and dragged it toward him. He pushed himself back from the table and stood slowly. The clamor in his head muffled the noise from the increasing hustle and bustle in the library. After another furtive glance at the ceiling dome, he started his walk toward the front lobby. He picked up his pace gradually, feeling more invigorated as he progressed.

He was ambivalent as he dreaded and relished calling Dance. He perceived Dance as solid, stanch, inert—the true reason he returned for counseling—not out of fear of being exposed for his voyeuristic escapades. Dance was his mentor, his guide in this other world. And he had not been totally earnest with him, as the dictates of psychotherapy prescribe.

He peered down an infinite tunnel. At the end was the library entrance. The lingering, free-floating, unjustified fear of a stranger approaching him, detaining him, persisted. Struggling with each step, he walked mechanically, but swiftly. *Focus. You need help. You can't do this by yourself. Help is close. Get to the phones. Get to the phones.*

Upon reaching the foyer, he grimaced at the four public phones lining a side wall. He preferred a closed booth, rather than these partitioned compartments. He rummaged in his book bag for Dance's office number—not his local school counseling center number—his office somewhere in LA. He dropped the coins in the phone, awaiting a dial tone, then pressed each number with deliberation. Each tone reverberated a surrealistic chant, finally leading to a ring signal.

"Dr. Dance's office," an nasally female voice answered.

Teetering on an ambivalent hump, he hesitated and remained silent. The female voice sighed an impatient, "Hello?"

"Yes, I'm one of Dr. Dance's patients here at the counseling center at Long Beach State. I really need to talk to him, urgently. It's an emergency. Is he there?" Marzee asked in a soft voice.

"Yes, he is here. What's your name, dear?" the receptionist's voice softened as well.

He resented being called "dear," considering the reference condescending and shallow, but now was not the time for trivial resentment. "My name? Marzee. Marzee Banks. Is he there?" he repeated with trepidation.

"My name is Susan, Marzee. I'm Dr. Dance's assistant. You sound like you are in some trouble?" Susan asked, with a genuinely concerned demeanor.

His trepidation phased to impatient anger as his desperation heightened. *No shit, I'm in trouble, bitch. Now get me the fuck who I asked for!* "Am I in trouble? Yes, I suppose you could say that," Marzee replied, holding back his irritability.

"Dr. Dance is in a meeting. He's not with a patient, though. Let me see if I can get him out to talk to you. He hates meetings, so your call may be just what he's looking for," she commented, laughing. "Can I put you on hold? It will just be a couple minutes, OK?"

He was neither amused, nor did he want to be placed on hold. "Yes, OK," Marzee answered nervously. Background music immediately filled the silence. He drifted away.

Sand fly, where are you? Are you admiring her concave stomach, protruding hipbones, and her tanned skin glistening on the beach?

"Marzee, this is Lorn Dance," the male voice announced.

Marzee startled, his lapse into fanciful silent reverie disrupted abruptly. "Oh, Dr. Dance," Marzee said. He was tempted to hang up. "I don't know where to begin," he commented, stammering.

"Marzee, Susan said you're in some sort of trouble? Are you alright?" Dance asked with alarm.

Jittery about discussing such pressing matters in public, he was worried Dance would hurry him. "I don't know. I feel like I'm in trouble. I'm not arrested, or anything like that. I've got to tell you what happened. But I'm not sure where to begin. Maybe you can tell me if I'm in trouble," Marzee replied.

"Please, tell me, Marzee," Dance responded, sounding somewhat relieved.

Marzee wished he could see Dance in person, pressing himself to continue with this uneasy soliloquy. "OK, there's some stuff I didn't tell you while in session. Stuff I was doing," Marzee said, pausing. "But, this IS an emergency. I didn't call you, like, for an added therapy session, or out of guilt for shit I didn't tell you earlier."

"I'm listening," Dance offered with continued calm.

"OK. Remember, I told you about my philosophy instructor, the German woman, who's so fine?" Marzee asked.

"Yes, I remember," Dance acknowledged.

Stalling and full of trepidation, he was aware of intruding on Dance's time. He had to be blunt. "Ok," Marzee said with uneasiness, "I've been following her; stalking her. Remember, I told you I had researched where she lived. Then I went over there. I went over there two, no, three times now. Once I peeped in her window at night. This last time, yesterday, I went into her house when no one was home."

"Ok, Marzee, I just want to make sure I've got what you told me straight. You've been stalking this instructor of yours. You think about her all the time. You found out where she lives. You went to her house and peeped. When you went into her house, no one saw you. No one was at home? No personal contact?" Dance asked, unaffected by Marzee's confession.

Recalling the reporting standards, he knew what he told Dance did not qualify as reportable to the authorities. *I'm not diddling any kids. I'm not abusing any old folks. I'm not threatening to cut that horse-faced bitch's throat.* "That's right. No one was at home. The door was unlocked. I didn't break the door or window or anything like that. It was already unlocked. It's not like I broke in," Marzee responded defensively.

"You had been stalking her up to our last session, so I'm assuming something happened around your going into her house," Dance inquired.

A sense of relief filled Marzee. A point of reckoning approached—he would broadcast his singular secret. "Yes, Dr. Dance. That's right. I was over there yesterday. I…" Marzee responded, faltering.

"Marzee, I'm not going to judge you, or think of you as a bad person. You can tell me what you've been doing. Please, tell me, so I can help you," Dance said.

Dance was his psychotherapist, yet he felt vested in preserving a pristine image with him—in looking good. He gathered his moral gumption to fully disclose his troubles. *Here goes.* "I got to thinking about her underwear awhile back. I was sitting, I don't know where. Oh, yes. The school library, but I was thinking about her, and all the sudden the only thing I could think about was her underwear. So yesterday I went there. I found her underwear in a dresser drawer. They were clean, smelling like fabric softener. I jerked off anyway. Strange thing, my lust for her didn't go away. I immediately had the thought—it just sort of flashed in my head—I had to have her unwashed underwear," Marzee declared, hesitating, shocked at what he had heard himself say.

"So you went there yesterday, looking for her underwear. And what happened after that?" Dance asked, urging him to continue.

Rolling with the momentum, his anxiety about the call had vanished. He even forgot he was standing in a public place. "OK, yes. So I was looking for her dirty drawers. I had to have them. I figured the laundry room would be my best shot. So

I vacated her bedroom with the clean drawers, and looked around the house, but—"

Anticipating what he had to say, he did not want to sound crazy. He felt like he was preparing to tell Dance he saw a UFO. "She came home while I was there," but he was quick to add, "No one saw me. I hid. It was what I saw before I hid, and what I heard them saying while I was hiding. It's crazy. I don't want you to think I was hearing things. It's like I dreamed this shit. It's crazy. You're going to think I'm schizophrenic, or something," Marzee announced, frantic.

"I'm absolutely sure you are not schizophrenic," Dance responded, reassuring him.

"OK, so I was looking for her laundry room, and I went through a door leading into a garage, thinking maybe the laundry was in the garage. At first I thought it was a one-car garage, but I saw the house from the front, I knew they had a three-car garage. From what I could see standing in the door, a wall, like an unfinished wallboard partition, separated the two-car part from the one-car part. The wall had a door, so I opened it. OK, so here's the first crazy part. They had some sort of physics laboratory in there, like a mad scientist's room, like in a movie. It was packed with shit, from top to bottom, wall-to-wall. Tubes, wires, controls, lights, dials on panels—other shit I never saw before— packed in tight. I told you before, I took college prep physics, so some of it I recognized. At first I thought it might be a photo lab, being that her

257

husband took lots of pictures of her," Marzee said, pausing.

His brain hyperventilated; his emotions sweat. The crux of the story had yet to be revealed, causing his anxious hesitation. He knew his therapist could not reject him for his eye's foray through strangers' bedroom windows at night, or even lapses into their empty homes, but he could not tolerate the prospect of being dismissed for delusional fantasy.

"You saw a room with unfamiliar objects in a strange house. And the objects you saw were in a garage, a workshop?" Dance asked with a what's-strange-about-that edge.

He wanted it out, but his prolonged expository stung more than any shame-laden confession. "Yeah, I guess a workshop. But it was more like a lab. I know I saw stuff for lasers, other optical equipment. But it was what I heard, what they said. Dr. Dance! Listen to me!" Marzee pleaded as he prepared to erupt.

"Marzee, I'm listening. You have my full attention," Dance replied, comforting Marzee he was listening.

"While I was in this room full of shit, the garage door next to this lab I was in—you know, the single car garage I entered from—it opened. Scared the shit outta me. I looked for a place to hide. Like I said, the room was packed with shit everywhere. I couldn't find a place to hide. Then I saw a door behind what looked like a big pump, so I climbed over the pump, and damn, the door opened! I went in, quiet as hell, closed the door, and I was in the laundry room. You know, the place I was looking for to begin with. There were a couple of small closets, so I quick, opened the door, squeezed in, and shut the door."

"So then I heard car doors open, and the garage door shut. You know, automatic opener. I heard voices. I could barely hear, so I put my ear to the wall. I recognized Utte's voice. There was another woman with her. The other woman had an accent also, but it was different from Utte's, not German."

"And Utte? She's your philosophy instructor?" Dance asked, seeming more ensconced in Marzee's anguish-filled tale of trespass.

Marzee snatched the respite offered by the hesitation. He was glad Dance asked questions, but he wanted to finish, to get off the phone. His emotions had reached a crescendo long ago—a level beyond frustration—and now he was numb and near surrender. "Yeah, right. But she also works at some gym as a trainer. I called there earlier, just before I left for her house, to check to see if she was working, to make sure she was not at home. I guess she must have left right after I called since she arrived home, I'd say less than an hour later. She came home with another woman. She called her Afsane. I looked up the name on the Internet. It's an Iranian name."

"Yes. I was in graduate school with an Iranian woman named Afsane. It's a common Iranian name for girls. Anyway, please continue," Dance said.

He doesn't get the picture yet. Goddamn. I hope he takes me seriously. His resistance to tell the full tale had engendered a deluded hope that Dance was a super-therapist, a mind reader, who already had surmised what he had yet to fully convey. "They also referred to someone else they called Mansour. Iranian, also, I found out. Anyway, they stayed by the car, talking a bit. Then they went into the room I bailed from—the one with all the equipment. Then they started talking the REALLY crazy shit," Marzee exclaimed, sighing. "I mean, really crazy!"

"Marzee, I feel you're holding back from the core of what you are trying to say. I'm still with you," Dance reaffirmed. "Please, continue."

His confidence had returned; his self-consciousness had dissipated. At the threshold of his belabored monologue, a vitality had returned unannounced, but welcomed. The anticipation of the call had been worse than the reality. "Utte was explaining the stuff in the room to the other woman. She said the equipment was a particle accelerator, designed and built by her husband. His name's John Thorndike. He's a physics researcher at UCLA. I looked him up too, just to verify. It's true. They said he, John, discovered a way of building a nuclear bomb by using lead instead of uranium, or plutonium, simply by making lead very radioactive and unstable. You understand? You get what I'm saying? They said they were building a nuclear bomb. That they were going to set it off in Los Angeles sometime soon. They're terrorists!" Marzee articulated in a low hiss. "And they fucking want to blow up Los Angeles."

"You overheard these two women say they had plans to set off a nuclear bomb in Los Angeles?" Dance replied, dropping his usual stoic demeanor for the controlled alarm displayed by a 911 operator upon hearing reports of a catastrophic accident in downtown LA during rush hour.

Marzee visualized Dance's expression. If he didn't have his full attention before, he had it now. "Yes, that's what I heard—no mistake. I couldn't make this shit up if I had to. Listen, if the KKK held a gun to my head, and said, 'Nigga! You better make up the wildest shit you can think of, or I'm going to blow your fucking brains out!' I wouldn't come close to this shit. They're terrorists!" Marzee continued in his high-pitch whisper.

"Marzee, I'd like you to come to my office, now. Can you do that?" Dance asked with a reserved officiousness as if he had looked up the proper response in a contingency manual.

Surprised by the unexpected request, he instinctively distrusted the sudden gesture of urgency. "Yeah, I guess I can do that. I have a class soon, but I'll come. I don't know where you are," Marzee replied. "But listen, I don't want to come there 'cause you think I'm crazy. You think I'm, like, a danger to myself or others. I read about that. I'm not crazy! I heard what I heard!" Marzee responded in a guarded tone.

"I'm not doubting you, Marzee. I want you to come to my office because you made some serious statements, serious accusations. Let's make certain we have the facts straight before we involve the appropriate agencies. Let me ask you something else—are you sure nobody saw you? Nobody knew you were there?" Dance responded, morphing to an official air from his usual therapist role.

Dance's change in demeanor puzzled and frightened Marzee. He no longer sounded like his psychotherapist. "Yeah, I'm sure. I waited 'til they left, obviously," Marzee replied.

"Marzee, I believe you believe you heard what you heard." he said, extending an uncomfortable pause. "You've been doing all the confessing. I have a confession for you. You know, I have another job. I only work at the counseling center part time—just to keep some patient contact," Dance said with a resolve counter to his usual manner as well.

Some shit's a-brew. He's setting the stage to tell me some shit. "Yes, I knew you came from somewhere else. That's what the lady at the front desk told me. I forgot where I got this other number from. Oh. I guess, you," Marzee replied.

"I work for the FBI, as a forensic psychologist," Dance replied with articulation, so Marzee could comprehend.

Motherfucker is a pig! Why didn't he tell me this earlier? I've been pouring my heart out to the fucking man. "The FBI!" Marzee exclaimed.

"I'm not an agent," Dance countered quickly. "I'm a consulting psychologist. I do profiling, that sort of thing."

Oh, that's good news. You're not a pig. You're a lackey for the pig. "Yeah, sure, I've heard of that," Marzee replied in a more relaxed tone.

"I work mostly on criminal cases. Real criminals, most-wanted-list types. I also do some work with Homeland Security, so I have some vital contacts. But I need to make sure we're on the right track before I call these people in to act. I believe you. On the other hand, I can't make a call, saying, 'hey, a patient of mine broke into a his teacher's garage, and while eavesdropping, heard her talking about blowing up LA with a homemade nuclear weapon.' Can you come here right away, so we can talk face-to-face?" Dance asked.

He wants me to come to him? Why doesn't he come to me? "Come there? Like come to where you are now?" Marzee asked incredulously.

"Yes, here. I'm in West Los Angeles, in the Federal Building, corner of Wilshire and Veteran. It's close to UCLA. Can you get here soon? I recall you drive," Dance responded.

"I drive, but not a car. I have a moped. That's a long way for me to come on a moped," Marzee retorted.

"You could come straight out Sepulveda. It'd probably take you about an hour at this time of day," Dance replied.

Remaining silent, his anxiety soared. Dance had introduced a new element of worry—his fear of police and police agencies. Venturing into the den of the enemy—terrorists on a different side—was deplorable.

"Another thing," Dance added, not waiting for Marzee to respond. "Remember when you first came into the counseling center at the college? You filled out some forms. One of the forms was an explanation of confidentiality. It said that what we talked about in our sessions was only between you and me, unless certain issues came up like child abuse, elder abuse, that sort of thing. Do you recall?"

"Yes, I remember those forms," Marzee answered.

"We'll have to discuss what you heard and how you heard it with other people. That means disclosing the nature of our counseling sessions. You understand?" Dance asked.

Reasons not to go mounted swiftly: telling others about his forays into Utte's house; telling others about masturbating in her house with her underpants over his head; disclosing his entire voyeurism history to others. His short-lived relief waned to torment. "Would I have to be very specific—I mean about the things I did?" Marzee asked pensively.

"You might. Frankly, yes. If what you are telling me is real—and I believe you—then we're talking about an issue of dire national security, not to mention the lives of millions." Dance spoke with increased gravity. "I could see if an agent could come there to pick you up, but I'd like as few as possible knowing about this issue initially, for your privacy and protection, and for security reasons as well. I think it would be better if you could come here to talk with me first."

Assuming expediency would reward his candor, he found himself implicated further. "Can't we just wait 'til you come to the school? I'm supposed to see you tomorrow, anyway. Don't you come here today?" Marzee asked.

"Marzee, when you called, you seemed very disturbed, hearing what you had heard," Dance replied. "Now you want to wait? You have nothing to fear here. No one's going to hurt you. Another thing—we have many databases—databases not publically accessible. While you're on your way here, we'll check on your Utte, and her husband, and the Iranian names you mentioned. These information guys do wonders. If they find links, given your information, well, the necessary agencies could be called into action even by the time you arrive. Please, come," Dance urged with the intensity of one trying to talk a jumper from a twentieth story ledge.

He was in a hole, a grave with slippery sides. Frustrated, tired, and scared, he resolved surrender was his only option. He resigned to his circumstances. "I understand. OK, I'll come," Marzee said.

"You know how to get here?" Dance asked with concerned apprehension.

"I've seen it before. Yes. Where do I go once I get there?" he replied.

"If no cell phone, call me using one of the public phones scattered about the building grounds. I'll come down to pick you up," Dance said. "I'll look for your call in the next couple hours?"

He felt uncommitted to a commitment he did not want to make. *He should come to me. He should come to me right now, especially after what I just told him. If he really believed me, he'd be on his fucking way right now.* "OK. It'll take me about ten minutes to get to my bike in the parking lot. Then it's a long way to West LA from Long Beach. Shit, then I gotta come back," he replied, begrudging the coerced obligation.

"We can return you and your motorbike in a van, or truck, or something. The important thing is to get here," Dance insisted.

"See you when I get there then." he replied, placing the receiver on the hook with an impotent finality.

266

He picked up his backpack, and slung one of the straps over his shoulder. Glancing around, checking through the entrance windows, he made a dash through the double doors. Avoidance of others was paramount.

Jogging slowly, he lapsed into the logistics of his trip—*parking lot, Sepulveda, Torrance, long ass drive, lots of lights, changes to Pacific Coast Highway, Hawthorn, Beach Cities, LAX, Inglewood, Westchester, Marina, Culver City. Goddamn!* Oblivious to his lack of rest, food, and sleep, he hastily plucked his helmet over his head, secured his backpack, started his bike's engine, and darted out of the parking lot, ignoring traffic.

The monkey's still on my back. Dance is fuck'n with me. What did I expect? Someone to wave a wand to take this shit away? They could do any goddamn thing they want once I get there. Shit, I could disappear. Nobody would be the wiser. I didn't even tell anyone where I was going, or what I was doing. Maybe I should call Sanders. My mama and daddy don't even know where I am. For all they know, I'm at school. Shit, I'll just be another face on a milk carton! What the hell am I doing?

As he meandered to Sepulveda Boulevard, his resolve to see Dance dissipated with each block. *Maybe Dance didn't believe me. Or maybe he did believe me like he said, and wanted some time to sort things out before I got there. Or maybe they want to put a hit on me. They're in cahoots with the terrorists, and really want the shit to happen, like what Sanders' father thought about 9/11. I might be a sitting duck.*

Suddenly panicked, he turned into the nearest side street, stopped between two parked cars, then scanned the area nervously—no one followed him. He looked in the sky for a helicopter, spotting only the occasional bird braving the mid-morning LA air, and the planes approaching Los Angeles International. He checked his watch: forty-five minutes had elapsed since he had spoken with Dance. The logic of travelling from Long Beach to West Los Angeles—visiting Dance in the middle of the FBI building—now totally evaded him. His sought-after consolation had morphed into debilitation—interspersed with paranoia. Rendered paralyzed in this semi-residential district, probably Torrance, he disquietly ruminated his conundrum.

But if they wanted me, he would have told me to stay put. They would have come to get me. Dance would not have had me riding across town for two hours on a moped. Maybe he was telling the truth. He needed time to sort things through. And if they were going to kill my ass, they would have done it by now. But if Dance DID believe me, then what I said was time-critical. They would need to get me as soon as possible. It doesn't make sense either way. So what am I doing? I don't trust pigs; I don't trust the government; I sure as hell don't trust government pigs. Just what the hell am I doing?

Tracking calls from public phones takes time. At least that's the shit I saw in movies. Dance didn't say he was an agent. He said he was a psychologist who did profiling, like for serial killers and terrorists. So this shit should be right up his alley. Since he's not an agent, he's got to check with someone who is. That means he has to tell someone about me—what I heard, how I heard it. Damn! I'm gonna call him back. Tell him I'm not coming there. Fuck that. I'm not going there! I'll hang up before they can trace the call.

The parked car in front of him departed, disrupting his trance. He was unaware of the time standing in that spot. His moped engine was still running. The visor of his unbuckled helmet covered his face. *I look too suspicious, too strange, sitting here in this neighborhood. Someone might call the cops. Then I'd be in a jail, instead of in an FBI building. Maybe a jail cell would be safer.*

He removed his helmet, and swished off the sweat pouring down his forehead with the back of his hand. All was in slow motion. *I thought I saw a phone booth around the corner just before I turned. Change. I need change.* As he walked toward the corner, he dug into his pockets looking for coins.

At the phone booth, he dialed Dance's number—heart beating wildly, the ring tone blaring in his ear. The same woman answered. Without hesitation, she transferred him.

"You got here faster than I had expected, Marzee. Go into the lobby in front of the elevators. I'll be right down," Dance said, skipping a formal salutation.

No longer ambivalent about going, he was quick to respond. "No, wait. I'm not there. I stopped on the way," Marzee replied.

"What's wrong?" Dance asked apprehensively.

"Something's not right. I could come to that place, and disappear forever. At least I have a little more time to think, you know, if I don't come there. Maybe I'll go home, to talk to my parents first," Marzee replied. "Coming there is like being invited to an ass-fucking party, not knowing that I'm the main attraction."

"No one's going to hurt you. Marzee, you have to understand: what you told me is bizarre. I believe you. I believe you because I know you. I know we've only met a few times, but I feel I know you well. You made some very serious allegations. Like I explained, I need to see you in person. And there's some paperwork for you to sign for us to move forward," Dance responded. "You might even turn out being a hero once we get through this thing." Dance sounded more like a salesman than his therapist now.

Dance's words were compelling, but not convincing. Marzee was steadfast with his decision. "Come to me, then. Come to the counseling center where everyone sees you and me together, just like we usually meet. Come here. Then we'll talk," he responded. The silence on the other end, lacking the usual slew of ready responses, indicated Dance was considering his proposal.

"OK. How about at 7 pm? Can you meet me there at 7 pm? I'll cancel my other appointments, and I'll come there," Dance said.

"Seven? Yeah. I'll meet you there at seven," Marzee muttered in a monotone. He hung up still numb, but at least resolved. Betrayal lurked behind the neurons of his consciousness, masked from his awareness, but he ignored its subtle tapping.

Chapter 13
Hearth

After he dropped the phone, he felt a new resolve—a tingle of hope he had not known since young boyhood, a fresh wind of enthusiasm. He would go home: to save his parents and save his soul. If what he had heard—eavesdropping in Utte's laundry room closet—were to come true; if any possibility were remotely possible, he wanted his family elsewhere. Aunt Jeanne in New York would put them up for a week or two. He mulled over telling them: once he explained the imminent danger, they would abandon their skepticism, their stubbornness, and comply. As a last resort, Dance or some of his FBI cronies would talk to them. But he wanted to get his parents out of town as soon as possible.

He had never known such hyper-vigilance. It sapped his energy, tiring him as he speculated about who was watching him from where and with what. This specter of danger—real or imagined—persisted relentlessly. He trotted back to his moped, determined to save his parents.

Come to Sand Fly! It's getting warm—sunny skies, ocean mist, sandy beaches. Come to me. See through my eyes. I will end your torment.

"No! Please! Leave me!" Marzee shouted, causing the woman on the porch across the street to take notice. "Please, leave me be," he whimpered, slumping toward his handlebars. This unfamiliar neighborhood assumed a new significance, as he realized he was close to one of his favorite beaches. His fear of Utte, Iranians, pigs, terrorists, his parents, the government, and the lady across the street withered into the background. He tasted the tan curves and luscious colors the sand fly promised. He started the motor.

The avenue leading to the west was minutes away. The sun shone brightly, ushered in by a mild Santa Ana condition. The warm breeze titillated his skin, still moist from sweat. *I can be at the beach in fifteen minutes. The buildings lining that beach are perfect; they offer good cover.* He drove out to the corner, and turned tight against the curb to avoid oncoming traffic. He could not wait; his anticipation soared. His heart raced for a different reason now. A horn blared, warning him of his too-close turn onto the crowded boulevard.

He had cruised Redondo Beach several times, eyeing some of the alley-adjacent backyards and beachfront homes and apartment buildings. His singular purpose had morphed instantly: get the beach to see what he could see; explore new territory. He hugged the bike lane, trying to steer clear of the congested traffic while making as much headway as possible. Upon reaching Redondo Boulevard, he maneuvered a jagged ninety degree path to the left turn lane, just making a turn before the light changed, and ignoring the horn-sounding disgruntled drivers. The beach lay straight ahead.

His moped had not known such high pressure and precision performance. He sped past a police car with a stopped motorist at the curb. Looking in his side-view mirror, he saw he had caught the policeman's attention. *Fuck him. He's not going to jump in his car after a moped while he's ticketing Joe Porsche.* Marzee had shifted his focus, assuming a new single-mindedness and reckless abandon. He had all but dismissed the stymieing predicament beleaguering him just one half hour ago.

He arrived at one of the alleys typical of beach communities; it reminded him of Utte's neighborhood. He jammed his brakes, stopping abruptly in a shady spot next to a beach access path. A bikinied woman and her dog walked nonchalantly past him, turning down the beach path. His acrid lust consumed him. *She's at least forty years old. Look at the shape she's in—her muscles, her tits. I wonder how much a tit job like that costs? Will she take her top off? She has to find a secluded spot. I can follow her so she does not suspect me. Did she notice me when she passed?*

He jumped off his moped, extending the kickstand simultaneously. His book bag, his helmet, the bike itself—all had lost value. His sole interest and motivation: follow this woman. To discover where she settled, to watch her arrange herself on the beach—spreading her blanket, applying her suntan lotion, opening her beach bag, sorting through her magazines, making her cell phone calls, positioning her sunglasses, finding a comfortable posture—and to satisfy the singular question: will she remove her top?

The scent emerged from his body, an odor characterizing his hunt-state. He referred to it as his "sausage smell." He nonchalantly dropped his helmet and book bag on the ground next his bike, and put the key in his pocket. He began tracking her. The sidewalk ended at the sand line, and the beach panorama extended before him. The sounds, smells, and associations engulfed his senses. The woman he was trailing disappeared into the dunes. He wanted to pray—he did not believe in God. He wanted to confess—the policeman did not follow. He wanted to stop—he had no brakes. He had only Sand Fly, and Sand Fly flittered toward the dunes, beckoning him onward.

He fell to his knees into the hot soft sand. A group of teenagers carrying surfboards passed him. A subdued voice: "Hey man, you all right?" Marzee nodded, kneeling, trying to pray, emulating prayer, hoping, maybe, if God exists, It would hear him, help him now. *I must stop. I must return. Save my parents. I heard what I heard. I'm in too deep, and I never intended for any of this to happen. But if I hadn't been there, I would not have heard it, so You must have a plan for me, and it sure as hell must not be looking at that woman's tits on the beach. Please help me. I know I'm just talking to myself, but maybe that's enough. Maybe that's enough to get me turned around, and back to what I must do.*

Tears coated his cheeks, dripping, dotting the front of his pants. He opened his eyes and looked up, squinting through blurred vision. His silent reverie affected him unawares. Like a weekend binger emerging from a blackout, he awoke in an alien, unfamiliar location, not knowing how he got there, or who his bed companion was, but terrified of what he may have done, and hard-pressed to return to normalcy.

Wetness stuck to him, indistinguishable from tears or sweat. He stood up. His pants tugged at his legs; his clothes even beckoning him to stay. He pulled the fabric from his skin. "Thank you," he uttered so faintly. He did not want himself, or anyone else, to hear. He faced away from the beach, his prey now long penetrated into her niche. His task was clear: remove his parents from the danger he knew was imminent. More beachgoers parted around him, like water flowing around a rock in a brook. Some dawdled, perceiving him as an oddity: rescuers or condemners—sympathizing or punishing. He stood alone; he had guidance— whether from within or outside—his direction was sure. *You're not up or down. I wish I could look somewhere to see you, to thank you in person. I never had the strength to turn completely away.*

He returned to his discarded moped, having forgotten he had dropped his belongings by the wayside. Appalled by his own actions, he paused to inspect his backpack and helmet. He slapped his pocket to verify the lump from his key was there.

He donned his backpack and helmet, extracted his key, started the engine, and accelerated, merging into the traffic. The pace was different than before—urgent, but not pressured by his obsession.

While driving, he mulled over the script to his parents, rehearsing how he was going to explain to them why they had to leave their home for safety; how he came about knowing what he knew; confessing all that they did not know about their son. He cruised to a stop at a crosswalk, allowing a group of girls headed for the beach to cross. This visage, which would have sent him askew moments earlier, was now invisible, as he was consumed by a new resolve. He resumed his pace. The wind invigorated his skin; the motion charged his fervor. He drove even faster.

Still caught in the crag mire of the beach community, he felt compelled to leave swiftly. He cut through eastward-directed side streets and alleys, trying to expedite his way out. He fancied taking the freeway, rather than persevering street traffic all the way back to Long Beach. *Fuck it. I will. I'll just stay to the side. Even if I get a ticket, it'll be faster. Closest freeway on-ramp from here? Redondo Beach Boulevard. I could be home in thirty minutes.*

He reached the freeway on-ramp, ignored the meters, and accelerated onto the freeway, staying inside the right-side emergency lane, and remaining vigilant for CHP and other law enforcement officers. He maneuvered his moped through the dense South Bay freeway traffic, being careful to drive on the shoulder, occasionally dodging parked cars—stalled, flat tires, sleepers, or the lost, desperately perusing maps of Los Angeles. He was making admirable headway, hoping to catch his parents at home within the next hour, and confide not only his secret life, but also the danger facing them.

He hated his neighborhood, and that temperament had generalized to Los Angeles. He had coddled silent childhood ruminations about blowing up his neighborhood, or at least certain houses. *Maybe Los Angeles should just fucking blow up.*

Suddenly, he spotted a CHP motorcycle with a pulled-over motorist directly in front of him on the shoulder. He stopped behind a Caltrans sign, peeking around it periodically to check if he could proceed. The officer drove off on his motorcycle, exiting the next nearby off-ramp. Marzee remained where he was, spying the same officer who re-entered the freeway moments later.

Once Marzee was certain the CHP officer was long gone, he continued his shoulder-confined trek along 405. After transitioning to the Long Beach Freeway, he suspected two more freeway exist before he would be free of the traffic morass. He was surprised he had made the trip on PCH and Sepulveda that far to the north; he was even more impressed he had circuitously returned via the freeway on his moped. He was just happy to be close to home.

The bumpy street reminded him of his childhood, riding his bicycle on hot summer afternoons with his friends, looking for mischief, playing with abandon. Starting in mid-adolescence, he experienced the onset of a dysphoric apathy whenever he approached home. Today he felt different: identity, membership, camaraderie, a sense of community, belonging, engagement. His moped bounced up his family's narrow driveway, and he rolled to the backyard. *Dad's home. Good. And Mr. Brown's still on his porch in the afternoon. I had forgotten. I missed him.* Marzee waved and smiled.

He collected his helmet, backpack and keys. At this time of day, his mother sat at the rear kitchen window, smoking one of her few daily cigarettes, reading the paper, listening to the radio, or chasing away the neighborhood kids stealing fruit from the backyard trees. He paused, looking at the screen, straining to see her outline in the window, but she wasn't there. In the past she had often caught him unaware of her presence, detaining or distracting him as he tried to get away. Without her knowing it, her distractions had deterred him from his otherwise untoward behaviors.

The bright sun and warm breeze did not deter him. He walked with steadfastness and intent along the back of the house to the side door, still trying to see his mother's form, to get her attention.

He expected a lunch offer at any second, as he was rarely home at this time of day.

The roses covering the trellis leading to the side door seemed particularly fragrant today. He yanked on the screen door, surprised that it was latched. Aggravated, he yanked twice more, hoping someone would hear him, and open the door. *I told them a weak ass hook on a screen door is not going to keep out someone who wants to get in to steal something. All this way, and they're not home. The car? The car's here.*

"Mama! Open the back door," Marzee yelled at the door. He waited for a response, then jiggled the door in vain.

His serenity was impregnable. Refraining from kicking the door, he calmly went to the front door, discovering it was locked as well. Since his parents were so predictable, this deviation was unsettling. A deluge of thoughts cascaded. *Did Dance tell my parents? Did they come and get them? Bad, but good. At least they have their safety in mind, but how do I explain? I didn't want a stranger to tell them my secrets.*

Suddenly uneasy, he fumbled for his door key. He turned the lock, and moved the door open gently, half-heartedly expecting to find his parents at home. "Momma? Daddy? Anyone home?"

No response—he went inside. *Dance! He told them.* Even if they had unexpected visitors— rare to never—they wouldn't leave home. *And no note, telling me where they are. Too insecure to*

even leave a note. Some salesman or Jehovah's
Witness would open the screen, out pops the note,
and the whole world knows they're not home.

Now desperate to discover the whereabouts
of his parents, he scurried inside. He ran from room
to room, finding nothing. At the stairs leading to the
basement a wire harness, like one used inside
computers, straddled the door well. Thump. Bang.
Thump. Bang. A noise from the basement sounded
like a hopelessly unbalanced clothes dryer.
"Mama?" *What the fuck? She left the dryer on*
downstairs. They just bought that. I hope she didn't
break it already. And what's that wire harness
doing here? Has somebody been fucking with my
computer?

His shoes squished on the stairs, the source
hidden by the dim, morose lighting of the stairwell.
Patches of dark magenta blotched the basement
floor. *I'm dreaming. I'm dreaming. I can only be*
dreaming. A supernova flashed within—a point of
impact where what cannot be real occupies the
space of reality. Mediation was impossible. The
clamor from the dryer, its horrific message, kept
him from dissolving the instantaneous, yet infinite,
illumination of dread and catastrophe percolating
inside him. His perception collapsed to a single
point, drawn from the grotesque, silhouetted oblong
cameo on the corner basement table. The instrument
of dissolution: his computer monitor faceplate.

An omnipotent paralysis seized him—
thought, action, feeling ceased entirely. He did not

know how long he stood in place, motionless. His senses, previously overwhelmed by internal preoccupation, oozed to the exterior, signaled most urgently by olfactory triggers, causing him to crumble and vomit.

The dryer, a vortex leading to pure chaos, had to be silenced. Its contents, planted by demons from hell's rival, could neither be viewed nor ignored. Zombie-like, he emerged from his knees, and shuffled to the dryer. *No stop button.* He opened, then closed the door quickly to stop it from tumbling—not sheets, blankets, and pillow cases. Steam from the brief exposure escaped through the gap. It enveloped him in the same manner escorts to Hades would overtake the wicked and damned immediately upon death. Once more he collapsed to his knees, heaving and vomiting violently.

He could not die. He could not sleep. He could not anesthetize himself. He longed for the sweet bliss of the surgical table, just prior to total sedation. He had stopped the noise. Now he had to find the energy to leave the stench.

Dad! He turned on his heel, and slipped to his hands and knees on the tacky red laminate. His scream echoed the torment of ten thousand tortured lives. "This can't be real," he sputtered, barely intelligible to his own ears.

Dad. He went to the sink, and rinsed his hands ritualistically for fifteen minutes. Then he traipsed back across the basement floor, glancing back at the table in the corner, teasing himself with the miniscule possibility it did not exist, only to instantly jerk away at the visage he did not want in his memory. He retraced his path back up the stairs. At the top of the stairs, he peered left and right half-heartedly. He had already searched the first floor. *Time machines should exist. Not to take you back into time, but to remove your memories. Take my memories away.*

He negotiated and pleaded with an apathetic and unmerciful chronicler. *Maybe Dad was not home. Or maybe whoever did this took him, and he's still alive. Why would someone do this? My parents were innocent; they knew nothing. Who could know anything? Me. They know I know. Why kill my parents? Why murder these beautiful people; they loved me; they raised me. My mom, how I loved her hot breakfasts; how I loved her crossword puzzles. Maybe I can save my dad. Please, you gave me the strength to leave the beach. Please, protect my father.*

He lumbered around the corner, trudged through the kitchen, and meandered up the stairwell toward his room. *Please. Please. Please, don't let me find him. Please, let him be somewhere else, alive.* At the top of the stairwell, he faced the closed door of his room. From under the door a vicious semi-circle protruded to the outside. Its meaning enervated his being, pervading his central nervous system from cerebrum to spine. He covered his face, weeping hysterically.

He gathered himself, still shaking and sobbing, turned the doorknob, and eased the door slowly open. His father lay motionless on the floor, facing him on his side.

"Daddy!" Marzee cried, hanging on to a hope his father may be alive. The carpet emitted a familiar squish as he dived toward his beloved father. He pressed his fingers to his father's jugular vein—no pulse. He pushed his shoulder, forcing him face up, and rammed his ear next to his chest, listening for a heart beat—nothing.

"Daddy," Marzee moaned. "Please, come back to me. Please come back to me. I can't live without you, Daddy. Please. Please. Please. Come back to me. Please, Daddy. Please, don't be dead." He cried on his father's chest, disregarding the heinous circumstance, and forgetting Dance, Utte, the Iranians, the bomb, everything. He put his arms around his father, hugging him, rocking him up and down, as if the motion would stimulate life.

As he swayed and rocked his father in meditative mourning, he felt the motion hindered by an object under his dad. He rolled his father over, revealing a large hunk of rectangular, box-like metal that had been placed under him. Slippery around its edges, he stretched his right hand, leaving his left arm around his dad. Stuck to the carpet by capillary force, he pried loose a six inch long metal box, about an inch thick and four inches wide. The markings labeling the box were obscured. He swiped it across his bedspread, cleaning it enough

284

to read a label: Western Digital. *My hard drive. They stuck my computer's hard drive under my father's body? Why? To tell me what? Why not just wait for me, and kill us all?*

Barely holding the device with his last vestige of strength, he attempted standing, and feebly balanced himself. Then he buckled, his stance weakened, and he collapsed. Still conscious, his gaze crawled along the floor in slow motion, avoiding its grotesque centerpiece. *If they're still here, they should come kill me now.*

"Come, you fucked up, sick motherfuckers. Come out! Show yourselves. Kill me! Kill me!" he babbled while still lying on the floor. *I just want to die. Please, come and kill me.*

He stayed on the floor, wishing he could remain there, dead. From his vantage point, he stared at a wall socket. *Electrocution. Not enough juice. Maybe if I do it in the bathtub with a hairdryer. We don't have a hairdryer.* From the socket under his desk, his eyes wandered to his computer, ransacked and torn apart—memory and motherboard had been crushed and mangled, with bits and pieces thrown about. He started another bout of weeping, thinking about what these purveyors of death and misery had done. He visualized his parents' anguish. *They knew. They knew I searched for Utte, that I paid for a background check, but why didn't they come after me? They knew I would be home soon. Why not just wait for me? Or just get me on campus. They know where I am.*

What did I do? If only I had thought of my parents this morning. I knew what I had heard. I fucked around, going to school, going to the library. I knew what I had heard. I fucked around calling Dance. Dance. Then the beach. I should've come straight home after calling Dance. Maybe I could've saved momma and daddy. Maybe I would've caught them in the act. Maybe saved one of them, or both of them. Or maybe they would've killed me too. That'd be just fine. I want to be dead. Who do I tell this shit to? If I call the police, they'll hold me. Everyone will say I finally went berserk. I can hear it now, those self-righteous clowns from the neighborhood, from church: "I knew it! I knew it. Ever since that boy was little, I knew he just wasn't right! Now look at what he's done. Poor Ione. Poor Morgan. Ummf, ummf, ummf. Those poor people."

Marzee arose from the floor, dazed but stronger; he sat on his bed. *I can't leave my momma and daddy here to rot. I've got to find who did this. They want people to believe that I did this shit. They want me out of the way. Why didn't they just kill me too? The bomb. They think they can pin that on me? That doesn't make sense. I'm no physicist. But people will believe it if they hear it. It doesn't matter if it's true or not. Doesn't matter if it makes no sense. If people thought about what makes sense, they wouldn't believe most of the shit they believe anyway. Dance. I've got to meet him, tell him. Maybe he can help. If I tell him, he'll involve the police immediately. I can't have that. I've got to find Utte and that bitch she was talking to.*

He remained motionless and somber, unable to move, preserving the hope the assassin would return for him. He languished in his guilt; he felt separated from his body, semi-real, ephemeral. Movement seemed distant, but imminent.

What if they called the police after they left? Or they were watching the house, and they called just after I arrived? Police would arrive; take me into custody; charge me with the murders; the terrorists would do the bomb thing. They would leave some evidence linking me to the bomb since they knew I had been in the house. Pigs could bust in any minute. I've got to get out of here.

He scanned the room with catatonic movement, lingering on items as he passed over them, fondling them with his eyes, closing off his awareness when he skirted the room's center. *I need a plan. One. I can't go outside like this. What then? Shower. Change clothes. Money. I know where they hid their money. Then pigs'll think I murdered AND robbed my parents. No. They wouldn't know where to look, so they wouldn't know. Need to act. What about their bodies? Nothing. I can't do anything about them. Shower. Change. Money. Leave. Call police? No. Then they'll start looking for me. I've got to find Utte to clear myself. Little chance if I find her, but that's my only option. Maybe Dance.*

OK. Shower. Clothes. Money. Leave normally. How about covering my tracks? No, I was here. I saw what I saw, did what I did. I didn't do anything.

Shower. Clothes. He stared at his hands, flipping them inquiringly, half aware, then smeared them on his sheets. He rose robotically, and stepped toward his clothes dresser, extracting underwear, socks, and a t-shirt. He slid open his closet door, hesitating, imagining someone might be hiding in there, ready to pounce. He pulled a clean pair of pants, a shirt, and a pullover. He pressed the shirt to his face, smelling the remnants of fabric softener.

"Mama!" he screamed. "I want my mama!" He sobbed into the garment briefly, then abruptly stopped. *Got to stay steady. Shower. Shoes!* He returned to his closet to grab the pair of sneakers his mother had purchased for him, but he had refused to wear because of the embarrassing decals. Looking back briefly, he closed the door as he had found it, and made his way to the bathroom downstairs.

He disrobed in a daze, dropping his clothes into a grotesque pile on the floor in front of the tub, meticulously separating tainted from untainted clothes. After adjusting the water temperature, he showered until he had exhausted all the water in the hot water tank. He shuttered a sob, recalling a familiar disgruntled chant from outside the bathroom door: "Boy, you don't need to take such long showers. You'll use all the hot water!"

After drying himself thoroughly, he positioned his wet towel, tarp-like, over his sullied clothes. When he finished in front of the mirror, he scooped up them into the wet towel and bound the corners, making a compressed bundle, hobo-style. Red splotches eked through.

I can't. I won't leave my parents, my home, like this. There's only one solution. He carried his bundle to the middle of the living room floor, dropping it in the center as if its position bore some ceremonial significance. Automaton-like, he closed and locked the windows on the first floor. Looking out the west window, he noticed Mr. Brown was still perched peacefully on his porch, enjoying the unseasonably warm fall weather.

Garage. The canister is in the garage. I can't go near the basement. The door to the back, it's just half-way down the stairs. But the smell, that horrific odor. OK, I'll hold my breath. He inhaled deeply, ran down the basement stairs to the side door landing, hastily fumbled with the latches, ran across the backyard to the garage, flung opened the door, and snatched the five-gallon canister of gasoline his father had kept filled for the lawn mower and emergency gas for the car. He dashed back across the lawn, holding the tank, trying to keep it from spilling from the overflow vent. When he arrived at the side door, he held his breath, and went inside.

He dropped the canister at the top of the basement stairs, and side-tracked into the kitchen, donning his mother's rubber gloves. He metered the spillage, dousing everything on the first floor—

furniture, floors, clothes—with gasoline. Careful not to step in blood, he did the same on the second floor. He saved the last for his father's body, splashing the gasoline as a priest waves a ceremonial sensor.

He returned to the kitchen. *My mama was so proud of her new stove. She just didn't understand how it lit without flame. I loved them so. They understood so little, and had no interest in knowing more.* Checking his watch at 3:45 pm, he set the timer on the oven to ignite at 4 pm. He pried open the top plate of the stove, and pulled loose the electronic igniter wire for the stove top burners, making sure the oven igniter wire was still intact. Then he turned all four knobs to high, and left the oven door open. The ominous snake hiss from the stove tops filled the room with the harsh, sweet aroma of natural gas. He spread a trail of gasoline from the kitchen to the already soaked living room carpet.

Gasoline odor inundated his smell. From the front closet he took a jacket, and tucked it under his arm. *Family pictures? No. The box is in the basement.* He faced the living room, taking what he knew was his final look at his life and home. *Last year, last month, last week, yesterday, three hours ago. No tears. No difference.* He turned, went outside, and locked the door behind him.

Chapter 14
Frank Sanders

The explosion reminded him of his life's history—the source of his values, beliefs, ambitions—decimated instantly. His resolve to remain on course abandoned him, and he pulled over, rolling next to the curb. He dropped his moped, and collapsed, crying. His grieving vacillated between remorse for the loss of his loved ones, and fear of the future. He struggled to recover, sobbing, lying face down on a lawn with his head buried in his arms.

I don't deserve this shit. I've been a good boy. Done all the things I was supposed to do. Went to church. Smiled and greeted all the people I wished would go to hell. Was a good student. Studied hard. Tried to be honest. Respected my mother and father. Stood during the national anthem. Stayed away from drugs. No trouble with the police. Did some charity work. Goddamn, I'm still a virgin. I'm not gay. What the fuck happened? Maybe I'm one of those multiple personality sickos. Maybe I did it after all. Maybe I killed my parents, but just don't know it. Those assholes with multiple personalities had brutal lives—beatings when they were two, burned with cigarettes by their mamas when they were three, raped by their daddies when they were four, made to live in the basement and eat dog food, sleep on a hard, concrete floor with rats running around when they're five years old. Hard,

*fucking lives. I didn't have that. My parents loved
me, never abused me. If anyone was mistreated, I
mistreated them. I didn't respect them as much as I
should have. I didn't love them the full measure they
deserved. So, no. It's not me. Someone else did that
to them. And I'm going to find them. And I'm going
to kill them. That's all I can do. That's the only
thing to do.*

Sirens sounded in the distance. A helicopter
flying overhead, seemingly en-route to his former
house, caught his attention. He glanced upward,
recalling the time he wanted to take flying lessons.
Fastened to where he lay, powerless to move,
incapable of thinking, he struggled to plan his next
step. Whatever impetus had moved him through his
parent's house moments ago had dissipated. He
needed it back.

*I could just call the police. I already talked
to Dance at the FBI. He's waiting to see me later
today. Why not simply tell them what I heard. Tell
them what I found at home. I broke down. That's
why I blew up my house. That's why I destroyed the
evidence. It doesn't work; pigs won't help me. I
have to help myself. I must find Utte and the
Iranians. I'll go there, force their hand. They die or
I die. Either way, I win. I need a weapon. My father
had a gun in the upper drawer. Too late. Gun. Who
has a gun? Sanders. Sanders has a gun.*

He rose, wobbly-kneed, and forced himself
to stand. He drove away, still feeling the ache of
what had passed in his life—it was all over now.

Even the neighborhood through which he drove had a waning familiarity as he passed through, invoking a nostalgia gained usually from a twenty-year absence. Houses, trees, buildings, people on the street, shadows, sounds, the air on his face, the smells, the time of day—all gone. With renewed vigor and single-minded purpose, he navigated through side streets and alleys to Frank Sanders' house.

Dust spewed behind Marzee's trail as he forged a path down an unpaved alley. Using Sanders' dilapidated garage as a marker, he cut his engine, and rolled to a stop. He fought waves of sadness, overcoming him without warning as he encountered random indicators reminding him of times past. *How old was I when Sanders put me on the back of his bicycle, and tore up and down this alley? Four years old, I think. He was probably fourteen or fifteen. What a thrill. How I loved his power. The way he made a bicycle go so fast? Just like it happened yesterday.*

He rolled the moped into the barely standing structure and dropped it in the dirt without using the kickstand. Sanders' German Shepherd, Cain, bounded into the back, teeth bared, barking and growling. When the dog recognized the intruder, he jumped on Marzee, licking, yelping, tail rapidly sweeping full semi-circular swaths.

He scratched Cain's head and neck vigorously, trying to maintain his balance from the dog's exuberance as he approached Sanders' back door. After Sanders' mother and father had died in an auto accident five years earlier, Sanders continued to live in their heirloom home, supporting his younger brother, Squeaky. Sanders sold grass, pimped a few girls, and was the neighborhood bookie, taking bets on sporting events and horses. Marzee believed he hadn't done badly for himself, though his parents had often put Sanders down for squandering the sacrifices they had had made on his behalf.

"Nigger! Goddamn! I thought you were dead!" Sanders shouted from the dirt-obscured screened window facing the backyard. "I just heard your house blew up with you in it!"

Marzee sported a feeble grin, opening the back door without invitation, and continued inside.

Sanders greeted him at the door. "Say, man. What's this shit all about, your house blowing up? You all right? What's going on? Your parents, they alright?"

Yearning to surrender to Sanders' arms, Marzee refrained—emotional confidant was a relationship they had not shared. Still, Sanders was his unspoken older brother—not in name or parent or court document, but in an implicit bond that had persisted in various manifestations throughout his childhood. Marzee had already decided: he had finished crying. "I need a gun," Marzee responded bluntly, still petting the dog.

"What it is, bro?" Sanders replied, still dumbfounded and without answers.

"They killed my mother; they killed my father; they destroyed my life," he choked, sitting down on the slashed vinyl-cushioned chair at the kitchen table.

"What? Who? What! Someone killed Mr. and Mrs. Banks? Let's go," Sanders responded on impulse, jumping up, not caring to hear any details. "I'll get dressed and get my shit."

Physical and emotional weakness inundated Marzee. After sitting, he was too feeble to move. "No, wait. It's not that simple," Marzee responded, motioning for Sanders to return to his seat. "Sit down, man. I'll tell you about it." He knew Sanders would sense his sincerity, and abide. "I fucked up. I'm a fuckup. Don't you know that?" Marzee asked, glancing at Sanders from his slump

"Fuckup? Man, what are you talking about? You're our future statesman, or scientist, or Nobel prize winner, or some shit like that. I—we've— mama, daddy, folks around here—we always been proud of you. What the fuck you mean, you're a fuckup?" Sanders asked, disturbed by Marzee's condition—one he had never witnessed from his younger friend.

Telling Sanders his secret tore him at the core, but the trauma numbed the agony. "I peek at people through their windows. I've done it for years," Marzee replied. "I jack off while I'm standing there."

Sanders stared back, unaffected. "Nigger. Everyone knows that. You're a little freaky. So

295

what? Great motherfuckers are all fucked up," Sanders responded, relieved as if that's all Marzee had to admit. "What's this about your house? Your parents?"

Marzee took a glimpse of Sanders through his fingers, his hands still covering his drooped face. *Everyone knows? What the fuck. Why didn't someone say something? Why didn't someone kick my ass early to get me out of that shit.* "My teacher at school, she's German. I started following her, stalking her," Marzee eked out, torn between the revelation just bestowed upon him, and the tragedy facing him directly.

"I don't understand," Sanders stated with brashness. "Man, you came here looking for a gun, I just heard your house is on fire, you tell me your parents were killed, and you want to fuck your teacher at school. Marzee. What-do-you-need?"

He inhaled deeply, sat straight in the chair, put his hands down, and faced Sanders. *I should have come to Sanders a long time ago. Fuck Dance and those other assholes.* "There's shit I never told you, lots of it—" Sanders started to interrupt, but Marzee waved him off. After he painstakingly related the series of events and convolutions leading him to his current state, he stopped abruptly, casting a beseeching gaze at Sanders, and shuttering.

"Some real shit has gone down," Sanders replied, looking more and more perturbed. "These people killed your parents? Why didn't they just kill you?"

"I don't know. Maybe they went there looking for me, then killed just who they found. I don't know. But I'm pretty sure they know that I saw and heard what they're planning. They're planning to set off some kind of nuclear bomb in Los Angeles."

"Goddamn! You need the FBI or CIA. Some white dudes with letters, guns, and shades. What the fuck are we doing talking about this shit?" Sanders remarked, seeming to reach for a phone.

"I already have an in with the FBI. I didn't realize it at first, but it was fortuitous. But given the circumstances of that contact, I don't think they will react. They'll think I'm just crazy. He was my therapist."

"Fort what? Whatever. OK, what do you need from me?" Sanders asked with an earnest expression.

"I need a gun and your cell phone. I have to return to Utte's, and bring the man down on them. The police have to find their nuclear lab while they're chasing me," Marzee explained.

"About the gun. Man, I know for a fact, you never fired a pistol. You'll shoot yourself in the foot. I'm going with you. We'll take my car. You can't go on that little piece of shit, putt-putt thing of yours anyway."

As much as Marzee wanted to protest, he could not. Sanders' help was a life-line—one he had probably sought unawares. "OK, agreed. How about your business? Your customers in the other room?" Marzee asked.

"That's what Lonetta's for—and—" Sanders opened his mouth, then touched the tip of his nose with the tip of his tongue. "She can handle things while I'm gone," Sanders replied smugly with a slight grin.

"We have to go to the beach—Wavecrest Lane. But we can't just drive up and knock on the door—" Marzee explained.

"Say, man. You know who you're talking to?" Sanders interrupted. "Speaking of stupid niggas, you just missed your pal, Freddie. He's the one who told me your house exploded. Niggas know instantly about bad things happening to their friends. It's like they rejoice in it. But they couldn't find Africa on a map if you had they mama at gun point."

The collision of facial muscles while attempting to exert a smile was undeniably unique, an experience Marzee had largely taken for granted. Sanders' comment created a glow, breaking the somber gloom dominating his mood. "Some of them couldn't find their mama, if you threatened to shoot them," Marzee responded, joining in the laughter they both shared briefly.

"Gimme about ten minutes," Sanders said, leaving Marzee in the kitchen while he went to the front of his house. Sanders' two-story wooden house was a multi-purpose facility: a book joint, a repose for those in need of sexual services, a source for small quantities of marijuana, and a Golconda for high quality boot-legged liquor by the shot. The local police left him alone, its members using the house frequently for their own discounted entertainment pursuits. Sanders rarely left the house, as "making sure niggas stay honest is the main job of a good business man." After five minutes, Sanders' girlfriend, Lonetta, stuck her head in the door.

"You alright, hun?" she asked with the sweet reverberation Marzee knew only a young black woman of Lonetta's caliber could deliver.

Confronted by the guilt her appearance invoked, he recalled peeping on Lonetta twice, catching her in the downstairs shower late at night. He had hoped to not see her. "I guess, as good as could be expected. Yeah. I'm OK. Thanks," he replied.

"Frank's taking a quick shower and changing. He said he'll be right back. You need anything? A beer? Drink? Something stronger?" she inquired, persisting in her angelic tone.

He wondered if Sanders had told her anything about what had happened to him. She must be thinking: If his house had burned down with his parents inside, shouldn't he be talking to the police or firemen or undertaker? But then, most of Sanders' people didn't ask questions, and Lonetta was one of Sanders' people. "Nah. I'm OK. I need a straight mind," Marzee replied.

"All right, sugar. You need anything, anything at all, you let me know," she said, emphasizing "anything at all."

He had frequently fantasized about Lonetta—her light-brown skin, smooth complexion, round curves and almond brown eyes. Having graduated from high school two years before him, he had daydreamed about her, visualizing her naked as he sat in class with sustained erection—the way she strutted down the hall—males stopping, dropping books, stumbling; females, frowning, disapproving posturing—folded arms and clinched fists on hips. He pictured the two halves of her sensuous, bulbous ass undulating in synchronous unison under her always skin-tight skirt, not one jiggling reservoir of fat, shred of loose skin, or mound of cellulite—only a pure silken chamois stretched over an Aristotelian form of quintessential woman. Even the white male teachers could not help but look. An affair between her and one of the white female teachers had been rumored, but its veracity was only for Lonetta, and maybe Sanders. "Anything at all" was a statement more torturous than soothing. She should have offered it back in high school instead of now.

After the promised ten minutes, Sanders bounded into the kitchen, a metal lockbox lodged under his arm. "I don't think we'll need these," he said, nodding toward the box, "but if we're dealing with the kind of shit you said, then maybe. Let's go in the basement. I'm gonna give you a quick lesson—do some quality control."

A free-floating urgency, a panic, pressed him to depart—to do something, anything. "I can shoot," Marzee responded with an air of indifference, trying to suppress the impatience. "I shot my father's gun a few times in the air."

"Let's go," Sanders said, ignoring Marzee's response. "No bullshit. Let's go. Follow me. If you're carrying heat around me, I'm for damn sure gonna know that you can aim it."

He followed Sanders down a narrow flight of stairs through a half-painted door close to the rear entrance. Sanders stopped half-way down, confronting Marzee. "Ignore the shit you see down here. You hear me?"

Marzee returned a bland stare, slighted by Sanders notice—whatever Sanders kept in the basement was Sanders' business. He would be neither shocked nor inclined to discuss the contents. Continuing to the basement, the implicit silence had satisfied Sanders.

The basement expanded beyond the confines of the house above. Several freezers lined a wall. A partially opened door at the far end revealed a tunnel. Stacked boxes of bootlegged liquor created a maze. "Follow me. I did lots of shit down here since you were here last. Damn. Must have been, what, six, eight years?" Sanders commented, leading the way.

"Yeah. I think. At least six years, since your father died," Marzee replied.

They arrived at a brick retaining wall, behind which was dirt, and further back, into the darkness, targets hung on clothes lines. Sanders opened the metal box he had carried under his arm, and extracted two forty-five automatic pistols. "My practice range," Sanders remarked, smiling coyly. "It relaxes me from the shit upstairs. Besides, when they hear me down here practicing, it calms them too, if you know what I mean." Marzee and Sanders chuckled at the image of Sanders' customers hearing gunshots from below them.

Suddenly, an elusive perception popped into his awareness—an insight he had not recognized until now. It seized him, stunned him. Sanders trusted him. Sanders fully digested what Marzee had told him, without requiring any substantiation from external sources. "These people, they're serious. They're not neighborhood niggas," Marzee said, turning to Sanders as he shoved the clip in. "It's the shit you hear about on the news. Those motherfuckers who flew those planes into those buildings a few years ago? You know, 9/11? These motherfuckers are worse. They're planning to set off a bomb somewhere in LA. Earlier, I was on my way to the FBI building in West LA, but I stopped, and called the dude I was on my way to meet. We're supposed to meet at school later at seven."

"You told him what you saw? What you heard?" Sanders asked.

"Yeah, I did, but something's not right. I can't put my finger on it, but it just ain't right. Now I'm not even sure about meeting him. I just want to find the motherfuckers who killed my parents." He fell to his knees, crying.

Sanders knelt next to him, remaining silent. He tugged on Marzee's elbow, urging him to stand. He threw a toggle switch on a beam next to him, lighting the area behind the retaining wall, revealing three fresh targets hanging at different intervals. "Watch me carefully," Sanders said. Assuming a composed and expert stance, he squeezed off six rounds, two into each of the three targets. "Now you do it," Sanders said, motioning for Marzee to follow through quickly.

He was numb from the two hours he had traversed the full gamut of an emotional spectrum—pain so unbearable he wanted to die, an unrelenting anger, and a dire desperation to seek revenge. Now he grasped cold-hearted numbness, like the cool clutch on the pistol grip. He assumed Sanders' identical posture, mimicking his mentor with comparable composure and accuracy. Six strident blasts rang out.

"Ma man," Sanders uttered fondly, offering a confirmation not easily earned, a compliment for his marksmanship. "After you reload, keep that one. Tuck it under your shirt, behind your belt. Then let's go."

As they trudged up the stairs, Marzee remembered Sanders from his past. He had been a

303

lifelong acquaintance, a friend from a distance, an enigmatic anti-social—not an unruly criminal—a nonconformist, playing by his own rules, yet remaining in an enclave Marzee considered a cesspool. He had avoided entering into an alliance of brotherhood until now. Sanders behaved as if the alliance had been inevitable—had always existed.

When they reached the front door, Marzee was glad he had worn a jacket, covering an otherwise obvious protrusion from his lower back. As he walked through the living room area, he felt self-conscious among Sanders' customers and guests. The gun didn't give him courage. He felt more vulnerable. "Where's the car?" Marzee asked, needing to break the silence since the basement.

"At a bro's house, down the block," Sanders replied. "I got just the ride for us. I keep cars everywhere, just not at home."

Having walked three blocks through the shaded, serene blue-collar African-American family neighborhood, Marzee was surprised when they reached their destination. "You keep a car at Kip's?" Marzee said, amazed that another abandoned childhood acquaintance was on Sanders' payroll.

"No account nigga needs a car occasionally. I need a place to store it. Works for both of us," Sanders said, withholding a smirk. He pulled his cell phone from an inside pocket of his suede jacket and pressed a speed dial number. "Say. I'm tak'n the car. Yeah. You inside? No! Stay there. Don't come out. I don't have time. Yeah, I know! I see him. He's with me. Nigga look dead to you?" He slapped the phone shut, shaking his head and cursing.

Marzee and Sanders traipsed through Kip's white picket fence gate, rounded the house, and walked down a short driveway to a closed garage. He could feel eyes on him from the house. Sanders unlocked the garage and rolled up the door, revealing a late-nineties white BMW M3. "Get in," Sanders said, motioning toward the passenger side. "It doesn't attract attention. Once you get the man's attention, you're fucked," Sanders explained, searching through keys one by one on a keychain. "You said the beach area, right?"

Marzee was apprehensive about directing Sanders—giving him instructions. "Yes, the beach. When we get close, I'll let you know, but we should be very careful. Maybe drive by the house, or—"

"Let's worry about that when we get near. We don't know what's going on there now. You said they got nuclear shit. We can't just pop by, like we're delivering a pizza," Sanders interrupted.

"When we're within a mile, I'll let you know. By the way, sometime soon, I should call the man I know at the FBI." Marzee hesitated, frowning. "He's also my shrink."

"Goddamn, nigga," Sanders replied, feigning disgust. "The shit you get into. Yeah, you should call him. He'll prob'ly know more than we do." Sanders tossed his cell phone into Marzee's lap.

After fifteen minutes of ruminating while Sanders drove, Marzee jerked his head up, startled that he had been dazed for an unknown period. The last time he had looked out the window, they were backing out of Kip's driveway. "We're coming up on the Coast Highway. If you turn right at the signal, we'll be about two miles away," he remarked.

"I'm gonna park on a side street once we get up here a bit. You think the police may be looking for you?" Sanders asked.

"I don't know. Maybe," Marzee responded.

"Well, maybe ain't good enough. We can't take any chances getting pulled over," Sanders replied. "Look. Ahead, in the sky. What's that? Two helicopters buzzing around." Sanders turned right onto a side street, made a couple more turns, and parked in front of a vacant lot, aiming the car in the direction of the aerial activity he had noticed. "My guess—that's where your nuke lab is."

Merely looking in the direction of Utte's house triggered an instantaneous barrage of images from his frequent forays into the residence. The memories now ricocheted from null receptors. "That's about where the house is," he said, gesturing in the direction Sanders had pointed out. "Something happened, somebody called, for them to be flying around. I better call Dr. Dance now." The phone had lodged itself behind him. As he groped around for it, the bulge under his belt reminded him of the serious business yet to be undertaken. "This phone?" Marzee inquired, holding it up for display. "It's a generic pre-pay, not in your name?" Sanders winced with feigned disgust, indicating the question did not deserve an answer. "I don't know if they can triangulate on an unknown number or not. They probably can. Just how long would it take to get a fix, I don't know. It wouldn't be cool, getting swarmed by feds while our black asses sit here, trying to be clandestine," Marzee explained. He had memorized Dance's office number, and he pressed the buttons.

"Dr. Dance's office," the same female voice answered, though more pressured and less assured than the last time he had spoken with her.

Tempted to hang up, he could tell something was different. "Hi," he said hesitating, "It's Marzee Banks."

"Yes, Marzee, one second, please," she replied promptly, as if expecting the call. Her temperament had shed the officiousness irritating him on their first contact.

"Marzee. Hey. It's Lorn. Where are you?" Dr. Dance asked.

Lorn? All the sudden he's my buddy?
"Where am I? Say, man. I'm not playing games. What the fuck. You know what happened? I—"

"Don't tell him about your parents," Sanders interrupted suddenly. Marzee rolled his eyes, perturbed. "Just don't!" Sanders insisted.

307

"What happened, Marzee? Is somebody with you? Where are you now?" Dance asked, having relinquished some the therapist suave by which Marzee knew him. "We've done some research. Listen. We've got to get together as soon as possible."

Intent on getting more information than Dance could get from him, he was suspicious, guarded, and confrontational. "Research, huh? How many people are on this line? How many listening to us now? We on speaker? You and your FBI buddies trying to trace this call? Last thing I'm going to do is tell you where I am. What's up? What'd you find out?" Marzee inquired insistently.

"Our therapist-client relationship? We're past that now. What you told me about the nuke—there's something to it. We need to talk, face to face. Some people need to ask you some questions," Dance answered, dropping his usual soft tone.

For all I know, THEY could have killed my parents. Scum of the earth, posing as the good guys. "We're talking about as close as we're going to get. I was on my way over there. I'm glad I changed my mind," Marzee responded. A long pause ensued on the other end of the line. Marzee heard hissing and whispers. "Hello? You still there?"

"Marzee. I'm going to be straight with you. You're in a lot of trouble. I'll let you know. It appears from the evidence collected, you're involved with the people you told me about. "

The nightmare scenario he had only conjured as a remote possibility, materialized, sending him to near panic. "Me? With them? I told you EXACTLY how I know about them. There is nothing else," Marzee replied, his voice two octaves higher.

"We went to the Thorndike residence. We found Dr. Thorndike, dead. We found your fingerprints on the murder weapon. We also found samples of your DNA there."

"My DNA? You mean cum, don't you? You found evidence that I jacked off there. Hell, I told you about that."

"Marzee, I believe you. That's even more the reason for you—"

"Mr. Banks. My name is Special Agent Jefferson. I'm head of the terrorism task force for Homeland Security in Los Angeles," an unknown voice suddenly interrupted. "We know about the particle accelerator equipment in the Thorndike residence. You're trying to do the right thing, calling us. Your relationship with the Thorndike woman is irrelevant. For whatever reason, it looks like you had a change of heart, tried to stop them, and they retaliated. How far did you get in disrupting their plan? Where is the equipment now? Are you aware of their time-table for setting off the bomb?"

Marzee snapped the phone shut. He felt like the time he had evaded capture by hiding in the car trunk. *Jefferson? And he sounded black.* He opened the car door, and vomited next to the curb. After regaining his composure, he grabbed the cell phone, and yanked out the battery cartridge.

"Say, man. What the fuck! That phone cost money," Sanders yelled, protesting Marzee's destruction of his cell phone.

"They think I'm involved. And Utte's husband is dead. They think I killed him," Marzee muttered, catching his breath. "Let's move away from here fast. I don't think that phone had a GPS transponder in it, but if it did, we'll have ten thousand government motherfuckers up our ass in two minutes or less."

Sanders drove meticulously, maintaining thirty miles per hour, navigating through the residential streets until he found a major avenue outlet leading them back to the freeway. "They don't know you're with me; they don't know what car you're in, or even if you're in a car. They prob'ly think you're still putt-putting around on that piece of shit you drive. Too bad you even called them. They might have thought your ass got blown up in the house," Sanders said, trying to coax a smile from Marzee.

Marzee sank into a spiraling vortex, digging for memories containing clues about his taunters. *Go deep, deep to when I was sitting in the closet. When I was sitting in that dark, fucking, laundry closet, trying to sniff that bitch's dirty drawers, I heard them say something, something that wasn't planned 'cause they didn't know I was there. The building has a permit for radioactive materials. What could that be?* "When I overheard them talking, they said they were collecting everything in a warehouse at San Pedro Harbor," Marzee said half-consciously, still groping his recollection for clues.

"San Pedro? Warehouse? Damn, man. That's my turf. I do all kinds of business over there. I know the area," Sanders offered with confidence.

Still focused on clue retrieval, he ignored Sanders' comment. "Problem is, how do you conceal that much radiation? Even lining and insulators won't shield that kind of radiation from suspicion, unless it's supposed to be there. Unless it's legitimate," Marzee remarked, pondering puzzle pieces.

Chapter 15
Smoke Screen

Guilt and shame tempered his mood—guilt for involving Sanders; shame for the circumstances fostering the involvement. He wavered from reluctant to steadfast as he mulled over their situation. "You're right. I prob'ly shouldn't have called, but now I know what I didn't know before," Marzee declared. "I realize now—Utte knew I was following her, stalking her all along. They went to my house looking for me. They didn't find me, so they killed my parents. They left the bodies as a calling card." He stared at Sanders, who returned an expectant expression. "They don't know what I know, so they needed to find me. That's why they ransacked my computer. My parents were a message—to come looking for them. And they don't know if I told anyone else. That's why they moved all their shit. And they killed their main man, the scientist who put all the shit together for them. She killed her own husband. Man! I watched them fuck through their back window. Her own husband. Cold bitch."

His guilt, his shame, his forlorn—orchestrated a clashing and disorganized symphony of emotions. "Sanders," Marzee said softly, nudging him on the elbow. "I need for you to listen to me. I mean really listen. Pull over right here." Comprehending Marzee's earnestness, he slowed the car, turned into a strip mall parking lot, and parked amidst a covey of other cars.

"What's up?" Sanders replied, turning to face Marzee.

"I got you into a world of shit, man. I'm sorry. I—"

Sanders squeezed Marzee's shoulder. "Ma man, you're all right with me. You're all right. We're both in this now," Sanders offered reassuringly.

Appreciative of his friend's genuineness, he still did not believe Sanders had grasped the circumstances fully. "This thing. It's not just the LAPD or Sherriff's Department. We're talking the highest levels of US government pigs—FBI, CIA, NSA, Homeland Security. God knows what else," Marzee said.

"Still just a bunch of white men employed by some initials," Sanders replied, rolling his eyes.

He admired the manner Sanders could reduce any situation to its common denominator, but he recognized Sanders had over-simplified the situation as well. "Yeah, but these white men have tremendous power at their disposal. They're fuck'n dangerous. They can do anything and get away with it. They could be watching us through a satellite right now. I guarantee, they're looking for us, they just don't know what to look for yet. And that's just a matter of time. If they've already been to your house, they probably know what car we took. They've already got our description and the vehicle we're driving. Hopefully, my blown-up house and parents' bones will keep them busy a little longer. But I'm telling you, that's where it's going. That's why that fuck, Jefferson, or whatever the fuck his name was—that's why he interrupted Dance. They see me as a link to a cell of terrorists bent on setting off a nuclear bomb somewhere in Los Angeles. Now, you tell me. How much do think they want to find me?"

"Is there a reward? Nigga, I should turn you in myself!" Sanders announced with a guffaw. Marzee couldn't help but laugh with him.

Deeper than gratitude, his love for his friend surged—a feeling he could not fully express. "Thank you for helping me. I should've come to you a long time ago," Marzee muttered, close to tears.

"It's OK, nigga. We're cool. Now, what the fuck we doin, goin shopping?" Sanders replied, impatient.

During the conversation he had overheard while hiding in Utte's laundry closet, he believed the women stated vital pieces of a puzzle. *It's just a puzzle. I can solve it.* "They moved their shit, and they said they were almost ready. They've got to be in some warehouse on San Pedro Harbor. But when I overheard their conversation, they weren't clear about where the place was." He turned, staring at Sanders, who sat expectedly staring at him. "Say, man! I discovered that they're Iranians from a simple name search using the Internet," Marzee

314

blurted, giving cause for this impromptu respite in a parking lot. "Just bear with me. There IS a method to my madness."

He closed his eyes and rolled his head around his shoulders, attempting to relax and squelch the noise, inside and out,. *Think. Concentrate.* "Utte said she wanted to surprise her Iranian friend. Think about it. They have to amass a large quantity of nuclear material in one location without it being detected. I read after 9/11 the harbors were the most unsecure places. You could slip anything through. Remember? That dumb motherfucker, Bush, wanted to hand over managing the harbors to his Arab buddies. White America was scared of terrorists sneaking nuclear material through the harbors, so they installed all kinds of radioactivity detectors, especially at San Pedro. So, if they're at the harbor, Utte and her pals are doing their thing under the U.S. government's nose.

"When Afsane asked where they were assembling the bomb, Utte said she wanted to surprise her. She said, 'think about when you worked with radiation as an engineer.' How would you hide radioactive material without all kinds of shielding in an area that's under scrutiny for radioactivity?" He paused as his thoughts morphed into a solution. "That's it! If you had some shit you wanted to hide, where would be the best place for it?" Marzee excitedly posed the question, not really expecting an answer.

"Shit? Like weed?" Sanders asked dumbfounded.

"No. I mean, real shit. Like, if YOUR shit were really valuable—like you think it is, anyway—and you wanted to hide it, where would be the place to hide your golden shit?"

"With other shit?" Sanders answered with uncertainty.

"Exactly. Their bomb factory is in the middle of other radioactive material—most likely, legal and documented. Now, what's radioactive that's not controlled by government security?" Marzee inquired with escalating intensity.

"Daddy had a watch that glowed in the dark. He said it was radioactive," Sanders said.

"Yeah, right. Watches with radium hands. I don't even know if they make those anymore. But a big fuck'n' warehouse was full of boxes of watches with radium-coated hands, then, yeah, that'd be a good place to start. Radioactive commercial products, and a lot of them."

"Say, man. I don't have to remind you, we're still not too far away from where all the bullshit went down. Maybe we shouldn't be sit'n here," Sanders remarked.

"Prob'ly the best place, unless a black-and-white cruises by," Marzee replied. "They may have issued an APB, but I don't think so. They don't want to panic the public, but they want me real bad." He scanned the area, focusing toward the business storefronts occupying the shopping center.

"See that Internet cafe over there? I just got an idea. I need to use the Internet. Let's park closer. We shouldn't walk across this parking lot. We're too much out in the open."

They cruised the lot until finding space close to the Internet Cafe—a space secluded between a large pickup and a U-Haul truck.

"I'll stay in the car. Don't make sense, me going in with you. Would just draw attention. I'm too dark to use a computer, no how," Sanders announced with resolve.

"That's bullshit, man!" Marzee protested with a stern reproach. "But it's prob'ly best we don't go in together. I'll be right back."

Sanders nodded, rolling his eyes, mindful of his correctness in the matter. Marzee cracked the car door open into the barely adequate clearance next to the truck. Relieved he was on the U-Haul side, the view from the street was blocked. He crept slowly to the edge of the truck for a furtive peek, then he scanned the sky—no helicopters. He ran the one hundred feet to the Internet Cafe storefront.

As he stepped through the entrance, he noticed a wall-mounted, flat screen TV airing CNN—seeing his picture and name on the six o'clock news would be difficult to handle right now. Quickly he scrutinized the booth-seated patrons. *Everyone's looking at their screens. That dude's playing WoW, that dude's looking at porn, she's looking up some shit. Ain't no one reading the news no how.* "How much for an hour?" he asked the inattentive attendant at the front counter. *Skinny, pasty, pony-tailed, stingy-haired, book-reading, thick-eye-glass wearing motherfucker. Any other day, I'd be in your ass for not looking at me.*

"Five dollars," the man responded apathetically, turning to check the unoccupied workstations. "Use number five."

Marzee slapped a five dollar bill on the counter, creating a strident cracking noise to purposely startle the attendant. As he walked to his assigned workstation he overheard the man say, "Thanks. I needed that."

Not smart. I don't need to attract any attention. A timer appeared in the upper right corner of his screen, counting down from one hour. *I can't stay here forever. I've got to connect Afsane with engineering, radioactive material, anything else I can remember.*

He brought up Google. *What I know: she was an engineer. She worked with radioactive material. She worked in Munich and she's not German, meaning she wasn't working on any government projects. That means she worked for a commercial company. They're hiding three hundred radioactive pellets. It's not a defense building. Utte mentioned warehouse. They store lots of shit at the harbor to be shipped overseas. Radioactive products shipped overseas. High quantity. Not watches.*

After trying various combinations of search terms, he painstakingly scrolled down and examined a list of hits from searching on "radioactive material" and "commercial uses," finally stopping at: "Smoke Detectors. Americium-241, used as an alpha particle source to ionize air." *Every house, hotel, motel, prob'ly dudes living in cardboard boxes have a smoke detector. That's it. Smoke detectors.* He continued reading the article. He reset his search box, and typed "smoke detector" and "Munich, Germany." Among the hits he noticed Siemens had a smoke detector facility in Munich. *Got it! Afsane was a smoke detector engineer in Munich. They're building the bomb where there's a bunch of smoke detectors.*

Clearing the search screen, he glanced at the timer. Forty minutes remained. *I could have worked for the NSA, or CIA, or even up in Dance's office.* He contemplated in a self-congratulatory day dream, and he drifted off momentarily.

His short-lived spell of tranquility was interrupted with a jolt. "Say, man!" Sanders hissed in his ear. "I had to bail. Pigs found the car. We gotta sneak outta here and find some alternate transportation. Quick."

Rather than resort to panic, Sanders' unscheduled appearance kicked him into an emotional stride. He looked down the aisle, staring out the front pane glass window. The lackadaisical clerk had approached the window, curious about the commotion outside. Three police cars had blocked Sanders' BMW. *No helicopter noise overhead.*

319

We've got to find cover fast. He scribbled on a notepad: restroom in back. Go.

Sanders dashed toward the back of the store before Marzee had completed the note. Marzee remained seated for several seconds, maintaining reconnaissance while Sanders cleared the way. The customers, entranced in their Internet pursuits, had not noticed Sanders' sudden arrival nor the activity in the parking lot.

That clerk has to be brain-dead, not noticing two black men wanting to use Internet facilities within fifteen minutes of each other in a predominantly white area, Marzee pondered. *I wish that asshole would get out of the way. He's blocking my view.* Tilting into the aisle as far as he could without drawing attention, he tried to ascertain the commotion outside. He twisted around to check Sanders, who had already gone into the restroom. He looked back to the clerk, who was still transfixed outside. He pushed back, and walked toward the back, passing both occupied and vacant workstation booths. At the bathroom door, he made another cursory glance toward the front, then went inside, and locked the door.

"Goddamn, that was close," Sanders exclaimed, breaking his usual stoic demeanor. "I caught a glimpse of a black and white cruising the other side of the parking lot. I got suspicious, so I got out and ran over here. Sure 'nough, he had spotted our car. My mama always said, 'Boy, listen to your gut. It never lies.'"

"I'm glad you didn't try the back door. I think it's alarmed. It would have caused a stir. Let's see if we can get through this window," Marzee suggested.

"We may have to use the back door if we can't get through this motherfucker. And we're gonna have to be fast," Sanders responded. "They're gonna be in here any minute."

Sanders stepped on the toilet seat for height. Pushing on the two-foot wide window with both hands, it slid opened six inches and stopped. Marzee had positioned himself to the side of the window, and noticed the security stops.

"We're gonna have to break it," Sanders whispered, pulling out his gun.

"No, wait," Marzee said. "These blocks slide to the side to let the window open." He unlatched the bolt, and moved the stops sideways. "It should open all the way now."

Sanders pushed the window as far up as it would slide. Upon punching out the screen, he poked his head through. "It's clear. Let's go." He squeezed head-first through the opened window. Marzee followed, each landing on his hands, then falling against the wall to right himself. Marzee's gun slipped from the grip of his belt, bouncing to the asphalt pavement.

"Damn. I'm glad the safety was on. Gun going off would sure blow our cover," Sanders commented.

Always apprehensive about surveillance aircraft, Marzee vigilantly scanned the sky for helicopters. "No shit," Marzee replied. "And we got no cover." Looking in both directions, they were confined within a long, narrow back lot, providing enough space for loading and employee parking. From their vantage point, they could see clearly in both directions. A brick wall bounded the rear access lot, facing the building wall from about twenty feet. "We gotta jump that wall," Marzee said, "And I don't know what's on the other side. But we gotta get outta here."

They sprinted to the wall, leaping it in unison, then hooked the top edge, and hoisted themselves over. Upon dropping to the other side, they landed in a concrete sidewalk-wide, V-shaped drainage ditch, bounded by yet another brick wall.

"From the top of the wall, I saw some office-looking buildings about one hundred yards that way," Marzee said, panting, pointing to their right. "Let's go."

Marzee and Sanders ran, balancing themselves along the slanted edges of the trench. Sanders recoiled from one side to the other, trying to avoid the shallow water in the middle. Marzee remained to one side, balancing himself, edging one foot in front of the other. He followed closely behind Sanders, struggling to not panic. The physical obstacles and the logistics facing them distracted him from being totally beleaguered.

"OK, stop. We're about where I think I saw the office buildings. They must have a parking lot," Marzee remarked, winded. "Let's go before some shit starts flying over us." He looked overhead, then back from where they had come. "No one following us. Guess they didn't get to that restroom, yet."

"Say, man. I told you I'm with you, but you didn't tell me about sloshing through no sewers. Goddamn, these shoes cost me five hundred dollars," Sanders complained.

"Good you didn't wear that two thousand dollar jacket I heard you brag about. We'd have to lay it over that barbed wire to get over this wall," Marzee replied with a dead-pan look.

"What the fuck you talk'n about? Nigga, I'd throw YOU over that shit before I'd use one of my expensive jackets," Sanders said, sneering. "We're gonna use that K-Mart look'n piece-of-shit you're wearing. Take that shit off. Let's get going."

Marzee pulled off his accurately-described tan jacket, but he was concerned about exposing the borrowed gun protruding from the small of his back. "One of us has to stand on the other's shoulders —"

"I don't trust standing on your puny, weak-ass shoulders. You might drop me into that nasty sewer shit," Sanders interrupted, stooping down, so Marzee could get a footing. "And, pleasssse, scrape the shit off the bottoms of your shoes first. This sweater costs more than you!"

Grabbing a near-by chunk of concrete, Marzee scrapped the bottoms of his shoes, then balanced himself on Sanders' shoulders, one foot at a time. As Sanders stood, Marzee could see over the top of the wall. He unwrapped his jacket from his neck, and draped it over the barbed wire lining the top of the concrete wall. "We're cool. It's a parking lot for the office building I saw. Before we jump over, we need to make sure no over-zealous rent-a-pig is patrolling," Marzee remarked.

"Hurry the fuck up! Yo' ass isn't as light as I thought," Sanders yelled.

"I'll prop myself across the top of the fence, then pull you up," Marzee responded. "Must be about six o'clock. Most people have left, but there's still a few cars here."

He doubled his jacket for extra thickness, protecting himself from the fence barbs. Placing it carefully over the wires, he pressed his stomach against his jacket cushion, and hung jackknife-style, across the top of the fence. He grabbed Sanders' hands, helping him repel up the wall. They both jumped off the top, Marzee snatching his perforated garment before leaping.

"There's a truck next to the wall. Let's get behind it," Sanders said.

After taking cover behind a small truck parked next to the brick wall fence, Marzee took aim at the four-story commercial structure he had seen earlier. He studied the back of the building, eyeing two sets of double doors facing them across four rows of sparsely parked cars. The onset of dusk triggered automatic lighting systems, which illuminated the parking lot and building entrance lights.

Hyper-vigilant about air reconnaissance, he responded to the barely discernible noise. "I hear the helicopter now," Marzee remarked. "They'll see us, even lodged between this van and wall. Let's get under this truck."

Laying belly-down, side-by-side, on the ground under the truck, Marzee and Sanders perused the area for available transportation. The adrenaline rush of hiding and escaping sparked reminders of past, persistent behavior now pathetic and abandoned. *Sand fly, you can't help me now.*

"Say, man! Assuming you don't know anything about jacking a car, I'm telling you right now, we need to find something quick and easy. No alarms, nothing to cut, and for damned sure, no Lo-Jack. We're not well equipped," Sanders remarked with atypical stress in his voice. Within seconds of his rant, he nudged Marzee, nodding toward a tattered, old-model Blazer pulling up next to the building entrance. "Check this out," Sanders remarked. "You know what that is? Mexican janitors. Our transportation has arrived. And look, all four of them went inside with their cleaning shit. I bet you one hundred dollars they left the key in the car."

Marzee didn't want to steal these people's car. It was their livelihood, and probably their only mode of transportation. But arguing with Sanders about waiting for another car was not an option. "No bet. I believe you," Marzee said drearily. He scooted to the edge of the truck undercarriage, and scanned the sky. "That helicopter is buzzing around the parking lot we just came from, but he's going to be widening his search radius soon. He prob'ly doesn't know what to look for."

"No shit. Let's hope they keep it that way. We got to get over there, get that car, and go. Goddamn. I came here in my BMW, and drive away in a fucked-up piece-of-shit janitor wagon. Ain't that a bitch," Sanders whined, shaking his head and pursing his lips.

"We haven't driven away, yet. Those janitors are all still inside. Since the helicopter's probably looking for two, we'd make it obvious if we both cross the lot together. Why don't you walk over there, take the thing, then drive over here, pull up real close to the truck, and I'll sneak in?" Marzee said.

"That ain't a bad idea, actually," Sanders responded. "I'll be right back with the transportation." Carefully looking side to side, up and down, he came out from under the truck. Cursing about debris on his clothes, he brushed off his pants and sweater, and walked calmly toward the cleaning crew's Blazer.

Marzee watched Sanders intently while still maintaining a vigilant ear on the distant helicopter—it sounded closer. He froze when a

326

woman emerged through one of the building's double doors as Sanders approached the Blazer. She ignored Sanders, and proceeded to her parked car. He was impressed with Sanders' disposal of fanfare and trimmings when he reached the Blazer. Without ado, he opened the door, started the engine, and drove toward Marzee's position.

The helicopter had widened its orbit to include their parking lot under its sweep. Marzee was scared, but confident—if he and Sanders remained under cover, they would not be detected. Sanders pulled up next to Marzee's hiding place. When the helicopter was at the far end of its circumference, Marzee crawled out and got into the passenger side. Sanders drove steadily through the parking lot, to the exit, and out to the adjacent street.

"You owe me a hundred dollars," Sanders said unflinchingly. "And buckle your seatbelt. We don't want no reason to be fucked with."

He complied and buckled his seatbelt, but he was dismayed by encountering still wet stains on the seat. "Fuck you. I told you, 'no bet.' I figured you'd be right. Say, man. Let's get the fuck outta here, and away from that helicopter's line of sight. If the Man searches that parking lot, those Mexicans you stole that car from are gonna be forced to tell them they just got jacked," Marzee remarked. "Besides, we were so busy running, I didn't tell you what I found out while I was in that Internet cafe. I know how they camouflage the radioactivity,"

Marzee said, hesitating and turning toward Sanders curiously. "Didn't you brag about knowing San Pedro Harbor?"

"Brag?" Sanders drawled defiantly. "Yeah, bro. I got business dealings there. I have a buddy— well, more of a business connection, if you know what I mean. He's old, been around there for years. But let me get us the fuck out of here first. OK?"

Jostled by the excitement of escaping the Internet Cafe, climbing barbed wire adorned brick walls, hiding under trucks, and stealing a car, Marzee had put his findings on hold. As he re-examined his discovery, a chill overcame him. "It just dawned on me. We don't know what the fuck we're doing. We're just driving into a dark fuck'n forest with no headlights," Marzee announced with tremulous voice.

"This ain't somethin' you can plan. You just have to do!" Sanders barked. "Don't start that negative, doomsday shit with me now, nigga. We've come too far, we're in too deep." He paused at a stop sign, then quickly made a right turn, accelerating into traffic. "I know where I am now, and I know where I'm go'n. Up a little further, we'll catch the freeway. I think we're far enough along so the Man won't catch up with us for awhile. So, tell me. What'd you find out?" Sanders asked, more upbeat that usual.

Leaving outcome to fate and destiny disturbed Marzee. He preferred planning, organizing, and mapping contingencies. Having no plan removed his false sense of control, and that made him very uneasy. Although he was pleased with his discoveries, having no set course troubled him. "I found out how they hide the radioactivity from detection. They're building their bomb where they build or store smoke detectors," Marzee responded. "Smoke detectors use a radioactive isotope called Americium 241. It's perfectly legal, so the radioactivity detected wherever the smoke detector facility is would be acceptable to whatever or whoever does the detecting."

"My man at the harbor, he'll know. He knows everything, ol' Saul," Sanders said, motioning to the road sign indicating Interstate 405 was another two miles.

Since Marzee didn't trust Sanders' assertion of an "all knowing, all wise" associate, his discomfort with the situation continued un-assuaged. "If I may ask, who's this wise friend of yours? You trust him? If he's so smart, what's he doing hanging around the harbor for so long?" Marzee asked.

"Say, man. You need to have a little faith. I know the dude. I trust him. He knows lots of shit," Sanders replied, scanning the road intensely. "But if you must know, I been importing shit from him for, damn, seven years now. Not drugs. Absinthe."

"Absence?" Marzee questioned. "You mean, he kills people? He makes someone absent?"

"No, nigga! Not absence. Absinthe. You drink it. It comes in a bottle," Sanders replied impatiently after articulating "absinthe." "They make it in Europe, but not here. It's alcohol with a psychedelic kick. It's good shit. And I'm the only nigga who imports the shit. It's illegal to distill in America. I sell it mostly to white folks, but niggas who try it? Shit, they just keep com'n back for more."

The developing darkness bathed its inhabitants in anonymity, helping Marzee feel less distraught. Sanders fumbled around the dashboard, searching for the headlight switch. The late hour reminded Marzee of his missed appointment with Dance. "What time is it?" Marzee asked.

"Seven forty-five," Sanders answered, glancing at his watch. "You need to relax. You didn't do noth'n 'cept jack off. The Man's not gonna execute you for that. You'll be a fuck'n hero, jacking these Arabs. Right?" He nudged Marzee on the arm, attempting to cheer him up.

I can't cry—I want to. I can't die—I wish it would happen instantly, right now. I feel like exploding. He shivered, thinking about the hours he had spent, cramped in the Mustang trunk. *Trust. I can trust Sanders. I always have. It's not faith. It's trust.* "I don't trust the Man," Marzee blurted. "No trust, end of discussion, period. Whatever they say, it's a lie. I trust you, so wherever you're goin, just take us there. I got no plan." He glanced at the speedometer: sixty-seven miles per hour. *Sanders is a survivor. I guess, from Darwin's point of view, that makes him—if not very smart, at least evolved.*

330

"As I think about seeing what I saw—my parents—
the story is more painful than the reality. The
image, the memory, hurts more than being there."

Sanders remained silent, maintaining his
driving vigil, watching for signs of interception, on
the road and from above. Marzee recognized
Sanders was pre-occupied and directed. He looked
to the side, watching objects whiz by. Then he'd
fixate on an object, holding it in focus until they
passed it, biding his time en-route to San Pedro
Harbor.

Chapter 16
Absinthe Makes the Hearth Grow Fodder

The drone of the freeway had hypnotized Marzee. He had fallen asleep while Sanders drove them to their destination at San Pedro Harbor. Startled by the cessation of motion, he awoke with a jolt. They had stopped. The sign in front of him read: Feuerstein Imports-Fine European Commodities.

"Good, bro. You're awake. I'm glad you fell asleep. You were goin fuck'n nuts, talk'n about movies and shit. We're at my business associate's place at the harbor," Sanders said, grinning. "He's here. I know he's here, 'cause he's always here. He ain't got nowhere else to go no how. He's gonna be pissed though. I gotta get him to open up the warehouse so I can pull this piece-of-shit inside. If those Mexican janitors reported it stolen, they done it by now. Got to be careful of your spy-in-the-sky shit!" he said jeeringly, pointing up.

A spring of joy boosted him, followed by downfall. *It was a dream, a nightmare. My parents.* "How long was I asleep?" Marzee asked, dazed and semi-conscious.

"Not long, maybe thirty minutes. I got off the freeway, took a couple of detours, side streets. I been here a lot, but since 9/11 they got roadblocks in some places. You know, random searches," Sanders replied.

332

Sanders' remark about "spy-in-the-sky" annoyed him. An irritating characteristic, Sanders devalued concepts he did not understand, even though he fully accepted whatever Marzee told him about technology. "That 'spy-in-the-sky shit' to which you referred, could zoom in on your black ass and put it on every TV screen in the world instantly. I'm glad you took precautions," Marzee said, stretching and looking around.

"I'm gonna run around the back. He lives in there, but he ain't supposed to," Sanders said smirking, deliberately ignoring Marzee's remark. "Stay here 'til I get back. He's nervous around strangers. Actually, more like paranoid." Sanders closed the car door gently.

As he glanced from side to side, he noticed Sanders had parked, cramped within a small loading dock. The miniature warehouses were densely spaced, and the paucity of area lighting made him feel more secure in the misty harbor night air. An avid student of leading edge technology, he knew even the veil of darkness could not hide them from infrared-viewing satellites. *If I can see my house using Google, the government can see my balls in the black of night.* He whimpered with this thought, remembering he no longer had a house, and a moroseness started to engulf him. Then Sanders suddenly opened the door.

"Saul's here. We gotta drive around the back. He's got a spare warehouse with noth'n in it right now, so we can park in there," Sanders announced. "How you doin'? You been out here cry'n, bro? You ain't think'n of offing yourself, are you? Not after all this shit you got me into."

Awkward, he felt like he was just caught doing something private and otherwise embarrassing. "Suicide? Nigga! Fuck you. If I wanted to kill myself, I would've done it by now," Marzee replied, upset by his own transparency. He calmed quickly. "You know me—revenge and glory—that's all I'm thinking now, revenge and glory."

"Good. Keep think'n that," Sanders asserted, starting the car.

They backed up through a cloud of exhaust smoke, which caused Marzee to hack. "Damn. This thing belches enough smog! I'm glad it was dark while we were driving. Didn't you notice all that fuck'n smoke?" Marzee yelled, marginalizing the despondency Sanders had detected.

"Fuck yeah, I noticed it. I noticed it when we were lying under that truck in that parking lot," Sanders replied. "Saul's gonna hate it. Wait. You'll see."

They crept through narrow passages between small warehouses and stacked shipping crates, finally reaching a small, carved-out clearing. A squalor, rotund pot-bellied man with near-shoulder-length, gray, stringy hair motioned them into the garage. As they drove slowly past him, he coughed, gagged, grabbed his throat, and dramatized dying of asphyxiation. Marzee liked him

334

immediately; he couldn't take his eyes off of him as they pulled into the narrow opening, barely scraping the edge. Though the man acted out his displeasure with the stolen car's excessive exhaust, he was keen on Marzee as well, and tracked him behind his thick lenses.

Since he didn't have enough clearance on his side to open the door, Marzee scooted over to exit after Sanders. Sanders side stepped along the car, cursing and complaining the entire time, as his clothes wiped against the vehicle. Marzee followed behind Sanders, trying not to crowd him. The anticipation of meeting Sanders' friend, and the man's sheer theatrics, had momentarily distracted him from his current woes.

"My gawd. Someone give me my Nobel prize. I just discovered the cause of global warming. What the hell are you doing driving such a thing! You, Frank, of all people! Divine and holy Frank! What are you doing? Never mind. I know. You've suddenly taken on the path of altruism and philanthropy. You've come to pick up a large shipment of absinthe, and you're going to deliver it to those less worthy than you," Saul declared, limbs and face alive with expression.

Marzee recognized this man must be special friend to Sanders, as Sanders hated being called Frank, and usually corrected or dismissed even the casual offender. Yet Sanders tolerated it from Saul. He even smiled coyly. The man's eyes glued on Marzee, he continued his monologue about the smoking car, pollutants, and the environment. Intrigued by Saul's histrionic performance, Marzee added the man's overall scruffy appearance to the composition: Mets t-shirt, indiscernible-color shorts to his knees, tattered sandals, and skullcap.

After waving off several attempts from Sanders to intervene, he stopped. "So, who do we have here?" the man asked, directing his query toward Marzee while bending, squinting his eyes and angling his head. "What are you? I can't tell your ethnic background. Let me hear you say something ethnic."

Dumbfounded by the request, Marzee looked to Sanders for direction. "Well, talk for the man," Sanders insisted.

"Pleased to meet you. My name is Marzee Banks," Marzee said, extending his hand.

"My hand is dirty, and so is yours," Sanders' friend said, declining the handshake. "You a mulatto? You're not an Arab, but you sound intelligent, too intelligent to be hanging around him," Sanders' friend said, gesturing toward Sanders.

Marzee glanced at Sanders, who nodded affirmatively. "I'm not a mulatto," Marzee answered. "Both my parents are—were—black. But they each had lots of other races mixed in, including African."

"African-American, Black, Negro, colored. Hell, I can't keep up. My name is Saul Feuerstein."

The German-sounding name reminded him of Utte, and the other events leading to this moment. He sank, and recovered. "It's German for Firestone," Marzee commented.

"Yeah, it's German for Firestone," Saul repeated mockingly. "Feuer means fire; stein means stone. Most German Jews changed their German-sounding names to English words when they got here. They didn't want to be reminded of *Deutschland*," he enunciated mockingly, "and even forbade their children to speak German! My family, for one, didn't go for that. They kept their original name intact."

Saul is wonderful. He can't be for real, he thought. *I wish Sanders had brought me here long ago, before all this.* Saul challenged Marzee, reminding him of playing the dozens with Freddie and Richard. "Your family's original name can't be German. Your ancestors emigrated to Europe centuries ago," Marzee recited, alluding to some history of European Jews he recalled. "Somebody changed something along the way, so your namesake is not that etymologically pure."

"And your ancestors 'emigrated' here centuries ago, not in first class cabins, I might add, and you can be sure, their name wasn't Banks," Saul replied, smirking, but acknowledging Marzee's discerning response. Then he furiously fanned at the air in front of his face. "Let's get out of here before we die of lung cancer," Saul insisted, motioning to the door.

337

The trio filed through the slit between the heisted Blazer and the door frame. Outside, Saul pressed a remote, which closed the a sliding aluminum door. Motioning impatiently for Marzee and Sanders to follow him, they obediently slipped through a short labyrinth between buildings to a narrow door. After fumbling through a jailer's set of keys, Saul turned a deadbolt, and all stepped inside.

The utter disarray of junk and mess stunned Marzee, disabling him momentarily. Facing him, old television sets lined one wall, piled floor-to-ceiling high. A cursory look-around yielded dishwashers, car parts, sofas turned on end, antique-looking lamps, computer monitors, tables, chairs, washing machines, and dozens of sealed wooden crates.

Saul stared at Marzee, as if absorbing him for a chemical analysis. "You and your friend are in trouble, or else you wouldn't have shown up like this," he said turning from Marzee to Sanders.

"According to ma man," Sanders replied, gesturing to Marzee, "we're all in deep trouble unless we do something quick."

"We? We includes me," Saul said, laughing nervously. "I'm always in trouble. I just don't bother to find out about what! This all sounds very serious—or mysterious. Maybe WE need a drink first. How about a shot of your next order of absinthe, Frank? You two, take a seat. Look around for a chair," Saul added, waving circles in the general direction of the table.

Marzee and Sanders scouted the bare concrete floor for chairs strewn about Saul's warehouse sprawl. Besides the single mismatched metal and vinyl kitchen chair conspicuously sitting in front of a half-eaten pastrami sandwich, Marzee didn't detect a lived-in ambience. He assumed Saul had disappeared into the kitchen, an area divided by juxtaposed metal cabinets. Sanders found some folding chairs, and they sat at the table with the pastrami sandwich.

"Marzee, I'm a slob, and I like it that way. I'm the original hippie," Saul yelled from behind the cabinets. "Frank. Your customers will like this new batch. Very pure, very smooth. And I've been told it achieves the desired effects."

Saul emerged from his kitchen behind the cabinets with an absinthe bottle and three jelly glasses adorned with popular cartoon figures. "Help yourself. It's Frank's money," Saul remarked, placing bottle and glasses on the table. "I don't drink." He eyed Sanders and Marzee. "So, what's this I'm in trouble for now?"

"You OK to talk, man? Or do you want me to start?" Sanders inquired with sympathetic consideration.

Not knowing quite where to begin, Marzee suddenly erupted into deep sobbing. As he heaved, images of his parents tormented him. "You—" Marzee said, trembling, not able to finish his sentence.

"He found his parents murdered at his house, today," Sanders explained, picking up after Marzee. "After he found them, he burned his house to the ground, and came to me."

"What! Oh my god. No!" Saul cried. "Your parents? Murdered? Your house, burned down? Who? Did you call the police?"

Still choked up, he shook his head to reply. Sanders squeezed his arm. "No, no police. It's a long, strange story," Sander responded. "Let's just suffice it to say, ma man here got his nose opened behind a woman. The wrong woman. She's a serious terrorist."

Struggling to regain his composure, Marzee stiffened his body, shook his head, and wiped his face vigorously with the back of his hands. "I'm OK now," he muttered in subdued volume. "Saul, it's a long, complicated story. The summary? I stalked the wrong woman. She was involved in an international terrorist ring. I saw the lab they make nuclear material in, and I overheard their plan to set the nuke off somewhere in LA." Saul's agape mouth didn't give him confidence his explanation was getting through.

"You hear about some idiots with an atom bomb in LA, and you come to me?" Saul exclaimed, looking wildly between Sanders and Marzee. "The only thing I can do is give you advice: let's call the authorities right now!"

"No! Wait!" Sanders yelled, holding Saul arm. "We're not stupid. We know that! He already called the FBI. Hear him out first."

Marzee hoped Sanders knew what he was doing by bringing them to Saul for help. He didn't know where to turn if Saul insisted on calling the police. With resolve, he mustered the energy to continue. "The terrorists knew I was stalking her, and they implicated me. They even made it appear as if I killed my own parents AND killed her husband. The FBI has proof I was in the house. They believe somehow I'M part of the terrorist ring. I know this because an agent told me, and Sanders and I saw them buzzing around this woman's house from afar. Calling them will only put me in their custody with the terrorists still out there." Suddenly he remembered the picture of John Thorndike he had printed in the library. He pulled it from his pocket and handed it to Saul.

Saul put on his glasses. He unfolded the paper and scrutinized it, squinting his eyes and moving it back and forth from his face. "I've seen this man around here," Saul commented thoughtfully.

"We didn't come to you for your wit and wisdom," Sanders remarked with stern familiarity. "We came here 'cause Marzee discovered they were building the bomb in YOUR neighborhood, around here. And now! What you just said about seeing him. Man! That means good brother here ain't crazy after all."

"You say, they're building it around here?" Saul gasped, dropping the paper to the table. He started to get up hastily.

With delayed effect, Saul's words trickled into Marzee's awareness. *He's seen him around here? That can't be coincidence.* "Listen to me. Something is wrong, very wrong," Marzee exclaimed. "If you call them, we're dead. Sanders said you could help, that we could trust you. You know the area AND you think you saw Thorndike."

"You two, both of you, are bright young men. I've known Frank here for years since he was a small boy. He's like a son to me. I knew his father. I believe you, what you're telling me, but I don't understand. There are people trained to handle these situations, just what you're talking about," Saul remarked with deliberation.

Convincing Saul to help them—and to not call the authorities—burdened Marzee's already tenuous stability. He needed assurance Saul was manageable. As Sanders conducted a side conversation with Saul, Marzee perused the room. His scan stopped at a desktop computer setup in a corner. "Saul, does that computer work, there in the corner? Are you Internet-connected?" Marzee asked with guarded interest.

"I couldn't do business without it," Saul responded bluntly. "You need to do something?"

Who was Jefferson? The intruding voice— the name—haunted him. His investigation had been cut short at the Internet cafe, and he had not

342

completed compiling the terms and names lingering in his personal cache. Eager to resume the research, he felt obliged to finalize his explanation to Saul. "One thing I left out. I was seeing a shrink, who unbeknownst to me, worked for the FBI. I had called him first, and was on my way to see him before I went home to check on my parents. Then later, while we were driving, when we saw the helicopters, I called to tell him not to meet me. Another voice broke in, interrupting me and this FBI-therapist. He introduced himself as Special Agent Jefferson. He tried to sweet talk me into turning myself in. So, to answer your question: Yes, I would like to use your computer to find out who this Jefferson is," Marzee explained.

Rising from his chair, Saul patted Sanders on his arm with assurance. "I'm not calling anyone. Come, I'll turn it on. Search 'til your heart's content," Saul said, turning to Marzee and motioning to follow him.

Marzee sprang from his chair, eager to get started. *Mama told me to trust my gut. She also told me to have all my ducks lined up before I make a move. My gut tells me something's wrong with Jefferson, and he's a duck who for damned sure needs to be lined up.* He stood behind Saul, who sat, tapping his fingers while his computer booted. After the system had fully started, Saul got up and motioned for Marzee to sit.

Marzee immediately brought up Google. At the search window, he typed "Jefferson" and "FBI," producing hundreds of hits. After several unsuccessful trials, he narrowed his search, typing: "Jefferson, terrorism, Federal Bureau of Investigation, and Los Angeles." Amazed that so many search terms converged to over a dozen hits, he clicked the first link: "Cecil Jefferson promoted to Terrorism Head, Los Angeles Division." A burst of adrenaline deepened his intensity. He read the article, mumbling occasionally as he read. *It'd be nice to find his picture,* he pondered. He followed other links, examining sundry articles while Sanders and Saul discussed matters unrelated. Switching to image search, he scoured the image databases, looking for a picture of Jefferson.

His gaze narrowed on the screen; his body stilled from a creeping shock. He stared in disbelief. He had found a photograph of Jefferson. "Motherfucker," he muttered, flabbergasted with what he had found. "Jefferson looks identical to Butler. This can't be! I've got to double-check." As he stared at the picture, he purposefully contrived differences in his mind's eye, comparing the image in front of him to his memory of his psychology instructor. None stuck. The images rendered the same individual. Butler and Jefferson were the same person.

"Damn, he's lighter than you," Sanders observed, taking an instant tack on Marzee's discovery.

Sanders' native insight had always impressed Marzee. From the low resolution digital photograph, Sanders had discerned Jefferson as a very light-skinned black, which had not been obvious to Marzee when he had been with him face-to-face. "You're right," Marzee responded with congratulatory recognition, "and he's my psychology instructor at school. He told me he's black, asked me to be part of his bullshit research. He's Dance's friend. He saw me doing my thing in an apartment complex across from campus. He's the one who referred me to Dance. But why?" He pondered a moment, then concluded. "Why? Because they work in the same office."

"I think I've seen him too," Saul said after donning his glasses and peering at the monitor. "I can't say definitely," Saul continued "but he looks familiar. But then again, I could have seen him in a grocery line, but he looks familiar."

Overwhelmed by his finding, a flurry of possibilities flooded his mind. He was certain—Jefferson was more than what he was led to believe. "This dude! This dude!" Marzee squeaked excitedly, pointing at the image. "I read about his career. He grew up in Compton. And I think I had it bad?" He smacked his lips, gloating in the comparison. "Can you imagine this nigga, with his complexion, growing up in Compton? This is one angry bro. His history is sketchy, but he first worked for the LAPD." Marzee mused at their similarities. "Hell, I considered doing that. I used to fantasize about pulling niggas over in their cars, frisking them, pulling bags of weed and pills and shit out of their pockets, handcuffing them, making them sit on the curb while they're being discussed, knowing their asses are fucked." He lingered in contemplation. "Yeah, I KNOW this dude now. But he went all the way. He was with LAPD for seven years, then he switched to the FBI. He was with them for ten years, then to Homeland Security seven years ago."

"My gawd. You found all that in, what, thirty minutes?" Saul exclaimed in genuine awe. "What's the problem with him? He sounds right to me. Neighborhood boy makes good. What's wrong with that picture?" Saul asked.

Marzee heard Saul, but he didn't respond. Something was wrong; he just didn't know what. He felt a rekindled sense of purpose, akin to helping his father solve his newspaper puzzles. If he kept pressing toward a solution, he would discover it. "When he was with LAPD, he went back to Compton, his old neighborhood. He was in charge of a gang division. He worked square out of Compton," Marzee remarked. "I'm still having trouble believing it's him, my psychology professor. If not, it's his twin, a spitting image. And now that I remember his voice on the phone, it sounded like my psych prof too." He paused momentarily, reflecting. "It's him, no doubt. But why? Why the front, unless—?"

"Unless he's undercover," Sanders interrupted. "And he's already watching your German girlfriend," Sanders offered flippantly, hitting Marzee on the shoulder. "Then YOUR weird ass stumbles into the picture. Shit, it's perfect. You ain't doin' noth'n but watching her. You're doin their job for them. Then report what you see to your fuck'n shrink, who works down the hall from this dude." Sanders' acrid levity bore more substance than he had intended.

"You two, you're spinning fairy tales, like little spiders spinning weak webs, but you're not catching any flies," Saul broke in. "Why didn't they level with him later, when he was on the phone with them? And why didn't they apprehend the German woman. And the Iranians? And most importantly, why didn't they protect you and your family? Seems like they would know you were in some sort of danger."

Consumed by an unsolved puzzle, the unseen factors heated his imagination. *Gut, intuition, sixth sense—something tells me Saul knows something. He's just not aware.* "Saul. What you just said. That's why I don't trust going to the authorities. That's why Sanders brought me to you. 'Cause they're building the bomb around here. And I think you know where it is. I'm not saying you're involved, of course not. But I think once you think about what I tell you, you can probably tell us something we don't know," Marzee declared with persuasive conviction.

"Me? I know where Islamic terrorists are building an atom bomb?" Saul bent his head down, exposing his skull cap. "You ever hear of a Jew terrorist? The only Jews involved with 9/11 were the ones working in their offices in the World Trade Center when those crazy Arab fucks flew those airplanes into them," Saul exclaimed.

"Ma man has something," Sanders inserted, agreeing with Marzee, then turning to Saul. "You know everything that goes on around here. If a seagull farts, you know whether he had sardines for breakfast."

Smitten by an idea, Marzee started furiously typing. "I should have done this search earlier," he said. "Smoke detectors. That's their cover, but I didn't search possible locations, especially any around here," he clarified.

"Smoke detectors? Siemens has a huge facility not far from here," Saul instantly volunteered. "They manufacture smoke detectors for Europe, then ship them over there. The environmental laws are stricter in European countries regarding—"

"Regarding radioactive Americium 241," Marzee interrupted. "They make the devices here, and ship them over there." Saul nodded a confirmatory grin.

A familiar sensation overwhelmed him, made him tingle, his armpits moisten, his heart palpitate, his mouth dry. *Feels like I'm searching, hunting. Not for naked women, or unobstructed bedroom windows, but the feeling's just the same.* "It's almost ten. Saul, do you know that facility? Where it is? How secure is it at night? You think I

348

can get in? To look around? I heard them say they would employ migrant workers for the final assembly. These people won't be aware of the risks," Marzee inquired with focused intensity.

"This plant you're talking about. It's about fifteen minutes walking distance from here," Saul replied impatiently.

Sensing Saul's reluctance, Marzee didn't want to alienate him. He looked to Sanders, who silently confirmed with a nod: he's OK. "With or without being seen?" Marzee asked delicately.

"Well, there's only so much cover between here and there. You have to be in the open occasionally." Saul rolled his head back, biting his lip as he pondered the question. "It's not like we're in the jungle here, swinging from vine to vine," he commented, pausing self-consciously. "No racial innuendos intended," he added apologetically. Marzee and Sanders smirked. "We can walk part of the distance. Absolutely no driving. Then take a small rowboat across a channel. The factory's on Smith Island. We can stay in shadow. There's lots of stacked crates along the way. I'll guide you there, but I'll have to let you two young men go it alone beyond a certain point. The climbing and jumping, I can't do it. But I can point the way from where I leave you off."

"That's what I'm talk'n about," Sanders remarked. "This IS a jungle, and you ARE the king gorilla!"

"Yeah, yeah. And you're the king of bullshit," Saul replied. The three laughed together, like boys staying up late in their dormitory room. "But we should wait until eleven thirty to start over there. There's a security guard shift change at midnight," Saul added.

Marzee lulled into contemplation, briefly relinquishing the agony of his tragic day. The prospect that Saul could be right—they were spinning webs of false assumptions—gnawed at him. Though parts of the puzzle were coming together, the picture was not complete. He struggled to create continuity from an incomplete picture. "How is it a big corporation like Siemens doesn't know what's happening inside their own facility?" he asked abruptly. "Can you imagine what would happen to their stock if it got out they were harboring terrorists?" He stared into space, as if pulling an answer from an unseen dimension. "Don't companies contract out their security services? Seems like Siemens would do the same. If everything else we've come up with is true, and we find them building the bomb there, it would make sense that the security service is being paid off," he muttered with reserved conviction.

"Where'd you get this guy?" Saul asked Sanders whimsically, gesturing with his thumb toward Marzee. "He's pretty smart. In fact, I noticed about a month ago, something was different with security over there. The patrol cars had changed."

"Don't say he's smart—his head's already too big. He's been hearing that all his life," Sanders replied, looking to Marzee. "Hey, bro. Here's a question. What do you intend to do once you find these muthafuckas? You ain't gonna just run down there, waving that gun I gave you, saying, 'Alright fools, I'm the nigga in charge now! Ya'll just go home.'"

Sanders had whimsically verbalized a concern badgering him all evening. Marzee had thoroughly planned his intrusions on Utte's house. But now he faced a life-threatening challenge. He should map his course to the extreme. A surge of adrenaline boosted his resolve. "It's impossible to plan with facts you don't have," he responded hastily. "I have to trust the process, what we're doing. My intent is to fuck them up in whatever way presents itself." Chuckling, they slapped each other's palm. Saul slowly shook his head in feigned disdain.

"You two schmucks need to have your heads examined. And mine too, for going along with this insanity," Saul remarked cryptically. "But I've got to admit, this is more excitement than I've had since I was a kid living in the Bronx, dodging gangs, dope dealers, and pimps."

Aside from the sheer rush of the quest, the need for, and lack of, basic planning and tactics worried Marzee. "Saul, from what you remember of the building, is there some way of getting in undetected, like through the back?" Marzee asked.

351

"Yeah, but you've got to climb a couple fences. I don't know about alarm systems. I hope the fence isn't electrified," Saul answered cautiously.

Marzee remembered a local drug addict—a childhood friend—electrocuting himself by climbing the fence of a neighborhood transformer station, and falling across the wires. He had watched the emergency workers extract the victim's charred corpse. "I think we'll need a distraction, something to draw attention to the front while I go through the back," Marzee said.

"You? Say, man. I didn't go through all this shit just so you could go it alone. For all I know, my house, my business, my woman. Everything is gone, taken by the Man," Sanders remarked with defiance.

The comment struck a nerve-sensitive guilt chord. A lack of empathy and self-centered resolve dominated his tactics, and he edged out anything unrelated to achieving his target. Sanders had not even asked to use Saul's phone since they had arrived. His pitiable appearance in Sanders' backyard jeopardized Sanders' life, his livelihood, his home, and whomever he considered family. Yet, Sanders remained steadfast—loyal to Marzee—not outwardly worried or curious about his own well-being. *I wish I were living long enough to pay him back. I wish I were living long enough to muster the moral restitution for all those people whose privacy I invaded without their knowledge. I wish I had more time.* "Sorry. I know you're coming with me. I'd have it no other way." He paused, turning to Saul. "So what do you think about the distraction idea?"

"I think it's a good idea. I'm not going to the front door, announcing, 'I heard you needed an old Jew to help you put your atom bomb together, so here I am. I'm your guy,'" Saul replied with a dead-pan face. "Although that might provide the distraction you need."

"How about a fire?" Sanders suggested.

"You mean, set the building on fire?" Marzee asked.

"No. I mean, like, set a fire close to the building, so everyone rushes to it," Sanders replied. "Maybe some gasoline."

"Absinthe. Set some of your absinthe on fire," Saul suggested. "It's flammable, and it'll eventually lead to me. Then, when the real investigation starts, they'll ask me questions."

"Why do you want—?" Sanders started.

Brilliant. Impressed with the incisiveness, Marzee grasped Saul's proposal. Restraining Sanders' comment tactfully, Marzee touched his shoulder. "He's saying, in case we don't come back. The terrorists won't recognize what burned. BUT whoever does the investigation will, and that will lead to Saul," Marzee interrupted.

"Fuck that! I'm come'n back. Ain't no deny'n that," Sanders recoiled with conviction. "But

353

I get it. Good idea. Goddamn expensive shit to burn though. Let's have another drink before we burn it."

"Put a few bottles in a bag. I've got a backpack around here somewhere. You only need two or three bottles. Put some padding between the bottles to keep them from rattling," Saul suggested. "Like I said, I'll go with you as far as I can to show you the way, but that's it. You're on your own after that."

Marzee glanced at the time on the computer monitor—almost eleven. He stretched his neck back and closed his eyes. *Sleep would be nice, death better. I feel numb. I want the people who killed my parents dead.*

Regressing to his far past, visions of Cecilia Golden danced in the dark backdrop of his closed eyes. He recounted the dozens of times he had crouched outside her bedroom window at night, watching her dress, undress, towel herself dry after a bath. She never had said a word to him—never a hint that she knew of his presence outside her window. But he knew she knew.

What if I went up to her, and said, "Hey Cecilia, you've given me countless pleasures, letting me watch you parade around naked. How can I repay you?" I wonder what she'd say? What's the price tag for what I've done? Jail? Social quarantine? Exile as a pervert? A lifetime of penance, seeking spiritual and moral absolution? If I wanted to pay for it in advance, who would I contact? It's not real. That's why I kept doing it. No

roller coaster ride, no bungee jump, no bobsled run,
no car race at two hundred miles per hour. Nothing
could buy what I've experienced. I didn't get it for
free. The bill collector has arrived. Now I've gotta
pick up the tab.

Chapter 17
A View to a Kill

"Say, man, Wake up. It's time to go. It's eleven thirty," Sanders yelled, shaking Marzee's shoulder.

He awoke with a jolt, panicked and dazed—fearful he had missed their crucial time table. "What? Did I miss?—" he cried, looking around wildly.

"We're packed and ready. Let's go. We just let you sleep. We're set. Saul even printed a map while you were asleep. C'mon, move yo ass!" Sanders said, continuing to shake him. "And make sure you're pack'n your shit."

The division between nightmare and wakefulness had become blurred. The pang of his parents, his home, his student ambitions lingered briefly, followed by the resolve for revenge. Since arriving at Saul's, he had not removed his jacket hiding the gun under his belt. He reached behind him, verifying its presence. He had become as numb to the pressure it exerted against his lower back as he had become numb to the agony of the day. "It's still there. How about you? You ready?" he asked Sanders in a defiant tone.

"Say, man. I'm ready. But let's go," Sander replied, ignoring Marzee's attitude.

"Yeah, you two. We need to catch the change of the guard. It's gonna work better since we're doing this absinthe thing, if you catch the new shift right at the beginning," Saul reminded them. "By the way, here. You may need this. But I for damned sure want it back. It cost me one hundred fifty dollars at Best Buy." Saul handed Marzee a compact digital camera.

Rather than expressing immediate gratitude, he was silently irritated Saul hadn't given it to him sooner. He needed a little time to acquaint himself with it. "Do I have time to take a piss?" Marzee inquired, holding out the camera. "While I'm pissing, I'll figure this thing out."

"The toilet is back there," Saul said, pointing to a far corner. "It's a garden-variety digital camera. You can figure it out once you get there."

He hated short naps; he was confused and disoriented right after awakening. Lighting Saul's drab, dingy yellowish bathroom helped arouse him, like holding ammonia under his nose. After unzipping his pants, he studied Saul's camera under the dim cast of the swinging light bulb. A tune resounded when he pressed the on-button. "Shit!" he whispered, half-startled. "That's got to go." The program functions displayed on the LCD panel reminded him of working with Photoshop, and his computer in his bedroom, and—. He shook off the train of thought.

"Say, man. How long does it take to piss? Let's go," Sanders hollered.

Marzee turned the light out and shuffled away from the bathroom, head down, focused on the camera's controls. The true value of the camera suddenly dawned on him. "Saul. Thank you," he said, approaching the others. "This was a good idea."

"No problem." Saul replied, nodding as if to say, "Finally you understand. What took you so long?" He glanced at his watch. "We really have to go." Saul opened the door.

The cool, moist, night breeze on his face signaled they were leaving. *I should feel fear, but I don't. Maybe it's because I don't know what we're going to encounter. This whole adventure into the night may be bullshit. What do I feel? I feel nothing. Maybe I'm in shock. Still, my senses should be sharper; I should be more alert. I feel disconnected and alienated. The cool, moist air helps. I sense something not real about myself, yet we're going out the door, into the night. I'd be at home, in my room, studying, preparing for bed. My mother and father would still be downstairs: she on her crosswords, he on his Jumble Puzzle. They don't exist; my bedroom does not exist; my house does not exist. I want to cry. I cannot.*

"It's foggy. We're in luck," Saul commented with optimism. "We got everything?"

"Yeah, except ma man here," Sanders replied, turning back to Marzee. "You alright? This ain't no time to go cuckoo on me."

In the past Marzee had cynically translated out-of-body experiences to mean distortions of reality by those who had described them. Peculiarly unconcerned, he now saw himself from outside his body, not connected to himself, not whole. Part of him wanted to panic; part of him was apathetic. "Bitch-slap me. Hard," he commanded Sanders. Through the mist he saw that Sanders flinched only momentarily at his request, then took him seriously.

Sanders un-slung the bag of absinthe from his shoulder, dropped it to the ground, and approached Marzee. He appraised him briefly, then hauled off, slapping him squarely across his left check. A clacking sound echoed between the narrow passage. Marzee swayed slightly, maintaining his footing.

The last time his ears rang so, his mother had lost her temper with him at the dinner table when he was ten, besetting her backhand across his face in a similar manner. His cheek stung with a burn. He shook his head vigorously; then he smiled. "Thank you, bro. I needed that. I was losing touch," he said. "Let's get on with this." He looked to Saul. "After you, sir."

Witnessing the slapping ordeal, Saul stared at Marzee and Sanders, then shook his head in disbelief. "Like I said before the boxing match, we're in luck. It's foggy. Good and foggy," Saul remarked with waning volume.

The fog stroked Marzee's face like a soothing brush, cooling his still smarting cheek. He mused that the slap actually did help him, and that he had gotten the idea from seeing it in movies. Perhaps, he thought, someone should have slapped him that hard a long time ago. He checked his pocket for the camera, imagining it may have been ejected from the force of Sanders' smack to his face.

He was glad Saul did not walk too hastily. As he moved away, his lumbering form dematerialized in the swirling mist, and he disappeared. Even wearing his jacket, Marzee felt cold, and the chill was augmented by the damp air. He zipped it to his collar as he started to walk. Third in line, he followed Sanders.

"Stay close. In this fog, if you lose sight of the man in front of you, you're gonna be up a creek," Saul warned. He continued talking with his head turned over his shoulder, as if his voice would be better broadcast to parties behind him. "Marzee. Too bad you didn't get a chance to look at the map I printed from Google Earth. I was going to wake you, but your friend said leave you be. Anyway, it's just a close up of this area. It's a satellite picture. I don't know the date, but nothing changed. This area is a labyrinth of shipping containers and portable storage bins. It's that way until we get close to the channel. I've got a small boat tied down below the channel ledge, out of sight from casual passersby."

He followed Sanders meticulously, zigzagging left and right, back and forth, feeling more energized as time passed. The sting on his cheek invigorated him, and the taste and feel of the fog made him come alive—more so, he inwardly mused, than searching for peeping opportunities.

"You said earlier we'll be out in the open. When? How long?" he asked Saul.

"I was getting to that. There's about a ten foot gap between the channel edge and where we'll emerge from the cover of these crates. We go across that, then we have to climb down to the boat. Just follow. I'll explain when we get there," Saul replied impatiently.

"Damn. I feel like a rat in one of those mazes," Sanders remarked. "'Cept they can see where they're going."

"I could do this blind-folded," Saul replied. "Don't worry. With my legs, I'm not going to sprint ahead of you, so just follow."

After ten minutes, the three stopped in a huddle, bounded within three feet of towering crates and bins on each side, and a nebulous mist facing them. Marzee could hear gentle splashing of water, and deep, synchronous fog horns in the distance. He loved the sound of fog horns. Different from the intrusive, annoying sirens of emergency vehicles, fog horns issued a foreboding, omniscient testimony to immovable dangers ahead.

"Frank. Walk more than ten feet in that direction, and you'll get wet," Saul said, grabbing Sanders' arm, and holding him back. "There's no railing there, so edge forward carefully, feeling with your feet. When you get to the edge, kneel down, and feel around under the edge. When you feel a bunch of rope, yank it up. Here's a small flashlight. Don't use it unless you have to. The rope is a rolled up ladder. Release it, so it rolls down. The boat is docked directly below."

"Goddamit. Now I've got to crawl around some more. These pants cost me five hundred dollars," Sanders complained, emphasizing 'five' in a whispered hiss. "Don't make no never mind, anyway. I already climbed over walls, and crawled on the ground under nasty ass, greasy trucks with this fool."

Marzee feared Sanders did not swim well, having witnessed his abilities at the community swimming pool when they were boys. Hyper-sensitive to another grievous loss, he worried the potential of Sanders' drowning was too great to risk. "I'll do it instead. I'm a better swimmer. If he falls in, he'll go straight to the bottom," Marzee stated in a low voice.

"I swim fine," Sanders rebutted. "Last time you saw me swim was ten years ago. I learned since then. I'm not gonna fall anyway. Stay here. Once I do all this shit, I'll yell "come," but not too loud, so listen. Both you come. Help Saul down first." He paused—the loss of facial expressions from the dense fog made the silence seem longer. "Saul, I thought you said you couldn't do any climbing."

"I can make it down the ladder, and back up on the other side. It's my arthritis. I'll show you where I have to draw the line later. Let's get going," Saul responded, as if a plethora of other pressing engagements were going unattended.

Marzee watched Sanders' form blend into the densest fog he had ever encountered. He heard Sanders' feet shuffle across the unknown paved surface as he slid them alternately toward the ominous channel edge, about which Saul had warned them. "I don't wanna hear no splashes, now!" Marzee whispered loudly after Sanders had completely disappeared from his view. Sanders chuckled softly, unseen.

After five minutes he began to worry. He had heard Sanders mumbling and cursing under his breath; then he had stopped. He was about to tell Saul he was going to see what was wrong, when suddenly Sanders hissed, "Come!"

In the brief period of their acquaintance, Marzee felt protective of Saul, fearing for his well-being, and guilty he had brought these troubles upon him to begin with. "Let me go ahead of you. Take my hand, and let me lead," he told Saul.

"That's what I was going to suggest," Saul responded. He took Marzee's hand. "Keep in mind, this is neither a date nor an AA meeting," Saul added.

They shuffled gingerly along the ground, shoe soles as feelers, making six inch scraping slides as they approached the channel wall ledge. "I can see you from down here. I'm in the boat," Sanders projected an exaggerated whisper from below them. "The bottom of the ladder is in the boat. Just get your asses down here. This shit's rocking back and forth, and I'm standing here trying to hold it steady,"

Sanders' voice relieved him, as he had worried about his friend's safety. He released Saul's grip, and passed his hand along the edge of the pier, assuring himself he was centered with the ladder. Then he sat to one side, stabilizing himself from the edge. "I put my foot at the middle of the ladder, Saul. Use my foot as a guide," he said.

Saul kicked gently forward until nudging Marzee's foot. Then he sat on the ground and inched along on his rear, pushing with his hands, until his legs hung over the edge. "I'm OK now. I've done this hundreds of times, just not in dense fog at midnight," Saul remarked, minimizing his earlier trepidation.

Marzee helped Saul ease down the ladder as he stabilized the ropes from above. "Got him. C'mon down," Sanders said softly. Marzee climbed down swiftly, settling into a large row boat with four benches. Saul sat on the back bench. Marzee and Sanders sat together on the second bench.

"This boat has a motor, but obviously we can't use it. So you two get to paddle. The oars are along the sides. And for God's sake, don't drop them in the water," Saul announced with a cryptic warning.

"I'm OK with rowing," Sanders said. "But how do you know where we're going?"

"This channel is not wide—about one hundred feet. We'll smack into a wall on the other side. It's easier climbing back up. There's concrete docks, and stairs along the wall, spaced every twenty feet."

Marzee searched the sides of the boat, retrieving the oars and handing one to Sanders. Noticing Sanders had stalled, he reached across to assist him in attaching the oar holder to the side. "Place the back of the boat against the retaining wall, then go straight across?" Marzee asked. "Or follow the horn?"

"Just go straight across. You two have to row in harmony, or we'll go in a circle," Saul said, chuckling.

"I got it, bro. No need to explain," Sanders remarked, stopping Marzee before he started a rowing lesson.

The boat slid through the still water as Marzee and Sanders paddled in unison. They seemed to synchronize to one another, each oar slicing through the water in rhythm. The thick fog condensed on his face and hair, dripping into his eyes. His cheek still burned warmly from Sanders' slap. Cruising blind, he trusted their guide's directions.

"Hear the water lapping against the wall? Stop rowing now. Let the boat glide," Saul suddenly announced.

Marzee didn't hear the sound, but he and Sanders stopped as directed. The boat jolted to an abrupt stop, startling Marzee, who hadn't anticipated such a short journey. They collided with a mirror-image wall, so similar he feared they had gone full circle. Apprehensive about their position, he peered through the fog searching for an anchor point. He spotted a pier-like platform three feet from them, jutting out from the wall. "To the left, a platform," he exclaimed louder than he had intended.

Metal loops protruding from the wall caught his attention. He quickly latched onto one before they rebounded too far. Marzee tethered them closer to the wall, Sanders maneuvered the boat closer to the platform, and Saul readied the rope for docking.

"There's a stair from where we're tying down," Saul remarked. "No more rope ladders. Frank, why don't you jump across to the platform. I'll hand you the rope."

After securing the boat, Sanders and Marzee helped Saul out. The three stood together as if absorbing each other's body heat. Saul rubbed his hands together briskly. To prepare himself, Marzee felt in his jacket pockets—right pocket, camera; left pocket, a folded piece of paper, he map Saul had printed. He felt the forty five automatic pressing into the small of his back. "Are we close?" Marzee asked. "I wish I had thought of going back to campus, and lifting a Geiger counter from the physics lab."

"You won't need it. I've been mulling over everything you guys told me and showed me," Saul said with a ruminative air. "Something different is going on over there. And the picture of

Thorndike—I HAVE seen him. If you're my age, and you've been around here for as long as me, you know when something's fishy. So, listen. We go up these stairs and cross a street. Then we have to go inside a huge warehouse. Don't worry, I have a key. You have to stay quiet. The guard's probably asleep, and right now there's nothing in there to guard anyway. Then we walk through the building. The Siemens plant is on the other side. Got it? Follow me and stay close."

As they climbed the rusty stairs affixed to the face of the retaining wall, Marzee amused himself with Saul's oversized, lumbering derrière inches from his face. He glanced back at Sanders, who had noticed Marzee's predicament. Sanders grinned, and motioned, "watch where you're going."

He almost fell flat on his face, stumbling while crossing the four-lane street Saul had briefed them about. They lingered on a narrow sidewalk by a metal door as Saul fumbled through his gigantic key ring. Waiting tortured Marzee, as he conjured worst-scenarios, like the worst possible time for a police car to cruise by. *A light-skinned nigga, a dark-skinned nigga, and an old Jew, standing around in the fog at midnight, trying to get into a locked warehouse. What the fuck would I do? Shoot a pig? I guess I'd have to. This day couldn't get much worse anyway.*

Sanders tugged on his elbow, pulling him along, as his daydreaming caused him to tarry after

Saul had opened the door. Saul paused, turned around, and forcefully put his finger over his lip, issuing an edict of silence. He ushered Marzee and Sanders inside, then he eased the door closed behind them.

Not being immersed in fog was comforting, though the inside of the warehouse was cold, damp, and dimly lit. Marzee marveled at the labyrinth effect produced by the cascading twenty-foot-high shelves. He stared down the aisle facing him, which created an almost infinite tunnel toward an unknown end. Saul motioned to follow, and the trio commenced the trek to the other side.

Grateful for having completed an uneventful journey to the opposite side of the stadium-sized building, Marzee looked to Saul for direction. They stood by an identical door through which they had entered on the other side. Saul opened the door, and gestured for them to go through. When he closed it, he did not shut it completely, purposefully leaving a gap.

"Move a little further along the wall, away from the door," he said once outside. "This is where I leave you," he declared with restrained certitude. "Your destination is across there." He nodded toward a diffusion-lit fog. "We're facing the west side of the Siemens plant. Marzee, get out your map. Frank, hand Marzee the flashlight." He waited while Marzee unfolded the paper and held the lit flashlight in his mouth. "The map is a close-up of where we are now. You've got a ten-foot fence to climb, but no barbed wire. No alarm. They have surveillance cameras, but there's none here where you'll cross. Again, we're lucky with this fog—the cameras at the corners of the building won't catch you in the fog anyway. There's a guard shack at the entrance. Here—" he pointed at the positions on the map, "and another back here."

"You guys need to set your distraction before you climb the fence. Both of you, run straight across from here to the fence. It's about twenty yards. We're in sort of a junk yard, so be careful. Don't trip. Once at the fence: Frank, you run along the fence to your right about fifty yards, start the fire, then run like hell back to Marzee. Then you both climb the fence. Get to the wall of the building." His finger tip followed the edge on the printed image. "Creep along the wall to the back here. That's it. There's no more detail, and I've never been inside there before, so you're gonna have to find your own way. My guess—this structure at the back of the building looks like a storage hut. You could use it to get on the roof. It's probably less conspicuous to enter from the roof."

Saul's departure vexed Marzee. He wondered whether he was so overwhelmed with loss that any additional separation seemed inappropriately amplified. At least he still had Sanders. He touched Saul on his shoulder. "Thank you. Thank you from the bottom of my heart," Marzee said. "When this is all over, would you mind me visiting?"

369

"Mind? I insist," Saul responded, reciprocating Marzee's shoulder squeeze, then he looked at his watch, drawing it to his nose. "You guys, get going. The time is ripe. I'll leave this door ajar. Come back the same way. I have a feeling you'll shake things up. I'm too old for this. I've got to get some rest."

"I'll be back for my product. I got customers waiting for that, and goddamned if I don't have to burn some of it! Order me some more," Sander remarked gruffly.

"Good luck, boys," Saul replied, disappearing through the door and leaving it ajar as promised.

"Let's go, bro," Sanders said. "Ready?"

Marzee's heart pounded; his armpits, sticky; his breathing, short. *This is the best part of the roller coaster ride—the chain clacking, the coaster slowly cresting the first hill, riders braced for the descent.* "Let's do this," he responded. "I'll count steps so we'll have an idea about when we get to the fence."

They ran with long strides, hunched as if scrambling across a battlefield. Stopping suddenly to avoid a pile of tires, they by-passed the obstacle and continued toward the fence Saul had meticulously described. Sanders cursed after colliding with an empty five-gallon can. Marzee saw the fence from five feet away. The glow from the building's area lights was brighter, obscuring the surroundings even more.

"We're here," Marzee whispered, holding Sanders back. "Let's climb this fence the same way as the last one. I'll use my jacket."

"No. I'll use mine. You got the camera in yours. Besides—" he paused thoughtfully, "well, fuck it. I'll use mine this time." Sanders pulled off the backpack, dropping it to his feet. When he took off his jacket and folded it across his arm, an object fell out of a pocket. "That's my knife. Grab it. I'll get it from you later." The bottles of absinthe rattled as he readjusted the backpack over his shirt.

Sanders applied a Spiderman grip to the chain link fence, scaling it with circus-act alacrity. Marzee had meant to warn him to check it for electrical charge, but Sanders sat astride it, his precious and expensive leather jacket protecting him from the protruding chain link spikes.

"It's cool. C'mon on," Sanders assured, readying himself to assist his friend.

He stuffed his hands and shoes through the fence loops, and hoisted himself within Sanders' grasp. Sanders pulled him far enough to the top, then jumped to the other side, allowing his friend enough room to slide across his jacket. Marzee slung his body over the garment, rotated himself around, carefully pulled Sanders' jacket from the fence top, and jumped down.

"Thanks, bro," Marzee said, handing him his jacket. "No worse for wear. I know how much that must have hurt."

"Say, man. It's no biggie. I'm not gonna wear it. Stuff it in the backpack. It'll keep this shit from rattling so much 'til we're done with it," Sanders said, turning his back to Marzee.

Folded neatly, Marzee pressed Sanders' jacket into the knapsack against the bottles of absinthe as Sanders prepared to create the absinthe-ignited distraction.

"I'll be right back. Be ready to run when I get back." He strode off, counting steps under his breath as he ran.

The sound of Sanders' steps vanished quickly, leaving Marzee isolated in the darkness and dense mist. The solitude infected his diminishing internal sanctuary, brashly underscoring the cold and loneliness in the biting midnight harbor moisture. He didn't like waiting, wondering, anticipating what would happen. He peered into Sanders' direction, trying to glean a glimpse through the fog. Occupying himself, he made patterns from the swirls of mist and light. *One minute. Two minutes. How long can this take? Pour out the bottles. Light the shit. Run like hell. Damn. Then we have to find a way inside.* He quelled a rising panic within him. He heard noises, human voices. Indistinguishable, the sounds ran together. He saw a bright, bluish glow from Sanders' direction. Suddenly, Sanders materialized from the mist.

372

"Goddamn, that stuff burns like hell. Burned my hands. Let's go!" Sanders hissed in an elevated whisper.

They sprinted from the fence, toward the lighted auras and nebulous form of a building. Marzee heard someone yell "fire." Allowed to gloat only briefly, he impacted a hard surface, stunning him slightly. They had bounded away so fast, they had run headlong into the building wall. Sanders had seen the wall before running into it, and avoided impact.

"Goddamn, fool. Watch where you're going," Sanders scolded derisively.

Embarrassed, Marzee shook off the stun. *This is serious business. I can't daydream. I have to think, concentrate, second to second.* "Fuck!" he muttered. "Hang on." He reached into his pocket for Saul's map, but then remembered the outline. "We move along the wall from here, to our left."

He swiped his face to remove the debris collected from the wall impact. Touching the wall with both hands, they side stepped in the direction they had studied on Saul's map. The fire had its desired effect, as the echo of voices increased from the fog-enshrouded source. Marzee heard, "Call the fire department," and another voice—an accent reminiscent of Afsane—quickly rejoined, "No!"

They crept along, hugging the wall until they arrived at a corner of the building. As anticipated, a smaller structure stood, juxtaposed within three feet of building's rear wall. Marzee

373

noticed gas tubes, hoses, and pressure regulators protruding from this satellite building. "This must be the shack Saul mentioned," he said. "From the looks of it, there's gas canisters in here." He paused, reaching in his pocket for the flashlight. "I'm gonna shine the flashlight along this wall." Before Sanders had a chance to retort, the light revealed a ladder within two feet, affixed to the wall. He returned the flashlight to his pocket. "This ladder goes to the roof of the shack. Once on top, I'm pretty sure we can jump this gap to get to the main building. There's prob'ly even a plank."

"Do it," Sanders responded encouragingly. "But I hope that light didn't attract any attention. They're prob'ly look'n for who lit that fire."

Marzee started climbing the ladder; Sanders followed closely. He had already considered the same threat, but figured the security guards would search for a *what* rather than a *who*, given that it was after midnight in the fog at San Pedro Harbor, making for a paucity of pranksters.

Once atop the roof, he felt more secure since any search parties would first scour the surrounding grounds, though the voices still remained at a distance. Directly across their position on the main building he spotted a rectangular light. "See that?" he whispered. "I bet that's a roof window. That's our way in. I've gotta use the flashlight again. We need to make sure we're walking in the right place."

"Yeah, go ahead," Sanders replied. "This shit is starting to worry me. And I don't like heights."

As Marzee had suspected, a narrow plank crossed the gap linking the shed with the main building. "Follow," Marzee said, switching off the flashlight. They tip-toed across the railed plank to the roof of the main building. As they approached the raised roof window, Marzee took wide strides, attempting to minimize noise from footsteps. As they moved nearer, he heard voices from inside— different from those on the ground—they rang familiar. Distinct, yet indistinguishable, each voice intertwined, creating a dissonant chord. His pulse gyrated. *These voices, I know them, like a bad but familiar odor.* He stopped, gesturing to Sanders to get down. As if jolted by a microsecond of high voltage, the voice-blitz shocked him. He hunched on his hands and knees, crawling the remaining six feet to the window. Sanders begrudgingly did likewise.

The window light glowed white, hauntingly outlining each individual mist droplet, like miniscule shells, jostling to and fro over the angled pane glass. Marzee and Sanders, now on their bellies, slithered toward the window frame. The conversation inside over-powered the sounds outside, where reactions to the fire continued to escalate. The moment consumed him as he moved within inches of looking inside. A ventilator shaft next to them amplified the conversation from within. He turned back to Sanders, and signaled "hush." Fearful of being seen, he hoped the fog's shroud, and hugging the window's rim, would be enough. He eased his head over the glass until the conversants were in clear view: Utte, Jefferson, and a thin, dark-haired woman.

"When's he coming back? Now's not the time to go running around looking for ghosts," Jefferson said. "We've laid the tracks. Our timing is critical. We must move within the next three hours. He's got to get that disposal truck here."

"The disposal company said they would have their truck here before three AM. It's on its way," the dark-haired woman replied. "Enough time for transport before sunrise."

Afsane! Her voice was as unique as when he had heard her from inside Utte's laundry room closet. Aghast at the visage below him, he turned to Sanders.

"You look like you just saw a ghost," Sanders whispered softly.

His belly ached, his head throbbed, he could barely support himself on his elbows. A deluge of emotion and thought confused him. "Utte, and Jefferson, and the other woman I heard. All three, together, talking," he replied in a lifeless murmur. Wide-eyed, Sanders shimmied to the window's edge for a peek.

As if his soul had departed him momentarily, then returned immediately, Marzee instantly felt reenergized. He suddenly remembered

Saul's camera, and scooted away from the window to retrieve it. Laying on his back, he fished the camera and flashlight from his pockets. "Turn it on and hold the light on the camera," he said to Sanders, handing him the flashlight. "I've got to adjust it quick." After a brief study of the controls, he turned a knob and switched the camera on. "I hope there's enough light," he mumbled, returning to his former position at the window rim. Jefferson was ranting to the two women when Marzee returned.

"I've got to go. This truck delay seems like more environmentalist bullshit. This is no time for delays. You've deposited the money?" Jefferson asked, facing Afsane.

"As you directed, in your Cayman Islands account," Afsane replied. "We've all got to go."

Jefferson punched some buttons on a Blackberry. He nodded apathetically, but with affirmation. "Here is the exact location for the dumpster. It's an apartment building in Compton," he said, hesitating, smiling. "Same building I grew up in."

"Your mother still lives there?" Utte inquired, as if she had heard the story before.

Jefferson oozed an acrid snicker at the remark. "Yes. My seventy-four-year-old mother still lives there," he replied. "She still lives in that rat's nest. I wish I could watch when it goes off. I wish there were a way. I want to see the looks on their faces, certain select ones. As they lie writhing in torment, I wish I could pull each up by the collar, look him, or her, in the eye, smile, and tell each one: 'You're going to die a slow, painful death from radiation poisoning—you, your family, and any little pickaninnies lying around. You're all going to die. And I'm responsible for it. I did it. You're dying because of me. Your pain and suffering is because of me. Rot in hell.' Not that they'd even know what radiation poisoning is," he hissed.

Unimpressed, Afsane cast an apathetic eye, then studied the paper Jefferson had handed her. "The disposal company will simply replace the dumpster there with our dumpster. No one will suspect?"

"Absolutely nothing," Jefferson replied."The dumpsters are identical."

"They'll hunt you, once they've put the pieces together," Utte said.

"'Once they put the pieces together' is the operative phrase," Jefferson responded. "The designer of the dirty bomb, your illustrious ex-husband, was killed by your stalker. The boy's fingerprints are on the murder weapon; the murder weapon was buried into Thorndike's chest; his DNA is inside and outside your house. The agencies will have their hands full before someone figures out what happened. And even then, do you think these bureaucracies will want the public to know their own hand-picked agent was involved in a terrorist attack more heinous than 9/11? I don't think so. I know our government."

"There's a difference between us," Afsane said, peering at Jefferson. "I do this for a love of my people; you do it for a hatred."

"Love, hatred. Both are ideals, which makes us both idealists," Jefferson replied sneering. "I've got to go make an appearance before I disappear. It has to look like I blew up trying to save my old neighborhood." He walked toward an over-sized, light-blue dumpster, patted it, and spun around. "If either of you dykes fucked me, you know I can always find you." He turned, striding away hastily.

Once Jefferson receded from view, Marzee slipped the camera into his jacket pocket. An indestructible aura surrounded him, as if nothing could harm him now. He felt his secret—his sand fly secret—could be on the six o'clock news, and he'd gloat about it. "We've got to stop this shit from happening," he said, turning to Sanders.

"I wish they'd called the fire department. I don't hear no sirens. That means they don't want to be found out, and it means—" Interrupted, Sanders eked a piercing gasp, reached for his throat, and fell over, bleeding.

"It means you're dead men, my little friend," Mansour said. In an instant, he pressed his knee to Marzee's chest, pinning him to the roof. The huge man had overcome him, and held a knife to his throat before he could resist.

Stunned by the sudden intrusion, Marzee reached impotently for his out-of-view friend. Mansour had disabled him so rapidly, his struggles were in vain. Incapacitated, he feared his chest would be crushed from the giant man's knee. The pressure of the knife on his throat distracted him from his inability to breathe. "Frank!" he gasped, yearning for Sanders to respond. A musty, stark realization seeped in like a fast moving, putrid odor: the massive, ominous form hovering above him murdered his parents. "You. You killed my parents," Marzee said, straining each word.

"I confess," Mansour replied, leering, his accent stronger than Afsane's. "And what a delight it was. Clever, didn't you think? Using fragments from your computer as an instrument of your parents death? I'd gladly relate slice-by-slice details to you, but, alas, I'm afraid we are pressed for time. How I hate being rushed in situations like this. You know, if your mother was typical of how women of your race die, no wonder you allowed yourselves to be enslaved by the Europeans. Now we take up the fight where you could not."

A crack sounded in the distance. Mansour veered to his side, relieving the pressure on Marzee's chest. Sanders' clinging-to-life shot had missed its mark. Mansour lunged toward Sanders' direction, holding the twelve inch blade over his head. He stabbed twice, then returned to face Marzee.

Marzee wanted to quiver; he wanted to cry; he wanted his parents and his home. He feared for what he would discover upon viewing Sanders. The image of the brotherhood he felt in Sanders' basement that day during target practice brought him to tears. He aimed at Mansour's head. The first shot grazed his neck. Mansour issued a bear-like growl, diving toward him ferociously. The second shot created a crisp, red circle in the center of his forehead. He fell motionless, clinching Marzee in a cocoon of his still warm, lifeless body.

Concerned the commotion had garnered the attention of Utte and the others, he tried to push Mansour off. Grunting and heaving, he could not budge the massive bulk of his body. With all his might, he rolled him over while wiggling from under him. He spun around, and clamored up to the window rim. He couldn't see Utte and Afsane anymore, and he panicked that they had heard the rooftop calamity. He noticed loud rumblings and the shrill alternating beeps a large truck sounds when backing up.

He crawled over to Sanders, who lay still and bleeding. "Frank. Frank. Please, don't be dead," he cried, shaking him.

Sanders turned his head, the gun he had aimed at Mansour still in his grip. "Did you kill that motherfucker?" Sanders whispered.

Reprieved by relief, he had a moment of optimism. "That bitch is dead," Marzee affirmed with a grim smile.

"Noise downstairs. You hear it? You gotta get out of here, to stop that shit," Sanders said.

Marzee illuminated Sanders with the flashlight, displaying the grisly maroon silhouette surrounding him. Terrified his friend would die, he was unable to call for help. Blood spurted from Sanders' neck and oozed from his abdomen; Marzee was helpless. "I've got to get you help," he said with desperation.

"Say, man. Fuck that. I feel better than I ever felt," he rebutted with a feeble voice. "Fact, I'm gonna say, I get to see my mama and papa now."

Marzee heard a sharp clunk, the impact of the gun falling the short distance from Sanders' hand. With the flashlight still on, he shone the light on Sanders' face. He suppressed screaming; he could not cry. Sanders' eyes were closed, his lips slightly parted. Recollecting he could always depend on that face whenever he was lonely or blue, his psyche's depth belched up the last silent despair he could render. He moved the beam from Sanders' face down to his throat, then traced the blood across the roof. Like a river tributary, it mingled with another stream—the one from Mansour's body. The combined flow coursed down the narrowly slanted surface, then deflected horizontally, outlining a rectangular shape—a hatch, allowing entrance to the floor below.

Chapter 18
G.I.G.O.

He yearned for any sign of life as he thrust his ear to Sanders' chest. He thought maybe the clanging and pounding from below obscured the heartbeat he desperately wanted to hear. *My friend, my brother. Please, come back to me.* Fury and agony welled inside him, reminding him of what he had to do. He kissed Sanders on his forehead and took one last look at his brother.

Chains clacking and the monotonous truck reverse warning continued below him. Since Mansour had appeared alone, Marzee concluded Mansour had acted on his own, without discussing his whereabouts with the others. *Why the candid conversation between Jefferson, Utte, and Afsane, knowing me and Sanders were up here? They'll be looking for Mansour after he doesn't come back. I've got to hurry.*

On hands and feet, he spider-stepped back to the window. Straining to see around the edge, he could only ascertain Utte and Afsane had vacated their previous location, probably to deal with whatever was making the racket. *They said a garbage truck was on the way to pick up a dumpster, and the bomb is in the dumpster. Jefferson said "dirty bomb." Yeah, I read about those—kill people without destroying property. What kind of a heartless, piece of shit could do that? Plant a nuclear device under the same apartment he grew up in? And his mother still lives there? And I thought I was crazy.*

The trail his of friend's blood, illuminated by the faint flashlight halo, had served a vital function. He turned around, casting the light in the direction he recalled. Through still foggy, he could discern a mechanism protruding from the roof surface. He squinted, hoping to pierce through the mist blanket which had benefited him up to now.

Fearful of being detected from below, he crept over the window to its upper edge. From that angle, looking directly along the ceiling, he made out a hatch opening corresponding to the position he had identified on the roof. A large building support pillar next to it extended from floor to ceiling. Attached tubular rungs alternated down the pillar.

Motion in his periphery suddenly caught his attention. Utte, Afsane, and a security man were struggling with a motorized sliding freight door. They recycled the door, closing it, then reopened it half-way. Through the opened gap, he spotted the truck awaiting them. The security man squatted in the opening, pushing the door up from its partially opened position to no avail. *It's stuck! He's calling others to help him.*

His pulse raced as he prepared for a leap into an unknown abyss. As this day had taught him, the answers unveil themselves in the process—the plan is in the doing. Scanning his mind for options, all funneled to these steps: *go down the hatch without being seen; try to get into the garbage bin; disable the bomb.*

As he rotated himself in order to scoot down to the roof hatch, he checked himself for blood. Since he had supported the full weight of Mansour's corpse, with a bullet hole through his forehead, he should have bled all over him. Though difficult to see on his dark-colored clothing in the fog, he was not blood-soaked enough to warrant a change of clothes. An inspiration, possibly a reprieve, leaped from the corpse. If Mansour carried a phone, he could lift it, and call for back-up.

He duck-walked, inching toward Mansour's body. The burden of not having enough time to think, let alone act, created a quandary. He hunched over his parents' murderer, his friend's murderer. The hatred and lust for vengeance caused him to shiver. He wanted to shoot him repeatedly while he lay there, dead and lifeless. He examined the man's massive, beach-ball-sized head, thankful, but amazed, that his single forty-five caliber bullet pierced this monster's skull sufficiently to penetrate his brain and to end his life.

Having to search him, but not wanting to touch him, created another quandary. He patted the dead man's chest and abdomen reluctantly. He felt around the front of his belt. He followed his belt around his side. Finding nothing, he gripped the front of his belt and tugged his body upward. Slipping his other hand under him, he rejoiced. *Found it!* He pulled, rotated, and yanked until it released from its retainer. To his chagrin, the phone had deflected Sanders' feebly-aimed bullet, rendering both bullet and phone useless.

He cast the light toward the window and retraced his path, checking below him once more before trying the roof hatch. Four more security men had joined the original three trying to get the freight door fully retracted. He heard Afsane screaming profanities. The search for the fire starters—he and Sanders outside with the absinthe—had apparently ended with Mansour. At a level deeper than anything he had ever felt or understood in his life, he knew he must act now.

Protective of the flashlight and battery power, he turned it off and put it in his pocket. The few square feet he had occupied on this coastal rooftop in the past thirty minutes had burned an indelible image. He could navigate blind. He scooted the six feet to the roof access door, and without thinking, turned the latch. He stopped abruptly. *Shit! That could have been connected to an alarm.* He listened carefully, hearing only the sounds from below—no alarms, no sirens. *Maybe it's connected to a silent alarm. The police would show up. I'm sure Utte and the rest wouldn't want to be swarmed by police now.* He yanked up on the handle. The bright fluorescent light from below saturated the mist, creating an eerie glow, and engulfing him in the alien light. Afsane's screaming, the noise from the door motor, the security men yelling back and forth, and the truck motor on the other side of the door produced a comedy of sounds, suggesting an ineptness he had reserved only for his friends, Freddie and Richard. Nevertheless, the calamity obscured his entry.

He stuck his head through the ceiling, and faced the runged pillar upside down. Suddenly hyper-vigilant, he whipped his head around, relieved to verify all was clear. Peripherally, he caught a glimpse of his target, the bright cyan garbage dumpster. As if an internal warning bell had sounded, he hastened his pace. Inverting his position and contorting his body, feet first, he scrambled through the hole in the roof. Stretched—feet inside on a pillar step and hands on the edge of the hatch door—he eased it closed. Behind the pillar, they could not see him, and he could not see them.

Before climbing down, he noticed he had left a blood print on the hatch handle. The handprint was a tell-tale sign he had been there. He worried someone would see remnants of his presence at a most inopportune moment. The inclination to clean off the handle swelled, causing him to freeze. Momentarily battling this needling obsession, he rationalized his way to refocus. *Think. It's small and twenty feet up. I don't have time to deal with it.* He rubbed each hand vigorously over his pants.

He had lost track of time: seconds seemed hours; hours ago were just a moment away. Dawdling on the pillar ladder had its own history, its own beginning and evolution. He forced himself to conclude it, ending another episode in a series of micro-eras he had experienced in his most recent past—juxtaposed, but disconnected, capsules of time. He scurried silently down the ladder.

Pressed against the column, he felt as if bullets bombarded his perimeter, and he hugged it even closer for dear life. Yet he had to take a look to see what was going on. He lay flat on the smooth, cold cement floor, stretching his body perpendicular to the three-foot wide column he had just descended. He poked his head around the left edge. Two janitors had joined the crew attempting to push the stubborn door beyond its sticking point. The truck driver from outside limboed under the four foot opening while holding a tool box.

"How fucking incompetent can you be?" Afsane screamed at a man, apparently the crew boss. "You knew opening this door was a critical part of this project. You're supposed to check critical parts! We need the fucking thing to work. Don't you think? What are we paying you for? Go find Mansour, you worthless piece of shit. Where's Mansour? Let's get this fucking thing fixed and out of here!"

Marzee searched for Utte, but she had left the scene. The image of her, harnessed in her sex machine, her husband below her, flashed through his memory. He felt alive, bursting with fear, anxiety, and exhilaration. *What the fuck am I doing here? That crazy bitch would shoot me on sight if she saw me.* He retracted his head, and looked around for a secluded telephone. He recalled catching the glimpse of the garbage dumpster earlier.

The light blue dumpster stood directly to his left, its front concealed by a large modesty curtain, but clearly visible from his vantage. *Is that the fuck'n bomb, or just garbage. No, it's the bomb. I never saw a garbage dumpster looking that clean and spiffy. And why cover it from view? That IS it. Now, how am I gonna get over there from here?*

He glanced quickly at the door crew who continued to battle the immovable mechanism. He ducked back in, and looked over to the dumpster. *About fifteen feet. I could make a run for it while they're all busy, but it's too risky. I've got to get over there without being seen.* He heard another sound—an electric motor becoming rapidly louder. In another glimpse, he saw Utte driving a large electric forklift. The group's attention segued to her, who positioned the forklift, driving it directly under the door in an attempt to force it open.

Like a soldier hustling for the cover of a foxhole amidst a barrage of bullets, he ran, slumped as low as he could bend. He dove behind the curtain, sliding the length of the dumpster before stopping. Worried he had been seen, he scrambled back to the other side, kicking the curtain in the process. *Fuck. Be careful*, he cursed to himself.

Head pressed to the floor, he peeked around the edge. The team's eyes were still on Utte and her forklift. She had placed the forks under the door edge, and had started to raise it. He heard crunching sounds—the door buckling from the pressure.

"Break it. Tear it down! Just move it. We've got to go," Afsane yelled, stressed and animated.

Marzee stood up, facing the large unmarked, turquoise container. Two horizontal, side-by-side hinged lids completely covered the top. He tugged up on the right lid. To his surprise, it gave way immediately. Reminiscent of spy movies in which he had reveled, an array of lights and counters bewildered him, like James Bond confused and befuddled by his enemy's technology. Afraid his tampering would have a disastrous outcome, he restrained from touching the any of the knobs and switches. Frustrated, he dropped the lid gently.

He side stepped six feet to the left, and opened the other side. Perplexed that the covers were not locked, he worried that a device of this import would have been more secure. A black vinyl-covered octagonal protrusion extended over from the other half, but a large space remained, containing a large, lumpy plastic bag. *I've got to ride with this thing. I've got to go with it, then jump out once they place it. I can find a phone there. Or just flag down the nearest fuck'n black-and-white.*

A loud crash startled him, disrupting his planning. He heard one of the men directing the others to move the door out of the way; he heard scraping metal. *I've got to hide in this thing. That shit in the bag. What's that? Fuck, I forgot. This thing is radioactive. I'm already exposed. Got to do it. Take my chances in there or die if they see me now.*

He scrambled squirrel-like up the dumpster's edge, landing head first on the bag. It's contents dampened his fall. His ankles remained between the lid and the edge. Twisting up, he held the lid open while he pulled his feet inward, then eased the lid closed. Outside, the beep-beep sound of the truck reverse warning resumed. He poked at the bag, trying to determine its contents. It was partly solid, partly grainy. *Fuck, I hope this shit isn't radioactive waste.* Frantic they would open the container for one last check before sending it on its way, he wriggled under the bag. To avoid his limbs sticking out, he drew himself into an embryonic position.

"Where is Mansour?" Afsane asked. "Did you find out what that commotion was?"

"He went to check on it. Some sort of fire outside," Utte responded, trying to calm her partner down. "He may have had to deal with fire officials. Better he do that, than them snooping around in here now. Maybe there was paperwork. I hope he used discretion."

The bitch is dead, bitches. Dead, dead, dead. His dead motherfuck'n corpse is bleeding on the roof. He's dead, and I killed him. He huddled in the pitch-black claustrophobic space, petrified they would discover him, yet fulfilled he had killed the murderer of his parents and friend. Another scraping sound hinted that they had moved the curtain aside. He could hear the truck draw near.

"I'll check the system once more, and set the final timer," he heard Afsane say.

"You're still certain you don't want to detonate remotely?" Utte asked. "The chance of signal interference is nil."

"The old fashioned way is more reliable in this case, my love," Afsane replied. "The timer will detonate the bomb, no matter where it is. I don't care about Jefferson's neurotic vengeance against his old neighborhood. If it explodes there, fine; if it explodes on the freeway, we still make our point." She paused, gesturing toward one of the security guards. "Keep him back while I make the last adjustments," she ordered.

All his nerves tingled with anticipation. Aware his muscles were twitching, he struggled staying still. He remembered past readings in his psychology text—in order to relax, take deep, long breaths. Inhale slowly; exhale slowly. *Maybe if I imagine I'm in my bed at home. Mama and daddy downstairs.* Soothed by the image, he relaxed and sobbed silently.

Blackness turned dark gray. He closed his eyes, hoping to fend off disaster with blindness. His plight spurred a memory of his past—a day in Kindergarten when his naïve teacher left his class with two third grade boys on the playground during recess while she went inside momentarily. Under the pretense of teaching the younger children how to play dodge ball, the older boys lined up the class, firing squad style, facing a brick wall. Then the boys hurled volleyballs against the wall, narrowly missing Marzee's head. The strident ring of the inflated ball rebounding next to his ear was etched indelible by his hyper-vigilant five-year-old senses, and underscored his helplessness, the strength and cruelty of the boys, and the teacher's betrayal. His fright now equaled then: the fear of not knowing when disaster would strike.

Inwardly, he conducted a final reality check: what he had seen in Utte's garage was real; what he had heard the two women discuss was real; Sanders and his parents were dead; he had witnessed conspiracy and betrayal, orders of magnitude beyond what he had ever read or imagined. He cowered inside the veneer of a weapon intended to wreak mass destruction. *Based on what? For what reality is this?* An inner voice whispered to him. *A statement of war? A statement of God? Whose God? One persistent and aggressive group's insistence on having their message recognized? One man's vengeance for feelings of persecution and his inability of resolve a chronic identity crisis?* A power loomed within him as he lay curled up, hiding from these assailants. As a Kindergartener, he should have fought back. He should have turned around, picked up the playground gravel, and hurled it at those boys. He must survive to make amends— to his classmates, to his community, to his parents, to Sanders, to himself.

He heard Afsane busying herself above, turning and clicking controls. Like Russian Roulette, every click and turn he heard was a hammer in search of a firing pin. She closed the lid. He heard a latch engage, then a low frequency hum commenced.

"He's inside? You checked?" Afsane whispered with an affectionate officiousness.

"Mansour checked. He's the one who did it," Utte answered with mild indignation. "Are you ready now? We've come this far. Perhaps we should let the package get delivered?"

Another clicking and latching sound against the metal container signaled to Marzee they were about to get underway. Relieved he had not been discovered, optimism moderated his anxiety. The sound of the truck warning beep resumed. Echoing inside, his canister jolted and bounced. He guessed grappling hooks had been attached, as the jolt was followed by the sound of chains, movement, and a change of angle. From inside he supposed the dumpster had been towed onto the truck bed, and locked into position.

"Here is a backup address and map, with instructions and details, in case you do not already have it," he heard Afsane tell the truck driver. "Place this garbage dumpster with the existing dumpsters at the building complex you'll find with this address. It's a large complex, a group of government project buildings."

"I got it," the truck driver replied. "Should I make any pickups while I'm there? Or is that it?"

"Nothing else, thank you. Just unload it, and leave it. The apartment manager there is expecting it. He'll get it later today. Thank you for your patience with the door. Here's a little something extra," Afsane replied, handing the driver a one hundred dollar bill.

Underway, Marzee stretched his legs and arms as far as he could. The weight of the bag under which he had hidden shifted as they bounced over speed bumps in the driveway. The truck slowed, then turned and accelerated. He wiggled from under the plastic bag. Lying outstretched, he settled into deep thought while trying to ignore a newly developed, low-level nausea.

She set a timer. What time is it? Maybe three, four in the morning. We're driving early morning from San Pedro to Compton. No traffic. Depending upon where in Compton, it can't take more than thirty minutes. When we get there, he'll unload the dumpster. What if I just starting banging like a motherfucker? Or I could just jump out now. What if he's one of them? He'd call them. I shouldn't trust him. He's the one delivering the bomb, so I don't know what he knows. I got no phone, so I can't just dial 911. So I wait for him to leave, then jump out and find a phone booth. Then dial 911. And say what? Tell them where I am and what I'm doing? Who would they send? Prob'ly think it's a hoax. Sending a black-and-white to

Compton at five AM. 'cause some voice says there's garbage dumpster disguised as a nuclear bomb? Maybe.

Don't blow your cover too fast. What if I wait 'til we're on the freeway? Then I jump out on the truck bed. What if the truck driver's got a gun? I've got a gun. No. Fuck! I left it on the roof. I jump out, and hail passing drivers for help. How about CHP? No. Not trusting any pigs. It all goes back to Jefferson. They'd call Homeland Security, and Jefferson would be here. He'd take my camera, and I'd lose the video busting his high yella ass. Then I'd be it 'cause they've got more evidence on me than I do on him without this camera.

Someone who can turn this thing off has to be at the scene. Someone important has to take me seriously. What keeps the Man honest? A rolling camera. Rodney King. That's what I need. A camera rolling when the Man arrives. A news crew! I'll give the video clip to the news first. Then call the Man. There's not much time. How much time? I get out of here, get to a phone booth. Phone booths in Compton? Forget it. Maybe a neighbor's help? No. I'd get shot at five in the morning, banging on someone's door with a story like mine. I've got to find a phone around there.

Seized once more by panic, he agonized over what would happen if they found the bodies on the roof now. Would they call the truck driver to stop? Would they come out to the delivery point after figuring out he's riding with the bomb? *No.*

They're trying to get as far away from here as possible. He twisted and turned, trying to find a comfortable position within his bleak, cramped quarters. He felt the truck turn sharply while the vibration increased.

The motion—without a frame of reference inside the pitch black cell—made him dizzy and weak. He had forgotten the last time he had eaten, yet his nausea worsened. More than anything, he despised vomiting. He'd do anything to not throw up, given other options. He deepened his breathing in an attempt to stave off what he feared was inevitable. His head started to spin; he closed his eyes and arched his head back as far as possible, so that the rear of his head rested against a corner.

What's happening? No food, I guess. I don't want to puke. Not stuck in a garbage can with my own vomit. Goddamn, that's disgusting. At least this shit isn't airtight. I can breathe OK, but I'm getting hot. He put his hand to his forehead to check his temperature. *I'm burning up. What's wrong with me? Anxiety? Panic? Stress causes all kinds of shit, even cancer.* Suddenly, he turned his head downward, into the corner, and vomited in frenzied waves.

He wanted out. Desperate to escape, and disregarding the consequences, he positioned himself on his knees in order to push the lid up if only for a bit of fresh air. The uneven contents of the black plastic bag accompanying him shifted, causing him to lose his balance and collapse. *Fuck*

397

this. I've got to see what I'm doing. He remembered the diming flashlight still in his pocket, and turned it on. The dim glow confirmed what he had already glimpsed when he had dived inside back at the warehouse: the octagonal end of the bomb protruding from the other half, and the lumpy bag upon which he rested. He cast the light on the upper edges of the compartment, noting the inner seals lining the lid perimeter. He shined the beam below him, searching for stable footing, so he could balance himself long enough to push the lid up. *If the driver sees the lid rise, he'd probably think the wind caused it.*

After he balanced himself on his knees, he turned off the flashlight, and returned it to his pocket. Then becoming as upright as his confines would allow, he pressed up on the lid. It did not open. He pushed harder, but to no avail. Racked with weakness, he groaned, pushing with all his remaining strength, but the lid would not budge. He collapsed, crying.

Too weak to be terrified, and disgusted by the stench of his vomit, he rested his head in the opposite corner. He decided crying was futile, sapping his much needed energy. His only option was to wait until the dumpster was in place. Then he'd bang against the sides as hard and as long as he could, hoping someone would come along to help him. He had to preserve his strength until that time. A different vibration from outside—he deduced the truck had changed its speed, possibly exiting the freeway. *Can't be that far from Compton now.* His nausea persisted.

A completely different vibration startled him. He sat up, alert. The sound, like the buzz of a distant chainsaw, repeated on and off. He put his head next to the protruding bomb, but the sound did not come from there. He put his ear to the plastic bag. Whatever was making the sound was in the bag.

Apprehensive about the bag's contents, and more concerned about his strategy once at his destination, he had avoided investigating it. He figured it contained radioactive waste, or else why would they want it to go along with the bomb? A grim reality of his sickness seeped into his awareness: this ever worsening nausea and weakness was caused by radiation. Yet, between his curiosity about the buzzing noise from the bag, and his desire to avoid further harm—his curiosity won out.

He lamented not having the foresight to bring along Mansour's twelve inch blade and Sanders' gun. He could have opened the bag with the knife; he could have shot his way out of his cell with the gun. At least he still had the nearly spent flashlight and Saul's digital camera. Almost faint, he pulled himself over the bag, and ripped a hole with his fingernails. Working in the dark, he eased his fingers from both hands into the hole and tore a wider opening. The sound had persisted, then stopped. Gingerly, he stuck his hand through, touching what felt like popcorn packing and a textile-covered object.

Mustering his fortitude in the darkness, he ripped opened the hole as far as his strength would permit, allowing the contents to spill. "Fuck it. I'm dead anyway," he muttered with shattered resolve. Hearing his own voice perked his awareness. He reached in his pocket for the flashlight, giving it a good shake before turning it on again.

Dance's lifeless face lacked his usual therapeutic insight. His empty stare, his eyes still opened wide from surprise by his killer's intentions, peered at Marzee through the hole he had just torn in the plastic. The yellow tint from the faded light created a ghostly specter, causing Marzee to squeal in terror. His demeanor morphed from fright to shock to disbelief to dismay to optimism within five seconds. Mortified by his therapist's corpse, a dark insight jolted him: the buzzing sound was Dance's cell phone. Ambivalently—if not guiltily—gleeful, he surmised whoever had killed Dance had neglected to remove it.

Ashamed for rifling his body to loot his corpse, he searched frantically for his phone. He tore at his clothes like a zombie to fresh carrion. As if he were a deep water scuba diver with empty tanks, he found a precious lifeline in his dead therapist's pants pocket. He fondled Dance's cell phone.

The flashlight grew dimmer; he turned it off. In hopes of squeezing more power out of the batteries, he unscrewed the battery compartment, put the end cap in his mouth—to assure not losing it—reversed the battery order, and screwed the cap back on. He needed the light to study Dance's phone—numbers, functions, menu.

Discovering Dance's body had distracted him from his nausea and weakness. Remaining motionless, he could barely hold himself upright. A jolt—probably the winch engaging—knocked him over. Aware of his weakened state, he clutched his lifelines of escape with vehemence. Suspicious of anything, he dismissed the notion of the truck driver opening the lid—his delivery instructions did not include examining the contents on site. He wondered if the man had been affected by the radiation as well.

The rattling was distinct—metal wheels rolling over asphalt. He bounced and jostled about inside until coming to a stand-still. He heard footsteps departing, and the truck driving away. Soundless moments passed. He was certain he had reached his final destination.

First assuring the phone and flashlight were well in his grip, he rolled on his back. With feeble, though concerted, effort, he kicked up at the lid, hoping to shake it free. The thick sheet metal bowed only slightly at the edges, allowing in diffused light.

He shook his head vigorously, fighting back a dizzy lightheadedness. "I've got to get serious. I got a phone now. Must make a call. Who? 911? No, that's still the Man. Fuck." Talking to himself

401

energized and grounded him. He sat quiet in the darkness, mulling over his dilemma. "I figured it out. The news. I'll call the news. What news?" He paused, thinking, propping himself up, trying not to pass out. "My mother. What was that news she watched in the morning? Yeah, it's morning now. I saw light. Those dudes in LA, the hot anne in the helicopter. What was it? Channel Five News. I'll call them. Get them here. Explain the situation. How? They'll hang up—think I'm fucking nuts." He hesitated, dropping his gaze toward Dance. "I got the ideal calling card with me."

He lit the flashlight and illuminated Dance. Shrugging off his numbness, he examined Dance's body, trying to determine cause of death. The bruises around his neck suggested strangulation. He pulled Dance's collar down further, fully exposing his neck.

"You've seen better days," he patted him on his cheek, then closed Dance's eyes. "Got to make sure you look dead."

The cell phone was damp from his grip. He flipped open the lid. *Fuck! Being in here is making me stupid. How could I forget the phone lights up when opened?* He turned off the flashlight.

Though he did not own his own cell, he had done enough hands-on window shopping to know all the functions. Months ago he had instructed Sanders on how to take a photo with his new phone, then send the photo along with a text message to a business associate. Now he knew the associate had been Saul. Dance's phone was not exceptional, and he was relieved to see the phone's camera features were intact.

After studying the menu on the LCD, he turned on the flashlight. He aimed the cell phone toward Dance. "Smile for me," he said sincerely. The phone camera flash erupted the darkness, momentarily blinding him. He had to wait a minute before he regained his acuity.

Death had numbed him. The picture of his dead counselor did not faze him. "Perfect," he said after his eyes cleared. "You're very photogenic."

He punched 4-1-1, and asked the information operator for Channel Five News in Los Angeles. After quibbling about which department, he settled on the City Editor's Desk. "On Sunset Boulevard. Here's your number, and thank you for using Verizon," the operator said with melodic officiousness. Once the automatic system recited the number, it connected him.

Weak, but determined, he waited for someone to pick up. He lacked the energy to convince someone he was genuine, so verbal persuasion could not be part of this equation. Whoever answered, he had to capture that person's attention unequivocally.

"News desk. John speaking," the male voice answered tersely.

"I have breaking news. This is not bullshit. Can you record what I'm about to tell you?" Marzee said in a low monotone.

403

"All incoming calls are recorded. My name is John Weiss. I'm the morning news editor. What can I do for you?" His voice softened. "And to whom am I speaking?"

Thank god, I didn't reach a receptionist.
"OK. I'll repeat. This is not a prank call. My name is Marzee Banks. I'm the Marzee Banks who lived in the house on Larch Street in Long Beach that blew up yesterday. You know about that incident?"

"Sure, we know about it. We covered it," Weiss replied with enthusiasm. "You're Marzee Banks? People are looking for you. No one knows if you're alive or not."

Afraid he might collapse while on the phone, he rationed his energy by speaking slowly and choosing his words. "Now you know," Marzee replied. "I called you because I don't trust calling the police, or any government agency. At least, not yet. You'll find out why later. There's much more here than meets the eye. Listen carefully. I want a news team with cameras and a helicopter at my location before anyone else. No police. No feds. News crew first. That's most important. I also want to be taken to a hospital immediately. I don't think I have much time left," Marzee continued, stammering.

"Marzee, I'm putting you on speaker phone, so some others here can listen, if that's OK with you," Weiss announced, pausing.

"Fine. The more the merrier," he responded faintly, clearing his throat. "OK, here goes. First,

404

I'm locked in a garbage dumpster with a dead man. He's works for the FBI. His name is Lorn Dance. I just took a picture of him with his phone camera. I'm calling, using his cell phone. You ID the number I'm calling from?" Marzee asked.

"You're calling from 310-999-2222," John responded.

"Excuse me, Marzee. This is Chuck LeGrange," another voice announced, cutting in. "I'm one of the morning anchors here. We're preparing to broadcast our morning show. We'd like to get the live coverage. Where exactly are you calling from, so we can come to you?"

"I don't know exactly. I'm trapped inside a dumpster. That's how I got here. The fact I'm using Dance's phone, the picture I'll send to you, and that I blew up my house should be adequate proof I'm for real. Do you agree?"

"Absolutely, Marzee," Weiss said. "Marzee, I've got to tell you, you're already news, with your house and all. Did you call another news agency before you called us?"

Tempted to reveal the entire situation up front, he restrained himself. "No, you're the first, and hopefully the last," he gasped. "Give me a number. I'll upload Dance's picture. In the meantime, you can look in your database to verify it's him. That sound reasonable?"

"It's very reasonable. Send it to 555-454-2233. Got that?" Weiss said.

Too weak to be scared, he did not want to die locked inside in a garbage dumpster. He wanted to plead with them to come and get him, no holds barred. Mustering his courage and remaining dogged in his resolve, he stuck to his plan. "OK. I've got to hang up to upload the picture. Call me back as soon as you've got it," he said. "But hurry. It's very urgent—for me, for you, for LA. Then I'll tell you where to send the news crew and an ambulance. BUT there's more. Much more. I want the team here first," Marzee muttered. "Think Rodney King, but bigger. OK?"

"Marzee, hang in there," John said.

"Marzee, Darcy Rodriguez, the producer here. To me, you sound very weak, in a life-threatening situation. Shouldn't we get help to you immediately? We believe you already," Rodriguez said.

Suddenly he heard rhythmic humming coming from the bomb compartment. Clicking, like a gasoline pump counter, accompanied the ubiquitous hum. Feebleness dampened his alarm. *Maybe I should just tell them where I am. It's not just me. It's all these people. No! News crew here first.* "Probably, but I'm gonna send that picture first. Pull up all the data on Dance," Marzee replied hesitantly. "One other thing. You're gonna have to locate me by the phone's GPS. I don't know my exact location since I'm locked in. Get whatever equipment you need ready, but you've got to have that camera crew here before you call anybody else.

Understand? Just, please, call back fast." He snapped the phone lid shut.

After ending the call, a profound loneliness overwhelmed him. Others' voices had an augmented impact on his sensitive state. Checking the phone's battery power relieved him—it indicated half full. He flipped through the menu options quickly, finally locating "Texting with Attachment." His eyes watered from fever, blurring the screen. After following the menu instructions, the message appeared: "Your message has been sent with Image01.jpg."

The persistent humming and clicking from the bomb posed the grim reminder: he could die any second. Distant memories phased in and out, like abbreviated dreams. On career day as a high school sophomore, he recalled asking an airline pilot: "How do you fly knowing you have the lives of all those people behind you?" The pilot told him he did not fly the back of the plane; he flew the front of it. That fleeting memory guided his attitude: his decisions and actions had to be aimed at his own survival. If he survived, everyone else would survive as well. And he wanted to live.

A familiar buzzing broke his light trance—Dance's phone. Faint, but jubilant, he was grateful Channel Five News had been expedient. "Thank you for calling back right away," he answered faintly.

"It's John Weiss, Marzee. We got the photo. You're legit, and we understand—you're wherever you are with Dance's corpse next to you. Marzee, let us help you. Let us come to you."

Taking as deep a breath as he could, he gathered his little remaining energy. "Listen to me carefully. Get the news crew here. I'm somewhere in Compton, locked inside a trash bin. A big turquoise garbage dumpster. It's probably the cleanest one you'll see. It's around some government project buildings. Home in on the phone's GPS signal. I'll leave the line open. But hurry. The charge is running down."

"We're on the way. We've got our news helicopter patched in. They've got the homing equipment. Just hang in there," Rodriguez broke in. "Hang on, Marzee. Our pilot says he's about ten minutes away with a news crew." She hesitated, faltering. "Marzee, we're gonna have to bring in the police at some point here."

"Promise me you'll be here. Your crew on me by the time the police arrive."

"Marzee, I promise you. You have my word," LeGrange added. "We're on the way as we speak. Here, listen to this," he said, holding the phone above his head, so Marzee could hear the helicopter noise.

Marzee, honey, you think long, you think wrong, his mother's voice echoed. "OK. I'm trusting you. Here's the main story: I accidently uncovered a terrorist ring in Los Angeles. I'm locked inside this dumpster—" he sighed, hoping his next words would not thwart his efforts. "—with a nuclear device. A dirty bomb. It's timed to go off sometime this morning. I don't know exactly when. Get experts here to defuse this thing. You've got to keep the cameras on them. An agent of Homeland Security was part of the plot. I recorded a video of him, talking with the terrorists. He doesn't know I recorded him. I have the camera with me. If they take it, there'll be no more proof. That's why you've got to get this camera and broadcast the video before the government gets it." He stopped, mulling over his next words. "I'm going to play it back while you're on your way. If anything happens before you have my camera in your possession, at least you'll have the audio. Just listen to it."

"Marzee. You just blew our minds. Did you say you're at ground zero of a nuclear bomb?" LeGrange asked after a brief pause.

He yearned to redeem himself, to explain personally what had happened. He was too faint to talk, and he had already decided the story sounded too far-fetched to be real. "Yeah. That's what I said. I'm gonna play the recording of the Homeland Security agent, Cecil Jefferson, talking with a German woman named Utte Thorndike. They killed her husband, John Thorndike, the brains behind the bomb. Just listen. And please, don't turn back." He dropped the opened phone on his lap. He fished out the flashlight and camera from his pockets, sapping the remainder of his strength. He switched the camera to playback mode. Relieved the volume was adequate, he set it next to the phone. He heard the

409

sound of a helicopter near. As the audio played, he longed for that time, when his friend and brother was alive, next to him. He ached, recalling his last time at the beach, hours before he last saw Sanders. Time compressed as his consciousness drifted away.

The sand fly hovered over the sand. Soft, glossy mounds of flesh speckled his horizon. Uninterested, he flitted and struggled against a steady ocean breeze, finally lighting on a pile of kelp. The other sand flies circled aimlessly, creating a bollix about the rotting debris.

My brothers, I am sorry. I shunned you, favoring those bronze bumps scattered on the horizon. I valued them. For what reason, I do not know. Brethren, please forgive me as I come to rest here amongst you. I will never leave you again. I am a sand fly.

Light embraced him, and voices, though close, were far away. Noise and energy surrounded him. His limbs were light and free. A voice whispered in his ear. His mother? His father? Sanders?

"Marzee, you're going to be OK."